KNOCKING ON THE DOOR
WITH 15-INCH GUNS

Only a small stretch of coast was entirely shrouded, as if cut off by a curtain. Everything there was hidden behind clouds of black smoke. Fountains of dust rose high into the sky. Nothing could be made out. Nothing at all. But behind that veil the American invasion was taking place. Only with the magic telescope of Sinbad the Sailor could the lieutenant-colonel have seen Second Lieutenant Arthur Jahnke in his half-buried dugout, Lance-Corporal Friedrich in his gun turret, Sergeant Hein by the mortar, and all the other men of 3rd Company, 919th Infantry Regiment, among the dunes of W5, upon whom the power of an entire fleet and an entire army was concentrated, where history was knocking at the door with death and destruction, ushering in a new chapter—the defeat of Germany and the victory of America.

THE BANTAM WAR BOOK SERIES

This series of books is about a world on fire.

The carefully chosen volumes in the Bantam War Book Series cover the full dramatic sweep of World War II. Many are eyewitness accounts by the men who fought in a global conflict as the world's future hung in the balance. Fighter pilots, tank commanders and infantry captains, among many others, recount exploits of individual courage. The present vivid portraits of brave men, true stories of gallantry, moving sagas of survival and stark tragedies of untimely death.

In 1933 Nazi Germany marched to become an empire that was to last a thousand years. In only twelve years that empire was destroyed, and ever since, the country has been bisected by her conquerors. Italy relinquished her colonial lands, as did Japan. These were the losers. The winners also lost the empires they had so painfully seized over the centuries. And one, Russia, lost over twenty million dead.

Those wartime 1940s were a simple, even a hopeful time. Hats came in only two colors, white and black, and after an initial battering the Allied nations started on a long and laborious march toward victory. It was a time when sane men believed the world would evolve into a decent place, but, as with all futures, there was no one then who could really forecast the world that we know now.

There are many ways to think about war. It has always been hard to understand the motivations and braveries of Axis soldiers fighting to enslave and dominate their neighbors. Yet it is impossible to know the hammer without the anvil, and to comprehend ourselves we must know the people we once fought against.

Through these books we can discover what it was like to take part in the war that was a final experience for nearly fifty million human beings. In so doing we may discover the strength to make a world as good as the one contained in those dreams and aspirations once believed by heroic men. We must understand our past as an honor to those dead who can no longer choose. They exchanged their lives in a hope for this future that we now inhabit. Though the fight took place many years ago, each of us remains as a living part of it.

INVASION—
THEY'RE COMING!

The German Account of the Allied Landings and the 80 Days' Battle for France

PAUL CARELL

*Translated from the German by
E. Osers*

BANTAM BOOKS
TORONTO · NEW YORK · LONDON · SYDNEY

INVASION—THEY'RE COMING!

A Bantam Book / published by arrangement with
E. P. Dutton & Company, Inc.

PRINTING HISTORY

Originally published in German under the title of SIE KOMEN!
and © 1960 by Gerhard Stalling Verlag.

Dutton edition published January 1963
2nd printing . . . . January 1963

Bantam edition/May 1964
2nd printing . . . . January 1967
3rd printing . . . . March 1967
4th printing . . . . January 1973
5th printing . . . . June 1984

Art by Greg Beecham, Tom Beecham, and Bob Correa.

Maps by Alan McKnight.

ISBN 0-553-24164-8

Published simultaneously in the United States and Canada

Bantam Books are published by Bantam Books, Inc. Its trade-
mark, consisting of the words ''Bantam Books'' and the por-
trayal of a rooster, is Registered in U.S. Patent and Trademark
Office and in other countries. Marca Registrada. Bantam
Books, Inc., 666 Fifth Avenue, New York, New York 10103.

PRINTED IN THE UNITED STATES OF AMERICA

O   0 9 8 7 6 5 4 3 2 1

CONTENTS

PREFACE

To be the chronicler of victories is a gratifying pursuit. But to report a campaign that ended in disaster and defeat is an invidious undertaking. There is always a strong temptation either to gloss over the lost battles or to rant angrily about the senseless sacrifices and try to apportion the blame.

Neither of these courses has been the author's intention. He wants to report what things were really like as accurately as possible on the strength of personal accounts and documentary evidence, and to present them in a manner that will interest a large reading public.

All this has been possible only through the help of a few hundred voluntary collaborators—from ordinary rankers to Army commanders—who had occupied some particular place in the vast, relentless drama. To all these the author owes a debt of gratitude: for their accounts, for the notes and studies they made available to the author, and for the operation sketch-maps, original orders, and situation-maps they had saved from the holocaust. Much new information was in this way brought to light for the war historian. Many a controversial question was clarified.

The views and judgments of some collaborators on certain aspects of the campaign occasionally diverged. On one point, however, there was always complete agreement between author, collaborators, and advisers: on the need to be guided solely by the question of how things really were, and why they were so.

P.C.

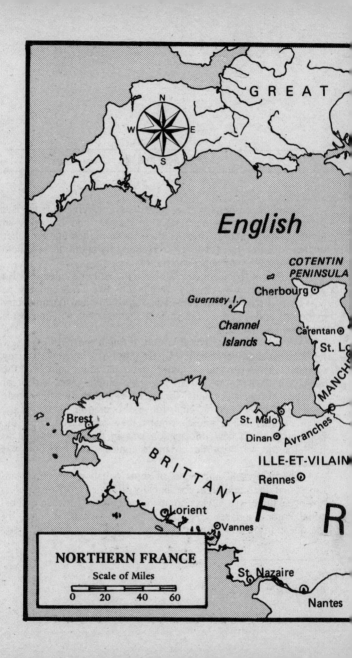

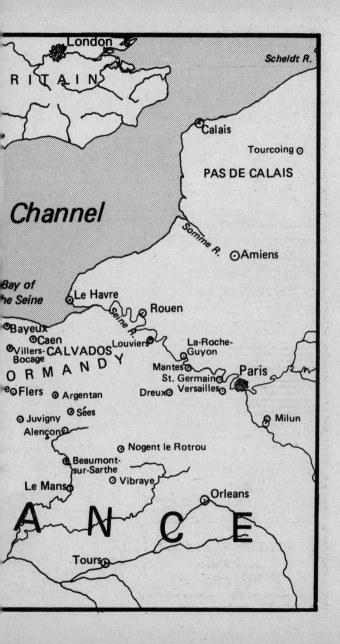

1
THE UNEASY WAIT

Bad Weather

The date was Saturday, June 3, 1944. Sergeant-Artificer
Günter Witte was lying in the grass among the dunes on the
Atlantic coast of Normandy, scanning the sky through his binoculars.
The midday sun was hidden by a haze, but it was a warm day, as
indeed one had every right to expect on the Cotentin peninsula at
the beginning of June. But storm clouds were gathering. It
looked as though the fine spell was at an end.

The roar of the long Atlantic breakers was punctuated by
hammer-blows. A party of the 1262nd Army Coastal Artillery
Regiment was emplacing a captured French gun outside Rozel.

"Hey, Witte, bagged anything yet?" Second Lieutenant
Wollschläger called up to the dunes. "No luck so far," the
sergeant-artificer replied. In the same instant, however, he dropped
the binoculars on to the haversack beside him. With a single
swift movement he rolled over on his stomach and snatched up
his French shotgun. Its twin barrels described a slow arc in the
sky from right to left. *Bang!* And again: *Bang!* A white ball of
fluff came tumbling down. Witte dropped the gun into the grass
and raced off.

"Got it?" his comrades asked when he returned a minute
later.

"Here it is," the sergeant-artificer said, grinning. "Look."
And he showed his comrades a dead pigeon. "Is it loaded?"
asked Wollschläger.

"Certainly, Herr Leutnant. Here we are." And Witte held
out to him the tiny metal capsule which he had detached from
among the plumage. He opened it. Inside was a scrap of
wafer-thin rice-paper. Written on it were numbers and letters,

and the message was signed with a tiny drawing of a fox. "Last time it was a raven or a magpie—or some other such bird," said Witte. He was an old hand at the game.

"Take it up to the château," the lieutenant commanded. "And be quick about it." Witte pedalled off on his requisitioned bicycle, along the road from Les Pieux to Cherbourg, to regimental headquarters in the little château of Sotteville, to hand over the carrier-pigeon with its message for England—a message for British Intelligence from the secret network of agents in France. These messages disclosed the locations of the gun-emplacements and pill-boxes that the Germans were building along the coast and inland, the identity of the army units stationed in the villages, and anything else that might be of interest to the enemy's intelligence.

Shooting down these flying postmen had become a popular sport along the whole coast of Northern France. Of course, only a few of them were shot down. Countless pigeons were safely reaching their lofts along the south coast of England. But of those that did not complete the journey home one was particularly valuable. Its failure to return was to cost the lives of many American soldiers. We shall hear about that presently.

On the morning of Monday, June 5, Major Friedrich Hayn, the Intelligence officer of the 84th Corps in Saint-Lô, noted in his log the report from 709th Division about the intercepted carrier-pigeon with its secret message. He put the aluminium capsule with the coded text aside in order to show it to General Marcks. On the next day, June 6, he would send it by courier to Central Intelligence in Paris. He was not to know that on the following day he would be busy with far more important things.

The major glanced at the large window on the far side of the room, and out to the cathedral with its impressive spires. He looked at the sky, which seemed to portend bad weather. Then he turned back to his work—situation-maps, air raids, enemy signals. More and more paperwork.

Like Major Hayn at 84th Corps headquarters, staff officers everywhere, in the châteaux around Paris, in Brittany and in Normandy, over in Belgium and in the Pas de Calais, in Holland and in Southern France, were on that June 5, 1944, studying reports and information about enemy air incursions and bombings, reports from the coastal sectors, and about the progress of fortification work. But their main interest was in the weather situation. For everything hinged on the weather.

The weather was the be-all and end-all. It would decide the

question that was worrying them all. Would they, or would they not, come? It was that question that kept them all where they were—the staff officers, the generals, and the fifty-eight divisions west of the Rhine. They were all waiting, all absorbed by the one problem. When would they come?

Whenever a general asked, "Any risk of an enemy landing to-day?" his staff officer would first of all look at the weather-chart. After all, the enemy had to come by sea. And there certain rules applied. If, for instance, the wind was higher than Force 4 and visibility less than three nautical miles, no landing operation was possible. Likewise, rain with a low cloud-ceiling would rule out that air cover which was indispensable to any armada attempting a landing. Nor would the enemy come sailing in at the height of the day. They would certainly come before day-break in order to approach the coast as closely as possible under cover of darkness. Hence it would have to be either low tide or high tide at dawn, according to the tactics General Eisenhower had chosen—a landing at high water or at low water. That, of course, was anybody's guess. On the whole, the German staffs tended to believe that he would land at high water, with the tide running behind him. That was one of many mistakes.

What, then, was the weather like on the Normandy coast on June 5, 1944? Reassuring, very reassuring. There was a wind of Force 5-6 and a rough sea of Scale 4-5. There was heavy cloud. Many places had drizzle. All headquarters from Paris to Brest were looking forward to a quiet night. Preferably with a bottle or two of Chablis.

Cheers! Or, as the French said, *A votre santé!*

The men in the gun-emplacements, the strongpoints, and the defence-posts along the many miles of coastline had no Chablis. At most they had Calvados, the local apple-brandy. They were looking out across the nocturnal mist-shrouded sea, keeping watch.

In the concrete dugouts along the Seine estuary the men were lying on their wooden bunks. It was hot and damp and sticky in these modern cave dwellings. The men were talking. Or else they were voicing their homesickness and resignation in true army style by singing the hit of the dugouts of Western Europe, the *Lili Marlene* of Normandy; it was called *Cute Little Bus Conductress*.

Seventy-five miles from the Seine estuary, on the east coast of the Cotentin peninsula, strongpoint No. 5 was held by a platoon of the 3rd Company, 919th Infantry Regiment. Second

Lieutenant Arthur Jahnke was making his tour along the foremost trench on the crest of the dune. A look-out was manning the scissor telescope.

"Anything?" Jahnke asked.

"No news, Herr Leutnant." Jahnke stepped up to the telescope. Across the foreshore he looked out towards the sea. The night was black. Rainclouds were shrouding the moon. Only now and then would it break through a gap in the clouds—the round disc of a full moon. For a moment it would steep the beach and the land beyond, the hedgerows, the orchards, and the willow-trees, in its pale light. For a few seconds it would be mirrored in the water of the inundated valleys. Then it would hide again.

"They won't come in this weather," said the look-out. The lieutenant nodded. They would not come in this weather. Furtively he touched the wooden balustrade of the observation-post. Then he returned to the stone building of strongpoint No.5, known for short as W5.

"They won't come in this weather." That also was the verdict of the meteorologists.

On June 5 Rear-Admiral Hennecke, Naval Commander Normandy, sent an urgent inquiry about the weather situation from his headquarters in Cherbourg to the chief of his meteorological station at Cap de la Hague. He was uneasy because the first week of June favoured a landing from the point of view of high- and low-water times, moon phase, and long-term weather prospects. Moreover, his radar officer, Lieutenant Wesemann, had reported a striking amount of activity on his screen during the preceding night. "It could be a major concentration of ships," had been his opinion. The radar signal had then been lost, evidently through interference. Even so!

However, the weather men sent Admiral Hennecke a reassuring signal: "Rough sea, poor visibility, Force 5-6 wind, rain likely to get heavier. Most probably we shan't even get our usual air raids."

The unpromising weather prospects had been further confirmed by a report that a convoy intended for Brest had not sailed because of the weather.

"And what's it going to be like to-morrow?" the admiral asked.

"There is little prospect of short-term changes in the weather during the next few days," was the reply of the meteorologists.

Hennecke brightened up visibly. "That means," he was

thinking aloud, "that the various conditions of tide, moon, and general weather situation necessary for a landing here in Northern France won't coincide again until the second half of June."

In Le Mans, at Seventh Army headquarters, Colonel-General Dollmann likewise asked his chief of staff, "Anything likely to happen to-day?" Major-General Pemsel had already inquired from Naval Group headquarters in Paris. He was able to quote to his army commander the reassuring forecast of the meteorologists, though he added a little doubtfully, "If only one could rely on those weather men."

Probably the army commander had not even heard that last remark. He wanted to believe that "they would not come." For he too realized the value of time gained. If they did not come that day, he calculated, several weeks would elapse before they would be likely to try to effect a landing. And time was what he needed—time to set up more obstacles on the beaches, to build more strongpoints, and to bring up more coastal guns. A lot remained to be done before that 600-mile-wide coastal gate to Europe was securely barred.

"Then we can hold our commanding officers' conference and the subsequent map exercise in Rennes tomorrow morning," General Dollmann said to his orderly officer. "See that everything is arranged. Every divisional commander is to bring with him two regimental commanders. I shall expect the gentlemen in Rennes at 1000 hours to-morrow."

The Seventh Army chief of staff was a mistrustful and cautious officer. In spite of the reassuring forecast of the meteorologists he was uneasy at the thought that for two days the entire front line of the Seventh Army was to be without its most important commanding officers. He therefore had a signal teleprinted to the various divisional commanders urging them not to set out on their journey to Rennes before daybreak. If, against all expectation, a landing was attempted, then surely it would come in the early hours of the morning. By daybreak everybody would know where they stood. Needless to say, this advice was not much use to the divisional commanders a long distance away from Le Mans. Over those bomb-pitted roads they would never get to Rennes by 10 A.M. From the battle headquarters of General von Schlieben's 709th Division near Valognes, for instance, it was a trip of 120 miles. For General Falley, of the 91st Air Landing Division, stationed at Château Haut, the distance was not much less. For this reason von Schlieben, with the consent of 84th Corps, set out during the afternoon of June 5,

Erwin Rommel

and Major-General Falley drove off at nightfall. "Nothing's going to happen in this lousy weather," he said to his chief of operations.

Even Field-Marshal Erwin Rommel, commander of Army Group B, the military overlord of the entire northern French coast, had allowed himself to be tempted by the bad weather to combine business with pleasure. On the morning of June 5 he had left his headquarters, the thousand-year-old château of the Dukes of Rochefoucauld, La Roche-Guyon, for Germany. He intended to pay a brief visit to his wife at Herrlingen, as her birthday was on June 6, and then drive on to Berchtesgaden in order to report to Hitler. It was to be a very important report. He was going to ask for reinforcements for his coastal front. Rommel intended to talk the Führer into transferring two additional armoured divisions and one mortar brigade to Normandy. In his diary is the entry: "The most urgent problem is to win the Führer over by personal conversation."

Rommel was worried about the situation on the coast. Unless reinforcements arrived both for the coastline and for his operational reserves the chances of throwing the enemy back into the sea once he had gained a foothold were slender. Rommel needed more and better divisions. He needed units with operational experience. How were his divisions of elderly reservists, the "East Battalions" made up of former Russian prisoners of war, the battalions of men with ear or stomach complaints, and the over-age crews of his coastal batteries to resist a large-scale attempted landing supported by naval guns, aerial bombardment, and subsequent close combat?

The average age of the men of the 709th Division, for instance, was about thirty-six; that of the American G.I.'s in the assault divisions (which were ready poised across the Channel in England) was twenty-five. The average age of the naval gun crews along the invasion front was as much as forty-five. Among them were men of fifty-six and more. These figures spoke for themselves. But was this disadvantage not offset by the insuperable Atlantic Wall? By that protective shield of concrete, steel, guns, and mines? Was the coastline not thick with menacing concrete fortresses equipped with powerful naval guns? And was the foreshore from Brest to Ostend not littered with ingenious death-dealing obstacles?

The answer, unfortunately, was no. In the summer of 1944 the Atlantic Wall existed only in the Pas de Calais. For the rest it consisted merely of a string of widely spaced strongpoints, some of them only half finished. Only a few of the heavy batteries were adequately protected or even equipped. Most of the equipment consisted of captured enemy guns, totally unsuitable against naval targets because of their calibre and their lack of fire-control equipment.

What worried Rommel more than anything was air power. He knew from the African campaign and from the fighting in Italy for the beach-heads at Salerno and Anzio what enemy superiority in the air meant. He knew from El Alamein how fighter-bombers could pin down entire armoured divisions. Neither Field-Marshal von Rundstedt, the Commander-in-Chief West, nor General Geyr von Schweppenburg, commanding the armoured forces centred on Paris, had any comparable personal experience. Rommel had that experience, and on it he had based his plan of defence ever since November 1943 when he was appointed commander of Army Group B and thereby overlord of the coast of Northern France.

His basic principle was simple. The front line was on the beaches. The invading troops were to be engaged at once, on the very coast, at their beach-heads, to avoid long and costly movements to the battlefield.

"The enemy is at his weakest just after landing," Rommel declared. "The troops are unsure, and possibly even seasick. They are unfamiliar with the terrain. Heavy weapons are not yet available in sufficient quantity. That is the moment to strike at them and defeat them."

Hence Rommel's insistence: All available weapons and troops must be employed at that moment. The enemy must be struck at his first step on land, or, if possible, even while still at sea. Instead of defence in depth, along traditional lines, Rommel demanded a linear defensive structure close to the coastline. Heavy armaments, artillery, tactical reserves—everything was to be employed to its full extent to engage the enemy on the coast. Rommel even called for a forward build-up of the armoured divisions, so that they would be able to intervene from the very outset in the defensive battle on the coast.

That was his active defence. His passive defence was the system of foreshore obstacles that he had invented. It was his old idea from the African campaign. Outside El Alamein he had planted his 'devil's gardens'—extensive barrier-zones with infernal obstacles, mines laid in three tiers, booby-traps touched off by trip-wires, harmless-looking stakes with tremendous explosive charges. The same idea—only more elaborate and on an even bigger scale—was to be used to defend the French coast against an invading fleet.

For the foreshore below the high-water mark he invented ramming cones with mines and steel saws designed to wreck all landing craft. From the old Czech defences, the so-called 'Czech hedgehogs,' he ordered steel-girder obstacles to be brought to the West by the hundreds of thousands and to be dumped on the beaches. He invented the most intricate mine constructions: the nutcracker mine on posts linked by wire (to be triggered off by the pressure of a landing craft against a stake) and mines to be detonated by gunfire.

Inland—in fields, meadows, and forest clearings—he ordered tall stakes to be driven into the ground to prevent airlandings. They became known as Rommel's 'asparagus.'

He was indefatigable in his inventiveness. To overcome the resistance of the older officers, who were not overimpressed by these new-fangled ideas, he ordered: "I hereby forbid all training, and demand that every minute be used for work on the beach obstacles." He knew what he wanted. "It is on the beaches that the fate of the invasion will be decided, and, what is more, during the first twenty-four hours."

Field-Marshal von Rundstedt and General Geyr von Schweppenburg held the opposite view. They wanted to fight the decisive battle far behind the coast. They wanted to keep the armoured forces and the tactical reserves well back in the interior of France in order to cut off the attacker as he was thrusting forward—in accordance with the orthodox strategic principle of encircling the enemy in order to destroy him. "Don't let them land," was Rommel's strategy. "Let them come," was Rundstedt's and Geyr's motto.

In this clash of opinions Hitler had made a decision that rejected General Geyr's plan but fell short of Rommel's requirements. The armoured divisions remained outside Rommel's command. True, they were not quite as far inland as Rundstedt and Geyr had wanted, but neither were they as close to the coastline as Rommel considered necessary.

All this the field-marshal turned over in his head as he was driving to Herrlingen on the morning of June 5. Together with his chief of operations he was planning how he could induce Hitler to change his defence strategy and how, above all, he could get him to reinforce the divisions in Northern France, if need be at the expense of the garrisons in Norway, in Southern France, or the Channel Islands.

Rommel knew that his strategy of "front line on the beaches" could not be realized if a single division—for instance, General von Schlieben's 709th—had to defend a front of forty miles. So long as there were two or three miles of no man's land between one defence-post and the next it was impossible to prevent an enemy landing, let alone throw him back into the sea. A well-tried rule of thumb said that a front line of six miles was as much as a division could hope to cope with. Rommel, of course, was aware of that. He therefore saw only one solution. Somewhere the European front had to have some gaps. Frederick the Great's principle was still valid: "He that would defend everything will defend nothing."

All this Rommel hoped to be able to explain to Adolf Hitler on June 6. But the opportunity never came. By June 6 it was too late. Events had started to move. But as yet no one suspected anything.

A Poem by Paul Verlaine

On the other side of the Channel Allied security officers were guarding the date of the invasion, the secret of D-Day. A large army of German Intelligence agents were trying to discover that secret.

And they succeeded. Even before the first aircraft took off from England on D-Day to drop their bombs over the Normandy coast the German Command in France knew that the invasion was on. Proof of it, in black and white, was literally lying on its desk. But it did not make use of it.

This is no fairy-tale or film plot. The full, sensational story may be found in the official American history of the invasion. Evidence can also be found in the war diary of the German Fifteenth Army. Treason and skilful espionage had unveiled the great secret. No German field officer, no officer commanding a strongpoint, and no ordinary trooper need have been taken by surprise by the Allied invasion on June 6. Here is the well-nigh incredible story of why, nevertheless, they were caught unawares.

The Allied Command had set up in France a widely ramified secret organization for collecting information and carrying out sabotage. Experienced regional chiefs were in charge of the various sections. Among these the Alliance of Animals was one of the most efficient information-gathering organizations. Its members bore the names of animals. The transmission of information was by radio or by carrier-pigeon. In addition to the spies there were the saboteurs. In some areas these organizations were linked with one another, in others they were kept strictly apart for security reasons. The sabotage organizations existed throughout the whole of France. They were divided into regions, complete with regional chiefs, section leaders, and thousands of collaborators. Their task was ceaselessly to disrupt the work on the German defences and, above all, to hold themselves in readiness for the main blow on D-Day itself.

A quarter of an ounce of sugar—just three lumps—dropped into the water of a concrete mixer, was enough to rob two hundredweights of concrete of its strength, for if calcium combines with sugar, instead of with carbon dioxide, a readily soluble calcium saccharate is formed. Thus, if a member of the French Resistance succeeded in getting himself employed by the Germans near a concrete mixer he could cause extensive damage to the defences by dropping quite small quantities of sugar into the mix or into the stored materials. The concrete shield of a gun-emplacement or the roof-slab of a dugout might be sufficiently weakened to crumble like sandstone if hit by a shell. But that was only one aspect of these sinister activities. For D-Day the London headquarters of S.O.E.—Sabotage Organizations in Europe— had worked out a special plan—the Green Plan. A few hours before the invasion 571 French railway-stations and junctions were to be destroyed and thirty main lines blocked at a single blow. Simultaneously the Tortoise Plan was to be put into effect. This envisaged the disruption of telephone-lines and the blowing up of crossroads, bridges, and viaducts.

It is obvious that the main problem in this kind of work was the signal for immediate action. After all, it was impossible to inform the numerous section leaders in the various regions of France of the top-secret invasion-date several days in advance. Quite apart from the fact that this date might have to be postponed at the last moment—as, in fact, it was.

Thus the idea was conceived of giving the order by radio. The chiefs of the sabotage organizations were instructed to listen carefully to the French transmissions of the B.B.C. on the 1st, 2nd, 15th, and 16th day of each month and to watch out for a code message. This code was the first phrase of Paul Verlaine's famous poem about autumn. If it was transmitted—that is, if it was read out among a multitude of other messages—this meant that the invasion was imminent. From that moment onward all transmissions had to be continually monitored for the second half

of the verse, the so-called B message. If that came through as
well, it meant the invasion would start within forty-eight hours.
From then all sabotage chiefs had to stand by for detailed orders,
likewise to be given by radio codes, for their specific operations
under the Green Plan and the Tortoise Plan.

It was a well-thought-out scheme. However, the Abwehr,
the German counter-intelligence service, got hold of the secret.
Too many Frenchmen were in the know, and one of them was on
the German payroll. He betrayed to Admiral Canaris, the head of
the Abwehr, this militarily most valuable poem in the whole
history of literature.

Canaris treated it as a precious gift. He soon knew the first
verse by heart:

> Les sanglots longs
> des violons
> de l'automne
> Blessent mon coeur
> d'une langueur
> monotone

That was the fateful verse that Canaris entrusted to the
chiefs of his monitoring-posts as their most carefully cherished
secret.

Thus it came about that not only the regional chiefs, the
section leaders, and the active saboteurs of the S.O.E. were
listening to the B.B.C. transmissions for that poem by Verlaine,
but also a team of specialists of the signals centre at Colonel-
General Salmuth's Fifteenth Army headquarters in Tourcoing.
They were not confused or distracted by the countless messages
which were merely blinds. They knew the correct text and were
waiting for it. Their patience was rewarded. The war diary of the
Fifteenth Army, which held the sector between Seine and Meuse,
contains five entries under the date of June 5. The first of these
states that the signals centre monitored the first part of the
Verlaine verse, *Les sanglots longs des violons de l'automne*, on
June 1, 2, and 3. The second entry, logged at 2115 hours,
states: "Second half of message, *Blessent mon coeur d'une
langueur monotone*, recorded."

The third, fourth, and fifth entries—at 2120, 2200, and
2215 hours, respectively—almost reflect the excitement of the
writer. They state that the sensational news, the great secret, had
been passed on to the commander Fifteenth Army, to O.B. West

(Commander-in-Chief West), all general headquarters, the 16th Anti-Aircraft Division, the military commanders in Belgium and France, as well as to Army Group B and to O.K.W. (the High Command of the German Armed Forces) at Rastenburg, in East Prussia. By 2215 hours on June 5 the High Command of the German Armed Forces, as well as Field-Marshal von Rundstedt, Naval Group headquarters in Paris, and Rommel's Army Group had been informed that the invasion was imminent.

As yet no shot had been fired. The bombers were just about to take off from their bases in England. The transport aircraft with their airborne troops were taxiing out to the runways. Pilots and paratroops believed their secret to be safe. But their secret had long been betrayed.

But there was no need to worry. It was to make no difference. A great effort had been made for nothing; the first victory had been thrown away by the German High Command. Admittedly, Colonel-General von Salmuth immediately placed his Fifteenth Army on full alert, but that army happened to be outside the scope of the impending events. Apart from him, nobody did anything. Nothing at all. Army Group B did not alert its Seventh Army and allowed it, hours later, to fall an unsuspecting victim to the most powerful attack in military history. The 84th Corps, against whose coastal divisions the first airborne and naval landings were directed, was left to be caught by surprise. Neither Admiral Hennecke, Naval Commander Normandy, with his vital coastal batteries, nor the radar stations were alerted. Rommel was not immediately recalled from Herrlingen. For fourteen decisive hours his Army Group was left without its head, without its directing and controlling force. Its chief of staff, General Speidel, was left to his own devices.

General Jodl at the Führer's headquarters might be excused for thinking that Field-Marshal von Rundstedt would give the alarm. But the field-marshal did not do so. He did not do so simply because he did not believe the report. The standard American history of the invasion quotes one of his staff officers as saying: "As if General Eisenhower would announce the invasion over the B.B.C.!"

The report, quite simply, was disbelieved. A verse by Verlaine—ridiculous!

Why, on the other hand, the staff of Army Group B should likewise have been infected by this lordly contempt for unconventional methods of warfare and have failed to alert its corps and divisions remains a mystery.

Thus the triumph of the German Abwehr was in vain. The night of June 5 was spent in routine activities, in a carefree and sometimes even convivial atmosphere.

Strong Formations of Enemy Bombers Approaching

In Cherbourg German officers and signallers were sitting in the underground battle headquarters of the Naval Commander, as on any other night. Every now and then Sub-Lieutenant Gunnar Blume, the situation-room and orderly officer, would come down from Hennecke's little villa, which was sited exactly over the underground tunnel housing the battle headquarters, and ask for news.

But there was no news in Cherbourg. Each time Blume was able to return above ground reassured. In the villa above, Admiral Hennecke was sitting with his staff officers in the spacious room whose windows during the day offered a wide view over the sea. Now the heavy curtains were drawn and the tables were laid for a light meal. Admiral Hennecke was entertaining visitors. Following a concert given by a troop-welfare party, the admiral had asked the performers and officers back to his house. Among them were two young women—Ursula Bräutigam, the imperturbable naval auxiliary who kept Sub-Lieutenant Blume's operations log, and Senior Lieutenant Wist's wife—the pianist of the visiting concert party.

Frau Wist saw the piano in Hennecke's mess room. It was well tuned. She played a few bars and, like a nostalgic dream of bygone days, Schumann's *Papillons* softly filled the air. Time seemed to stand still.

But it was not standing still. An orderly was threading his way through to Blume. He was wanted on the telephone. When the lieutenant returned he leaned over to Hennecke: "Very heavy air-raids on towns and roads in the coastal area, Herr Admiral. Other strong bomber formations are reported from the Calvados coast."

Hennecke nodded his head. The war was demanding attention. The war had no time for Schumann's *Papillons*. The admiral glanced at his watch. The time was 2330 hours. "Strong bomber formations." He could not get the phrase out of his mind.

In the air the enemy was coming and going just as he pleased. And who was to stop him? Only that day Hennecke had learnt from Paris that the second *Gruppe*[1] of No. 26 Fighter *Geschwader*,[2] which was commanded by the successful Commodore Priller, "the mathematician of the air," had been switched to the south of France for rest. The first and third *Gruppen* were on their way to Reims and Metz. That left the entire fighter defence in the hands of No. 2 Fighter *Geschwader*, the Richthofen *Geschwader*. But Field-Marshal von Rundstedt had always reassured his generals: "On the third day after an invasion, at the latest, you may count on the support of 1000 aircraft." And Rundstedt had referred to Hitler's firm promise: "On the third day after D-Day, at the latest, I shall render the invasion front capable of breaking the Anglo-American air superiority."

Thus it came about that Field-Marshal Sperrle, according to the operations log of June 5, was commanding an air fleet which on paper possessed 496 machines, but of which only 319 were operational: 88 bombers, 172 fighters, and 59 reconnaissance aircraft.

"I can't keep my fighters in France waiting for an invasion," Goering had said. "I need them for the defence of the Reich." And so he had employed his fighter units against the Allied bombing offensive on Germany proper. As a result the Second Air Corps had no aircraft at all available in the West. The idea was that on D-Day they would be switched from Germany to the airfields in the battle zone.

Those were Admiral Hennecke's thoughts, and he no longer enjoyed his little party. He went down into his tunnel headquarters, which, though no more than half finished, was already a highly elaborate and absolutely safe command-post. In the right-hand tunnel a field hospital had been installed and equipped; on the left were the situation and map rooms and the various command-posts. There were direct telephone-lines to every battery on the coast. There was even a direct line to the Führer's headquarters at Rastenburg, in East Prussia.

The duty officer passed the admiral the reports that had come in from the observation-posts of the Navy's coastal batteries in the sector from the Bay of the Seine to the Normandy Islands.

"Loud engine noise of approaching bomber formations."

---

[1] Normally about twenty-seven aircraft.
[2] A *Geschwader* consisted of three *Gruppen* and had approximately ninety-three aircraft.

"Light reconnaissance aircraft penetrating over a broad front."

"Target-markers being dropped behind the front."

Even the small observation-post by the Quettehou light-house reported overflights by pathfinder aircraft and transports.

"A real field-day," Hennecke grunted. He was feeling a little uneasy. "Blume, just run upstairs and ask them to wind up the party. Make my apologies to Frau Wist, but I rather think we may have to listen to a different kind of music presently."

The party was over. The guests were driven back to their quarters.

Thus, the night of June 5-6 passed in a strange mixture of moods, in a sombre atmosphere of unsuspecting gaiety and uneasy suspicion.

Field-Marshal Rommel was not the only one to attend a birthday celebration.

In the Panzer Lehr Division of Lieutenant-General Fritz Bayerlein, which was deployed in the area of Nogent le Rotrou between Tours and Le Mans as an O.K.W. reserve, two officers of 902nd Regiment were giving a joint birthday-party at their quarters at Vibraye. One of them was born on June 5 and the other on June 6. It seemed a splendid opportunity for an early start and a late finish. The Burgundy was excellent, and every-body was having a wonderful time.

Bayerlein's division was an excellently equipped fighting unit. The only Panzer division of the Wehrmacht to be 100 per cent armoured, it had 260 tanks and 800 armoured tracked vehicles. The N.C.O.'s were hand-picked and trained with thoroughness. Their average age was twenty-one and a half. "With this division alone," Colonel-General Guderian, Inspector-General of Armoured Forces, once said to Bayerlein during the post-mortem on a *Kriegspiel* (map exercise), "with this division alone you will throw the Anglo-Americans back into the sea. Into the sea," Guderian had deliberately emphasized. "Remember. Your objective is not the coast but the sea."

When the birthday-party at 902nd Regiment was in full swing, with the Burgundy flowing freely, the men tuned in to *Soldatensender Calais*, the British propaganda-transmitter for the German forces. There was usually some hot jazz between the news items. But that night Second Lieutenant Bohmbach was unlucky. *Calais* evidently had no time for merrymaking. He tried the B.B.C. But there, too, he found no music. Urgent voices were reading out messages, presumably intended for the French

Resistance. Unintelligible phrases in a flowery code. "John loves Mary." "Have no fear of colours!" "The dice are on the table." "The beetroot has been peeled." This was followed by advice to the French civilian population on how to behave during air raids. They were to leave the towns where German troops were stationed, especially headquarters towns, and take shelter in the open country. "Leave the towns," the radio urged.

For a minute a slight feeling of uneasiness came over the birthday celebrations. The urgent warnings had made the men nervous. Supposing something was in the air?

However, a telephone inquiry to regimental headquarters and another to Division yielded the reassuring reply: "Nothing doing. No alert." So they switched off the unintelligible Frenchman and let the champagne corks pop.

June 6 was also the birthday of Sergeant-Signaller Klaus Lück of the 22nd Panzer Regiment. His regiment belonged to the reconstituted 21st Panzer Division, that old élite unit of the Afrika Korps which had remained behind in Tunisia. The 21st were the armoured unit nearest to the coast in Normandy. The division was still far from well equipped. The drivers were cursing the French tanks which had to be specially fitted with radio equipment. The artillery troop had to practise with Russian anti-tank guns. Only slowly were the Mark IV tanks with their 75-millimetre short- and long-barrel gun reaching the division.

Conditions were no better with the grenadier regiments.

Panzerfaust

Their fleet of vehicles was very modest. But at least they had the new *Panzerfaust*, that bazooka-type grenade intended as an infantry weapon against armoured vehicles. The grenadiers were again able to do honour to their ancient name. "Our best weapons are our old corporals, sergeants, and N.C.O.'s," was a crack of which Second Lieutenant Höller was inordinately fond. He was an old Africa campaigner from the original 21st Panzer Division. He was now in charge of the heavy section of 8th Company of 192nd Panzer Grenadier Regiment, which was holding the area between Caen and the coast, on the left bank of the river Orne.

Many men of Rommel's Afrika Korps who had survived the shambles and managed at the last minute to escape captivity in Tunisia were in the 21st Panzer Division. There were also Russian campaigners and old hands from Crete. They were a well-tried lot. Their divisional commander, Major-General Feuchtinger, was at first in Rennes, and later at Saint-Pierre-sur-Dives—still a little too far in the rear for the liking of the old tank troopers, considering that the coastal area was to be the division's operational zone.

Regimental headquarters of the 22nd Panzer Regiment under Colonel von Oppeln-Bronikowski was at Falaise. The two tank battalions were fairly widely scattered along a line from Tours to Le Mans. The companies were stationed in sleepy little villages among willow-trees and apple orchards. Many of them realized that they were in an easy billet and knew how to organize their little pleasures. Others were kept under strict discipline and cursed their over-zealous company commanders. Among the latter kind was the 4th Company under Captain Hoffmann, at Epancy, nineteen miles south of Caen. That night Hoffmann had again laid on an extensive round of patrols.

Corporal Heilig, on the other hand, who had fought in Africa with the legendary 361st and there had worked his way up from the despised position of a former Foreign Legionary to corporal, had an easier time in the 1st Company. "There's plenty of time for dying once the bullets start to fly. Until then we'll live," was his motto. During the night of June 5-6 he had therefore cycled from Verson to Caen together with his friend, Lance-Corporal Briten. It turned out to be a most uncomfortable outing.

Sergeant-Signaller Lück made his last check of the line to the regimental telephone exchange at 2230 hours. He too asked, "Any news?" And he too received the reply of an unsuspecting front: "Nothing special, sergeant, apart from a few reports of enemy bombers approaching the coast." Lück said good-night and went up to his room in the old château. There his apple-brandy was waiting for him, to be taken as a nightcap while he read a birthday letter from his wife, saved up until midnight. When he heard midnight strike from the church tower of Falaise he downed two fingers of Calvados, opened his letter, and lay down on the old sofa. "Dear Klaus. . . ."

Night lay over Normandy. A night without stars. Major Friedrich Hayn stepped out of 84th Corps headquarters in Saint-Lô into the small garden. For several hours he and his clerk had been busy drawing the situation-maps which his chief, General of Artillery Erich Marcks, wanted to take along with him to Rennes for the Seventh Army's intended *Kriegsspiel*. The subject of this map exercise was "Airborne Landing." Parachute-General Meindl was to be in charge.

It was an ironic twist of fate. An airborne landing as the subject of a *Kriegsspiel* planned for an hour when that very contingency would have become cruel reality! And just then the most important commanding officers would be away from their headquarters.

Hayn's eyes swept over the deep-cut valley of the Vire, over the pastures and the orchards with their apple-trees. The Intelligence officer of 84th Corps thought of Anklam, the small town where he had been the headmaster of the secondary school. His reverie was interrupted by a four-engined bomber roaring low over the river. From the near-by AA-gun-emplacement, on the tower of the local school, the 20-millimetre tracer-shells streaked up into the night sky straight into the bomber. Just above the clerical seminary of Agneaux, above the western bank, the machine caught its packet. A burst of flame was followed by a crash. Like a solemn knell the twelve strokes of midnight rang out from the cathedral.

The major entered the bunker. The chief of staff, Lieutenant-Colonel Friedrich von Criegern, and the chief of operations, Major Hasso Viebig, were already waiting. For here, too, a birthday was being celebrated. The general commanding 84th Corps, General Marcks, born on June 6, 1891, was fifty-three. The celebration was brief. Marcks, a brilliant officer of the old school, not greatly in favour with O.K.W. because of his earlier connexions with General von Schleicher, but kept on the active list because of his great ability, was not given to celebrations.

His meals were severely restricted to the official rations. Whereas an invitation to General von Schlieben at 709th Division headquarters was much appreciated by officers throughout the corps, since Schlieben had a reputation as a gourmet, there was no great rush to dine at corps headquarters. But that did not in the least impair General Marcks's popularity—striking evidence of the man's personality.

As the chimes rang out from the cathedral the officers filed in to offer their good wishes. Standing, they drank a glass of Chablis. Then the general returned to his map table with creaking steps. He had lost a leg in Russia and wore an artificial limb.

Marcks too had been ordered by Seventh Army commander to attend the *Kriegsspiel* in Rennes on June 6. He wanted to be well briefed. "The maps, please, Hayn," he said to his Intelligence officer. The major unfolded his situation-maps—enemy situation, air situation, special map showing own gun-positions, map of minefields and flooded areas.

The general kept thinking about the previous day's large-scale reconnaissance by the Allied air forces. Since 2200 hours, moreover, reports had been coming in about massive incursions in spite of the bad weather. What did it mean? That was the great secret. The secret whose solution had long been lying on the desks at Saint-Germain and La Roche-Guyon. But it was not passed on to the commander of the key corps.

And while General Marcks at Saint-Lô kept wondering about the enemy bomber formations, while Admiral Hennecke in Cherbourg was examining the incoming reports, while Second Lieutenant Jahnke at strongpoint W5 west of Sainte-Mère-Eglise was relaxing on his bunk, while Sergeant-Signaller Lück of the 22nd Panzer Regiment in Falaise was sipping his Calvados, while the officers of the 902nd Panzer Grenadier Regiment angrily switched off the B.B.C., and while in troop quarters along the Seine, Orne, and Vire estuaries the sentimental tune of *Cute Little Bus Conductress* was drowning the whine of the mosquitoes, the green light flashed on in the leading machine of the 82nd U.S. Airborne Division.

Mauser Kar 98   Major General James Gavin glanced below him. Then he jumped. His parachute opened with a jerk. The General could not see anything in the darkness. But he knew that just then, at that very minute, thousands of parachutes would be opening. Alongside him, behind him, right in the centre of the Cotentin peninsula. And some fifty miles away, east of the Orne, British parachutists would at the same time be stepping out of their machines, and gliders would rush down to the ground with a swishing sound. An army was dropping out of the night sky.

They are coming!

Alarm—Paratroops Landing!

Lieutenant-Colonel Hoffmann had just glanced at his watch. The time was forty minutes past midnight. June 6 was less than three-quarters of an hour old. For the past hour there had been a continuous drone of aircraft above the battle headquarters of 3rd Battalion, 919th Grenadier Regiment, east of Montebourg.

Another wave was approaching. The roar grew louder.

Hoffmann stepped outside the bunker. He gave a start. Six giant birds were making straight for his battle headquarters. They were clearly visible, for the moon had just broken through the clouds. "They're bailing out." For an instant Hoffmann thought the aircraft had been damaged and its crew was going to jump. But then he understood. This was an airborne landing by paratroops. The white mushrooms were floating down—straight at his bunker.

"Alarm! Enemy parachutists!" The men at 3rd Battalion headquarters had never pulled on their trousers so fast before.

"Alarm! Alarm!"

The sentries' carbines were barking. They were firing at the parachutes floating down from the sky. Then the moon hid itself. Darkness enveloped the descending enemy. Hoffmann grabbed a rifle. Then the darkness was rent by the first burst of fire from an American sub-machine-gun.

The battle for Normandy was on.

Fifty miles south-east of the battle headquarters of 3rd Battalion, 919th Grenadier Regiment, on the far side of the Orne, things were also fairly noisy. The German sentry on the eastern end of the bridge over the Caen canal at Bénouville jumped as some fifty yards in front of his concrete sentry-box a spectral aircraft swooped towards the ground without any engine noise. A moment later there was a crash and a splintering sound, then quiet.

The sentry snatched his carbine from his shoulder and loaded. He held his breath, listening. "A crashed bomber," was his first thought. After all, enemy bomber formations had been roaring overhead in from the coast for well over an hour. From the Caen direction came the noise of explosions. Anti-aircraft guns were barking from the neighbourhood of Troarn.

"They've had it," thought Private Wilhelm Furtner. Then a searing flash blinded his eyes. He no longer heard the burst of the phosphorus grenade.

His comrades in the dugout by the approach to the bridge leapt up. They raced to their machine-gun. They fired a burst at random. They saw nothing. Suddenly they heard voices calling: "Able-Able." They did not know that this was the recognition signal of A detail of a combat team of the 6th British Airborne Division, one of whose gliders had just crash-landed there in front of them. The lance-corporal of the guard was about to lift up the telephone to give the alarm to his platoon commander on the far side of the bridge. But there was no time. Two hand-grenades came sailing in through the aperture of the pill-box. Finished.

It was a neat job. But then Major John Howard's men had practised it long enough. Back in England they had built a model of the bridge, accurate down to the last details, which they had ascertained from air photographs and agents' reports. Then for weeks throughout the spring they had rehearsed their attack on the bridge with a stopwatch.

Everything went off perfectly. Above all, the surprise.

A detail cut the barbed wire at the approach to the bridge. There was no point now in keeping quiet. The hand-grenades were bound to have roused the guard on the far side. With shouts of "Able-Able" the Tommies galloped across the bridge.

They heard other gliders crashing. They also heard the rallying cries of B detail: "Baker-Baker." And a moment later they could hear C detail as well: "Charlie-Charlie."

The German machine-gun was blazing away over the bridge. The first Tommies were falling. But the bulk of them got through. A short skirmish. The guard on the bridge was overwhelmed. The crossing of the Caen canal at Bénouville was in British hands. Only Lance-Corporal Weber got away. He tore through the village to the commandant. "British parachutists have seized the canal bridge." What he did not know was that the near-by bridge over the Orne at Ranville had also been seized by men of the 5th British Parachute Brigade in a surprise attack. At 2nd Battalion, 192nd Panzer Grenadier Regiment, at Cairon the field telephone rang: "Launching immediate counter-attack against enemy parachutists at Bénouville bridgehead."

At the Dives bridge, on the Varaville-Grangues road, another sentry was peering into the night. The watch at the bridge was mounted by the 2nd Battalion, 744th Infantry Regiment, which was barely a platoon in strength. The men had every reason to curse the bridge. Four weeks previously 3rd Battalion had organized a night exercise without warning neighbouring units, and staged a dummy attack on the bridge. The sentry, of course, could not have known that the shots that suddenly came from the approach to the bridge were blanks. He had thought the balloon had gone up in earnest and opened up with his machine-gun. There had been several wounded and two men killed. There was a terrible rumpus and some very unpleasant investigations. All that flashed through the mind of the sentry on the bridge when, shortly after midnight, he saw three men with blackened faces charge up the embankment. "Silly fools," he called out to them contemptuously. But then he jumped. Too late. He was given no time to call out or to scream. Without a sound he collapsed, stabbed by a long paratroop knife. From then onward it was an easy matter for the Tommies. Five minutes later the bridge was blown sky high.

The same thing happened at the bridge over the Dives at Robehomme. Even the important bridge at Troarn, which carried the main road from Caen to Rouen and Le Havre over the river, was blown up by sappers of Major Roseveare's combat team.

It was exactly 0111 hours when the field telephone rang on General Marcks's desk at 84th Corps headquarters in Saint-Lô. Marcks and his staff officers were still sitting over their maps. The general himself picked up the receiver. He listened. He raised his head and motioned his chief of staff to listen in with him. The call was from chief of operations, 716th Division. Hurriedly the words tumbled out of the earpiece: "Enemy paratroops have landed east of the Orne estuary. Main area is Bréville-Ranville and the northern edge of the forest of Bavent. Main objective apparently the Dives bridges and the crossings over the Orne. Counter-measures are in progress." The news had the effect of a thunderbolt. Was it the invasion? Or were they merely strong liaison groups dropped to link up with the French

Resistance? These were the questions to be answered. After a little hesitation Major Hayn shook his head. "Too close to our front line. The Resistance people would never risk that." His conclusion was: "This is the invasion." General Marcks nodded. "Let's wait and see."

They were still arguing the pros and cons when Colonel Hamann, acting commander, 709th Division, came through on the telephone: "Enemy parachutists south of Saint-Germain-de-Varreville and at Sainte-Marie-du-Mont. A second group west of the Carentan–Valognes main road on both sides of the Merderet river and on the road at Sainte-Mère-Eglise. Headquarters of 3rd Battalion, 919th Grenadier Regiment, holding prisoners from the 101st U.S. Airborne Division."

The time was 0145 hours. Five minutes later, at exactly 0150, the telephones were also ringing in Paris, in a big block of flats on the Bois de Boulogne. The chief of operations of Naval Group West, Captain Wegener, summoned his officers to the situation room. "I think the invasion is here," he said calmly.

Admiral Hoffmann, the chief of staff, did not even wait to dress. He grabbed a dressing-gown and rushed into the situation room. The reports from the radar stations under Lieutenant von Willisen were unanimous: "Large number of blips on the screens."

At first the technicians thought the huge number of blips must be caused by some interference. There just could not be so many ships. But presently no doubt was left. A vast armada must be approaching the Normandy coast.

"This can only be the invasion fleet," Hoffmann concluded. He ordered: "Signal to C.-in-C. West. Signal to the Führer's headquarters. The invasion is on."

But both in Paris and in Rastenburg the news was received sceptically. "What, in this weather? Surely your technicians must be mistaken?" Even the chief of staff of C.-in-C. West scoffed: "Maybe a flock of seagulls?" They still would not believe it. But the Navy was certain. Naval headquarters alerted all coastal stations and all naval forces in port: "The invasion fleet is coming!"

At 84th Corps, likewise, all doubt had vanished. "Alarm coast," General Marcks instructed his chief of operations, Viebig. This was the code word for the invasion. And now everything proceeded smoothly—an operation rehearsed countless times. The corps's alert was given over the service telephone. The civilian telephone network was put out of action. Divisional staff officers everywhere rushed to their map tables.

"Alarm! They are coming!"

At regimental headquarters sleepy sentries leapt to their feet. "Alarm!"

Field telephones passed the signal on to battalions and batteries of artillery; thence to companies and troops, and down to the platoons in the foremost positions, on the coast, in strongpoints and dugouts.

Field police combed the cafés and restaurants of Caen: "Come on, everybody. The balloon's gone up!"

Corporal Heilig and his friend Lance-Corporal Briten of the 22nd Panzer Regiment, who had managed to get out of Caen just before the bombing started, pedalled their bicycles furiously over farm tracks, past hedgerows and orchards, back to Verson. They got there just in time. No. 1 Company was falling in outside the church.

No. 4 Company in Epaney were already getting their tanks out of their camouflaged positions. Corporal Weinz, whom Captain Hoffmann had sent out on night patrol with five men, was just returning as his tank was being manhandled on to the road at the edge of the little town. There was a curious reason for their rapid response to the alarm. Captain von Gottberg, the officer commanding the 1st Battalion, 22nd Panzer Regiment, had just stretched out on his bunk when his telephone tinkled. He wondered why it did not ring properly, but nevertheless picked up the receiver. Thus he eavesdropped on a conversation between his regimental commander, von Oppeln-Bronikowski, and the divisional commander. General Feuchtinger was passing on to Oppeln the alarm ordered by Corps.

Gottberg was up at once. He mobilized his companies. Thus No. 1 Battalion, 22nd Panzer Regiment, was ready to move within a very short time. They were now standing by for orders.

The 2nd Battalion did not have to be roused from sleep. Major Vierzig was on the move with his tanks towards the starting-line of an exercise scheduled for the morning of June 6, east of Falaise—naturally with blank ammunition. He received the alarm by dispatch rider. He sent his companies back to their quarters to draw live ammunition. Then he too stood by.

The entire 22nd Panzer Regiment, with 120 tanks, was standing by ready to move off and ready for action. It was close behind the British dropping zone where the Tommies were still blowing up or capturing bridge after bridge, occupying crossroads, and establishing themselves in tactically important positions.

"Lieutenant, let me see your hands"

Second Lieutenant Arthur Jahnke in strongpoint No. 5—W5 for short—on the eastern coast of the Cotentin peninsula, in the sector of 709th Division, could not sleep. The ceaseless drone of aircraft had made him jumpy. He stepped out of the stone building of the strongpoint and looked up at the overcast sky. He could hear bomb bursts and AA fire in the distance and a continuous rumble above the clouds. Jahnke rang up the neighbouring strongpoint, W2. Second Lieutenant Ritter answereed the telephone. He too could not sleep. "I have a feeling that something's up," he said. "But nothing that concerns us," replied Jahnke. "I hope you're right," said Ritter. "I'll come and have a tot of your cognac to-morrow just to prove I was right," Jahnke ended the conversation. Well, that's one free drink, he thought to himself, smiling. He was not to know that his patch of dune, surrounded by barbed wire and held by a platoon of 3rd Company, 919th Grenadier Regiment, would within a matter of hours assume an historic significance as the spot where the Americans first set foot on the soil of France in the struggle for Europe. Once more Jahnke turned towards the sea and listened. "Low water," he said. And they would not come at low water. That he had straight from the horse's mouth—from Rommel in person.

When the field-marshal had inspected strongpoint W5 on May 11 he had been far from cheerful. The sector held by the division did not seem to him sufficiently fortified. There were not enough ramming blocks and pile barriers dug into the foreshore. Not enough 'Czech hedgehogs' had been laid. Not enough 'asparagus' driven into the ground to protect clearings and fields against airborne landings. Rommel's bad temper was unloaded on von Schlieben, the divisional commander; on Lieutenant-Colonel Keil, the 919th Regiment's commander; and even on Lieutenant Matz, the company commander. Rommel's famous sense of humour, his persuasive arguments which usually fired the enthusiasm of officers and other ranks, his inspiring vision—none of these had been in evidence.

He had not even handed out cigarettes. Only Jahnke, who had won the Knight's Cross as a platoon leader in Russia, and who had arrived at the Western front as a result of a wound and subsequent posting to a reserve unit, had refused to be intimidated.

He had reported to the field-marshal about their fortification work, and pointed out that with every spring tide the 'Czech hedgehogs' and the mined stakes were washed up again. Barbed-wire obstacles in depth? "Such wire as we get is used for obstacles," Jahnke said, pointing to the wire hedges built in accordance with his experience from Russia. But the field-marshal's anger was too deep-seated. "Let me see your hands for a minute, Lieutenant," he said suddenly. Second Lieutenant Jahnke, a man of twenty-three, was a little taken aback. But an order was an order. He stripped off his grey suède gloves and held out his hands to the field-marshal. They were torn, with bloody scratches and calluses. The lieutenant had learnt in Russia that an officer lends a hand with the laying of wire obstacles every bit as much as a private. Indeed, over here in the West he had demonstratively done his share, for the long years of occupation in France had not exactly engendered much enthusiasm for fortification work among the German units.

The sight of Jahnke's hands had robbed Rommel of his last chance to vent his anger. He nodded. "Well done, lientenant. The blood on an officer's hands from fortification work is worth every bit as much as that shed in battle." The blood on an officer's hands. . . . The second lieutenant with the Knight's Cross, who had only newly arrived from the Eastern front, had uttered his regulation *Jawohl* and had kept his thoughts to himself. If only the men were given proper instruction in fortification work! But many elderly reserve officers, whose active service experience dated from the First World War, were still building 1917-type positions. Jahnke had frequently been exasperated by it. And not only by the fortification work.

He had discovered to his amazement that the French fishermen were authorized to stroll along the macadamized road right through his strongpoint on their way down to the shore. Jahnke forbade it. The village commandant in the rear shook his head: that new chap was taking everything so seriously. Those decent local people—why shouldn't they fish? And when Jahnke actually got his guns to open fire one night as a practice alarm the whole of regimental headquarters was in a flap. "That Ivan," they said jokingly, "that Ivan has clearly gone off his rocker. Just can't wait for the show to start!"

But Jahnke had grinned and gone on practising and building fortifications in accordance with the field-marshal's instructions, even though the increasingly heavy air raids left little doubt as to what would become of the magnificent and laboriously constructed positions with their trenches and wire obstacles if a bomb carpet were laid over them. The effect could be studied in detail at 1st Battery, 1261st Army Coastal Artillery Regiment, under Lieutenant Erben outside Saint-Martin-de-Varreville. Not a stone had been left standing there. The position, complete with all its guns, had been pulverized. "Wouldn't be so funny if they caught us," Sergeant Hein had said to Jahnke.

Since then they had been really afraid of the nightly bomber incursions which were getting heavier all the time.

The troops, of course, would not believe that anything could go wrong. After all, their strongpoint looked well fortified from the crest of the dunes: the impressive 88-millimetre gun, the bunkers with their flanking 50-millimetre guns, the 75-millimetre anti-tank gun, and the machine-gun nests, the flamethrowers, and the Goliaths. Why, even the FK-16, the field gun from the First World War, positively radiated military prowess.

"Surely they won't walk smack into a fortress," the men were saying. Jahnke did not think so either. He returned to his quarters in the stone building. He curled up on his camp bed and lit a cigarette. He thought of Russia. He was glad to be in France. They even had a shower next door, though it was just a watering-can cunningly rigged to the ceiling.

75 mm. Anti-Tank Gun

The telephone rang. Jahnke lifted the receiver. He leapt up from his bed. Battalion was passing on the alarm. The message added: "Enemy parachutists probably dropping behind your position also."

"Alarm!"

"Action stations! Double sentries along the strongpoint perimeter! Patrol to move off at once to reconnoitre the situation!"

"Probably an operation in support of the French Resistance," said Sergeant Hein. True, he had not yet come across a single armed Resistance man, but there was a lot of talk about their secret army.

Jahnke agreed with him. There was a good reason why the big invasion need not be expected that day. "When they come it will be at high water," Rommel had said to him during a recent inspection. It seemed to stand to reason. At high water the landing craft could run up right against the base of the dunes, close to the barbed wire. At low water, on the other hand, every attacker would have to cross some 800 yards of perfectly flat beach. Eight hundred yards! In the face of machine-guns and anti-tank guns—not to mention the mortars.

No. They would come at high water. But now the tide had just turned and was running out. It seemed unthinkable that paratroops would open the invasion at that moment. It didn't make sense. Hence this was not the big landing operation.

Those were Jahnke's thoughts as he stood waiting.

Half an hour later the carbines and machine-guns opened up among the flooded fields at his rear. It was the patrol. They had run into two dozen American paratroopers who had tried to work their way across the swamp. The poor wretches were up to their waists in the water. As the machine-gun bursts spattered around them and the first few dropped the others raised their hands. With nineteen prisoners the leader of the patrol returned to the strongpoint. "Hands above your heads. Faces to the wall." The lance-corporal ordered the captured Americans to line up inside the stone building. The prisoners were frisked, and all their belongings were closely examined. Their two wounded, whom the Americans had carried in with them, were taken to the first-aid post in the bunker.

Jahnke immediately rang battalion headquarters. "Nineteen prisoners of the American 2nd Battalion, 506th Parachute Regiment—" and he was about to add: "—of the 101st Airborne Division" when the line clicked and went dead.

The underground cable which had only recently been laid

by French workers under the supervision of German engineers
had been cut. W5 had contact only with its neighbouring strongpoints right and left.

Corporal Hoffmann of the medical corps was meanwhile
giving first aid to a seriously wounded Negro. The poor man
must have been in terrible pain. He had been shot through the
chin. Hoffmann nodded to him reassuringly. "You'll be all
right." The black man looked terrified. The corporal turned to
his medicine box and met the eyes of a slightly wounded
lieutenant. The lieutenant grinned. In fairly good German he
said, "You are in the medical corps and you carry a pistol?
That's against the rules!" Hoffmann, like Jahnke, was an old
hand from Russia—and on the Russian front every member of
the medical corps carried a pistol. It was more effective protection than an armband with a red cross.

Hoffmann realized at once that the American officer was
right. "Maybe it's also against the rules that I'm bandaging you
in spite of my pistol," he grumbled. At that moment Jahnke
entered the bunker. He heard the last few words.

"What's up, Hoffmann?"

"He's complaining about my pistol."

Jahnke glanced at the enemy officer. "You're quite right,"
he said. And turning to the corporal he added: "Take your
cannon off, Hoffmann."

The corporal took off his holster belt. He was grinning.
"Let's hope the bombs remember that I'm in the medical
corps."

They did not remember. Corporal Hoffmann of the medical
corps was killed shortly afterwards.

Jahnke had a troop bunker cleared in the dunes farther back
and ordered his prisoners to be taken there. The door was barred
and a guard mounted outside.

Towards 0245 hours Corporal Hoffmann came up to Jahnke.
"The wounded are curiously restless. They keep wanting to
know the time. And they keep asking when they're going to be
moved." The guard outside the bunker with the prisoners likewise reported that the two officers in particular demanded to be
moved.

"I wonder what the hurry is?" Jahnke asked.

"Maybe they don't like it here," the guard said, grinning.
"Or maybe something else is due to happen yet, Herr Leutnant."

A Regiment jumps into the Swamp

By daybreak 84th Corps realized that the airborne landings were no second-rate operation, no commando raid, and no bluff.

Reports showed that entire divisions had landed on both flanks of the corps's area. To the right of the Orne and Dives, in the sector of the 716th and 711th Divisions, the 6th British Airborne Division had been identified. On the left, in the sector of 709th Division, the 82nd and 101st U.S. Airborne Divisions had been identified in the strength of four regiments.

The combat teams were trying to gain control of the principal bridges and roads across the flooded area to the hinterland in order to seal off the coast from all possible supplies and from support by tactical reserves. In a few places they had succeeded in this. This could no longer be taken lightly. This was deadly serious. The air drops evidently represented a bold strategic operation to protect the flanks of an impending seaborne landing between the estuaries of Orne and Vire.

The conclusions of 84th Corps were correct. D-Day had come. The greatest amphibian operation in history was being preceded by the most adventurous, spectacular, but also the most costly air operation.

Altogether, 9210 aircraft—not including bombers and reconnaissance planes—left England during the night of June 5-6, 1944. For two and a half hours without pause the immense air armada passed over London.

The coastal front was spluttering with bomb bursts. Over Caen hell was let loose. Bridges, roads, and especially airfields in the French hinterland were under a ceaseless hail of bombs.

Vast fleets of gliders sailed through the air. Everything had been accurately calculated, worked out in detail, and rehearsed. A great deal went according to plan. But not everything.

The Americans dropped two airborne divisions—17,000 élite troops with field guns and armour-piercing weapons—behind the German line on the Cotentin peninsula. Their objective was to establish a strong position in depth behind the German coastal line of 709th Division, to keep open the exits through the artificially flooded areas, and to cut off the German 91st Air Landing Division from the American beach-heads. Moreover, communications were to be cut, roads and bridges blocked, and the German coastal front cut off from supplies and reinforcements.

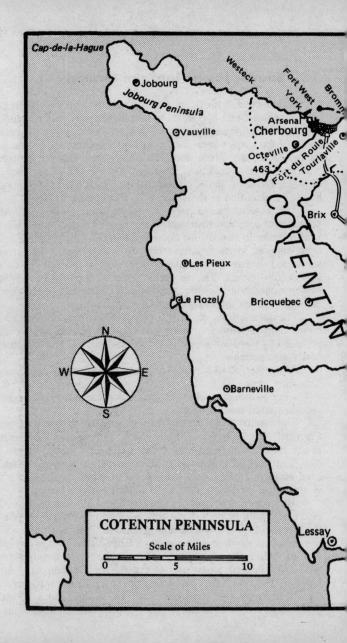

COTENTIN PENINSULA

Scale of Miles

0   5   10

But the gigantic airborne landing operation was launched under an unlucky star.

Heavy, low-lying clouds prevented the pilots of the advanced formations from making an accurate approach. The glider formations, too, were broken up. That was the beginning of the disaster. The objectives of the drops were the bridges and causeways in the flooded areas of the Merderet river along the road from Sainte-Mère-Eglise to Pont l'Abbé. If the men jumped half a minute too soon or late they would land in the swamps or in the water. That was precisely what happened. The 507th Regiment, without exception, jumped right into the middle of the flooded area. The grass grew so thick upon the swampy ground that, looking down from the air, one might well believe it to be a lush meadow. But a man coming down by parachute, with seventy pounds of equipment on his back, would be swallowed up at once. Only a few succeeded in getting out the bog. The regiment's heavy equipment was lost entirely. Wounded men drowned helplessly. Crash-landing gliders vanished with men and equipment.

General James Gavin, the thirty-six-year-old commander of the 82nd Airborne Division's parachute assault, also stepped out into the void. While over the Channel he had seen the machines of his advanced formations and had known 7000 men to be behind him. Over the Channel Islands, however, they had run into flak, and presently low cloud had slid between aircraft and ground like thick porridge.

At the last moment Gavin's machine got a clear view. Below him the general saw a glittering sheet of water. He heaved a sigh of relief: the Douve. The green light, the signal for jumping, flashed on. He drew a deep breath and stepped out. But like the general and his pilot, so nearly the whole armada had made a mistake. The 507th Regiment had dropped into the water of the flooded area along the Merderet.

They waded through the swamp. Some men lay drowned in the ditches. Others blundered about the banks of the river looking for the bridge that they were to have secured.

Only one thing went right: the little town of Sainte-Mère-Eglise fell to Gavin's men. A German AA transport unit which had been stationed there withdrew after a brief skirmish with a few scattered detachments of the 505th Parachute Regiment, which had dropped right in the middle of the little town, abandoning to the enemy that important township on *route nationale* 13, the road from Cherbourg via Carentan to Paris. This blunder of a flak lieutenant was to have far-reaching consequences. It presented the American airborne landing operation with its first decisive success.

General Taylor's 101st Airborne Division was not much luckier than General Ridgway's 82nd. It lost 30 per cent of its strength and 70 per cent of its equipment in the landing. Rommel's 'asparagus,' the stakes he had ordered to be driven into the ground, were the doom of countless gliders. They were impaled and splintered; they dug their noses into gardens and fields; they crashed into hedgerows and sunken lanes. In small groups the various units tried to reach their operation areas or the coastline. They fought running engagements with German patrols. They attacked villages and headquarters. They took prisoners or were taken prisoners.

The Frogs of Saint-Marcouf

The heavy naval coastal battery of Saint-Marcouf was an important pivot of the German defences on the east coast of the Cherbourg peninsula. It had been planned as a showpiece of the Atlantic Wall and was intended for use against naval targets. Its equipment included four 210-millimetre long-barrelled guns, six 75-millimetre AA guns, and one 150-millimetre gun. Unfortunately this powerful barrier behind the beach of La Madeleine was not yet ready on June 6. Nevertheless, the 400 naval gunners and their equipment represented a by-no-means negligible defensive power against attacks from the sea.

The first gun emplaced in the bunker had been ranged on April 19. Its roar was heard far and wide. The foundations held. The men nodded. On the following day the war began in earnest for the battery. Every evening the bombers came over from England out of the setting sun and made straight for their positions. They dropped their eggs into the churned-up nests of the bomb craters. But the 400 men of Saint-Marcouf, a motley crowd from many units, most of them over thirty-eight, were gradually developing a stubborn *esprit de corps*. In spite of the air raids they continued to fortify their positions. They planted 'asparagus.' They uncoiled barbed wire. They built bunkers. They laid belts of mines on the dunes and planted esparto grass on top of them. They toiled hard in the sunlit coastal landscape with the sea breeze fanning their faces. The roar of the breakers came from below the bluff.

"Get a move on there, get a move on," was the sergeant's never-varying refrain. "Get a move on!" But in spite of it all they did not get enough concrete, they did not get enough ammunition, and they had no steel loophole flaps for the bunker openings, the vision slits of the command-posts. They had no swivelling armoured cupolas and no modern fire-control instruments. "Let's hope the enemy waits till we are ready," tall Corporal Hermann Nissen used to say every evening. He was not to know that the enemy, across the Channel in England, was waiting for only two things—the right moon and a suitable tide.

At last the moment came.

On the evening of June 5, 1944, the sun set without the customary simultaneous call of "Enemy aircraft!" It was the first evening in weeks without enemy bombers.

With a sigh of relief the men went to their quarters in the little town of Saint-Marcouf and the village of Crisbecq. This had been the normal routine since April 19, since the bunkers at the gun-position offered room and cover only for the crews of the two fully installed guns and the AA guns.

The sentry took up his position in a sheltered corner of the bunker. A faint drone was audible from afar. Karl Sellow cupped his right hand over the bowl of his pipe. Then he took a puff.

Luxuriously he blew the smoke into the night air. It was 2300 hours. In another hour he would be relieved. But what was that drone over to the west? Surely those fellows were not suddenly coming from a different direction? It would be a damned nuisance; especially as the night had started so peacefully.

"Enemy aircraft!" So it was them after all. The drone swelled to a deafening roar. Thus began the worst night Saint-Marcouf ever experienced. Over a hundred aircraft attacked the position. According to official Allied records 600 tons of bombs were dropped on the battery site. Six hundred tons!

The onslaught lasted thirty-five minutes. All six AA guns were smashed. The ground was ploughed over.

Shortly after midnight a runner from the little château of Saint-Marcouf burst into Ohmsen's battle headquarters. He was breathless and shaken. "Herr Oberleutnant, direct hit on the château. The quarters are wrecked. Lots of men are buried. The ruins are burning. There are many dead and wounded."

Ohmsen was worried. That was the last straw. "Oberleutnant Grieg," he said to his gun-position officer, "take all available men. Get them to draw spades and shovels. And hurry up. We can't afford any losses now."

Lieutenant Grieg wasted no time in telling his men to fall in. Helter-skelter they rushed out into the night with spades and shovels. But they did not get far. Back at the battery the men were trying to patch up two damaged AA guns when Grieg's men returned.

"What's up?"

Grieg rushed over to Ohmsen. "Herr Oberleutnant, we came under fire. I presume from enemy paratroops."

"Paratroops?" Ohmsen was doubtful. "Get a fighting patrol ready! Oberleutnant Grieg will lead the patrol. Under him two N.C.O.'s and twenty men. Weapons: sub-machine-guns and hand-grenades."

The first hour of June 6, 1944, that historic and bloody Tuesday, had begun also at Saint-Marcouf. Cautiously the men picked their way through the darkness. Silence. Only here and there came the croaking of a frog from the marshes. A short distance away two other frogs answered. Yet another was croaking quite vigorously next to Lance-Corporal Albert Müller. Strange, Lieutenant Grieg reflected, he had never known so many frogs there before.

The patrol fanned out. At the same instant things began happening on the right wing. "Halt," came the voice of the end man of the line. Then a crash and a groan. Grieg rushed over. "What's going on here?" he whispered. "An American," a lowered voice replied. And there he lay on the ground. Herrmann and Müller had got him. He had used a kind of toy snapper to croak like a frog—evidently the recognition signal for his comrades. On hearing the German challenge he had tried to escape, but Müller had hit him over his tin helmet with his sub-machine-gun. He was now kneeling by him. He picked up the tin snapper and pressed it. *Croak*, it went. Müller pressed it again. *Croak*. The signal was answered from the swamp. That was when their ruse was conceived. They went on pressing the snapper, silently stalking the answering frogs and picking up one American after another from the swamp—until there were no frogs left to croak.

Towards 0130 hours the patrol returned to base without losses. Each man had brought a frog with him: they had taken twenty prisoners. A truly impressive bag. "Croak, croak," Lieutenant Grieg said, chuckling. Then they locked up the twenty Americans in an empty bunker.

The prisoners belonged to five transport units of the 502nd U.S. Parachute Regiment. Among them were the company commander and the complete company headquarters personnel. The remaining hundred men, who had fought their way through the swamp as far as Saint-Marcouf or had come down in the middle of the village, were now trying to reform for an attack on the battery position.

Interrogation of the prisoners revealed that the combat group had had the task of occupying Lieutenant Erben's gun-position 1/1261 near Saint-Martin-de-Varreville, four miles farther west, behind strongpoint W5. Either in error, or because it had seemed easier, they had decided to attack Saint-Marcouf instead. The orderly officer of 2nd Battalion, 919th Infantry Regiment, with a hastily formed assault team of eight men, had forced the Americans out of Saint-Marcouf and driven them off the road back into the pathless swamp.

Ohmsen and his officers were wide-eyed with amazement when they saw the equipment taken from the prisoners—tiny walkie-talkie sets in the shape of pocket torches, compasses as tunic buttons, the New Testament on India paper, and silk scarves with maps printed on them. Most interesting of the lot were the maps. Even the fields in the hinterland where Rommel 'asparagus' had been planted only a few days before were accurately marked. But that was not all. Ohmsen had never computed the exact map co-ordinates of his machine-gun posts; yet the Americans had accurately surveyed them by aerial photography and plotted them on their silk maps. Ohmsen and his men had a foreboding of more surprises to come.

Two and a half miles farther inland, at the neighbouring strongpoint of Azeville, things were rather lively at the 9th Battery, 945th Army Coastal Artillery Regiment, with its four 122-millimetre guns in their fortress-type emplacements.

Lieutenant Kattnig, the gun-position officer and strongpoint commander, was busy writing a letter in his bunker when the air-raid alarm was given by the flak-post. He rushed outside his bunker and was amazed to see an armada of transport aircraft spewing out parachutists.

"All weapons, fire!"

Kattnig raced over to the command-post. But before him, in the most literal sense, a man dropped out of the sky. Kattnig whipped out his pistol and stepped on the shroud-lines. The man seemed dazed and raised his arms: an American officer.

He refused to answer questions. In sullen silence he let himself be locked in a bunker. At the same moment firing broke out outside the barbed wire surrounding the post.

Kattnig was no longer able to get through to Division by direct wire. He had to make his report via the observer-post situated at the Saint-Marcouf battery.

Meanwhile Lieutenant Hansjörg Habel of the neighbouring battery arrived with a handful of men. His battery was in field positions, and the air drop had been right among their tents. His men had been overwhelmed by the Americans. Habel's account did not exactly make the men of Azeville feel friendly. "They won't get in here," Sergeant Louis Schürger declared emphatically.

Merville—a Costly Mistake

The British too had their Saint-Marcouf. Its name was Merville. In December 1943, when Lieutenant-Colonel Terence Otway was first summoned by his divisional commander, General Richard Gale, he had never heard the name of Merville. But before long he became as familiar with the village as if he had spent his whole life there.

At Merville, east of the Orne, a mile and a half from the coast, was a battery of 1716th Artillery Regiment with a complement of 130 men. On the strength of agents' reports Allied Intelligence had come to the conclusion that this battery was equipped with 150-millimetre guns and hence represented a serious threat to the planned seaborne landing of the 3rd British Division in the Ouistreham–Lion area. "The battery must fall before the landing," was the order. Considerable machinery was set in motion in order to silence Merville before the seaborne landing began. That was the task to be accomplished by Lieutenant-Colonel Otway with the 9th Parachute Battalion of the 6th British Airborne Division. The operation was a battle in its own right. It was lavish in effort, costly, and essentially pointless; but it has been much quoted in military history and is still receiving a good deal of prominence in the most recent British and American publications. It therefore deserves closer study.

The general plan was as follows: Otway's reinforced battalion, in all some 750 men, were to drop between Merville and Gonneville shortly before 0100 hours, meet at predetermined rendezvous points, and then take the strongpoint according to an exact timetable. The execution had been worked out with loving care, rather like some modern battle between cowboys and Red Indians. Its climax was to be the landing of an assault force of

150 mm. Gun

sixty men by gliders right on top of the battery at the very
moment when the attack was mounted from outside.

Aerial reconnaissance had shown the strongpoint to be
surrounded by a barbed-wire hedge fifteen feet thick and five
feet high. In front of that was a wide minefield. And in front of
that were more barbed-wire obstacles. And, as if that was not
enough, there was another minefield a hundred yards deep and
surrounded by wire.

The defence-post included one-man foxholes and connected
beach trenches. Of the four gun-bunkers only the easternmost,
No. 4, was equipped for close-combat defence. The battery was
protected by automatic weapons. An automatic 20-millimetre
gun stood on the roof of one of the pill-boxes, right in the centre
of the battery. It was intended for action against air and ground
targets.

According to the Allied plan the position was to be eliminated
at all costs before the seaborne landing. Lieutenant-Colonel
Otway was therefore ordered to take the battery by 0515 hours at
the latest. If he did not succeed the Navy would start shelling the
position at 0515. That showed the importance attached to Merville.

The position of the battery at a crossroads, on open ground,
made effective camouflage difficult. The massive anti-tank ditch
marked out the post unambiguously for Allied air-reconnaissance.
By repeated aerial photography they kept tabs on the progress of
fortification work. When towards the end of March the photo-

graphs showed two of the gun-bunkers completed and the other two under construction, a systematic and wasteful aerial bombardment began. It is not without interest to consider the exact effect of it. Of roughly 1000 bomb bursts only 50 lay within the battery territory, and no more than two hit the targets intended to be hit—the gun-emplacement. Neither of them achieved penetration. This was instructive illustration of the high cost and small return of carpet bombing of reinforced concrete objectives in open ground.

Lieutenant-Colonel Otway was twenty-nine. His battalion of 35 officers and 600 men had the reputation of an élite unit. It was reinforced now by a company of picked, battle-seasoned Canadian parachutists. All in all they were 750 men.

Throughout two months, by the sweat of their brows, Otway's men practised the attack. They had built a model which even included the cows, and where every farm track had been correctly scooped out by bulldozer. They practised and practised, by day and by night, the same operation over and over again— the full, complicated sequence of actions. Every man knew his functions and every one of his movements—the reconnaissance teams, the taping party with their mine detectors who were to mark out the cleared path through minefield and wire, the "breaching" teams who were to clear passages through the obstacles, and the assault force to be landed from three gliders inside the strongpoint at the exact moment of the rush from outside and who were to take the guns by surprise. In addition, there were two reconnaissance teams with two German-speaking N.C.O.'s whose task it was to cause confusion by misleading commands.

The equipment was as lavish as the planning. All the weapons and equipment of technical warfare were employed— flame-throwers, anti-tank guns, radio jeeps, scaling ladders, assault demolition charges, special explosive sticks, an ambulance, microphones, and loud-speakers.

In order to wear down the German defenders and extensively damage the obstacles even before the attack, more especially in order to render the minefields ineffective, 109 heavy Lancaster bombers were scheduled to bomb the battery between 0030 and 0040 hours. A total of 382 tons of bombs, including block-busters of nearly two tons, were to crush the fortifications. The airborne landing was then to be made under protection of this aerial bombardment. While the battalion rallied, the so-called taping party was to advance with the mine-clearing party, clearing and marking out three paths through the minefield. The leader of the reconnaissance team was instructed to keep the battalion commander at the landing-point informed about the situation. The signal for the attack was a bugle-call. For identification each member of the assault parties had a luminous skull-and-crossbones painted on his chest.

The most detailed timetable was that for the glider-borne assault force. It looked like this:

> At 0324 hours: at 6000 feet above the German battery the tow-plane will cast off the glider with the assault party and flash a light signal.
> At 0325 to 0330 hours: at the bugle-call "Reveille" a mortar will fire star-shells towards the battery position in order to facilitate landing.
> At 0328 hours: at the call "Fall in" all fire will cease with the exception of the star-shells and the fire of the diversion team.
> At 0330 hours: at the call "Lights out" firing of star-shells will cease. The first glider will land. The charges in the obstacles will be detonated. Assault.

That was the plan.

And this is how it went in practice. Shortly before midnight the landing and reconnaissance parties took off from England. In front of them roared the Lancaster bombers. But the very first item on the programme went wrong. The aerial bombardment of the battery missed its target. Instead of the guns and the minefields the village of Gonneville was reduced to ruins. The reconnaissance party dropped right among the bombs and only just escaped annihilation.

Lieutenant-Colonel Otway and the main section had no inkling of the disaster. They felt sure that after all their trouble and planning nothing could go seriously wrong. But they soon found out that they had overlooked one small point—that the Germans would shoot back. And that was precisely what happened. They opened up with 88-millimetre flak. Many of the pilots took drastic evasive action. The paratroops with their heavy loads tumbled about in the machines like nine-pins. There was a good deal of confusion in the transports. Not without difficulty did the men get out of their machines. Others flew too far to the east. Several aircraft missed the dropping zone altogether. The glider with the heavy special equipment had torn loose from its hawser while over the Channel and had crashed. Widely scattered, the parachutists reached the ground. The last of them were as much as thirty miles from their target. Only very few of them came down on the scheduled dropping point.

Lieutenant-Colonel Otway had made a good landing but he had a vain wait for his battalion. At the end of an hour and a half 150 men had at last assembled. Only 150 out of 750! So 600 were missing. Otway nevertheless decided to attack—a testimony to the man's toughness, courage, and discipline. Naturally the whole plan had to be scrapped. The course of action was now dictated by realities. From the available strength two groups of fifteen men each were formed who were to breach the obstacles; four assault teams of twelve men each were then to storm the position.

They had cautiously assembled in a ditch on the edge of a cornfield, 500 yards from the battery-post. The time was 0330 hours. At the battery command-post the alert of the divisional artillery commander had long been received. The battery commander and gun-position officer had doubled the sentries. And before long they spotted movements outside the perimeter. The alarm was sounded throughout the position and the battery's machine-guns began to stutter.

At that moment the gliders with the assault force came flying in. The towing-planes flashed their lights to signal the casting off of the hawsers. Noiselessly the gliders wheeled down to the ground. One of them skimmed over the battery position at a height of a hundred feet, and 20-millimetre flak opened up from the roof of a crew bunker. The tracer went straight into the belly of the glider. Smoke poured out. The big bird swerved and crashed a long way off in the fields. Now the second glider came into sight. Since Otway had no mortars to light up the battery area the pilot mistook the village—still burning from the bombing raid—for the landing point and set down its party some four miles from their objective. Of the third glider there was no trace at all. It had made a forced landing on the wrong side of the Channel, still over England.

Thus, the final surprise assault was off. Otway therefore ordered his men to attack. Explosive charges were flung into the obstacles. The assault parties advanced on the strongpoint firing all their weapons.

The long period of waiting and the ceaseless alerts had blunted the caution of the German garrison at Merville also. The main entrance to the battery site was only skimpily barricaded.

As a result a small British party succeeded in penetrating rapidly into the battery. At the same moment Corporal Windgassen arrived at the strongpoint entrance with a reconnaissance unit of army flak. The 20-millimetre flak troop had run straight into the British airborne landings on its way from Franceville to Caen. The troop leader had decided to make for Merville. With five men Windgassen had gone ahead to reconnoitre. Meeting British troops at the barrier, they were so much taken by surprise that all they could do was raise their arms. Corporal Kurt Richter of the medical corps found a lot of work waiting for him.

From the bunker where Windgassen and his men were lying together with the British wounded they could hear the noise of battle in the strongpoint. Their German comrades were engaging the British assault party from the glider that had crash-landed behind the position.

In the trenches and dugouts the artillerymen were engaged in bloody hand-to-hand fighting with the attackers. Two of the gun-bunkers had their rearward steel bulkheads open so that the British only had to fling in their demolition charges.

It was all over in thirty minutes. Otway's men were victorious. Twenty-two Germans, all of them wounded, were marched out as prisoners from the position. The remaining men, about a hundred, had been killed in the fighting. Of Otway's 150 men 66 lay dead on the battlefield.

It was a dearly bought victory.

And with victory came the terrible revelation: the Merville battery did not have any 150-millimetre guns after all—only 75-millimetre field guns. It would not have constituted any serious threat to a British seaborne landing. For shelling targets at sea it was not suitable at all. The intended British landing beach was not even visible from the battery, and with its firing-range of four miles it could have opened only indirect fire on the easternmost part of the beach. An error, an error of magnificent magnitude, had guided the planners of the operation against Merville. As so often in war, the entire costly enterprise had been just an error.

In the landward direction the guns could not fire at all from their emplacements—unless, of course, they were dragged out of their bunkers. The whole position was equipped only for defence against a tank attack from the seaward side.

Yet another mistake upset the calculations of the British planners. After the capture of the battery Lieutenant-Colonel Otway fired the prearranged signal, to indicate that the battery had fallen. However, he received no confirmation that his signal had been understood by the reconnaissance aircraft. He therefore withdrew from the position so as not to become a victim of his own side's naval bombardment. Presently a German combat group of the 736th Grenadier Regiment recaptured Merville by a counter-attack.

It turned out that in the excitement the British had not wrecked the guns as thoroughly as they might have done. The equipment was by no means entirely useless. Makeshift repairs were put in hand at once.

On the following day, June 7, the German grenadiers defended the battery against a British commando party which had orders to mop up the area. They resisted stubbornly but were overcome. A renewed German counter-attack, supported by self-propelled guns, again brought the strongpoint under German control. Until the beginning of July it was to change its occupants several more times. It was hotly contested and drenched with blood. For in war one costly mistake begets a dozen others.

W5 joins Action

Dawn was breaking. The hedgerows of Cotentin and the orchards of Calvados were emerging from darkness. But one could not trust any hedgerow, any orchard, or any cornfield.

Scattered paratroops were lying in their hideouts, keeping out of sight. Stray patrols from various German reserve battalions in the dropping zones near Sainte-Mère-Eglise and in the area of Ranville, east of the Orne, were mounting posts in cornfields and outside villages.

"Come on, step on it," Major-General Falley said to his driver. "It's nearly daylight."

"We're practically there, Herr General," Major Bartuzat assured him. They were racing along the Coutances-Périers-Etienville road, back to where they had started from.

Six hours earlier General Falley and his supply officer had set out from 91st Air Landing Division headquarters at Picauville, so as to get to Rennes in time for the Seventh Army's *Kriegsspiel*. The ceaseless stream of bombers overhead had worried the general. An experienced instructor at the Military Academy and a front-line officer, he felt that these sorties against the hinterland did not bode well. The marker flares dropped by the pathfinder aircraft confirmed his suspicions.

"This is no routine raid, Bartuzat," he had said to the major as the drone of the bombers drowned even the noise of the car's engine.

Falley did not know that General J. H. Doolittle's 8th Air Force with three divisions of strategic bombers—a total of 1083 B-17s and B-24s—protected by 1347 fighters and carrying 3000 tons of bombs—was about to smash a way through the German defences for the invasion. He did not know, nor could he count the aircraft. But he suspected that something exceptional was afoot. And he knew that only some 320 German aircraft were available to oppose that aerial steamroller.

The thought of the few dozen German fighters made him feel sick.

"Turn back," he had ordered his driver. "We're going back to headquarters."

Over the roads of the *départements* Ille-et-Vilaine and Manche the car tore towards Château Haut, north of Picauville. They could hear the noise of battle in front of them and the roar of aircraft overhead. Behind them, in the Carentan-Bayeux-Caen area and along the coast, a very heavy aerial bombardment appeared to be in progress. The skyline was shrouded in the smoke and dust of explosions.

The car turned off the main road. A short distance away lay the château. But, surely, this was machine-gun fire and the rattle of submachine-guns. Falley whipped out his pistol and leapt out of the car. "Careful!" Major Bartuzat called out. Too late.

"Hands up," yelled a man with a submachine gun at the ready. The general managed to fire two shots from his Walther pistol. Then the submachine gun opened up. Falley and Bartuzat were mown down. Thus, in the early dawn of June 6, the battle for France claimed its first general.

The commander of the 91st Air Landing Division was dead before he could issue a single order.

In strongpoint W5 Second Lieutenant Jahnke was listening to the drone of the bombers. His battle headquarters was no bunker, but merely a hole in the sand shored up with planks behind the anti-tank wall. From where he stood the sea looked a hazy grey. Corporal Hein was coming along the trench.

"I have an uneasy feeling, Herr Leutnant," he said. "Shouldn't we put all men on action stations?"

"Why?" asked Jahnke. "Even if the invasion comes they're bound to bomb and shell us first. Better leave the men under cover as long as possible."

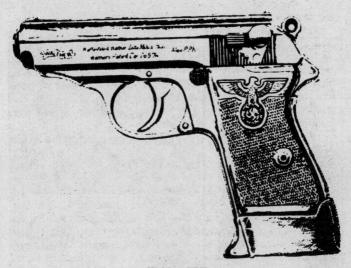

Walther PPK

Hein nodded.

"Have special rations issued to them," Jahnke ordered. "Food is always a good idea, and we've got plenty in store—enough for at least a week."

A new wave of twin-engined bombers was coming in from the sea in impeccable fly-past formation. "Going to cross the coast north of us," Jahnke thought aloud. But he had hardly finished speaking when to his horror the first wave wheeled right and, flying down the coast, made straight for the strongpoint.

Jahnke ducked into his foxhole, still watching the giant birds through his binoculars. Now!

The bomb bays opened. As if moved by invisible hands the bomb doors folded back. And almost at once the bombs came tumbling out, dropping with their curious wobbling motion.

Whining.

Binoculars down and face pressed into the ground.

An infernal roar. Flashes like lightning. Smoke. Stench. "That lot dropped this side of the macadamized road," Jahnke automatically registered. And already the next wave was coming in. More crashes and bursts.

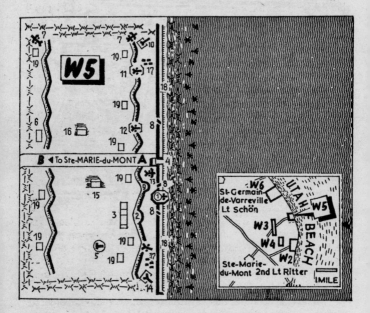

Strongpoint W5 was 400 yards long and 300 yards deep. At low water there was 800 yards of beach; at high tide the water came right up against the barbed wire. Underwater obstacles consisted of 'Czech hedgehogs' and ramming posts. A. Seaward defences. B. Landward defences. 1. Captured machine-gun in armoured cupola. 2. Command-post with scissor telescope. 3. Stone-built block covered with camouflage netting, housing officers' quarters, telephone switchboard, mess-room, and showers. 4. Road-block consisting of concrete cubes. 5. 80-millimetre mortar in concrete emplacement. 6. Reinforced bunker, used as first-aid post. 7. Heavy machine-gun. 8 Flame-throwers. 9. Fire control for flame-throwers. 10. 50-millimetre armoured-car gun. 11. 75-millimetre field gun. 12. 75-millimetre anti-tank gun. 13. 88-millimetre army flak. 14. 50-millimetre armoured-car gun. 15. Cookhouse. 16. Air Force post. 17. Goliaths. 18 Tank obstacles. 19. Armoured quarters. Both flanks and the landward side protected by wire obstacles and mines.

"Far side of the road this time."

But the next stick was again on the near side, and the screech seemed to come straight at Jahnke's dugout. Louder and louder. Going right through him. And still continuing. And then it happened. A giant fist grabbed the lieutenant and flung him against the wall of his dugout. Smacked him right on the turf and covered him with a cartload of sand.

"Must get out," was his first thought. He dug himself free. His shoulder felt as if it were on fire. His left arm was numb. And already the next wave of bombers was approaching. Jahnke raced over the dune. He tumbled into a very flat bomb crater. Almost unconsciously he registered that the enemy must be dropping his notorious anti-personnel bombs—bombs with advanced detonation and high fragmentation effect. "Get out of this shallow crater—no cover here," Jahnke said to himself. He ran over to the concrete block which barred the macadamized road and which formed a safe angle with the anti-tank wall. He threw himself down in the little hollow that the wind had scooped out in the sand at the base of the concrete block. His body was covered here as though by a projecting roof. Among the bomb bursts he could now hear the crackling and popping noise of a fireworks display.

"The ammunition bunkers," Jahnke realized. The ammunition was going up.

Suddenly everything was quiet. Jahnke picked himself up from his sandy hollow and ran through the strongpoint, which was still shrouded in smoke and dust.

All the fortifications they had laboriously dug and built through the weeks had been churned up like a children's sandpit. The 75-millimetre anti-tank gun was a heap of twisted metal. The 88-millimetre gun had taken some bad knocks. Two ammunition bunkers had blown up. The machine-gun nests had been buried by avalanches of sand.

Casualties, fortunately, were small, since the men had been sitting in their bunkers. True, the bunkers had been hit, but the bombs had not pierced the reinforced roofs.

The mess corporal's assistant came running up to Jahnke. He was an elderly man from the Ruhr.

"Everything is wrecked, Herr Leutnant! The stores are on fire. Everything's wrecked!" he cried, his face pale. And in a serious voice he added, "We've got to surrender, Herr Leutnant."

Jahnke was twenty-three. But he had learnt on the Russian front how to lead men. He could sense the rising panic. And panic was a soldier's worst enemy. More strongpoints fell to panic than to enemy weapons. That was a thing he knew from Russia.

"Have you gone out of your mind, man?" Jahnke said to him. "If we had always surrendered in Russia in this kind of situation the Russians would have been here long ago." And, raising his voice, he commanded: "All troops fall in for entrenching!"

"It's got to be done, chaps," he said to his disgruntled or shocked men. For most of them this was their first experience of the deadly reality of war. The elderly reservists who had been posted to the coastal divisions with the higher numerals were pale, and there was fear flickering in their eyes. But they started to dig.

Jahnke rang through to the next strongpoint along the coast, W2. Second Lieutenant Ritter answered. "Things seem to have been pretty lively your way."

"What about you?" Jahnke asked.

"Nothing much here," Ritter replied. "Looked as if they were after your lot."

And indeed they were after W5.

"Enemy aircraft!" The warning came again while Jahnke was still on the telephone.

"Take cover, everybody!"

A new wave came roaring in from the sea.

"They're only a few feet above the water!"

Over the coast they zoomed up and at once banked. Immediately the infernal concert started—rockets. They were firing only at the two corner bunkers with their 40-millimetre armoured carrier-cannon. The rockets slammed against the bunkers. They smacked through the apertures. The left bunker blew up at once: evidently a direct hit, through the aperture, among the stored shells. The bunker on the right was enveloped in smoke and flames. When the attack was over both bunkers and guns were only rubble and scrap metal. The crews had been killed or severely wounded.

That was at 0400 hours.

Everywhere in the strongpoint voices were calling for the medical orderly. Hoffmann was running across the dunes with his stretcher.

This was the modern aerial bombardment—the battle of *matériel* of the Second World War. Altogether the Allied air forces flew 10,743 sorties on June 6, dropping 11,912 tons of bombs—in other words, 11,912 tons of death and destruction. Within the short span of a few hours the same load of bombs crashed down on the German defences in Normandy as was dropped throughout the whole of 1943 on Germany's most heavily bombed city—Hamburg. The people of Hamburg who experienced the death nights of the districts of Hammerbrook, Hamm, or Rothenburgsort and those who trembled in the air-raid shelters during the infernal night of 40,000 dead may form a vague idea of what the German troops in their machine-gun nests, infantry trenches, and bunkers along the Normandy coast had to go through on that morning of June 6, 1944.

The bombs were to clear the way for the Allied invasion forces. Advanced detonation caused their blast to be directed sideways, to sweep everything aside without making deep craters in the ground. That was important, since deep craters would hamper the advance of the invasion forces with their heavy weapons. In the towns and villages behind the coast where the Allied Supreme Command suspected German reserves or head-quarters the same method was used. The purpose there was to increase casualties and, at the same time, to achieve the complete blocking of all through-routes by collapsed houses. This was done successfully in Saint-Lô and Périers; but the effect was particularly devastating in Caen, the ancient town amid a sea of cornfields. German supply columns were no longer able to move through the town on their way to the coast. On a reconnaissance drive to the front Major Hayn saw a dying city. The suburb of Vaucelles with its bridges over the Orne and its canal was a burning chaos. German infantrymen were only able to leap through the gaps left open by flames and crashing beams. Out of the black smoke rose the venerable towers of the Abbey Church of St. Stephen and the Church of the Holy Trinity—the former founded by William the Conqueror in the eleventh century. He was buried in St. Stephen's. A simple stone slab commemorated the man who, setting out from Normandy in 1066 with his famous 619 Norman dragon ships, had conquered England. That was an invasion in the opposite direction. William "the Bastard," then still Duke of Normandy, ferried 60,000 men across to England in his sailing-ships—Normans, Frenchmen, Bretons, Flemings, and a few German contingents. At Hastings, on October 14, 1066, he defeated an English army in that memorable battle which lasted from morning until late at night and which cost King Harold and his brothers their lives. William became King of England and was dubbed "the Conqueror." And now, 878 years later, the English and their allies were returning to William's grave with thunder and lightning. A hail of bombs was shaking the walls and towers of St. Stephen's. William's city was being reduced to rubble—belated retribution for the Battle of Hastings.

The Allied bomber strike as a trail-blazer for the invasion army now approaching aboard 5000 transports and landing craft fully reflected America's material superiority. The seaborne assault units were to set foot on French soil with the least possible risk in order to establish the initial beach-heads. Not a stone of the German defences was to be left standing; not one bunker and not one gun was to survive the inferno. Wire obstacles were to be atomized; not a man of Rommel's coastal divisions was to come out of that hell alive. Nothing was to be left that could offer any resistance to the disembarking Allied troops.

"Safety first"—that was Eisenhower's motto. Safety for the men under his command. It was the tactics of abundance, the tactics of mobilizing a fabulous mass of inanimate material against an enemy so as to spare the lives of one's own men. "Safety first"—that was the motto of the modern battle of *matériel* and of the whole struggle for Normandy.

As the smoke of the bomber offensive lifted and a pause occurred in the raging inferno they came.

Off the five selected landing points there appeared 6 battleships, 23 cruisers, 122 destroyers, 360 motor torpedo boats, and a few hundred frigates, sloops, and patrol boats. Under cover of this greatest armada in naval history sailed the most gigantic accumulation of ships ever seen by human eyes—6480 transports, landing craft, and special-purpose vessels. The defenders in their coastal positions now saw before them the originals of all the silhouettes they used to be shown in lectures—assault craft, anti-aircraft vessels, gunnery vessels, and infantry landing craft. The guns of the warships now began their bombardment across the landing fleet. It was an impenetrable box of steel sealing off the invasion coast from supplies and reinforcements.

Was it possible that along the beaches between Vire and Orne there was a single German hand left to press the trigger of a machine-gun, to fire an artillery piece, or to throw a grenade? And yet—fire was still coming out of the pockmarked crater landscape.

The time was 0415 hours.

"Enemy warship approaching." With a high bow-wave an American destroyer was racing inshore.

Sergeant Hein came running up at the double. "Permission to fire the field gun, Herr Leutnant?" he called out to Jahnke. Jahnke nodded.

"Fire!" *Crump* went the field gun.

Short.

Crump!

Still too short.

The destroyer now turned broadside on, and from it, in quick succession, came three barks. The first salvo dropped in the dunes behind the strongpoint. The second fell short into the water. But the third was bang on target: the FK-16, the old field gun, was smashed to smithereens and its crew killed.

All they had left was the damaged 88-millimetre AA gun. Its crew was feverishly working on it.

As if wanting to take a good look from above, an artillery-spotter aircraft flew over the strongpoint and back out to sea. It was lost from sight.

But evidently it delivered its message. The heavy naval bombardment began. Continuous, uninterrupted hell. Blow upon blow the huge shells crashed into the strongpoint. Trenches were levelled. Barbed wire was torn to shreds. Minefields were blown up. Bunkers were drowned in the loose sand of the dunes. The stone building with the telephone exchange crumbled. The fire-control post of the flame-throwers received a direct hit. Many men broke down under this hurricane of fire.

They pressed their hands against their ears. They screamed. They cursed. Others lay in the sand, weak with despair. Posts were no longer relieved.

And then a cry went up: "The ships!"

The cry had a galvanizing effect. The ships. Jahnke pressed his eye against the scissor telescope. What he saw seemed beyond comprehension. The landing fleet. Ships big and small. Countless ships, each with a barrage balloon flying from its stern. So that was it. There was no doubt left. They were also coming by sea in spite of the bad weather. And they were coming at low tide. The 'Czech hedgehogs,' the wired ramming blocks with their mines, the stakes with the primed shells, and all the other cunning underwater obstacles they had built were now standing high and dry.

"Rommel's blundered!" flashed through Jahnke's head.

They were coming at low water. And they had to cross 800 yards of flat beach, a wide-open field of fire.

But what use was a field of fire if one had hardly any weapons left to fire? Second Lieutenant Arthur Jahnke could have screamed with fury.

"Must lay down a barrage!" A runner was sent off by bicycle. Lieutenant Schön, positioned at Saint-Martin-de-Varreville, two miles behind W5, with his 13th Company and a 122-millimetre battery of 1261st Artillery Regiment, was to put down a barrage fire on the beach from all his guns upon the signal of two green Very lights.

Goliath

The landing craft were now detaching themselves from the invasion fleet. They could be clearly made out in the telescope.

Jahnke fired two green Very lights from his signal pistol. They waited. But no artillery barrage came. They could not know that the runner never arrived at Schön's emplacement. He had been chased by a fighter-bomber, and the aircraft had been faster than the bicycle. He had been hunted down like a hare and eventually shot off his bike.

The time was 0520 hours.

The broad naval barges with their banks of rocket mortars were firing their screaming missiles at the strongpoint. Gunboats were moving in, firing continuous salvoes.

The first landing craft had reached the shallow water. They ran aground. The men leapt out. They threw off their life-jackets. Evidently they were engineers. They made straight for the exposed foreshore obstacles to detonate the booby-traps, and so clear the approaches for the ships which would come in at high water.

Jahnke was thinking: a range of 500 yards. Experience in Russia had taught him that they should be allowed to come closer. To within a hundred yards. At that range the invaders would be at their mercy. But he saw wave after wave of them coming in. He could not afford to wait.

"Open fire!" he shouted to the right and left. "Open fire!" the order was repeated and passed on through trenches and machine-gun nests.

Inside the turret of a half-buried captured ancient Renault tank Lance-Corporal Friedrich was sitting behind his machine-gun. He wore spectacles as thick as magnifying-glasses. But every one knew that what Friedrich aimed at he hit. His bursts were quite short. The running men just saw the spattering sand in front of their feet before they were caught in the fire. The machine-gun on the left wing of the strongpoint was now also stuttering. It forced the disembarked engineers to get down on the sand. It caught the leading group of the second wave. They were mown down by the side of their boat.

The mortars were belching out their 80-millimetre shells.

But what was that? Strange monsters were approaching through the water. Amphibious tanks. Huge rubber skirts had turned them into nightmarish spectres. They had reached the sand. They were rumbling up the open beach towards the anti-tank ditch. Was there no hope of getting the 88-millimetre gun to work again? At last. Its barrel was traversing. "Fire!" To the men in W5 it was like music—that unmistakable *crump* of the 88, the queen of all guns of the Second World War. The leading tank ran straight into its shell. Not a direct hit, but enough for the tank to be flung aside, disabled.

That's the stuff. Keep it up. "Fire!"

But no second shell left the barrel. The first round had given the bomb-damaged gun its *coup de grâce*.

The second wave of tanks was now on the beach. They were concentrating their fire on the positions they had spotted. First the machine-gun on the right caught a direct hit. Next the mortar was put out of action. Only Friedrich in his Renault tank turret was still blazing away at the beach, pinning down the disembarked infantry on the water-line.

And then they got him too. The Renault turret was hit. It sounded as if a church bell had cracked. The fragments shattered the machine-gun and tore up the lance-corporal's leg. Nevertheless, he was to be one of the few to survive.

"It looks as though God and the world have forsaken us," Jahnke said to the runner by his side. "What's happened to our airmen? What is our artillery up to? What about that observer of 901st Artillery Regiment up on the church tower of Saint-Marie-du-Mont? He must be asleep."

He was not asleep. But the fighter-bombers had long ago shot him out of his vantage-point. And the battery whose fire he was to have directed had been smashed by carpet bombing.

"Well, then—our last resort," Jahnke said to Sergeant Hein.

The last resort was the Goliath tanks. "Our vest-pocket wonder-weapon," the troops used to call these remote-controlled miniature tanks. They had a range of 600 yards and carried nearly two hundredweights of dynamite inside them, detonated by remote ignition. They were an effective weapon against bridges, troop concentrations, and obstacles. On rough ground they were hardly visible as they hobbled towards their targets like tortoises. They were much too small a target for artillery-fire. Unfortunately, their steering was rather delicate.

Jahnke ordered the Goliaths to be employed. The dwarf tanks rumbled off. The men at the remote-control boxes tried to guide them towards the enemy armour. But the steering did not work. The delicate relays had been damaged by the concussion of the aerial and naval bombardment. Not a single one could be brought near its target. They remained lying on the foreshore. Even so, one of them was yet to claim an appalling toll of blood.

The naval guns were blazing away. This was the drumfire of the First World War. Yard upon yard was raked over. The men lay on their stomachs, their faces pressed into the ground, waiting for the end. Those are minutes that even the most hardboiled soldier never forgets. He feels forsaken by every one, alone, entirely alone with his fear and the reality of war—a war which, on those occasions, he curses a thousand times. But this is something nobody can understand unless he himself has pressed his face into the dirt, unless he has heard the Horsemen of the Apocalypse galloping overhead, unless he himself has argued with death because it would not even leave him time for a short prayer.

Sainte-Mère-Eglise—a Fateful Turning-point

Anyone viewing that kind of inferno from a distance, a distance of either space or time, can see only the general panorama that leads to victory or defeat.

Lieutenant-Colonel Friedrich von der Heydte, the commander of the 6th Parachute Regiment, likewise only saw the panorama at 9 A.M. on June 6, 1944. In the early hours of the morning he had driven from his headquarters to Saint-Côme-du-Mont, a small town nine miles behind strongpoint W5. The noise of battle from there had been heard as far afield as Carentan. Von der Heydte climbed the church tower. He raised his field-glasses to his eyes and thought that what he saw was a vision: before him, stretching out into infinity, lay the invasion fleet protected by hundreds of barrage balloons, the invasion fleet off Utah Beach. He saw the powerful battleships, the cruisers, and the destroyers. He saw the flashes of their guns. He also saw the countless boats moving between the larger vessels and the coast. "Like the Wannsee on a fine summer's day," he said to himself.

Only a small stretch of coast was entirely shrouded, as if cut off by a curtain. Everything there was hidden behind clouds of black smoke. Fountains of dust rose high into the sky. Nothing could be made out. Nothing at all. But behind that veil the American invasion was taking place. Only with the magic telescope of Sinbad the Sailor could the lieutenant-colonel have seen Second Lieutenant Arthur Jahnke in his half-buried dugout, Lance-Corporal Friedrich in his gun turret, Sergeant Hein by the mortar, and all the other men of 3rd Company, 919th Infantry Regiment, among the dunes of W5, upon whom the power of an entire fleet and an entire army was concentrated, where history was knocking at the door with death and destruction, ushering in a new chapter—the defeat of Germany and the victory of America.

All that, of course, Lieutenant-Colonel von der Heydte could not see from his church tower at Saint-Côme-du-Mont. But he knew that the curtain of smoke indicated the danger-point—the point at which the mighty armada out at sea was aiming.

He ordered his regimental headquarters to Saint-Côme-du-Mont and moved his regiment forward.

The 6th Parachute Regiment was deployed at the foot—or the narrowest part—of the Cotentin peninsula, in the Lessay–Mont Castre–Carentan area. The regiment represented the safety bolt on the peninsula's southern door. The area was twelve miles wide and nine miles deep—a considerable piece of ground for a single regiment.

Shortly after midnight the combat group farthest to the north-east had reported the descent of enemy parachutists, in at least company strength, in the area between Saint-Côme-du-Mont, Baupte, and Carentan. In combat groups and assault teams the advanced battalion penetrated into the dropping zone. They heard the wireless signals of the American units, put through in clear, demanding heavy weapons, ammunition, and reinforcements. That revealed the desperate situation of the Americans. Even before dawn the men of the Parachute Regiment brought in their first prisoners. Von der Heydte drove over to Carentan to interrogate them himself. It was important to get the earliest possible information about the enemy's intentions.

He reached Carentan at 6 A.M. He found that the prisoners belonged to the 501st Regiment, hence to the 101st Division, and at once realized that the employment of this crack division was no isolated operation. They were a strange lot, those prisoners. Painted on their jumping overalls were battle slogans such as "See you in Paris," or else life-size pin-up girls were painted on their backs. During interrogation most of them acted very confidently. Their pockets contained the most tempting and also the oddest things that the German troops had seen for a long time: chocolate, of course, in any quantity, as well as hard candies, American cigarettes, stimulants, water-purification tablets, instant coffee, tea tablets, soup cubes, and lavatory paper. And, not infrequently, alluring Paris photographs.

The men had all been drilled for the possibility of captivity. They answered no more than the questions they were bound to answer under military law—name, age, rank. That was all. Naturally, most of them talked a little, some nervously and others provocatively, some with sneers, others with easy *bonhomie*. But their interrogation yielded no tactical clues. Even so, it was enough to form a rough picture.

Von der Heydte informed 84th Corps. He was unable to make a telephone connexion with 709th Division.

"This is the invasion," Heydte said to Major Viebig, the corps chief of operations. "This is the invasion," General Marcks telephoned to Seventh Army.

But the higher commands were still doubtful. They still would not believe it. They had made up their minds that the invasion would come at the narrowest point of the Channel, in the Pas de Calais.

The combat groups consisted each of a parachute battalion with 75-millimetre anti-tank guns and one battery of 88-millimetre anti-aircraft guns. But, as they had been stationed at considerable distances from each other and were continually subjected to attack by enemy aircraft, they arrived in the Saint-Côme-du-Mont area at intervals of more than an hour. The battalion commanders were briefed and, as their combat groups arrived, sent forward into action, the first battalion in the direction of Sainte-Marie-du-Mont–La Madeleine, the area of strongpoint W5; the second battalion in the direction of Turqueville, where the 795th Georgian Battalion had its positions. The third battalion was kept back to protect the flank.

At first the action of the two battalions progressed well. Presently, however, they came under heavy fire from Sainte-Mère-Eglise and Sainte-Marie-du-Mont. Would they be able to save strongpoint W5?

Meanwhile the 1058th Grenadier Regiment and the Assault Battalion Messerschmitt had joined action with the air-landed enemy at Sainte-Mère-Eglise, and the 1057th Grenadier Regiment was sent into action from the west against the air landings along the Merderet river.

It is difficult now to reconstruct who gave the order for joining action—84th Corps, or 91st Air Landing Division to which the regiments belonged, or 709th Division. In any event, the units were sent into action too late, and, what was far worse, no artillery was moved up with them and no armoured or anti-aircraft support was given them. A fatal mistake. It underlines the fact that the two German divisions directly affected in the American air-landing zone were without their leaders at this decisive hour: Falley had been killed and Schlieben was still on his way back from that accursed *Kriegsspiel* which was to have been held in Rennes.

The German units were unable to advance against the mortars and automatic weapons of the American paratroops who had established themselves in the hedgerows and orchards. They were pinned down.

When Schlieben returned to his headquarters towards noon and received the reports about the first countermeasures he immediately realized the danger of the situation and tried to make good the mistake by bringing up two heavy artillery batteries and armour.

Would they be in time to save strongpoint W5?

Poor Jahnke was waiting in vain. Towards noon on June 6 only a few sporadic rifle bullets were being fired from the churned-up trenches and infantry dugouts on his dune. Useless rifle bullets against the tanks which by then were standing outside the anti-tank wall. As if on a practice range, they were firing point-blank into the strongpoint. The American infantry had also moved up right against the anti-tank wall. But they did not yet risk leaping over it.

An assault team of fifteen to twenty men was lying near one of the abandoned Goliaths. They were poking fun at the wonder-weapon. One of them flung an egg-shaped hand-grenade at it. He missed. Everybody roared with laughter. It was the next man's turn. He too missed. Thereupon one of the Americans crawled up to the miniature tank. He lifted the forward hatch and wedged his hand-grenade in it. He pulled the pin and ran back to his group. They did not know that it contained two hundredweights of explosive. Seconds later the entire group lay scattered about the beach, torn to pieces, their lungs burst. With renewed fury the tanks blazed away at the strongpoint.

"This, then, is the end," flashed through Lieutenant Jahnke's mind. Then he felt as though some one was slowly pulling a black curtain over him. In his half-buried dugout he had not heard the shell being fired, but he had just seen the impact flash on the edge of his earth hole. He had felt a blow in the small of his back. The cascade of sand was coming down on him like a nightmare. This, then, was the end. He did not know how long he lay underneath the sand. He regained consciousness when some one started to pull him out by the legs. Saved. He braced himself against the sand. He tried to move. Somebody was still pulling him. Suddenly there was air. And light. He coughed up the dirt. And before him he saw the steel helmet of an American. Lieutenant Jahnke recorded his impressions with complete detachment, like a scientific instrument. But since his soldier's instinct had been formed by the war in Russia his first reaction was: get away—anything rather than captivity!

He saw the machine-pistol on the ground. He made a dive for it. But something kicked him from behind and a calm voice said: "Take it easy, German!" Second Lieutenant Jahnke, twenty-three years old and never much good at English at school, could not help laughing. "Take it easy," the American had said. All right for them to take it easy, Jahnke thought as he tried to flick the dirt off his uniform with his hand. Then, as ordered, he held his hands up above his head and submitted to his pockets being emptied.

Down on the beach he found the remnants of his strongpoint garrison. A miserable handful of prisoners on the far side of the

Mat Laying Tank

anti-tank wall. He wanted to join his men. But a sergeant of the "leathernecks," the famous American Marine Corps, barred his way. He took him by the arm and dragged him some fifty yards away from his men, casting hostile sideways glances at his Knight's Cross. The Cross was dangling from his collar, the ribbon torn, held up only by the shoelace with which, like most other officers, Jahnke had secured it underneath his shirt collar.

He felt like a man walking in a dream. Gigantic bulldozers were being disembarked from special craft. Tanks were rumbling along, carrying before them a huge framework from which iron balls dangled at the end of long chains like enormous flails. These tanks were designed for clearing passages through minefields. He saw other huge tanks with enormous reels of coarse sisal matting. These were unrolled whenever the tank encountered sand drifts or soft ground, making its own temporary runway, over which it would then advance. Just like Baron Münchhausen pulling himself out of the bog by his own bootstraps.

The monsters were rumbling up the beach, no doubt to silence the more northerly strongpoints. Others were bumping over the wrecked anti-tank wall towards the macadamized road, aiming inland, to where Lieutenant Schön with his 13th Company was supposed to stop them. But he would no more be able to halt them than Lieutenant Matz with his reserve of 3rd Company, who, together with most of his men, had been killed by the naval gunfire barrage while attempting a counter-thrust.

Jahnke had sat down on the anti-tank wall. Anything for a cigarette now! Suddenly he started. An officer was calling to him. "Hi, lieutenant, come over here!" He was led behind a tank to be interrogated. "How many heavy guns did you have? How strong was your complement of men?"

The lieutenant shook his head. Thereupon the captain produced from his pocket a silk scarf and held it up against the light: "Take a look at this. We've got it all here, everything that was there in W5!" he said. It was no more than the truth: from the 88-millimetre gun down to the Renault tank turret everything was marked.

And on top of the sketch-map was the word Utah. "Utah! Surely that's a State in the U.S.A.?" Jahnke said to the officer. "Do you come from there?"

"No," the American laughed. "No, no." Jahnke understood. Utah was the code-name for the beach-head. He was the first German to know. Utah.

"If you know everything, what more do you want from me?" Jahnke asked after a glance at the map.

"You're not going to answer questions?" his interrogator asked.

"I shall answer no more questions than did your men whom I took prisoners during the night. And I hope you'll respect my attitude as I did theirs."

Jahnke had already spotted the two officers, his former prisoners. They had waved to him and called out a cheerful greeting. But the man guarding Jahnke had not allowed them to come near. He had seen them try to negotiate with the sergeant, but the sergeant had merely shrugged his shoulders. Not allowed. And even parachute officers did not argue with the hardboiled leathernecks.

Nevertheless, Jahnke realized that with these witnesses near by he could safely invoke the rules of war. This knowledge encouraged him.

"So you won't talk?" the officer once more angrily grunted.

"No," Jahnke said emphatically.

"Oh, go to hell!" The sergeant again took him by the arm and led him back to the anti-tank wall. The sergeant sat down in an infantry foxhole. At the same moment there was a bang. Chunks were flying through the air. German guns were shelling the beach. It was the 10th Battery, 1261st Army Coastal Artillery Regiment. One battery was not very much, considering what might have been achieved by concentrated artillery fire. But here, too, there was just not enough *matériel* available, and the confusion of command made things worse still. The Naval Commander was responsible for fire control against naval targets, while the Army was responsible for fighting ground targets. This arrangement produced an endless string of errors.

From his battle headquarters on a hill overgrown with gorse Colonel Triepel, commander of the 1261st Regiment, had been watching the landings in front of W5 through his scissor telescope. He ordered his 10th Battery with its 170-millimetre guns to shell the beach. "The trajectory of the shells lay straight over the regimental command-post. We were some ten or eleven miles from the target. The excitement produced in the target area by every burst was clearly visible," Triepel reports. And, indeed, it would have been difficult to miss.

The Americans were flinging themselves down behind their tanks or rolling into hollows of sand. They were shouting out orders and altogether seemed greatly astonished to find themselves so unexpectedly under fire again. Shell after shell smacked into their concentration of vehicles. With horror Jahnke saw that some of his own men had also been hit: killed or wounded in captivity even! Jahnke too was hit again. A shell-splinter tore open his side. A large red patch spread on his uniform. A hot stab of fear went through him—a belly wound! Unless he was operated on within six hours his survival of the American bombs and naval guns would have all been in vain. He would die from a lousy German shell-splinter.

Jahnke probed with his hand under his uniform. He felt warm blood. Cautiously he drew a breath. Deeper still. It was painful. There was a sharp jab of pain. But his stomach wall did not seem to have been pierced. Probably only a flesh wound. Relieved, he unbuttoned his tunic and placed his bandaging wad on his wound. His American guard crawled out of his sandpit, lay down alongside the German lieutenant, and packed his own wad of lint under Jahnke's tunic. Then he crawled back. He lit a cigarette and tossed it over to Jahnke. Jahnke fished it out of the sand and inhaled the rich fragrant smoke of a Chesterfield. If he had not been prone already it would have knocked him down. Abruptly the shout of his guard, "Hi, you, German!" brought him back to reality.

The sergeant had leapt out of his pit and was standing to attention. Jahnke too got up. And now he saw the general. It must have been Brigadier-General Theodore Roosevelt, junior.

An officer was drawing the general's attention to the German lieutenant. The general looked across. Jahnke raised his hand to salute. As he was wearing nothing on his head he put his fingertips to his forehead. The general lifted his hand, but then he evidently changed his mind, for he dropped his arm again and did not return the salute. He could be seen to be issuing an order. An officer was running at the double to where the radio control-post had been set up. Half an hour later Jahnke knew what the general's order had been: the Germans must be moved out of here! Two boats were coming ashore to pick them up.

Infantrymen do not like to get their feet wet. In accordance with this principle Arthur Jahnke took off his boots and socks when his guard motioned him to wade out to the tank landing craft. "Taking you off. P.O.W. camp. War over!" the sergeant said, grinning. War over, Jahnke reflected. He saw his men wading out to another landing craft. Protocol was being strictly observed: even now officers and other ranks were kept strictly apart.

The landing craft took them to a destroyer a good way out to sea. Jahnke climbed up the gangway, his boots and socks still in his hand. Up on deck he wanted to put them on again so as not to face the naval officers like some bedraggled shipwrecked mariner. But the ratings had no feeling for his sense of propriety. One of them kicked him in his behind. He fell forward. They laughed. Suddenly an officer shouted from the bridge. Amd at once they helped him up. He stooped down once more to pick up his boots, and thus, in his bare feet and with his wound bleeding again after his fall, he stepped before the waiting officers of the U.S. destroyer. They saluted him, and there was no mistaking that his Knight's Cross excited great interest. With a gesture a lieutenant motioned him into the wardroom, and as a sequel to the most exciting twenty-four hours of his life, marking the conclusion of his military career, Arthur Jahnke had his first piping hot, fragrant real bean coffee.

The destroyer was steaming northward. Utah Beach and what used to be W5 disappeared in the haze.

In Jahnke's mind, however, one question would not be silenced: how had it all been possible? Why should the German forces have thought that invasion was impossible in this weather when those fellows had come after all? Jahnke could find no answer. He did not know—and nobody on the German side knew at that time—that the date of the invasion had been the object of a dramatic struggle within Allied headquarters. That the decision had been balanced on a razor's edge. That everything, perhaps even the success of the operation as a whole, had hung by a thread. These, then, are the facts.

Originally the Allies had scheduled the invasion for the beginning of May 1944. But when Eisenhower and Montgomery took over their commands they both came to the conclusion that the envisaged beach sector was much too narrow and the budgeted number of troops too small. Eisenhower, in particular, demanded more shipping capacity, and the ships had to be brought together from all over the world. But in the end there were still not enough for him. He insisted that the invasion date be postponed by another month, which would make available another month's output of landing craft. The postponement was agreed to in spite of Churchill's fierce opposition. The British Prime Minister was afraid of political difficulties with Moscow, since he had firmly promised Stalin the Western invasion for the beginning of May.

The exact date of the landing in June had to be determined on the grounds of tidal conditions. The question merely was: should the landing be made at high water or at low water?

From numerous aerial-reconnaissance photographs Allied headquarters were aware that new gun-positions and beach obstacles of all kinds had been under construction on the French coast since the spring of 1944. It was obvious what Rommel intended those obstacles for. If an invasion fleet arrived on the incoming tide or at high water, when the obstacles were submerged and invisible, many landing craft, troop ferries, gunboats, rocket boats, amphibious tanks, and flat-bottomed barges would hit those insidious obstacles, break up against the ramming blocks, rip open their hulls on the T-girders, or be torn to pieces by mines and pressure-detonated charges. The entire landing operation might end in disaster. Eisenhower and Montgomery therefore decided on a landing at low water. The advance across a beach devoid of all cover was to be made possible for the infantry by means of tanks. Moreover, the plan envisaged that, immediately prior to the seaborne landing, the German defensive positions would be eliminated by heavy aerial and naval bombardment. Once a landing had been effected, the beach obstacles were to have been instantly removed so that the landing of troops could be continued during the rising tide.

As for the timetable of the seaborne landing, the fleet had to approach the coast under cover of night, but on the other hand it required one hour's daylight for the preliminary bombardment and the landing manoeuvres. The airborne troops, for their part, who were to be dropped at important key-points behind the lines in order to seize bridges and block roads, needed moonlight for their operation. On the strength of all these prerequisites June 5 was worked out as a suitable date. It was the date when the desired conditions of the tide and moon phase coincided.

The British and American secret services employed a thousand tricks to mislead the German signals experts in their calculations of the most likely time and place for the invasion.

An entire ghost army, complete with dummy hutments and dummy ships, was built up, and even after the first landings in France it strongly suggested that further enormous troop concentrations were standing by in the county of Kent in order to strike at a different point. Sure enough, this ghost army was spotted by German aerial-reconnaissance. It had a disastrous effect on the

German assessment of the question as to whether the Normandy landing was not, after all, a diversionary manoeuvre to cover a main landing at Calais.

Thus, everything was most ingeniously planned and calculated down to the last detail. The technical resources available to the Allies were insuperable. Behind them stood the unlimited economic capacity of America, functioning without enemy interference. As a result, everything went according to plan right up to June 5—everything, that is, except the weather.

The weather god appeared to be on Germany's side. Throughout May the weather had been fine. Originally Captain Stagg, the chief meteorologist of the Allied Supreme Command, had forecast favourable weather also for the first week of June. On Saturday, June 3, Eisenhower sent a signal to the American chief of staff, General Marshall: "We have a genuine chance of good conditions." But then the weather broke. The meteorological team predicted strong winds, low cloud cover, rain, and poor visibility for June 5, 6, and 7. Yet these were the only days on which low tide was at the required time.

At 2130 hours on June 3 those ships of the invasion fleet which sailed from remote ports were already at sea. Tens of thousands of soldiers were aboard the transports in the big ports of Southern England.

Should they set out? Or should the operation be postponed by twenty-four hours? That was the question posed by the weather. A crucial question, determined not only by military calculations but also by consideration for Stalin, who kept demanding an invasion and was beginning to suspect the Western Allies of dragging their feet and wanting to prolong the war so that Russia would bleed herself to death.

At 0430 on June 4—0530 Double British Summer Time—Eisenhower had still not made up his mind whether, in view of the unfavourable forecast, the invasion should or should not take place. Operation Overlord—the code-name for the invasion—was, in the most literal sense, hanging in the air. The Allied Supreme Command met. The weather forecast was no better. General Montgomery was in favour of going all the same. Admiral Ramsay, however, the Commander-in-Chief of the naval forces, doubted whether his smaller units could get across the Channel safely, in view of the rough seas predicted. And Air Chief Marshal Leigh-Mallory pointed out that the air forces might not find it possible to discharge their decisive rôle adequately. Only two hours were left—after that the bulk of the armada would have to leave port, or else June 5 would have to be written off.

In the end Eisenhower ordered the whole operation to be postponed by twenty-four hours. The ships already at sea were ordered back. Units sailing down the Irish Sea on a southerly course about-turned and sailed north again. One flotilla of minesweepers had got to within thirty-five nautical miles of the Normandy coast when the order to turn back reached them. One convoy with landing craft did not receive the order at all and continued blissfully unaware on its dangerous course. Destroyers were sent chasing after it, but they failed to find it. In the end some aircraft succeeded in halting the convoy, but by then it had got close in to the Normandy coast.

What now? The problem had not been solved by stopping the invasion: it had merely become more difficult. On Sunday, June 4, at 2130 hours (Double British Summer Time) the decision was made. It was made by Eisenhower not, as the legends have it, after profound soul-searching or from a personal heroic resolution. It was made on the strength of the meteorologists' verdict. From their far-ranging weather observations over the Atlantic they had established the presence of a small ridge of high pressure, wedged, as it were, between two depressions coming in from the west. This high was bound to bring an improvement in the weather for Monday and Tuesday—June 5 and 6. Eisenhower thereupon ordered: "H-Hour will be 0600 hours British time on Tuesday." And that is why the invasion came at a time when all German higher commands believed it to be impossible because of the weather prevailing on Monday.

While the U.S. destroyer with Second Lieutenant Jahnke on board was ploughing her way through the seas towards the English coast, back in Normandy, now the crucial theatre, a dispatch rider stepped up to Lieutenant-Colonel von der Heydte, the commander of the 6th Parachute Regiment: "1st Battalion has reached Sainte-Marie-du-Mont." That meant they were within four miles of strongpoint W5, on the macadamized road. Only four more miles to the coast. All that was needed was for von der Heydte's 2nd Battalion to wheel round at Turqueville and to advance over the causeway through the flooded area—and Utah Beach, the American bridgehead, would be sealed off. Success was so close.

But the 2nd Battalion could not wheel round. Its left flank came under heavy fire from Sainte-Mère-Eglise. There the American paratroops of 507th Regiment had assembled and dug in. The little town, far too readily abandoned by a German AA transport unit, was rapidly becoming the pivot of the first battle.

Captain Mager had to try to eliminate the threat to his flank. He therefore turned not towards the coast but towards Sainte-Mère-Eglise in order to capture it. However, the battalion was unable to cross the open, flat ground south of the little town or to penetrate into it. Darkness fell. Mager's battalion was forced to dig in. But the 1st Battalion could not advance beyond Sainte-Marie-du-Mont without its flank being protected.

That damned little town, Sainte-Mère-Eglise! Because of it the 6th Parachute Regiment could not make its last successful leap towards the landing beach. And the assault battalions of 91st Air Landing Division and 709th Division likewise came to grief against this fatal keypoint.

"We'll take it in the morning," Heydte's parachutists were saying. "We'll manage it in the morning," was also what Colonel Beigang of the 1058th Grenadier Regiment said to General von Schlieben when the general placed Lieutenant-Colonel Seidel's two heavy motorized artillery battalions 456 and 457 under his command.

"We'll crack it in the morning," said Major Messerschmitt, the commander of Assault Battalion A.O.K. 7, when he was told at Azeville that Captain Hümmerich with his Panzerjägers was on his way to join him.

In the morning!

2

HITLER THINKS IT'S A BLUFF

Sortie by E-Boats

Fifteen miles east of the American Utah Beach, where the VII U.S. Corps had to fight for every inch of the ground, was the beach of V U.S. Corps. It lay between the two coastal townships of Vierville and Colleville. It's code name was Omaha.

Shortly before 0200 hours Rear-Admiral Hall's flagship, the *Ancon*, carrying the headquarters personnel of the invasion forces, reached her anchoring place. The transports manoeuvred into their prescribed stations. "Stop engines." Anchors were dropped. The destroyers were circling the fleet like sheepdogs guarding a flock. Barrage balloons rose up. A seemingly endless armada was rocking on the waves of the Channel. "Prepare to enter boats," came the order for the infantry, engineers, and special commandos. The men staggered over the decks. They looked up at the sky anxiously. Would the German planes show up? After all, there had never been a target such as this. The German pilots need but release their bombs: they would be bound to hit something.

But the German Air Force did not show up. It did not show up for the simple reason that there was no German Air Force worth the name in the West. Eisenhower's air force, on that D-Day, enjoyed not only air superiority but air monopoly. The British and American air fleet had at their disposal in England on D-Day a total of 3467 heavy bombers, 1645 medium, light, and torpedo bombers, 5409 fighters, and 2316 transport aircraft. These units made 14,674 sorties on June 6. An incredible figure—14,674. Their losses were 113, due chiefly to German flak.

And what was there on the German side to oppose these

numbers? A pitiful handful of German machines. General Junck, the commander of 2nd Fighter Corps, had for several weeks been asking for at least two fighter *Geschwader,* so that he might prevent the destruction of transport and supply centres—all in vain. The German Luftwaffe Command could not let him have anything. It did not have anything. It needed every fighter plane to oppose the Allied attacks, which had been going on since the middle of May, on the German hydrogenation plants at Pölitz, near Stettin, and Leuna, near Halle, in order to prevent a further decline in the production of German motor and aircraft fuel.

That was why Eisenhower's invasion fleet could safely ride the waves off Normandy. That was why Allied amphibious tanks could calmly set out to swim to the shore. That was why the landing craft bobbing about on the waves could calmly be filled with infantry.

Not a bomb, not an aircraft cannon, not a machine-gun, disturbed the swarming regatta at sea.

Field-Marshal Sperrle had a total of 319 aircraft available for operation on June 6. Of that total 100 were fighters. Twelve German fighter-bomber sorties—literally twelve sorties—were made into the area of the Allied beach-heads. Ten machines were immediately involved in aerial combat and had to drop their bombs prematurely.

Thus the early light of dawn on June 6 revealed one of the most decisive aspects of the campaign, an aspect which was to become decisive for the entire subsequent course of military operations: the weakened Luftwaffe units were no longer able to pierce the vast Allied air umbrella which covered Eisenhower's invasion. The ratio was one to fifty. The German Luftwaffe was outmanoeuvred. The most important weapon of the Second World War had been knocked out of the hand of the German Command. The Luftwaffe had been broken by the excessive demands made on it. In the east and in the south it was involved in the heavy defensive ground fighting. It was obliged to hold reserves ready for action over the Reich and to engage in the most costly air battles against the bomber streams of the R.A.F. at night and against the bombers and fighters of the 8th and 15th U.S. Air Forces flying in from Italy and Britain during the day. The Allies had conquered the air. And it was in the air, and from the air, that the fate of the invasion was decided.

The fact that the few German fighters that took off to engage the enemy, often many times a day, succeeded neverthe-less in shooting down numerous enemy aircraft testifies to the courage and skill of individual fighter pilots. It does not, however, alter the fact that the German forces in Normandy simply lacked two vital arms—an air force and a navy.

One German naval operation, a very small operation, illustrates what could happen, and the risks to which Eisenhower's enterprise was exposed in spite of Allied superiority.

The naval forces in French coastal stations were alerted by Naval Group West headquarters in Paris towards 0150 hours. The alert also reached Lieutenant-Commander Heinrich Hoffmann, the leader of the 5th E-boat Flotilla in Le Havre. The first reports about the approach of enemy naval units were followed by the order: "Leave port to reconnoitre!" With three boats—T28, the *Jaguar*, and the *Möwe*—Hoffmann set out at 0330 hours. Like sharks the "naval hussars" drove through the waves. They roared up the Channel, and at 0430 hours came up against a smoke-screen. They raced through—and before them lay Eisenhower's invasion armada. In order to hide from German coastal artillery it had surrounded itself with a smoke-screen. —

E-Boat

Hoffmann and the other two skippers had the shock of their lives. As far as the eye could see—one enormous, unending fleet.

"It's impossible. There can't be that many ships in the world," said Heinrich Frömke, the rating in charge of the *Jaguar*'s pumps. The vast armada was guarded by six battleships, and around these circled two dozen destroyers. Commander Hoffmann aboard T28 stared at the scene, mesmerized. But he went in to attack, just as if this were merely a naval exercise.

The British battleships *Warspite* and *Ramillies* spotted the German E-boats and opened fire.

Zigzagging, the German flotilla advanced. As they swung round they released their torpedoes; eighteen deadly tin fish shot out from their tubes. The look-outs in the British warships saw the impending disaster. By brilliant manoeuvres they evaded the torpedoes. But one Norwegian destroyer did not get out of their way in time. She was hit amidships and blew up. But Hoffmann and his E-boats had already vanished through the smoke-screen.

The boats of the 5th and 9th Flotillas, stationed in the harbour bunker of Cherbourg, likewise left base. These bold, fast fighting craft had three 2500 h.p. MB511 diesel engines which gave them a speed of 50 m.p.h. They were armed with two torpedo tubes, flak, and machine-guns. But they too were unable to accomplish anything against the floating fortresses which shielded the invasion fleet on all sides. True, both flotillas subsequently broke through to Le Havre, but they were smashed up there by special operations of Allied Bomber Command. Senior Lieutenant Johannsen, the leader of the 5th Flotilla, was killed in the bombing. But an hour before he had been awarded the Knight's Cross.

Lance-Corporal Hein Severloh, a farmer from Metzingen, near Celle, was standing in the personnel trench of strongpoint WN62, scanning the dark, hazy sea in front of the dunes of Colleville through his battery commander's field-glasses.

Sergeant Krone was sitting in the entrance to the bunker that housed the observation-post of 1st Battery, 352nd Artillery Regiment.

"See anything, Hein?" asked Krone.

"Nothing's happening. Not a thing. The big one is still hove to absolutely motionless. But there are more ships coming up now. And our naval gunners from Port-en-Bessin are firing light signals—two red and two green. Maybe they want to make quite sure. But the ships aren't replying. So perhaps our boys in Port-en-Bessin are now convinced that those fellows out at sea belong to the other side."

Every word of Hein Severloh's running commentary was passed on by Krone through the open bunker entrance to Lieutenant Frerking. The lieutenant was sitting inside the bunker at the telephone, waiting for his moment. The moment when he would give the four 105-millimetre howitzers of his 1st Battery, back in positions near Houtteville, the target indication and fire order.

"They're taking their time," remarked Second Lieutenant Grass, the observation officer.

"Maybe we aren't on their list," the battery commander said, laughing. On getting the alarm from Major Pluskat they had immediately driven up from their comfortable billet in Monsieur Fernand le Grand's farmhouse at Houtteville. The strongpoint, under Sergeant Pieh with about nineteen men of 726th Grenadier Regiment, was already on the alert.

"Bombers above the clouds," Sergeant Krone called out. They listened. The air above them was vibrant with the noise. And then began the inferno of bomb bursts. They ducked their heads. But only two bombs fell within the position of the strongpoint. Everything else came down on the open ground behind them. They looked at each other and sighed with relief.

Frerking rang up the gun-emplacement. The telephone was answered by Sergeant Meyer—Ernst Ludwig Meyer, as he invariably introduced himself to avoid confusion with all other Meyers. "What's happening your way?"

"Not a single hit within the whole battery site," Meyer reported.

Frerking looked at Grass. "Not a gun scratched. The whole lot went wide, just as it did here." Grass was jubilant. "Maybe they weren't really after us."

He would have been less optimistic if he had known the truth. They had just been saved not by military design but by the proverbial fortunes of war. Chance had worked in their favour.

A force of 329 B-24 bombers had been instructed to smash the strongpoints along the four miles of Omaha Beach and to silence the batteries and their emplacements with 13,000 superheavy bombs. Because of the low cloud cover they had to make a "blind" bombing—by means of instruments. Duration of flight and exact bomb-release time had been calculated to the second. At the very last moment, however, 8th Air Force headquarters lost their nerve, and, fearing that the bombs might drop among their own lines, among the disembarked troops, they ordered the dropping time to be postponed by a few seconds. Only a few seconds—and 13,000 bombs missed their targets. They were to prove expensive seconds. They were to cost General Eisenhower the lives of many American soldiers.

Hein Severloh and Sergeant Krone had each lit a cigarette. "Aren't we to have any breakfast to-day?" Frerking called out through the open bunker door. Severloh pulled an army loaf out of his haversack. He cut several thin slices and spread them thickly with butter. There was a strange silence. The curtain of haze which had covered the sea lifted. Frerking came out of the bunker. He wanted his breakfast. But first he picked up the binoculars. He leant back against the bunker wall. "Holy smoke," was all he said. "Holy smoke—here they are." And he saw what hundreds of officers and troops in the strongpoints and defence-posts behind Omaha Beach were seeing at the very same minute. And all of them uttered the same cry of amazement and shock: "The invasion fleet!"

Lieutenant Frerking stood in a trance. "But that's not possible, that's not possible," he was muttering. Then he thrust the binoculars into Severloh's hand and rushed into the bunker. And now the lance-corporal saw what had so shaken his battery commander—the invasion fleet. Ships as far as the eye could see. Big ships and little ships, with turrets, super-structures, funnels, aerials, and grotesque barrage balloons. Like some mysterious city in the first light of day, gilded by the first rays of the rising sun, an unreal, golden, glittering city. Abruptly Lance-Corporal Severloh called out: "The big one is coming ashore! Landing craft on our left, off Vierville, making for the beach!"

In the same instant the air began to ring with a new note. It was like the deep swelling sound of a church organ. The heavy naval guns were putting down a protective barrage in front of their disembarking forces.

The first shells dropped close behind strongpoint 62. The newly dug foundations of a bunker appeared to be their target. "Go on, fill it up," Severloh grunted.

Sergeant Pieh, the platoon leader of the strongpoint garrison, came running up. He was bleeding at the throat. "Just a little splinter, nothing serious." He waved away questions. "Everything all right here?"

Severloh grinned and said, "So far."

Pieh looked across to the large transport which had anchored off the strongpoint.

"They're getting into the water now," he called out. He raced back to his command-post.

Calmly Severloh reported to the observation bunker: "Landing troops disembarking from the big transport."

Sergeant Krone came out. He looked towards the sea. "They must be crazy. Are they going to swim ashore? Right in front of our muzzles?" And, indeed, they swam a distance of 200 yards. Then they gripped their shoulderbelts and waded through the water, which came up to their chests. And not a shot was fired from strongpoint 62. As soon as the aerial and naval bombardment was over, Colonel Goth and Colonel Korfes, the commanders of 916th and 726th Grenadier Regiments, which were holding the coastal sector of 352nd Division between the Vire estuary and Port-en-Bessin, had called all strongpoints—the telephone-wires were found to be entirely intact—with the strict order to all commanding officers: "Hold your fire until the enemy is coming up to the water-line." The men behind the guns and machine-guns were obeying the order. The 352nd Infantry Division was waiting behind Omaha Beach.

Severloh behind his MG-42 in strongpoint 62 was waiting too. Inside the bunker Frerking was sitting at the telephone: "Target Dora, all guns, range four-eight-five-zero, basic direction 20 plus, impact fuse," he instructed the gun-position officer back at Houtteville. Calmly he added, "Wait for the order to fire!" Severloh was crouching behind the machine-gun. On the slope over to the left was the trench with the three machine-guns of the strongpoint garrison; in front of it was the mortar position. On the forward side of the dune were the infantrymen. Behind the observation-post, close by the signals bunker, two more of these useful mortars were emplaced. And then the moment had come. The Americans from the transport were now knee-deep in water. The range was 400 yards. "Target Dora—fire!" Frerking shouted into the telephone.

Hein Severloh, a lad of twenty-one, was no passionate soldier. He was a farmer. Heroics had never appealed to him. He was the company commander's batman and had shown his abilities in 'organizing' butter, eggs, cider, and Calvados. But now he had to fire a gun. The war had assigned to him a new part. And he fired. He curled his forefinger round the trigger, and the first burst streaked from the muzzle. The bullets smacked into the water. They caught the first wave of Americans. They sprayed them from end to end. Over to the left the machine-guns of the strongpoint were stuttering. The mortars began to woof away. Screaming, the shells of the 1st Battery at Houtteville came sailing over, laying down a barrage of gunfire on the beach.

Bloody Omaha

Fox Green was the name given in the American operations plan to the length of beach in front of strongpoint 62. Two assault companies of the 16th U.S. Infantry Regiment were to gain a foothold here. They had jumped into the water from their landing craft in the firm belief that there was no German gun left intact on shore, that there was not a machine-gun to open up on them, and that not a single German grenadier was left lying behind a rifle. As Hein Severloh's MG-42 mowed down the first wave in the shallow water, American hopes of a quick success at that point evaporated.

It was exactly low water. The tide was no longer receding, but the flood had not yet begun to rise. The dead, therefore, remained lying in a few inches of water, and the wounded crawled behind them for cover against the bursts of machine-gun fire. Anyone gaining the dry beach in spite of the murderous defensive fire immediately pressed himself into a hollow of sand or tried to get what cover he could behind the sleepers of a field railway. That was the point towards which Lieutenant Frerking from his observer-post up in the bunker was now directing the barrage of his 105-millimetre howitzers from Houtteville. By 8 A.M. not a single American infantryman had reached the base of the dune in front of strongpoint 62. Over to the west of Colleville, in the Vierville area, along the stretch of beach marked in the American maps as Dog Green, the situation was exactly the same as at Fox Green. Assault battalions of the 116th Infantry Regiment were to have taken that beach with the support of amphibious tanks. But the rough seas had been too much for the amphibious tanks. Their mother ships had lowered them too far offshore. One after another they had sunk. Only two of them had gained the beach, and they had been instantly shot up by German artillery.

Thus the plan to have the armour clear the infantry's path over the stony beach and up the steep dunes had failed. But plan

Amphibious Tank

or no, the infantrymen had been launched into action. Chilled through, wedged tightly together, they were being ferried to the beach in the small landing boats. Over their heads the naval bombardment roared away. But everything seemed to go wrong: the naval gunfire overshot the German front-line positions. More disastrous still was the mistake made by the naval craft carrying rocket mortars. The fire of the German coastal guns prevented these broad naval barges from getting close enough inshore. Consequently they launched their rocket salvoes from too great a distance. And instead of smashing into the German positions the rocket-shells with their wide-radius fragmentation effect burst right in front of the waterline, forming, as it were, an impenetrable deadly curtain of fire in front of their own infantry.

With a trail of spindrift from their bows the first wave of large landing craft was racing shoreward. Six of them. Two were hit by German gunfire and sank on the spot. The other four reached the first sandbar, ran aground, and dropped their ramps. The G.I.'s leapt into water which was waist to shoulder deep and waded towards the beach. Here too they walked straight into the fire of the German machine-guns.

No one could hope to describe the scene better than the American infantrymen who went through this inferno and survived it. In the account of 1st Battalion, 116th Infantry Regiment, we read:

> As if this were the signal for which the enemy had waited, all boats came under criss-cross machine-gun fire. . . . As the first men jumped, they crumpled and flopped into the water. Then order was lost. It seemed to the men that the only way to get ashore was to dive head first in and swim clear of the fire that was striking the boats. But, as they hit the water, their heavy equipment dragged them down and soon they were struggling to keep afloat. Some were hit in the water and wounded. Some drowned then and there. . . . But some moved safely through the bullet-fire to the sand and then, finding they could not hold there, went back into the water and used it as cover, only their heads sticking out. Those who survived kept moving forward with the tide, sheltering at times behind under-water obstacles and in this way they finally made their landings.
>
> Within ten minutes of the ramps being lowered, A Company had become inert, leaderless and almost incapable of action. Every officer and sergeant had been killed or wounded. . . . Within twenty minutes of striking the beach A Company had ceased to be an assault company and had become a forlorn little rescue party bent upon survival and the saving of lives.

Things were the same in the Vierville-Saint-Laurent sector, at Dog Green, and exactly the same again farther along at Fox Green and Easy Red. All the units in the wake of the assault companies suffered the same fate. Their landing boats were blown sky high. The amphibious tanks exploded under the concentrated anti-tank gunfire. Anyone who made the beach huddled, severely shocked, half crazed with fear, in a hurriedly dug hollow in the sand, or tried to find cover behind the dead bodies of comrades. Shouts of "Stretcher, stretcher!" rang out through the smoke and over the stutter of machine-gun bursts. But the stretcher-bearers were themselves lying dead or wounded in the sand and in the water.

Even if a tank got through the foreshore obstacles it would get stuck on the narrow strip of sand between water and mined shingle because the German fire had prevented the engineers from clearing passages through the minefields. Thus the assault regiments of the 1st U.S. Division and the teams of engineers clung to a strip of beach barely a hundred feet deep. They could not get a step farther. The 352nd Division under General Kraiss was barring their advance. But the plan was unrolling. And that plan demanded that wave after wave of troops should be landed at Omaha Beach, regardless of casualties.

One assault team of the famous Rangers tried to capture the murderous gun-emplacements on the steep bluffs of the western end of Omaha. From special mortars they fired ropes with grappling hooks and rope ladders to the top of the cliffs and the scarps of the dunes. They had brought with them free-standing extension ladders from the London Fire Brigade in order to conquer the dangerous cliff-face. It was like a medieval siege. The German defenders cut the ropes and tipped over the assault ladders. They rolled down boulders on top of the climbers. They sprayed them with machine-gun fire and tossed hand-grenades down the cliff. It was a massacre.

Omaha Beach was less than four miles long—some 18,000 feet. And four hours after the first assault there were 3000 dead or seriously wounded lying on that strip of sand and shingle. A dead or badly wounded man to every six feet—an appalling trail of sacrificed lives. At 0930 hours British time the operational report of V U.S. Corps summed up the situation in discouraging terms: "Assault units in state of dissolution. Heaviest casualties. Enemy fire preventing leap across beachline. Disembarked units crowded together within narrowest space. Engineers unable to clear passages through minefields or to demolish foreshore obstacles. Armour and vehicles immobilized on the narrow beach. In addition to units of 716th Infantry Division, units of 352nd also identified."

The conclusion of this report was: the Atlantic Wall was holding.

General Omar Bradley, commanding the U.S. First Army, stared at the report with dismay. How was that possible? How could they have so misjudged the German defenders' power of resistance? How was it an assault team of the 116th Regiment cracked a beach strongpoint and found in it men of the 352nd Infantry Division when they had all firmly believed that the entire sector between the Orne and Vire estuaries was held by one single division—the 716th? How could Allied Intelligence have made such a blunder when it was usually so accurately informed about the German defences? How indeed? The reason for this fatal error was an intercepted carrier-pigeon.

In May Field-Marshal Rommel had been authorized to move the motorized 352nd Division from the Saint-Lô area, far behind the coast, into forward positions in the left-hand sector of General Richter's 716th Infantry Division, which until then had held the long frontline between Orne and Vire single-handed. General Richter, however, had been instructed to leave the 1st and 3rd Battalions of his 726th Grenadier Regiment in their old positions. Under their regimental commander, Colonel Korfes, they were placed under 352nd Division. Behind them Rommel stationed battalions of 916th Grenadier Regiment and reinforced the left wing with units of 914th Grenadier Regiment under Lieutenant-Colonel Heyna. In this way the Allies' chief agent for the coastal sector Colleville–Vierville was deceived about the reinforcement of that part of the front. Towards the end of May he finally realized his mistake when he discovered part of a new unit east of the Vire estuary, complete with headquarters at Littry. The agent was appalled. Hurriedly he dispatched a carrier-pigeon with this vital information. To make quite sure he dispatched yet another with the same message. But for once chance seemed to be fighting on the German side. It guided the shotgun of an anonymous German trooper of the 716th Infantry Division. He got both carrier-pigeons. He very nearly won a battle.

None of that, of course, was known to General Omar Bradley aboard his flagship, the *Augusta,* at 9 A.M. on June 6. He knew only that things were going very badly on the beach. Just as he was considering calling off the costly assault, half a dozen further mistakes were to decide the outcome of the battle of bloody Omaha Beach.

Error and chance have been the mightiest generals in all wars. This is as true of the ancient Persians, Greeks, and Romans as it is of Wallenstein and Gustavus Adolphus. In Tolstoy's *War and Peace* we find this truth introduced as one of the principal factors of history in all military trials of strength. In the Allied invasion, too, chance was to be of decisive importance.

At the Führer's headquarters the general opinion in the morning of June 6 continued to be that the fighting on the Normandy coast was merely an enemy diversionary manoeuvre and that the real invasion was yet to come in the Calais area. For that reason the German reserves must not be frittered away against a "dummy attack." Field-Marshal von Rundstedt, C.-in-C. West, also tended to share this belief, even though experienced front-line commanders, as well as divisional and 84th Corps Intelligence, declared quite unambiguously: the Normandy landing is the invasion.

In vain did the divisional commanders ask for help. They begged, they entreated, they cursed—all in vain. "It's a disgrace," General Marcks, normally a man of great self-control, fumed when he was refused permission to employ the 21st Panzer Division. And the only man with the proverbial desert-fox instinct to grasp the situation, and with the authority to get his assessment accepted, was away from the front. Again the hand of blind chance. An error in the judgment of the weather prospects had kept the one man away from the great drama who had the courage, authority, and power to override instructions from the Führer's headquarters. After many months at the front, as we have seen, he was spending a few hours of his wife's birthday, June 6, at her home in Württemberg, and from there he intended to call on Hitler to make his report. Twelve hours too late for decisive intervention in the crucial phase of the invasion, he returned to the front.

Error had eliminated Field-Marshal Rommel for the first few hours. Just as capriciously it opened the door to success to General Bradley. As the critical situation of the attackers on Omaha Beach was moving towards its climax Bradley received a few inaccurate but rosy reports from naval observers. There was also a signal to General Huebner, the commander of the 1st U.S. Division, which stirred the desperate Army headquarters into action. Colonel Talley, deputy chief of staff of V Corps, signalled: "The assault craft are milling about off the coast like a stampeding herd of cattle and dare not venture on land. Such vehicles and armour as have reached the beach cannot advance any farther while the German guns remain intact. They have got to be silenced at any cost. Otherwise we'll lose the race."

Bradley drew the correct conclusion. He ordered the fleet to bombard the coast, without consideration for his own troops on the beach. It was a decision dictated by the hour. Now the strongpoints and gun-emplacements became the pinpoint targets of ruthless shelling by 15- and 16-inch naval guns.

In the headquarters bunker of 916th Infantry Regiment Colonel Goth was sitting among his staff officers, silent. Like some primordial thunderstorm the shells were crashing around their concrete pill-box. The colonel glanced at the luminous dial of his wristwatch: 0820 hours. No one spoke. Like summer lightning the flashes of shell-bursts in continuous succession came through the apertures, steeping the scene in a ghostly light. A second later it was plunged back into diffused twilight. It was impossible to tell whether the sun was shining or whether there were clouds in the sky. The sky and the horizon were shrouded in black smoke, fiery flashes of lightning, and pungent fumes.

"Now they're finishing us off," Goth said. "Is the line to Division still working?"

The signals N.C.O. flicked a lever at the telephone exchange and said: "Connexion with Division, Herr Oberst."

Goth spoke to General Kraiss: "Naval guns are smashing up our strongpoints. We are running short of ammunition. We urgently need supplies, Herr General." Instead of an answer the line went click. The connexion had been cut.

At the gun-position of 1st Battery, 352nd Artillery Regiment, Corporal Peesel was standing by No. 1 gun, giving his orders with complete calm. The 105-millimetre gun was making a brave noise. But for how much longer?

"Go steady with the ammunition," came the order from Battery.

"As if we didn't know," Peesel grumbled. "Those damned fools, why on earth did they have to take our shells away?" A fortnight before the invasion half the stock of ammunition had been collected from all coastal batteries and moved farther back. To safe ammunition-dumps!

Now the stocks were petering out. Colonel Ocker, the commander of 352nd Artillery Regiment, telephoned to say that he was sending 1st Battery a truck with fresh supplies. "It's on its way already," he added. It was on its way, all right. It got to within a very short distance of the gun-emplacement. Then it drove straight into a 16-inch naval shell—and with a brilliant flash the truck and its load blew up sky high.

When Lieutenant Frerking, speaking from strongpoint 62, ordered his battery to fire a salvo against an approaching wave of landing boats, his gun-position officer replied, "Sorry, Herr Oberleutnant. Order from the commander. Because of shortage of ammunition individual rounds only are to be fired." How could one oppose landing infantry by a few odd shells fired from individual guns? Another decisive mistake of the German counter-invasion measures emerges clearly—insufficiently concentrated use of artillery.

By noon Hein Severloh had fired 12,000 rounds from his machine-gun. Down on the beach men lay dead. The white figure 1 painted on each helmet, indicating the 1st U.S. Division, could be seen from the strongpoint. But inside the strongpoint things were also in a bad way. The naval bombardment had smashed the mortars, levelled out the trenches, and decimated the infantrymen. Now the Americans were bringing up large, flat-bottomed craft and unloading machine-gun carriers and tanks. The first jeep with a mounted machine-gun had just reached the beach. Lieutenant Grass shouted over to his left, to where Sergeant Pieh was lying, "Rifle grenade, quick!" Pieh handed the lieutenant the firing-cup which fitted to the carbine muzzle. These rifle grenades had become the infantrymen's personal mortars. And Grass knew how to handle them. Having started the war as an N.C.O., he was familiar with a rifle.

First shot. The grenade tore into the jeep.

Another shot. The first tank stopped dead. And now to rake it with MG fire. But already the next tank was rumbling ashore. Its gun was traversing. And with a loud crash its very first shell went straight through the aperture of the observation-post bunker. The battle for strongpoint 62 had begun. And this battle against tanks could not last long. The MG-42 was hit. Some of the fragments flew into Severloh's face. The sights of the machine-gun had been torn off. Never mind. In any case they now had only the ammunition-belts which were intended for use at night, with every fifth round a tracer. That was every bit as good as a foresight. But of course it gave away the machine-gun's position to the off-shore destroyer, which presently planted shell after well-aimed shell straight in front of Hein Severloh's dugout.

On the beach the tanks were now fanning out right and left. The neighbouring strongpoints in the east, WN61 and WN59, with the observer-posts of the 2nd and 3rd Batteries, had ceased to fire. There was no view to the left from WN62. But there, also, everything seemed to be quiet. The men inside WN62 did not know that the Americans had already gained the dunes on both their flanks. Lieutenant Frerking sent a last message through to his battery: "Gunfire barrage on the beach. Every shell a certain hit. We are getting out." But back at the gun-position there was no ammunition left. Only Corporal Peesel and Corporal Alpen had saved a few shells for No. 1 and No. 2 guns (On

Kar 98 Grenade Launcher

the following day Peesel shot an American observer out of a fir-tree with his last round.) Then they blew up their guns and made off on their horse-drawn limbers.

Behind the beach Frerking ordered his men to withdraw by intermittent leaps and bounds. Under the hail of fire from enemy tanks and naval guns it became, for most of them, a leap into death—including Frerking, Grass, and Pieh.

Hein Severloh and one signaller got through. They worked their way through open country. They marched along sunken farm tracks. They crawled through ditches. Finally they turned up at the battle headquarters of 1st Battalion, 726th Regiment, between Colleville and the coast. They had their wounds dressed. They made their reports. And they heard the battalion commander declare, "We're waiting for the tanks. Then we'll kick those Americans out again."

Tanks from the Sea

In the summer of 1942, when Erwin Rommel and his African Panzer Army had gained the last ridges of El Alamein in their drive towards the Nile, no one on earth would have given twopence for Britain's chances of holding Cairo. British headquarters personnel were burning their papers. Refugee trains to Palestine and Jordan were overcrowded. The British Commander-in-Chief, Auchinleck, was planning to take his army back behind the Nile and towards the south. Rommel was certain of victory. So certain, in fact, that during a brief stay in Berlin he attended a reception for foreign journalists and, putting his hand on the doorknob, said to them jokingly, "This is how I've got my hand on the door to Alexandria." On the Nile, however, an event of far-reaching importance had occurred: fate had placed Bernard Montgomery upon the stage of military history. Montgomery had reached the stage by fortune—the sudden death of Auchinleck's appointed successor, General Gott. And this man Montgomery, thus placed against the rules at the head of the British armies in Africa, was determined to apply to Rommel, that pampered darling of the goddess of war, and to his bold army, a recipe against which neither death-defying courage, nor skilful improvisation, nor even cunning would be of any avail. That recipe was a battle of *matériel* with a few thousand guns, a few thousand aircraft, and hundreds of thousands of shells. It was this wall of steel put up by anti-tank guns, heavy artillery, bombers, and armour which halted the German advance at Alam Halfa and smashed the Afrika Korps at El Alamein. The British victory in Africa had been a victory of material superiority.

Ever since General Sir Bernard Montgomery had known the invasion front was commanded by Erwin Rommel he realized that this opponent could be beaten again only with the recipe of El Alamein—by the crushing strategy of a battle of *matériel*. "At the spearhead of the first invasion troops we must have tanks and heavy artillery," was therefore his thesis.

And because the craft carrying the heavy guns and the special tanks against mines, against the soft sand of the dunes, and against the barbed-wire hedges would be endangered by Rommel's underwater obstacles, Montgomery upset Eisenhower's original plan of landing at high water. He thereby foiled Rommel's plan just as he had foiled it at El Alamein.

The German defences had been designed exclusively for a landing at high water. Nobody believed that the enemy would land at low water when he would have to cross an entirely clear field of fire 800 yards deep. For that reason all weapons along the coast had been so emplaced that they covered the foreshore. Montgomery deliberately accepted the risk of heavy casualties on the deep beach exposed at low tide for the sake of bringing his heavy *matériel* to bear. Events were to prove him right. Without the support of armour his first wave would probably have shared the tragic fate of Omaha and Utah. Even so, Montgomery's calculations did not work out everywhere.

The British Second Army under General Dempsey was scheduled to land on the western part of the Calvados coast between Arromanches and Ouistreham, north of Caen, on a nineteen-mile strip of beach. Armoured columns were to break through the German line, link up with the air-landed units east of the Orne, occupy the important road junctions of Caen and Bayeux, and reach positions twenty-two miles inland by the evening of D-Day. The southernmost key-point of this plan was a small town whose name we shall encounter again and again—Villers-Bocage.

In the first light of dawn, as the smoke of the night bombardment dispersed over the towns behind the coastline, the landing operations of the British Second Army began on the beaches named Gold, Juno, and Sword.

The naval bombardment began forty minutes before sunrise. In the half-light came the bombers. They were followed by the fighter-bombers. And these, in turn, by the torpedo aircraft. The battleships maintained their deafening concert of gunfire. And then the Tommies landed. First of all on Gold Beach. But here there were no infantrymen or sappers swimming or wading through the water. No! The spearhead of the landing was the 8th British Armoured Brigade. It was faced by General Richter's 716th Infantry Division, which was responsible for the defence of a coastal sector twenty-one miles long.

"Fire!" Corporal Behrendsen hissed at the man behind the heavy machine-gun. "Fire!" The machine-gun post was half buried in sand. Behrendsen himself had been wounded. The telephone was somewhere underneath the sand and could no longer transmit any orders. But then, what use would the telephone have been since all wires had been broken by the aerial bombardment anyway? There was no contact left between companies, battalions, and regiments of 716th Division.

"Fire!" The machine-gun hammered away. It swept the sand. "A bit higher!" And now the burst caught the group of Tommies running alongside the tanks. They heeled over like trees. They shouted. They flung themselves to the ground. Now a German 75-millimetre field gun was also firing at the beach. Its first shell struck the water. A landing craft drove straight into the next one. An explosion. Flames. Smoke. The boat slewed round. It hit the beach broadside on. It turned over. Burning bodies were rolling on the sand.

But those accursed tanks which were coming in all the way from the deep water were not to be halted. They crept on and on, like tortoises. Others carried enormous reels with chains and steel balls. "Damn," Behrendsen cursed. The time was 0630. The first tank had gained the dry beach.

That was the picture over on the right, on Sword Beach. And the picture was exactly the same in the centre, on Juno Beach, and over to the left, on Gold Beach. Everywhere Montgomery's disembarking troops were encountering fire from the crater-pitted moonscape.

Such German strongpoints as were still intact continued to resist, but as a fighting unit the 716th Division had been smashed by the murderous aerial and naval bombardment. The 736th Grenadier Regiment and the 2nd Battalion, 726th Regiment, in particular, had suffered heavily.

The minefields had been detonated by the bombardment and had thus become useless as barriers. The 15- and 16-inch naval shells had pulverized even solidly built concrete dugouts.

The German line was torn open in two places. The strongpoints of 441st "East Battalion" collapsed as its Russian auxiliary troops simply ran away, leaving only the German officers and N.C.O.'s with a handful of Balts to defend the positions. A remark by General von Schlieben, in a report made some time before, was borne out in full: "We are asking rather a lot if we expect Russians to fight in France for Germany against the Americans."

Through those gaps, where no longer a finger was raised to oppose them, the tanks of 8th and 27th Armoured Brigades and infantrymen of the 3rd Canadian and 3rd British Divisions were moving over the beach and up the dunes. Away from the sea. Right through the German line. If any German strongpoints were still firing on their right or left they simply by-passed them. "Keep going," was their order. Forward, to the principal highroads, to Bayeux and Caen. The day's objective seemed within reach.

But Montgomery's calculations had been over-optimistic. True, his steamroller was advancing. But at many points the defenders made successful bold swoops against his flank. British tanks were destroyed. Roads were barred to the infantry.

Major Lehmann and his 2nd Battalion, 726th Grenadier Regiment stood like a solid road-block in front of the important hill of Sainte-Croix. At last a Canadian armoured thrust overran the command-post. The major was killed. The adjutant defended the bunker with a handful of men until nightfall. Then they fought their way out.

The 2nd Battalion, 736th Grenadier Regiment, holding Tailleville, tried to halt the 3rd British Division which had broken through. The battalion headquarters personnel were surrounded. Then they threw the attackers back again. At 1548 hours a last message reached Division: "Hand-to-hand fighting inside command-post." That was the last news.

At Riva Bella, the extreme flank of the British landing, the 3rd Battalion, 736th Grenadier Regiment, supported by the 150-millimetre guns of 10th Battery, 1716th Artillery Regiment, made a counter-attack towards the coast. They got as far as Lion. They fought around the village church. But they were cut off and had to fight their way back. They collapsed, bled white.

General Richter, the divisional commander, was sitting at his battle headquarters. He did not know which strongpoints were still offering resistance. No news was coming through to him. No runners arrived.

Suddenly his telephone rang. He snatched up the receiver. And all the men in the room heard clearly the words spoken hastily into an instrument in some frontline bunker, over on the coast. It was Colonel Krug, the commander of 736th Grenadier Regiment. "Herr General," he was saying. "Herr General, the enemy are on top of my bunker. They are demanding my surrender. I have no means of resisting, and no contact with my own men. What am I to do?"

General Wilhelm Richter swallowed hard. Feuchtinger, the commander of 21st Panzer Division, Kurt Meyer, the commander of the 25th S.S. Panzer Grenadier Regiment, the orderly officers present—everybody was watching him. With deliberate calmness, almost solemnly, he said "Herr Oberst, I can no longer give you any orders. You must act upon your own judgment." And softly he added *'Auf Wiedersehen.'* And he replaced the receiver.

The Dam bursts

At 1300 hours Major Hayn at corps headquarters in Saint-Lô had shown General Marcks the reports received from the three invasion sectors. The corps commander made his report to Army Group. He left no doubt about the seriousness of the situation on the American landing sector in front of Sainte-Mère-Eglise. The British landings off Bayeux he likewise described as very dangerous. But about the central sector, about Omaha Beach, he dictated the words: "The landing at Vierville has been practically repulsed."

So optimistic were the reports coming in from Omaha.

Two hours later small parties of American infantrymen appeared behind the German line. They were utterly exhausted. Some of them were taken prisoners, but others penetrated two or three miles inland and dug in along important roads.

What had happened? Surely 352nd Division was holding? How had the Americans got through? What had suddenly tipped the scales away from the brink of utter defeat at "bloody Omaha"?

There were a number of weighty reasons for that turn in the fortunes, reasons illustrating the fundamental cause of the German defeat, reasons which could not be brushed aside by any amount of heroism by the German soldiers.

First of all there was the inexhaustible fire from American heavy weapons. No matter how many tanks and antitank guns were set ablaze by the men of 914th and 916th Grenadier Regiments and the two battalions of 726th Grenadier Regiment fighting within the area of 352nd Division—new ones instantly took their place. Secondly there was the inexhaustible stream of attacking troops. The first few companies which were mown down were followed by other units. The American Command was by no means reckless in the matter of risking human lives—quite the contrary. But General Bradley was determined to force the issue, and therefore ordered wave upon wave to advance into the German fire. Consistently he practised the method of frontal attack against the German defences. And he did not have to worry about reinforcements. Tens of thousands of men were waiting in the ships. Waiting to go into action against a single German regiment. The German defenders behind Omaha Beach were up against these two inexorable facts. There was just one regiment in action, and whenever that regiment had a bunker smashed there was no new one to spring up from the ground. If it lost a machine-gun there was no replacement to come in.

Time and the inexhaustible material resources of the Americans were bound in the long run to wear down the German defence, unless an immediate German counter-attack was mounted with fresh forces to throw the weary Americans back into the sea. For a while this would have been entirely feasible on Omaha Beach. The disembarked Americans were face to face with death: for hours on end they lay on the sand amidst a withering fire, unable to move forward or back, desperate at first, and later resigned. That was their lowest point. That was the much-quoted moment of weakness, the correct tactical moment for a counter-attack. But the moment was missed. And the Americans overcame it. Quite suddenly an American lieutenant got up to his feet on Easy Red Beach and said to his men, "You guys going to stay here until you're all dead? Like to see me attack alone?" And with an assault charge he ran to the barbed-wire hedge. The charge blew a hole into it. "Come on, let's go!" And they ran. They gained the crest of the dune. They leapt from shell crater to shell crater. They attacked the German strongpoints from behind. They filtered past a firing German bunker. They flopped down in the dunes. Crawling on their bellies, they cleared passages through the mines, and in Indian file crossed the minefields behind the much too sparsely held German line. If a man was killed he was left lying, and of the leading company alone forty-seven men were killed. The wounded were left lying too. The others just stepped over them. They must not step off the cleared path! Thus the men of the 1st U.S. Division walked, crept, or reeled out of the death-trap that was Omaha. A mere

300 men it was—300 men who slowly got the American advance moving again.

By the afternoon groups of men who had thus filtered through were deep in the hinterland. For the most part, however, they were repulsed or taken prisoner. They had no armour and no heavy weapons because the German infantrymen of 352nd Division were still holding out among the dunes, barring the few exits negotiable by tanks. The units which had seeped through were not a fighting force to be taken seriously. Not yet. The German counter-attack, which surely must come at any moment now, would simply sweep them away.

On the British invasion sector, admittedly, the situation was more serious. At Utah Beach, too, tanks had already broken through. Even so, it was still anybody's battle.

A classical military doctrine says: When an attacker has gained the far bank of a river he is in a state of weakness. He has not yet organized himself for defence and his position still lacks depth. This moment of weakness is the ideal moment for a counter-attack.

What rivers were in old-time land warfare, a beachhead was in modern amphibious operations.

Omaha Beach revealed this fact most clearly. But on the other beaches too the disembarked companies, which had suffered heavily from seasickness, the shock of their first casualties, and the over-exertion of the first attacks, went through that physical and psychological depression that paralyses all power of resistance. But where was the German counter-attack?

Since the early hours of the morning General Marcks had been almost continuously on the telephone from 84th Corps to Seventh Army, to Army Group, and even to General Jodl at the Führer's headquarters. "I need every available armoured unit for a counter-attack," he implored them. He was thinking principally of the 21st Panzer Division, Rommel's reconstituted battle-tested fighting force from Africa. As an O.K.W. tactical reserve it was the nearest unit to the invasion front. Immediately behind it was the 12th S.S. Panzer Division "Hitlerjugend" under S.S. General Witt, and farther to the rear was Bayerlein's well-equipped Panzer Lehr Division. Three armoured divisions in all. Used in a concerted drive, in the spirit of Guderian's motto "Not driblets, but mass," it represented a force capable of dislodging the invading enemy.

O.K.W.—the German High Command—however, hesitated

to release its tactical reserves. Berchtesgaden—or, for that matter, Field-Marshal von Rundstedt in Paris—was still not convinced that the Normandy landing was the great invasion. They still believed that it was a diversionary attack, a bluff, and they continued for a long time in this belief—with disastrous consequences.

And yet the pattern of the enemy's operation contained a sufficient number of clues. When the evening situation report for June 6 was discussed at 84th Corps, Major Hayn explained: "Three airborne divisions have been identified beyond doubt. That makes three-quarters of all airborne units we know to be based in England. There are, moreover, the crack units of the 4th and 1st U.S. Divisions. It is out of the question that the enemy would sacrifice some of his best assault troops for the sake of a mere feint." Turning to Lieutenant Kretschmer, he added, "Just take a look at Major Wiegmann's report from the Caen area. This is what it says. The 3rd British and 3rd Canadian Divisions had been identified before noon. Now we also know that the 50th Northumbrian and the 7th Armoured Divisions are present. That leaves only the 51st Highlanders and the 1st Armoured Division to make up Montgomery's entire old Eighth Army from North Africa! If this isn't the invasion—then what units are they going to use for it?" He had made his point, and the staff officers were convinced. Lieutenant-Colonel Vorwerk, the Seventh Army Intelligence officer, endorsed Hayn's opinion. Even Lieutenant-Colonel Meyer-Detring, the Intelligence officer of C.-in-C. West, said, "I agree with you entirely." But that was as far as it went. Rundstedt himself, and even more so the O.K.W. and Hitler, remained sceptical.

But why, at least, did not the 21st Panzer Division attack? It was deployed in the area of operations, and even though it was directly subordinated to O.K.W. it was still bound by the universal military rule that an enemy who has penetrated into a unit's area of operations must be attacked. That kind of action was not subject to permission.

The 21st Panzer Division had been alerted by its commander, General Feuchtinger, as early as 0100 hours. But exactly when it received the order to join action has remained a controversial question to this day—which is not surprising, considering that O.K.W. from its green baize table in the Führer's headquarters was governing all the way down to the front-line units. Added to this, the network of command was confused, not to say chaotic. There was no question of a precise, unambiguous chain of command. The result was vague orders. Switched into the direct chain of command from O.K.W. to its tactical reserves were various other levels of command—C.-in-C. West, Army Group B, and Armoured Group West.

Had there been in the area of Caen a commander of tank troops with clear and total power of command over all armoured forces, then there would have been a genuine chance of wiping out at least the Omaha beach-head. Admittedly, such a tank commander must have had his headquarters near the front, and he would have had to operate in the way Rommel used to operate in Africa in a great many seemingly hopeless situations: leading a concentrated armoured force straight into the enemy, pressing on and on, hitting the enemy wherever he showed up. This old recipe of Rommel's, however, was not applied in Normandy in time. The armoured divisions were employed in driblets, they were tied to the apron-strings of a far-away headquarters, and they had to operate in accordance with theories thought up behind an office desk. Rommel, the man who knew the answers, had been put in charge of an army group—a bureaucratic machinery of command—where his true talent for commanding men in the field found no opportunity of application. His gift was for leading armoured formations from the spearhead: boldly, with lightning speed, regardless of conservative rules of strategy. It was just this boldness and speed of Rommel's tank tactics that were needed now. The enemy ought to have been struck just then in a vulnerable spot, while he was right in the middle of his own operation, and thrown off balance. Where was the great strategist?

The 21st Panzer Division, though an O.K.W. reserve, was placed, in the event of a direct attack, under 716th Infantry Division on whose shoulders rested the coast defence in the British landing sector. General Feuchtinger thus found himself in the unenviable position of having to serve two masters. The result was as might have been expected.

As early as 0120 hours during the night of June 5–6, General Richter—as is proved by his records—ordered the commander of 21st Panzer Division by telephone to get his nearest units to attack the air-landed enemy forces and smash them.

At 0200 hours Richter amended his order to Feuchtinger: he was to use the whole of the 21st Panzer Division against the enemy who had landed from the air east of the Orne and clear the area entirely.

Feuchtinger, however, felt that as an O.K.W. reserve he was bound by the order that no operation was to take place without express O.K.W. approval. And this approval did not come. Precious hours were lost—hours during which the battalions of 716th Division on the coast bled themselves white. Those Rhenish-Westphalian infantrymen of 736th Grenadier Division who survived the hail of bombs were presently annihilated by British and Canadian assault guns, flame-throwers, and close-combat specialists. The artillery regiment of the division was smashed by naval bombardment and its engineer battalion was decimated. But the 21st Panzer Division, though ready to move off, stood rooted to its starting positions. At long last, after continuous remonstrations and angry arguments, General Feuchtinger decided at 0630 hours to act on his own responsibility. The commander of the 22nd Panzer Regiment, Colonel von Oppeln-Bronikowski, was at long last able to order his Mark IV tanks to move off. Dispatch riders tore into the villages around Falaise and Caen, where the companies had been standing by for hours in market-squares and village streets, well-camouflaged, with tank engines all warmed up. Order to advance!

The men leapt into the tanks. The skippers were bracing themselves up in the turrets.

"Distance forty yards. Column, move off."

The 22nd Panzers are off

To anyone studying to-day the first orders of the commander of 716th Infantry Division it becomes clear that until well into the morning of June 6 he saw the main danger in the British airborne landings east of the Orne. General Richter regarded it as his chief task to use the forces under his command to eliminate that danger. That the German reserves were, as a result, deflected away from the coast may well prove to be the most important contribution made by the 6th British Airborne Division during the early hours of D-Day. Shortly after 0200 hours General Richter directed 2nd Battalion, 192nd Panzer Grenadier Regiment, towards the bridge of Bénouville. Together with the 1st Panzerjäger Company of the 716th and a battery of the heavy artillery battalion of the 989th, the grenadiers were to recapture the bridge from the British paratroops and push across the Orne into the area of the airborne landings.

The operation started swiftly. Lieutenant-Colonel Rauch had his 192nd Regiment standing by. The 2nd Battalion under Major Zippe moved off a few minutes after 0200. The 8th Heavy

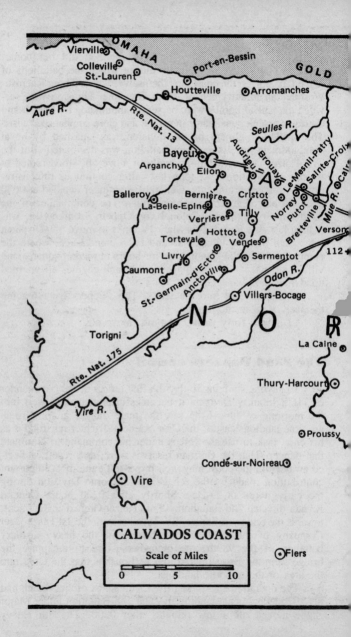

Company under Lieutenant Braats with its three self-propelled 75-millimetre guns, a 20-millimetre flak troop on armoured carriers, and a mortar troop equipped with captured French mortars drove rapidly from Cairon towards Bénouville. Dispatch Rider Atteneder had broken his own record when alerting the heavy anti-tank troop of 8th Company. "Half a minute less than last time," he reported to Lieutenant Höller, the troop commander. But in spite of all their efforts they arrived too late.

Towards 0330 hours they came up against the first British who were already across the bridge of Bénouville and had advanced westward. They pushed them back into the village of Bénouville and sealed off the western approach to the bridge. Unable to attack, the Panzerjägers, grenadiers, and engineers established themselves in defensive positions in a forest plantation and in a park on the outskirts of the village, and from there they engaged the stubbornly fighting Tommies, who were clearly determined at all costs to hold the bridge. The British were being reinforced all the time and also had some heavy anti-tank guns and field guns. They even had some tanks coming over the bridge. Sergeant Guse set one British tank on fire with his 75-millimetre gun, but a second one broke into the village and gave the British infantrymen cover against the German grenadiers. By mid-morning the German units were in the centre of Bénouville.

"With twenty tanks we could kick those Tommies out," Sergeant-Major Tanner was cursing among his mortars, which were drawn up behind the park. Sergeant Guse nodded. What had happened to the tanks?

By the time that General Feuchtinger—after those arguments with 716th Division and 84th Corps—decided to move his Panzer regiment it was daylight. A few more hours passed before all the companies, strung out over a large area, had received their marching orders. After that radio silence was imposed. From then onward all orders had to be transmitted by dispatch riders—a procedure entirely correct in theory, but utterly wrong in the particular circumstances.

Towards 0800 hours the 1st Battalion under Captain von Gottberg with its eighty tanks was moving northeast along the roads. Caen, shrouded in fire and smoke, was by-passed. Captain Hoffmann's 4th Company made contact with the first Tommies. Corporal Kortenhaus was instructed: "The company is placed under Lieutenant-Colonel von Luck's battle group which, together with units of 125th Panzer Grenadier Regiment and the engineer battalion of 716th, is attacking the air-landed enemy from the south and wiping him out." A clear order.

The 2nd Battalion, 22nd Panzer Regiment, under Major Vierzig, was also moving north-east with forty Mark IV tanks. Thus, while wave after wave of Montgomery's assault troops were disembarking on the coast, the most efficient German tactical reserve was operating against the wrong enemy. Vierzig's battalion had been on the move during the night to take part in a division exercise. The battalion commander, now a dental surgeon in a West German city, clearly recalls the events.

"Towards 0100 hours I had moved my battalion into the scheduled exercise area six miles east of Falaise. Over Caen and the coast the sky was red with the glow of fire. We heard the ceaseless detonations of the Allied aerial bombardment. But this did not strike us as unusual since such attacks had become quite a regular feature. There had been no special alert on the evening of June 5, whereas on most other days we had been getting alerts of urgency 1 to 3. Towards 0220 a motor-cycle dispatch rider arrived from my headquarters. Order from Regiment: 'The battalion will immediately return to its stations and stand by for action.'

"From 0400 hours onward the battalion stood by, ready to move and ready for action. But nothing happened. The telephone was no longer working. We waited. Towards 0600 an orderly officer whom I had sent to Regiment came back with the news that the Allied invasion had begun. At last, towards 0900, the battalion received orders in writing to move off at once towards the north-east. The order said: 'Air-landed enemy troops east of the Orne to be wiped out.' I sent dispatch riders to the companies. Then the long column got going.

"Because of the danger from enemy aircraft we kept a distance of a hundred yards between vehicles. During the move we were lucky. At first there were no fighter-bomber attacks. We approached the area of the airborne landings without having suffered any losses."

Not a single shot had been fired by the 75-millimetre guns of 22nd Panzer Regiment's Mark IV tanks against the British paratroops east of the Orne when a new order came: "About turn!"

While they had been moving to the north-east 84th Corps had been authorized by O.K.W. to make use of the 21st Panzer Division. General Marcks did not believe in using tanks against the British air-landings. Instead he ordered an attack to be launched towards the coast, against the real centre of the action—Montgomery's landing area. Only the armoured 4th Company was left to operate east of the Orne. Everything else: about turn. Direction: Caen. Radio silence until contact is made with the enemy.

What had until then been the vanguard now became the rearguard, and the former rearguard became the spearhead. As a result the battalion commander found himself right at the end of the long column. Up in front was Captain Herr's 5th Company.

Like the very devil 2nd Battalion raced past ditches, through orchards, and along sunken lanes.

Colonel von Oppeln, the regimental commander, and his headquarters personnel were with 1st Battalion, hustling it along towards the front. They struggled through the wrecked town. They were well spaced out for protection against fighter-bombers. They had lost touch with 2nd Battalion. At last they reached the jumping-off line north of Caen. It was afternoon by then. The afternoon of June 6—and at long last the first armoured counter-attack was to be made against the British bridgehead. Eight hours after the landing—at least six hours too late.

Near the little town of Lebisey, Major Vierzig spotted the 1st Battalion with its three companies all poised for attack. Without hesitation he placed himself with his tanks on their left flank. Not a shot had been fired as yet. That meant that radio communication was still forbidden. Vierzig set out on foot to locate Gottberg's battle headquarters. He found him, and together the two commanders climbed a near-by hill where regimental headquarters had been set up.

"A real old-time generals' hill," Vierzig chuckled as they spotted also General Marcks, the general commanding the 84th Corps, together with his orderly officer.

Anxious about the development of the situation, the general had come from Saint-Lô to see things for himself. Towards 1430 hours, having found both battalions of 22nd Panzer Regiment ready for action, he walked over to its commander, Colonel von Oppeln-Bronikowski. "Oppeln, if you don't succeed in throwing the British into the sea we shall have lost the war."

The colonel felt uneasy. Was victory or defeat to depend on his ninety-eight tanks? A mere ninety-eight tanks! He saluted. "I shall attack now."

General Marcks drove over to 1st Battalion, 192nd Panzer

Grenadier Regiment, and placed himself at the head of the armoured scout-cars. "Press on to the coast" was the watchword. General Marcks was taking on himself the mantle of Erwin Rommel. And fortune seemed to smile upon an outstanding leader.

The thrust went exactly into the gap between Juno and Sword beaches, which had not yet linked up. Exactly between the 3rd British and 3rd Canadian Divisions, at the joint between the two units, Marcks succeeded in splitting the beach-head. Units of 1st Battalion pushed through right to the coast. Near the villages of Lion and Luc the grenadiers reached the sea at 2000 hours on June 6. "We've made it!" they called out from their vehicles. "We've made it!" They found the last remaining strongpoints of 716th Division which were still holding out. They jumped into the levelled trenches and half-buried bunkers. "If our tanks join up with us now we shan't get dislodged from here again so easily," they were saying. If!

But the tanks were not so lucky. Gottberg's and Vierzig's companies ran straight into the advanced perimeter defences of Sword Beach. The leading tank of the regimental headquarters section received the first direct hit and blew up. The Canadian anti-tank gunners were firing like demons.

A serious drawback of the Mark IV tanks with their 75-millimetre long-barrel gun was making itself felt: excellent and penetrating as the gun was, its optics only went up to a mile and a half. That was not enough against the powerful British anti-tank guns established in favourable positions between Périers and Biéville. Oppeln's tanks had to advance on rising ground where the only cover was provided by a few ditches. The enemy's artillery and anti-tank guns were up on top, firing downhill. One tank after another was eliminated. Outside Biéville five tanks were blown up within a few minutes. It was obvious that it was not possible to force a break-through.

A glance at the situation-map of this first armoured battle reveals the drama and the tragedy of the moment: the road to the coast was still open, and 1st Battalion, 192nd Panzer Grenadier Regiment, had fought its way through to the beach. It was now waiting. Waiting for the tanks.

Similarly at Bénouville on the Orne the 8th Company, 2nd Battalion, 192nd Panzer Grenadier Regiment, was still holding out in the afternoon. Admittedly the other companies and battalions had been moved into the Périers neighbourhood in order to

support the tank attack; but 8th Company with its heavy weapons
had dug its heels in and was standing firm. It too was waiting for
the tanks.

At the air base of Douvres, a mile and a half from the coast
and on the flank of the British Juno Beach, 230 Luftwaffe ground
troops together with a few infantrymen, three anti-tank guns,
three 50-millimetre guns, a dozen flame-throwers, and twenty
machine-guns were holding out under their imperturbable
commander, Lieutenant Igle. They repulsed all attacks. Douvres
was like a thorn in the enemy's side. For ten days Igle and his
men held the position. For ten days they waited for the German
counter-attack.

But 22nd Panzer Regiment was unable to accomplish the
break-through in the face of the powerful line of tanks and
self-propelled guns built up by the British and Canadians in front
of Périers and Biéville. The regiment clung to its positions.
Because of a shortage of infantry units it could no longer be
withdrawn from the front in order to attempt an attack elsewhere.
The regiment was thus forced on to the defensive. Colonel von
Oppeln ordered: "Tanks to be dug in. Position must be held."
Only in this way could the forceful attacks of the 27th British be
repulsed.

Montgomery realized the danger. Unless the German wedge
driven into the beach-head was eliminated things might turn

50 mm. Anti-Tank Gun

critical. If the corridor from Caen to the coast, represented by 1st Battalion, 192nd Grenadier Regiment, were to become the pipeline of German supplies, filling rapidly with German armour and artillery, then this might well be the end of the British beach-head.

In view of this danger Montgomery did not hesitate a moment. He employed his glider fleet and dropped regiment after regiment of British airborne troops into the German corridor.

The disastrous effects of the total absence of the German Air Force now became patent. There was no reconnaissance and there was no air cover for the columns on the ground. Thus everything happened as it was bound to.

The armoured forces of the only Panzer division employed were too small to exploit the successes of 192nd Panzer Grenadier Regiment on the coast and at Bénouville and to turn it into a decisive victory at the British beach-head. Without reinforcements, and presently without ammunition, the grenadiers were forced to fight their way back again under a devastating bombardment by British aircraft and naval guns.

Once more Lance-Corporal Wlcek, a gun-layer at Bénouville, furiously aimed his 75-millimetre gun. *Crash*. The Tommy tank blew sky high. Then came the order to retire. Once again a position could no longer be held. The 8th Company was being taken back to the defensive line of 22nd Panzer Regiment.

Would the German Command at last understand that the dangerous situation demanded an all-out effort, the concentration of all available armoured reserves? Or would it persist in regarding the assault between Orne and Vire as a dummy attack and wait for the "true invasion" at Calais?

3
MISSED OPPORTUNITIES

The Nightmare Trek of the Panzer Lehr Division

General Bayerlein's Panzer Lehr Division, stationed seventy-five miles south-west of Paris, was also an O.K.W. reserve. Its rôle during the first decisive twenty-four hours was revealing.

At 0230 hours on June 6 the telephone rang at divisional headquarters in Nogent le Rotrou. General Warlimont of Jodl's staff passed on the following order to Bayerlein: "The Panzer Lehr Division is to be alerted for an advance in the direction of Caen. You will receive further orders from Army Group B."

How totally unsuspecting the German High Command had been with regard to Allied intentions in the West is revealed by the fact that, a few hours prior to that order, the O.K.W. had deprived the Panzer Lehr Division of its best tank battalion with its brand-new *Panther* and *Royal Tiger* companies, and ordered them to be switched to the Eastern front. Bayerlein immediately stopped this transfer on his own responsibility. Such units as had not yet been entrained were ordered back to their stations, and those on the move already were ordered to return. Even so, it took five days for the battalion to arrive at the front. Five precious days.

While the units of the Panzer Lehr Division were assembling Bayerlein drove over to Seventh Army at Le Mans. There a surprise was awaiting him. All night long O.K.W. had kept the division standing by. Now Colonel-General Dollmann demanded that it should move off at 1700 hours—in daylight. Bayerlein objected. An experienced commander and Rommel's chief of staff in the African campaigns, he had come to realize on his drive to Army headquarters where the main danger lay—in the

104

air, in the clear summer sky which was buzzing with fighter-bombers. Bayerlein proposed to wait until nightfall before moving off. Dollmann refused. The division, he argued, must arrive in the area south of Caen in the morning of June 7. In vain did Bayerlein try to convince him of the illusory nature of his calculation. Well and good if they had been allowed to move off as soon as the alert was given, at 0200, when it was still dark! But now? In daylight?

In view of the threat from the air and the bombed roads, Bayerlein pointed out, the division's average speed could be, at best, five miles per hour. The tanks were some ninety miles south of Caen. How long, therefore, would it take them to get to the operation area? Certainly they could not be there before June 8. But Dollmann insisted on his order and, moreover, proposed a change in the approach roads. On this point, however, Bayerlein was adamant. To redirect the division now would mean certain chaos. Bayerlein drove back and ordered the division to move off.

"Drive on the roads or alongside the roads, but see that you get to the front as quickly and with as few losses as possible," he instructed his officers. And presently the crack Panzer division was moving towards the Western front to come to the aid of 21st Panzer Division.

Even now Bayerlein, usually such an urbane person, gets

Panther

really angry when he recalls the sacrificial trek of his division—a trek marked by very heavy losses even before action was joined.

This is Bayerlein's own account:

"I was driving in front of the middle column with two staff cars and two headquarters signal vans along the Alençon–Argentan–Falaise road. We had only got to Beaumont-sur-Sarthe when the first fighter-bomber attack forced us to take cover. For once we were lucky. But the columns were getting farther apart all the time. Since Army had ordered radio silence we had to maintain contact by dispatch riders. As if radio silence could have stopped the fighter-bombers and reconnaissance planes from spotting us! All it did was prevent the division staff from forming a picture of the state of the advance—if it was moving smoothly or whether there were hold-ups, and losses, and how far the spearheads had got. I was forever sending off officers or else seeking out my units myself.

"We were moving along all five routes of advance. Naturally our move had been spotted by enemy air-reconnaissance. And before long the bombers were hovering above the roads, smashing crossroads, villages, and towns along our line of advance, and pouncing on the long columns of vehicles. At 2300 we drove through Sécs. The place was lit up by flares hanging above it like candles on a Christmas-tree, and heavy bombs were crashing down on the houses which were already burning. But we managed to get through.

"Towards 0200 we were getting to Argentan. The scene was as bright as day—what with fires and explosions. The little town was quaking under the ceaseless hail of bombs. We got as far as the southern outskirts; after that it was impossible to get any farther. The whole of Argentan was burning. We were in a witch's cauldron. Behind us the road was blocked too. We were trapped in a blazing town. Dust and smoke reduced visibility to nil. Sparks were flying about our vehicles. Smouldering beams and wrecked masonry blocked all roads. And still the enemy planes were hovering in the sky. Their flares flooded the burning houses with a brilliant light. We could hardly breathe with the pungent smoke. We had to reconnoitre a way out on foot. Teams of engineers were working on the heavily damaged bridge over the Orne. At 0300 we succeeded in escaping from this fiery cage across the fields in the direction of Flers. Towards dawn the bombardment abated. The road via Ecouché-Briouze-Flers was still passable. At 0400 we were in Flers, which had also suffered heavily. By 0500 we got to Condé-sur-Noireau. As for the vehicle columns of the division, there was not a sign of them anywhere. They were laboriously picking their way along bombed roads. Like Argentan, all road junctions behind the invasion front had been reduced to rubble, evidently in order to prevent the arrival of reinforcements for the Caen area.''

Bayerlein was accompanied by his indefatigable orderly officer, Captain Alexander Hartdegen, likewise an old hand from Africa who had been through the fighting at Tel el Mampsra with General Thoma. This is how he describes the second day of the divisional staff's disastrous journey:

''After driving right through the night, without any sleep, General Bayerlein, his driver Corporal Kartheus, and I were waiting for the vanguard of 901st Panzer Grenadier Regiment at Condé-sur-Noireau, thirty-one miles south of Caen. There was no trace of them anywhere. I drove back along the road. The little town of Condé had been reduced to a smouldering heap of ruins. The road bridge, too, had been destroyed by bombs. And since 0500 the fighter-bombers had again been cruising in a brilliantly blue morning sky. The Panzer Lehr Division had been placed under the 1st S.S. Armoured Corps. All night long we had been looking for the battle headquarters of Sepp Dietrich, the corps commander, to find out what his plans were and to get our orders. But we could not find it. Not till the late afternoon of June 7 did we discover it in a small wood north of Thury-Harcourt. Dietrich ordered Bayerlein to get one combat group each into the areas of Norrey and Brouay, on the Caen-Bayeux railway line, by the morning of June 8. From there we were to launch an attack on a broad front together with the 12th S.S. Panzer Division 'Hitlerjugend.'

''At last, towards the evening, we found the vanguards of our division near Thury-Harcourt. The grenadiers had arrived first. The tanks were still a long way behind.

''General Bayerlein discussed the situation with the regimental commanders and towards 2200 hours we drove to our battle headquarters at Proussy. This drive showed us clearly what the regiments had been through on their move. Dozens of wrecked vehicles, now no more than steel skeletons, lay by the roadside burning and smouldering. The sector from Caumont to Villers-Bocage was a road of death. Burnt-out trucks, bombed field kitchens and gun tractors, many of them still smouldering, with dead bodies strewn alongside. This was the appalling backcloth throughout our journey. Corporal Kartheus stepped on the gas hard: 'Let's get out of here.'

Danger: Low-flying Aircraft!

"The summer nights in Normandy were short [Captain Hartdegen's report continues]. We had just reached Hill 238 and were bowling along the road when we saw three fighter-bombers in the dawn sky. They had evidently spotted us, for they were streaking along the straight road at low altitude, straight at us. The brakes screeched. As a dozen times earlier that day, General Bayerlein let himself drop into the roadside ditch out of the moving car. I caught sight of a concrete culvert, raced towards it, and dived into the pitch-dark pipe head first—a real godsend of a cover. Kartheus also managed to get out of the car just before the aircraft cannon spat out their first shells. In an instant the B.M.W. staff car was ablaze. The next plane streaked right along the ditch, opening up at us as it dived. The 20-millimetre shells burst immediately in front of my concrete pipe. The corporal had just called out to Bayerlein: 'Crawl away from the car, Herr General, get away from it'—then he was silent.

"Unless a man has been through these fighter-bomber attacks he cannot know what the invasion meant. You lie there, helpless, in a roadside ditch, in a furrow on a field, or under a hedge, pressed into the ground, your face in the dirt—and there it comes towards you, roaring. There it is. Diving at you. Now you hear the whine of the bullets. Now you are for it.

"You feel like crawling under the ground. Then the bird has gone. But it comes back. Twice. Three times. Not till they think they've wiped out everything do they leave. Until then you are helpless. Like a man facing a firing-squad. Even if you survive it's no more than a temporary reprieve. Ten such attacks in succession are a real foretaste of hell.

"Our staff car was a gutted heap of metal on the road; it was smouldering and smoking. Corporal Kartheus lay dead in the ditch. As if by a miracle General Bayerlein got away with a few cuts and shrapnel wounds. As for me, I was saved by the culvert."

Captain Hartdegen knelt down by Corporal Kartheus. "Nothing we can do for him, Herr General," he said to Bayerlein. The general nodded and wiped the blood off his cut forehead.

"We must cover him up," Bayerlein said.

"Yes, said Hartdegen, glancing at the corporal's face. But what with? He hesitated, then took off his cotton pullover and spread it over the dead man's head and chest. The staff car was still smouldering and smoking.

"Let's get away from this smoke signal," Hartdegen suggested. Some fifty yards from the dead corporal they dropped into the ditch. Their hands were still trembling and their knees were like jelly. "And how do we get away from here?" Bayerlein asked. Hartdegen offered to make his way across to Coulvain, where they had left the headquarters personnel of 902nd Panzer Grenadier Regiment. Just then a German jeep pulled up. Gutmann, the regimental commander, had watched the low-level attack on the flat road and had anxiously sent the car along the moment the fighter-bombers had left. In this way the divisional commander again had a car—even if it was only a jeep.

Night fell over the road. Merciful night. Protection from fighter-bombers. They moved off to Proussy, where Major Kaufmann, the chief of operations, had been awaiting them with concern for the past twenty-four hours.

Meanwhile the battalions of the Panzer Lehr Division were struggling on along the roads into the battle area. Lieutenant Hans Eberhard Bohmbach was reminded of his double birthday-party with his friend Rollinger as he moved forward through the drizzling rain with his 1st Battalion, 902nd Panzer Grenadier Regiment, nearer to the front—the vital invasion front.

They had left Vibraye towards 1700 hours on June 6. They had been on the move throughout the evening and throughout the dark, cloudy night. But then came a brilliant summer day. And with the sun came the fighter-bombers.

The battalion suffered its first heavy losses before it had fired a single shot itself. The men in their open armoured personnel-carriers were simply picked off one by one. Unless the battalion was to be wiped out before it got anywhere near the front there was no alternative but to hide out in a patch of wood and await the night. The night of June 7-8—just as Bayerlein had predicted.

Towards midnight a dispatch rider arrived at the battalion. At last they got some information. Regimental headquarters of the 902nd, with Colonel Gutmann, the dispatch rider explained, was north of Villers-Bocage on the eastern outskirts of Tilly.

Tilly! Lieutenant Bohmbach tried to find the place on his map. He was not to know that the name would soon go down in military history. "Here we are—between Caen and Bayeux."

Bohmbach set out to get his orders for the battalion. He drove past gutted trucks, field kitchens, and staff cars. He paid no particular attention to the skeleton of the B.M.W. which still showed the twisted flagstaff of a command pennant on its bonnet—Bayerlein's car. The moon had come out among the clouds as Bohmbach reached the bombed-out little town of Villers-Bocage. He encountered weary groups of 716th Infantry Division marching away from the front. "The Tommy tanks are on our heels," they called out to Bohmbach—the kind of alarmist rumour invariably spread by retreating units. Bohmbach paid no attention to them. He pressed on in the direction of Tilly. Dawn was breaking. He looked at his map: Juvigny.

"Fighter-bombers!" his driver shouted. He flicked into low gear and drove the car into the ditch alongside the road. And already those cursed birds were swooping down. Past them. The ditch had saved Bohmbach and his driver. They heard the bombs burst on the crossroads they had just passed. They could hear the planes pull out, bank, and dive down again. Who were the victims this time? The grenadiers had no medicine against the fighter-bombers. During the first alarm an experienced old lance-corporal, in charge of the leading armoured personnel-carrier of the escort company, had broken column and driven off into the field to aim a burst of fire from his two machine-guns at the attacking Spitfire. And, to his utter amazement, nothing had happened. He had opened up again. The aircraft had flown straight through his fire—one had only to watch the tracer—but the effect had been nil. No wonder. Engine and cockpit had been armoured against small-arms fire.

Thus the fighter-bombers had become a frightful weapon against infantry. The warning "Low-flying aircraft!" was the nightmare of all units on the move. The dangerous birds were everywhere. No one was ever safe from them except, perhaps, by night or when it rained.

When Lieutenant Bohmbach at last jumped into the five-foot dugout that served as his regimental commander's battle headquarters near Brouay the last thing he saw in the sky was once more an aircraft. This time it was an artillery spotter. A minute later its purpose became plain: heavy naval guns began to bombard the area of Brouay where the 902nd Panzer Grenadier Regiment not only had its headquarters but where its advance units were standing by ready for action. For a whole hour death and destruction rained down upon the regiment before it had fired a single shot.

At his temporary divisional headquarters in Proussy, a little château surrounded by a few farmhouses, north of Condé-sur-Noireau, General Bayerlein informed his chief of operations, Major Kaufmann, about the situation of the division and the location of the various units. He explained the orders he had issued for the attack scheduled for the following morning, June 8. Colonel Scholze with his reinforced 901st Panzer Grenadier Regiment was to gain the area of Norrey, while Colonel Gutmann with the reinforced 902nd Panzer Grenadier Regiment was to move into the Brouay area. They were then to link up with 12th S.S. Panzer Division "Hitlerjugend" and, on its right, the 21st Panzer Division for the full-scale attack towards the coast.

The full-scale attack! It had to come off this time—not like when 21st Panzer Division had tried. The Panzer Lehr and the "Hitlerjugend" divisions were to get the German counter-measures out of the bog again where they had got stuck through mismanagement.

Confused Orders

Witt's 12th S.S. Panzer Division "Hitlerjugend" was a well-equipped unit. The grenadiers were young boys between eighteen and nineteen. They believed in their cause and had confidence in their weapons. They had no inkling of the tug-of-war that went on in the High Command—and if anybody had told them they would have been furiously angry. They were about to pay a heavy price for their innocence.

Both the choice of assembly area and the first operational orders issued to 12th S.S. Panzer Division clearly reveal the conflicting views still held in the higher German commands.

In April the division had been switched from Belgium to Normandy. It was to be stationed in the area of Lisieux, eighteen miles behind the coast. That would have been an excellent assembly area. If only it had been there on June 6! But General von Geyr, the commander of Armoured Group West, had the division moved another thirty miles farther to the south. His decision reflected the old quarrel between Rommel and himself: the former wanted to have the reserves quite close to the coast, while the latter wanted them stationed a good way back in order to gain elbow-room for manoeuvre. In his calculations Geyr had not made allowance for the overwhelming air superiority of the Allies—though, in fairness, it came as a surprise to all troops in Normandy.

Thus Witt's decision was exactly twelve miles too far away from the zone of operations to go into action on June 6.

As early as 0300 hours, 711th Division, commanded by Lieutenant-General Reichardt and stationed on the right of 716th Infantry Division between Orne and Seine, had sent a signal to General Witt: "Enemy airborne landings behind our left wing." And then came a strange postscript: "Enemy dropping uniformed straw dummies." That was one of Montgomery's deceptions. Altogether he was a past-master at that kind of trick. Although his division had not been ordered into action, Witt immediately alerted his units. At 0400 hours exactly they were ready to move. The tanks were waiting. The grenadiers were waiting. But nothing happened. The 25th Panzer Grenadier Regiment reconnoitred in the direction of Caen.

At 0700 came an order from Obergruppenführer[1] Dietrich, the commander of the 1st S.S. Armoured Corps, placing the division under 81st Corps in Rouen and instructing it to assemble in the Lisieux area. The unit commanders were shaking their heads in bewilderment. Why Lisieux? Surely reconnaissance had shown the enemy to have landed on both sides of the Orne and to be pressing towards Caen? Besides, a move without previously elaborated marching plans was bound to waste a great deal of time. But orders were orders—and there was no telephone communication with Army Group B. There was thus no way of making one's misgivings known.

New marching orders were worked out and taken to the units by orderly officers. Between 1000 and 1100 hours the units were ready to move off. And that was on June 6—early enough for a rapid counter-attack to the coast.

It was precisely the time when 22nd Panzer Regiment of 21st Panzer Division was being launched towards the western bank of the Orne.

At about 1500 hours an order was received from Army Group B to the divisional commander to the effect that the division should not, after all, assemble in the Lisieux area, but west of Caen. Objective: support for a counter-attack of 84th Corps. Witt cursed furiously. His regiments were already on the move. How were they to be recalled? By the time the new order reached the reinforced 25th Panzer Grenadier Regiment it had reached the area west of Lisieux and the time was nearly 1600

[1] An *Obergruppenführer* of S.S. troops was the equivalent of an army general.

hours. The remaining units received the order at various times at different points along their route.

Thus the 25th Panzer Grenadier Regiment had to cover yet another forty-four miles to get to its assembly area—an area that was only half that distance away from the regiment's initial position that morning. As a result it could no longer be employed on June 6. The day had been wasted in marching.

As if to add insult to injury the division was once more placed under the 1st S.S. Armoured Corps, and from it received the order to go into action at 1200 hours on June 7, on the left flank of 21st Panzer Division, for an attack to the north with the aim of throwing the disembarked enemy back into the sea.

The order came a full twenty-four hours too late to help the attack of 21st Panzer Division at Périers to achieve success. All that time was wasted before a perfectly obvious operation by a strong and ready armoured division was in fact launched. Twenty-four hours frittered away. During those twenty-four hours the chance of successful opposition to the airborne and seaborne landings was missed. Generalship from a far-away office desk had prevented what any authorized commander of armoured forces in the field would have done at once: order the 21st Panzer Division to break through to the coast with all available forces early in the morning of June 6, immediately after the seaborne landing, and make it wheel to the west, regardless of further airborne landings in its rear. By placing 21st Panzer Division under the 1st S.S. Armoured Corps the necessary reinforcements would have been ensured.

The 12th S.S. Panzer Division and the Panzer Lehr Division could similarly have gone into action not later than 1000 hours on June 6, under the command of 1st S.S. Armoured Corps in accordance with long-prepared operational plans. Witt's decision had been standing by since 0400. Bayerlein, as we know, had been alerted by General Warlimont from the Führer's headquarters as early as 0230 hours. Thus, at the very least, 25th S.S. Panzer Grenadier Regiment, reinforced by a tank battalion, an artillery battalion, and a heavy flak battery, as well as an equally strong armoured combat group of the Panzer Lehr, could have been ready for a counterattack at Caen in the evening of June 6. Fighter-bombers would not have ruled out this operation since there was haze and drizzle during the early part of June 6 and—unlike the clear evening—a rapid and on the whole unharassed move towards the front would have been possible.

Quite apart from all this, the question arises: Even if there were no fighter aircraft available, where at least was the German flak? The answer to this question again illustrates the lack of co-ordination in the transmission of information between the higher commands.

General Pickert's 3rd Flak Corps was under orders, in the event of a landing on the Normandy coast, to move into the bridgehead immediately with its flak units. The batteries of the corps were on the Somme. Its headquarters were south of Amiens. Three regiments, about six battalions, were available. That represented a considerable fire-power and a useful support for attack or defence.

In the morning of June 6 General Pickert had still not been informed about the landings. He left his headquarters on a tour of inspection. Not till his return in the afternoon did he find the first reports, and those with the reservation that it was still not clear whether this was in fact the great invasion. Still not clear! Pickert drove to Paris. In the afternoon of June 6 he eventually got his units to move off into the area on both sides of Caen. The batteries arrived at the front on June 8 and 9, badly mauled. Their casualties had been over 200 dead and wounded. Before they had fired a single shot! How different things might have been if the bulk of the corps had been at the front on the evening of June 6!

It is, of course, easy to operate with ifs and might-have-beens. Besides, things look a great deal clearer now than they did on that June 6, 1944. Nevertheless, many experienced critics share the belief that a swift counter-attack by the named units of June 6 could have sufficiently compressed the British beach-head to give subsequent German operations at least a chance of success. Especially as the Allied air superiority was able to inflict painful losses on German columns on the march and in assembly areas, while it could not be brought to bear so fully during the close clinch of battle, when friend and foe were closely interlocked.

However, things had worked out differently—and the question now was whether the omissions of June 6 could still be made good on June 7 or 8.

Ardenne Abbey

Lieutenant-General Witt believed that a thrust of his splendidly equipped 12th S.S. Panzer Division would do the trick. His orders for the attack on June 7 lacked nothing in lucidity or optimism. Following an exposition of the situation of the German and the enemy forces, item 3 read as follows: "The Division will attack the disembarked enemy together with 21st Panzer Division and throw him back into the sea." The deployment orders were precise and carefully thought out. They concerned the 25th and 26th Grenadier Regiments, the two armoured battalions of 12th Panzer Regiment, and the reconnaissance battalion, as well as the engineer battalion and the flak. The attack was timed for 1200 hours on June 7.

Before the attack Witt and Feuchtinger had a conference to co-ordinate their operations. Feuchtinger had brought with him the commander of his 22nd Panzer Regiment, Colonel von Oppeln, to report about his experiences. It was decided that 22nd Panzer Regiment should join in Witt's northward attack at the moment when their lines came abreast. The northward thrust was then to be jointly followed through right to the sea.

What then became of this operation, launched with so much confidence?

The forward units of the reinforced 25th Panzer Grenadier Regiment reached the western edge of Caen in the early hours of the morning. The town was still burning. The streets were blocked by debris. As the sun rose the fighter-bombers began their ceaseless attacks on the approach roads. The pilots picked their targets with great care. Above all they were out to hit the fuel trucks; for if the fuel trucks were destroyed the German tanks were immobilized. Without fuel they were helpless. For that reason the regimental commander of the 25th, Kurt Meyer, generally known as "Panzer" Meyer, had been using Volkswagens exclusively for carrying fuel to his fighting forces ever since daybreak. These small and highly manoeuvrable vehicles managed to get through by dashing from cover to cover.

The regiment set up a battle headquarters on the western edge of Caen. Meyer went forward to an advanced headquarters in the Ardenne Abbey.

He climbed up one of the towers to survey the scene. As he raised his binoculars to his eyes an incredible picture presented itself to him. Spread out before him, as if built up from toys, was a landscape criss-crossed by hedgerows and dotted with orchards. On the coast, unloading operations were in full swing. Huge ships were lying alongside jetties, just as if it were peace-time. Countless barrage balloons were floating in the sky, carrying steel cables to protect the fleet and the beaches from air attacks. A needless precaution!

But Meyer saw something else: enemy armoured units were taking up formation in front of his sector. "This is going to be quite a party," he said to himself. He cast a glance behind, inland, from where his own division was due to advance. He saw the Caen-Falaise road, straight as an arrow. But there were no fighting units moving along it. The tanks and armoured infantry carriers were somewhere under cover, waiting to make the leap to the front undisturbed by fighter-bombers.

Meyer again turned his field-glasses to the front. He started. Surely there was an enemy tank moving up through the orchards. Now it had stopped. It was at the most 200 yards away from the grenadiers of 2nd Battalion who were in position behind a hedge, well camouflaged. Not a shot was fired. The battalion's fire discipline was good, and it was soon to be rewarded. The solitary tank was clearly flank cover for an armoured unit which now emerged from the little village of Buron, making for the Caen-Bayeux road. Its objective evidently was the airfield of Carpiquet which a German Luftwaffe unit had abandoned without fight. The British tanks were moving right across the front of Meyer's 2nd Battalion. They were exposing a long, unprotected flank. That was the dream of all Panzer grenadiers. It was the ideal condition for anti-tank gunners.

Meyer sent an order to all battalions, to his gunners, and also to the 2nd Battalion of the Panzer regiment: "Fire not to be opened except on my express orders."

Down below, in the abbey garden, Standartenführer[1] Max Wünsche, the commander of 12th Panzer Regiment, was standing in his command car. Whatever Meyer reported to him over the field telephone from the tower he passed on to his tanks over his radio. One company was inside the abbey grounds, another, well camouflaged, on a rearward slope close to the road along which the enemy armoured unit was unsuspectingly advancing.

The British were entirely unconcerned. Before them was only one objective—the airfield. His eyes glued to his binoculars, Meyer passed on every movement of the enemy detachments. The tension was so great and overpowering that Wünsche was passing on the instructions to his tank commanders almost in a whisper, as if those noisy monsters out in front might hear him.

Meyer made his plan quickly. He had to take a chance. The enemy, attacking with one armoured regiment and an infantry

---

[1] Rank in S.S. troops equivalent to lieutenant-colonel.

brigade, was to be destroyed by the German forces straight from their favourable assembly position, and this would be followed by an immediate counter-attack. It was against the division's timetable, but instant action was imperative.

21st Division was informed by dispatch rider.

The enemy armoured spearhead was approaching the Caen-Bayeux road. Hoarsely Meyer called into the field telephone, "Attack!" Almost at once Wünsche rapped out, "Attention: tanks advance!" And with that order hell was let loose. The anti-tank guns began barking.

The tanks rumbled and clanked. Then they stopped and fired. The leading enemy tank was blown up. The second tank was on fire. Its crew were tumbling out and flopping into the roadside ditch. Among the enemy tanks—Canadians of the 27th Tank Regiment of the 2nd Armoured Brigade—there was complete chaos. Tank after tank was shot up. The accompanying infantrymen—Highlanders of the 9th Canadian Brigade—tried to fall back to the village of Authie and to dig in there. But the grenadiers of Meyer's 3rd Battalion were too fast for them. The German attack was in full swing. Already the first Canadian prisoners were shuffling into the abbey garden, their hands raised above their heads. Was fortune at last going to smile upon the Germans?

The Canadians suffered heavy losses. According to their own subsequent account the leading company of North Nova Scotia Highlanders was completely shot up. The other companies, too, had very heavy casualties. The tank regiment lost 30 per cent of its effective strength and twenty-eight Sherman tanks.

But Meyer's grenadier companies were now also running into enemy artillery fire. On a reconnaissance by motor-bike Meyer discovered to his horror that the right flank of his advanced 1st Battalion was no longer covered. The tanks of 21st Armoured Division had got stuck at Epron. To make matters worse, enemy armour was now striking at this open flank, bringing about a dangerous crisis in the 1st Battalion. The anti-tank gunners managed to avert the immediate danger, but any further advance was out of the question.

On the left flank, too, enemy armoured formations were deploying. These were part of the 7th Canadian Brigade, attacking the Caen-Bayeux road west of the little river Mue and threatening to break into the assembly area of 26th Grenadier Regiment. So far only the reconnaissance company of the 26th had arrived, since the battalions had been slowed down by heavy air attacks.

The area was being held only by scattered infantry units of the decimated 716th Division, and it was clear that these were no effective protection against attacking tanks. In the circumstances Meyer had but one choice: to break off his attack.

Thus, as June 7 drew to a close in the area of Caen, yet another opportunity had not been exploited. All the hopes of the German Command were now centred on June 8, the third day of the Allied invasion, the day when at long last the three armoured divisions—the 21st, the Panzer Lehr, and the 12th S.S.—were to launch their full-scale concerted attack against the British bridgehead which by then had grown to a depth of six miles.

Duel with the Navy

In the American plan for the landing on Utah Beach the heavy 210-millimetre battery of Saint-Marcouf and the near-by army coastal battery of Azeville with its four 122-millimetre guns had a small chapter to themselves. Both positions were to have been taken by American assault troops in the morning of D-Day. But when June 6 drew to an end Saint-Marcouf was still firing. It was shelling the landing beach and it was shelling the Iles Saint-Marcouf off the coast where the 4th U.S. Division was piling up stores. The G.I.'s were cursing and the American staff doctors were worried. "That damned battery's got to be silenced," they said.

"That damned battery" upset the entire American timetable.

Blackened with smoke and bleary-eyed, the naval gunners sat in their bunkers. The past twenty-four hours had been like a bad dream. First the attack by parachutists. Then the Navy. Was it really only yesterday morning that they had first sighted that armada? It seemed like eternity.

Staff Sergeant Baumgarten, the fire-control officer of the Saint-Marcouf battery, would never forget the scene. Lieutenant Ohmsen picking up the telephone towards 0500 hours and calmly reporting to Admiral Hennecke, the Naval Commander in Cherbourg: "Several hundred ships sighted in the Bay of the Seine. Question: Any German vessels at sea?" After a short pause the answer came: "No. None of our vessels at sea. Any vessels sighted bound to be enemy ships. Permission to open fire. Ammunition to be used sparingly. Message ends. Out."

After that all the talking was done by the guns.

At 0500 exactly visibility was so good that accurate aiming was possible. Visibility meant a great deal to the battery, since it

MISSED OPPORTUNITIES 119

had neither radar nor up-to-date fire-control equipment. As in the days of old-time gunnery, they had to fire with the aid of a trench scissor telescope—a collapsible telescope with a scale calibrated in degrees. The battery's great luxury was a home-made range-finding clock for calculating the range by impact timing. Thus equipped, Saint-Marcouf faced the greatest invasion fleet in history.

Ohmsen ordered all three guns: "Fire!"

Just as if his order had been heard aboard the battleships and cruisers out at sea the enemy salvoes came crashing over on top of them. And they were right on target.

The American fleet had clearly been waiting with their guns fully aimed. The range had been accurately calculated. They had merely held their fire until it was clear that they had been spotted. And the moment the muzzle flashes of Saint-Marcouf had been seen the order to fire had been given to all guns on the battleship *Nevada* and on a dozen cruisers and destroyers.

But Saint-Marcouf had also found its range. Its next salvo straddled the target. Direct hit on a cruiser, between funnel and bridge. Smoke poured from the ship. She stopped dead. Then her bow and her stern rose at the same time. She broke in two right in the middle. Destroyers raced to her aid. They ran straight into the fire of the Saint-Marcouf guns. "That's the stuff," Ohmsen shouted. "Keep it up."

The ship hit by Ohmsen's 210-millimetre guns turned out to have been not a cruiser but a destroyer, but the mistake was pardonable at the great distance.

But the gunners out at sea knew their job too. Shortly after 0800 the battery's first gun was eliminated by a heavy calibre hit right in front of the bunker. Ohmsen's men were consoling themselves: "An American warship for one gun! That's not a bad swap." With two guns they continued the shelling. Target: destroyer astern.

"Direct hit!" came the delighted shout from the fire-control post. Yet another destroyer approached—to help the sister ship and to tow her away. But that destroyer, too, was sunk by the well-aimed fire of the near-by 4th Battery of 1261st Army Coastal Artillery Regiment under Lieutenant Schulz at Quineville. The regimental commander, Colonel Triepel, was watching proceedings from his headquarters on a gorse-covered hill. He reported. "The destroyer tried to evade the shelling by zigzagging. But she suffered hit after hit. One shell apparently struck her rudder, for she kept going round in circles. Eventually she stopped. She listed to port. Her after-deck was slipping deeper and deeper into the water.''

The Americans lost three destroyers off Utah Beach.

To tackle the Saint-Marcouf battery the Americans employed against it the battleships *Nevada*, *Arkansas*, and *Texas*. The last two alone carried ten 14-inch guns, twelve 12-inch guns, and several dozen 5-inch guns. They were veritable mountains belching forth fire, death, and destruction against Saint-Marcouf.

At 0900 hours the moment had come: after prolonged, concentrated fire one of the *Nevada*'s 14-inch guns succeeded in scoring a direct hit through the loophole of No. 2 gun. It was a lucky shot for the Americans. And a real calamity for No. 2 gun. The effect was terrible.

"Direct hit through the loophole" may sound rather sensational, but a naval battery designed to fight targets at sea does not have the usual fire-slit. A heavy gun like that must be able to traverse through 180° and to elevate through an arc of 60°. Moreover, it must be capable of being raised or lowered by several feet. The 'loophole' in which the gun-barrel performs this manoeuvre is therefore more or less the size of a barn door—about twenty by twenty-six feet.

The armoured-steel loophole-plate to fit into this large opening had been dispatched from the supply depot at Bad Segeberg, but had never arrived. It was probably lying at some bombed railway junction, just as the battery's up-to-date fire-control equipment was.

With both pill-box guns silenced, Saint-Marcouf was no longer able to shell targets at sea. Ohmsen therefore trained their last gun, a free-standing 210-millimetre, on the landing strip. It was six miles to Utah Beach—to where strongpoint W5 had just been overwhelmed, and where American tanks, trucks, and troops were tightly pressed together, preparing to break out along the coast towards the north. In his account of the invasion Admiral King, C.-in-C. U.S. Navy, admits that "the enemy from 1100 onwards brought the beach under accurate artillery fire."

"What's the time?" Ohmsen asked.

"Seven o'clock, Herr Oberleutant," Baumgarten replied.

The telephone rang. Lieutenant Kattnig from Azeville was on the line: "My No. 3 gun has been silenced by a direct hit on the emplacement. The ten-foot-thick concrete roof has been smashed and the gun buried with its crew."

Ohmsen had no time to say much about his own situation.

He could hear machine-guns opening up within the strongpoint. "Alarm! Enemy attack from direction Crisbecq." The time was 0707 hours.

The Americans had launched an attack from their positions at Saint-Germain-de-Varreville—one battalion by the coastal road against Saint-Marcouf, another somewhat farther to the west against Azeville. They penetrated into the village of Saint-Marcouf. Ohmsen had got one of his flak guns working again and was firing at the charging infantrymen. The U.S. battalion suffered heavy casualties. But those American assault troops were tough customers. Along the poplar-lined track they fought their way forward from the village of Saint-Marcouf toward the battery.

Barbed wire and trenches had all been levelled by the hail of bombs and shells. The flanking machine-guns were smashed up. From the landward side the battery was entirely exposed. In short bounds the Americans were closing in.

"Alarm! Prepare for all-round defence!" Ohmsen ordered. That was the battery's emergency signal. Now everything was at stake. The attackers penetrated into the battery area. The German gunners were trapped in their bunkers. On the road to Crisbecq German and American infantrymen were lying within a hand-grenade's throw of each other.

The naval gunners, middle-aged reservists all of them, acquitted themselves like an infantry company of the line.

All the officers and N.C.O.'s were wounded. Lieutenant Ohmsen had a bullet through his hand. There was no doctor. He had been killed on the way to Saint-Marcouf from the neighbouring battery. Two medical ratings were looking after the wounded. And many a survivor of Saint-Marcouf owes his life to them.

The Americans, meanwhile, had come close to the fire-control bunker of the Azeville battery, which was situated within the Saint-Marcouf battery's area because from Azeville itself the coast could not be seen.

From his dugout Ohmsen saw an enemy assault group climb up on top of the Azeville fire-control bunker. He realized what the Americans were trying to do: thrust detonators into the apertures, light the fuses, and roast the occupants. That was exactly what would presently happen to all his gun crews.

In the face of this desperate situation Ohmsen took an equally desperate decision. His signaller with his walkie-talkie set was by his side. Ohmsen ordered: "Signal to Azeville battery: request gunfire on my own position. Ohmsen."

Aghast, the signaller stared at the lieutenant. "Get on with it, man!" he snapped. And by way of explanation, he added, "We shall have some losses ourselves. But it's our only chance." The signaller transmitted the message.

The Azeville battery was also surrounded by the enemy, but Lieutenant Kattnig received the signal. He saw at once what Ohmsen was up to. "Schürger," he said to his old staff sergeant. "Schürger, we're going to make those fellows dance." Calmly, as if this was a range exercise, he placed some well-aimed shells right in the Saint-Marcouf battery area.

The effect was startling. The Americans were bewildered. A burst close to the fire-control bunker of the Azeville battery swept off the men who had climbed on top. Where was the fire coming from? The American infantrymen's first thought was that they were being pounded by their own naval guns. And that made them furious. Nobody likes being killed by his own side's bullets. Their reaction, therefore, was understandable: helter-skelter the G.I.'s abandoned the battery. They even left their weapons and equipment behind.

This dramatic change of fortune acted like a tonic on the men of the battery. With their captured weapons—which included small, portable mortars—they equipped themselves like an infantry unit. As a further godsend, Lieutenant Geissler appeared on the scene with the 6th Company, 919th Infantry Regiment. They had fought their way through to the battery and now swelled Ohmsen's forces.

Jointly infantrymen and gunners pursued the Americans. They knew the terrain and struck at the retreating enemy's flank. The American regimental commander realized the danger and threw in a reserve company on his left wing. But it did not help. The Germans kept up the pressure. The Americans retreated faster and faster. Their retreat turned into a rout. The G.I.'s were shot up. Ohmsen's and Geissler's men took ninety prisoners. The remainder of the Americans were driven far beyond Dodainville, where at last they fell back upon reserve units of their 22nd Regiment.

The men of Saint-Marcouf believed they could sense the fury of the fighter-bombers which swooped down again and again at their battery during the rest of the day. They believed they could hear the anger of the naval gunners who were ceaselessly pounding them. But they enjoyed their grim satisfaction. They had shown those Yanks! They did not know how things stood on the other sectors of the front. They did not know that the grenadier battalions of the 1058th and 922nd Regiments, as well as the 6th Parachute Regiment and the 7th A.O.K. Assault Battalion were pinned down at Sainte-Mère-Eglise and Azeville. Pinned down by the American naval gunners and covered by the first American tanks pushing inland from the coast. General von Schlieben by then realized that the enemy bridgehead could no longer be wiped out by counter-attacks with local reserves. He was preparing to defend the Montebourg-Sainte-Mère-Eglise and Fontenay–Rovenoville roads and was organizing combat groups to confine the bridgehead as far as possible. He too was hoping that armoured units and operational reserves would soon arrive for a counter-attack.

Mercifully, night fell over Saint-Marcouf and Azeville. It spread its blanket over the wounded and the dead. But the living—those still capable of work—were standing by their wrecked equipment, carrying out repairs.

They were getting their machine-guns into working order again. From various parts they rebuilt one of the 210-millimetre guns. It would be able to fire again. It would fire again in the morning, the third day of the invasion, when the German armour would launch its big counter-attack. Surely that counter-attack must come now.

Last Message from Bayeux

June 8 was a Thursday. The Catholic world was celebrating Corpus Christi. But on the Normandy coast the bells were silent. There the war raged. It was a day of much courage and many weighty decisions.

During the night Tilly had been smashed by Allied bombers. The enemy wanted to cut off all supplies to the north. With increased pressure Montgomery's tanks were pushing towards Bayeux in order to reach the *route nationale*, the great highway from Cherbourg to Caen.

Just before noon the telephone rang at 84th Corps headquarters. The corps switchboard asked for the Intelligence officer. "The Bayeux exchange is on the line, sir." The voice of a girl came through, a telephone auxiliary: "Herr Major, British tanks are now passing the soldiers' club. They are right in the middle of the town." Major Hayn was nearly speechless. "How on earth do *you* know? Is there no one left at any headquarters?"

"All staff officers have joined the fighting. British armoured forces have broken through our main frontline and are attacking the town. I'm the last one here." And then she added, "Now the Tommies are driving past the building outside. You can hear for yourself, Herr Major." Coolly the girl held the receiver out of the window. The Intelligence officer in Saint-Lô listened and heard the deep-throated rumble and clanking of the enemy tanks. No doubt about it: that was enemy armour. It could only be the 50th British Division.

"I'm afraid I've got to ring off now," said the girl on the other end of the line.

Forgetting all military etiquette, the major shouted into his instrument, "Damn it all, girl, what's going to happen to you?"

"Oh, I'll disappear all right through the orchards at the back. Message ends." A click, and the line went dead.

Bayeux had fallen. Of that, after this dramatic incident, there could be no doubt. The British had captured the first major town in Normandy. They had cut the great artery running parallel to the coast and were now able to wheel towards the important communications centre of Caen.

Hayn was about to take the bad news to his chief, Lieutenant-Colonel von Criegern, when there was a crackling and spluttering noise outside the bunker door. An ambulance carrying German and American wounded had been strafed by fighter-bombers and was burning furiously. The wounded were screaming. They were dragged out of the vehicle. Two Americans were dead. All had severe burns. Into that confusion at the entrance to headquarters burst an orderly officer of 352nd Division with a staff sergeant and two Russians from 439th "East Battalion": "Where is the Intelligence officer? The battalion commander, Major Becker, has sent him two kitbags full of captured American documents."

How had he got hold of them? The staff sergeant reported laconically: in the battalion's area on the Vire estuary near Géfosse-Fontenay a shell riddled landing craft had been washed up. Aboard had been half a dozen dead American naval officers. One of them was a 'beachmaster'—an officer responsible for a particular sector of landing beach. His body had slumped across a case, and in that case had been papers, evidently secret documents. "Here they are, Herr Major," he said, tipping a mountain of documents, damp and in part sticking together, upon the major's desk. Even at his first glance Hayn saw entire pages covered with code words, figures, and a timetable. No doubt this was a major catch. Interpreters were mobilized at once. After less than half an hour Sonderführer Jobel burst into the office in great excitement: "Herr Major, we've got the whole plan of operations of the VII U.S. Corps!" The Intelligence officer could hardly believe his ears. Still sceptical, he ran his eyes over the first page. "My word, Jobel!" he breathed. It was as Jobel had said. A downright unbelievable piece of luck.

The Plan of Operations in a Washed-up Boat

The entire plan of operations, neatly set out for each separate phase from D-Day onwards, with day-by-day objectives on the Cotentin peninsula, was lying on the desk at 84th Corps. Revealed to the German Command were the intentions of the enemy—not only of VII Corps, but also of the neighbouring V American Corps and the XXX British Corps. Under this plan the Americans were first to link up their separate Utah and Omaha beach-heads at Carentan. Next they were to link up with the British at Bayeux and in this way establish a continuous bridgehead. Subsequently, VII Corps was to push through to the western coast of the Cotentin penninsula, towards Coutances, and, while setting up a provisional defensive line to the south, swing its main forces over to the north to capture Cherbourg.

General Marcks and his chief of staff studied the plan carefully. "Abstracts to be sent to all divisions at once," Marcks ordered. "Major Hasso Viebig, the chief of operations, will take the original to Rommel and then to Field-Marshal von Rundstedt at Saint-Germain."

That same afternoon Viebig, chased by fighter-bombers, made his dash to the Seine. He had been instructed to hand over the precious find, give a detailed account of the situation on the front, and urgently demand Luftwaffe support. As a special prize Hayn was also able to give him a slightly singed book in red-linen covers—*The German Forces,* the American handbook about "the enemy side." This was the first time that the American instruction booklet about the German forces in the field had fallen into German hands. It was found to give full credit to the Germans' military achievements, especially in Russia.

For once the god of battle seemed to smile upon the German Command. But what use were papers, what use was the knowledge of the enemy's plans if one was unable to foil them?

True, the enemy's timetable was upset more than once during the next few weeks. Objectives scheduled to be taken in a matter of days were taken only after many weeks. But it proved impossible to turn the discovered secret into a decisive victory. For that an entire arm was lacking—the air force. Nothing could offset its hopeless inferiority. Thus the lucky find of the Cossacks of 439th ''East Battalion'' and the historic moment in the Intelligence branch of 84th Corps proved of little avail. The battle took its course. Headquarters staffs had to watch the enemy's plan of operations unrolling step by step.

Half-way through the afternoon of June 8—at a time when General Marcks, Rommel, and Rundstedt knew from the American plan of operations that Carentan was an important enemy objective—von der Heydte's parachutists, who were still fighting for Sainte-Mère-Eglise, began to run short of ammunition. Facing them were the Americans, who were now attacking with strong armoured formations from Utah Beach, and behind them were the well-nigh impenetrable swamps. The regiment's supply depots, its field kitchens, its transport, and even its ammunition-dumps lay behind the flooded area.

Reluctantly the C.O. decided to abandon his heavy equipment and vehicles and withdraw all the mobile units of his regiment—wading and swimming across the swampy zone—to defensive positions on the eastern and northern edge of Carentan. There the parachutists established a barrier on *route nationale* 13 between the two American bridgeheads, and at the same time blocked the road to the British sector.

As a result, Carentan became one of the most hotly contested points on the invasion front. The survivors of the 502nd U.S. Parachute Regiment are not likely ever to forget the crossing of the causeway carrying the highroad from Saint-Côme-du-Mont through the low-lying swamps. Ceaselessly the Americans were putting pressure on the German positions. Shelling alternated with aerial bombing. The enemy attacked from Utah Beach in the north. Simultaneously he attacked from Omaha in the east. The German parachutists lay in shallow hollows of the ground. If they tried to dig in deeper their foxholes would immediately fill with water. Fighting for a farmstead south-west of the blown-up bridges, between the edge of the town and the swamps, was particularly fierce. The farm was situated in a large orchard and was surrounded by hedgerows. True, the terrain offered cover to the defenders, but on the other hand it made it easier for the Americans to work up to it. The regiment had its advanced battle headquarters in the farmhouse, and in the orchard outside there was much hand-to-hand fighting. Farther back, in an old cider store on the edge of the town, the regiment's medical officer, Dr. Ross, and the medical officers of 2nd and 3rd Battalions were operating, bandaging, giving injections, or bending over the dying. Two American doctors, taken prisoner by the regiment, were assisting. In a single day, in the course of twenty-four hours, more than 1000 wounded—Americans, Germans, Georgians, as well as a number of French civilians—were attended to at the regiment's forward dressing-station. The patients could be moved only at night. During the day the wounded men lay groaning in the basement of the dressing station.

Thus the men of 6th Parachute Regiment resisted the enemy's pressure towards the south.

In their push to the north, however, the Americans were still being held up on June 8 by the battery of Saint-Marcouf and the Azeville strongpoint. Although both positions were surrounded, Ohmsen's and Kattnig's gunners, supported by Geissler's infantrymen and Hansjörg Habel's assault battery, refused to give in. In point of fact Lieutenant Kattnig at Azeville had been authorized by Colonel Triepel to evacuate their wrecked battery position, but since an exchange of messages with Lieutenant-Colonel Keil, the sector commander, contained an assurance that infantry, anti-tank gunners, and engineers were on their way to reinforce him, he decided to continue holding his position against the 12th U.S. Regiment. When at last the reinforcements arrived they were no more than a few men: the rest had been wiped out en route. Nevertheless, Azeville and Saint-Marcouf held out throughout June 8.

The Americans were anxious at any price to crash through this annoying obstacle. At 1340 hours they attacked Saint-Marcouf. Step by step they advanced behind a creeping barrage of gunfire. In this way they eventually penetrated into the strongpoint. Their assault troops carried poles with demolition charges which they pushed into the fortifications and lit the fuses. But they used these infernal poles over-generously, and when they got to the main pill-boxes and operational bunkers they had used them all up. The bunker crews resisted furiously in close combat.

Once again Kattnig helped from Azeville. Again, upon Ohmsen's request, he directed the fire of his still-intact 100-millimetre gun at the American assault companies inside the battery area of Saint-Marcouf. Geissler led his infantrymen in a counter-attack on the left flank of the Americans. The G.I.'s were thrown off balance. They were pretty well spent. They were unable to stand up to the pressure. Once again the attacking battalion fell back as far as Dodainville.

The American reports about these operations are revealing. The assault battalion of the 4th U.S. Division lost over 50 per cent of its strength. The regimental commander was furious and suspected a German trap. He feared that this might be the beginning of a full-scale German counter-attack and was very pessimistic about the general future of his beach-head. The Americans had discovered that Saint-Marcouf had been reinforced by Geissler's infantry units, and this worried them. They saw in it a part of a big German plan, for they could not imagine that there were no German operational reserves of any importance behind it.

"It was lucky for us the Americans misjudged our situation," Ohmsen, to-day a lieutenant-commander in the Federal German Navy, recalls. "The Americans assumed the presence of well-equipped reserves, whereas in fact there were no units at all in the area. The shelling of their own lines had also shaken them considerably."

Not till June 9, an ill-fated Friday, did the Americans succeed in taking the Azeville battery by assault. After an artillery bombardment of 1500 shells they attacked with flame-throwers. The garrison had used up their ammunition. In vain did Sergeant Schauer get one of their flak-guns into working order again. It fired only one round—and then an enemy shell struck its emplacement. Resistance collapsed.

Ohmsen's Trek to the Gorse-grown Hill

The heavy losses sustained by the attacking units discouraged the American divisional commander from renewing his assault on Saint-Marcouf. Instead, the Americans tried to smash the battery by pounding it with naval and army guns. In the evening the American 22nd Infantry Regiment got ready to push past Saint-Marcouf in the direction of the German coastal strongpoint of Quineville. Saint-Marcouf was to be eliminated by special units composed of one infantry company, one company of engineers, and one anti-tank company each, as an independent commando operation.

But once more the timetable broke down. The commando units waited for air support, which failed to materialize. As a result, operations remained confined to light skirmishes. During the night the Americans directed a continuous stream of 20-millimetre tracer-shells at the battery so that any repairs to its defences were out of the question. After much laborious work the sergeant-armourer succeeded in getting one gun in working order from the wrecks of several others. It placed its shells among the American supply columns and thus caused renewed confusion.

Saint-Marcouf was a painful thorn in the flesh of the Americans. But the Germans had no way of strengthening that thorn. Ohmsen and his men were standing on a lost post: only they did not know it.

On June 11 the telephone rang in the command bunker. The weary men jerked up: it seemed incredible that the instrument should still be working after all those bombs and shells. But the telephone-lines in Saint-Marcouf functioned to the very last minute. All the battery's cable connexions survived the severest punishment.

Ohmsen is still proud of the way in which he had laid those cables when the battery was built—some thirty to thirty-five inches deep, in very narrow trenches which were not filled in. In this way the wires were exposed. Repairs were quite easy. But repairs, as it turned out, were not necessary very often because Ohmsen's experts had laid the cables quite loosely, with plenty of slack. In the event of a near-by bomb burst the wires were thus able to whip about without snapping. Communications to the Naval Commander in Cherbourg were along a deep underground cable by way of solid switching-gear. In spite of its twenty-five miles' length it remained intact, as indeed did many trunk-communication cables of the army which often continued to serve their purpose long after the Americans had occupied the territory.

As Lieutenant Ohmsen lifted the receiver all eyes in the bunker were on him. Ohmsen pressed the earpiece firmly against his ear. Admiral Hennecke in Cherbourg was on the line: "Tell me, Ohmsen, how many men have you left in the battery?"

"Seventy-eight, Herr Admiral, including such wounded as can be moved—although some of them would have to be carried. In addition I have some seriously wounded who cannot be moved."

"Ohmsen," Hennecke was speaking urgently, "Ohmsen, do you think you could break out?"

Before Ohmsen had a chance of replying Hennecke continued, "You must try it, Ohmsen. It's about six miles to our own lines. Try to get through this very night."

Ohmsen did not hesitate for a second. "Yes, Herr Admiral," he replied. Then he replaced the receiver.

There was not much to think over. Ohmsen ordered his battery, and Geissler his infantrymen, to fall in. Rifles and machine-pistols were handed out. Food rations were distributed. "Anybody who wants to do so can have his private belongings burnt together with the secret papers."

Then the handful of men of Saint-Marcouf set out on their trek through the night. They waded through watercourses. Their wounded they carried high over their heads on hurriedly constructed stretchers of poles, sheets, and blankets.

"Careful there, don't jolt them," Lance-Corporal Johannes Brockmann of the medical corps kept reminding them. Even so it was a bad journey for the wounded. The men wheeled northward. Their objective was Quineville, the gorse-grown hill near La Pernelle. That was where Lieutenant-Colonel Keil's 919th Grenadier Regiment had its headquarters. There also was Colonel Triepel, of 1261st Army Coastal Artillery Regiment, under whom Saint-Marcouf came for artillery purposes.

It was a long night. But it passed, as also did fear. At first light they were in front of their own lines.

MP-40

On the following morning, on June 12, 1944, the American commander decided to send in a newly landed regiment of 9th Division against those stubborn coast defence strongpoints.

Major-General J. L. Collins wanted to overrun the German defensive position outside Montebourg, capture the important road junction of Montebourg, and thus gain control of the road to Cherbourg. The big Atlantic port was the great objective of the VII U.S. Corps.

At corps headquarters the officers were bending over their maps. They were listening to their commander. From the very first day, he explained, those batteries had greatly interfered with the unloading of men and equipment. The entire timetable had been delayed by several days. Besides, it was not a pleasant feeling to have German pockets of resistance in the rear of the attacking troops.

The officers nodded. They understood the situation. They were prepared for anything. Two hours later, however, a reconnaissance unit of the 9th U.S. Division reported: "Saint-Marcouf battery evacuated."

All they found was twenty-one seriously wounded German soldiers—well looked after by the battery's medical N.C.O., who had volunteered to stay behind. The Americans were not displeased with their easy victory—nor, for that matter, were the German wounded. The American Army communiqué reported the capture of Saint-Marcouf. It did not report that it came six days later than was scheduled.

"Parachutists only need knives"

Carentan fell too. At almost the exact time when the men of Saint-Marcouf abandoned their fiercely contested strongpoint to make their way towards the north, Lieutenant-Colonel von der Heydte found himself compelled to withdraw his badly mauled parachute battalions from Carentan. The news of the withdrawal evoked horrified dismay at 84th Corps and Seventh Army headquarters.

The vital barrier on *route nationale* 13 between the American and British bridgeheads had fallen.

How was it possible? How could it have happened? How could the parachutists have given up such an important position?

To this day the question is discussed in all reviews of the war. And yet the answer is perfectly simple. It can be put in von der Heydte's own words, uttered on one occasion in the O.K.W. when his demand for better equipment was turned down with the observation: "Parachutists only need knives." Von der Heydte had then retorted, "Parachutists are only human." And that, in fact, was the answer. The parachutists were only human. They were brave, death-defying, and even reckless—but they were only human.

During the night of June 9–10 the remnants of the 1st Battalion, a mere twenty-five men—twenty-five out of 700—had found their way back to regimental headquarters and reported the annihilation of their battalion. It had been surrounded in Sainte-Marie-du-Mont, attacked by enemy forces, split up into separate groups, and literally wiped out. One-third of its men had been killed or had drowned in the swamps. The rest, nearly all of them wounded, had been taken prisoners.

On June 10, at noon, an American officer with a flag of truce appeared in front of the positions of the 2nd Battalion north of Carentan and, on behalf of General Maxwell Taylor, the commander of the 101st U.S. Airborne Division, demanded their surrender. The letter had been written in German. Von der Heydte sent his reply in English: "What would you do in my place?"

The regiment had only itself to depend on. It had to operate without artillery, tank, or air support. Ammunition was running short, especially for mortars and machine-pistols. There was plenty of artillery ammunition, but no guns to fire it. The guns had been smashed by the fighter-bombers and the naval bombardment.

In response to an SOS to 84th Corps a supply column got through with French mortar-shells. But the calibre was wrong. The inventive parachutists nevertheless managed to use them by wrapping each mortar-shell in a blanket. Luckily there was a blanket store in Carentan, so at least there was no shortage of blankets.

During the night of June 10–11 the parachutists thought they were witnessing a miracle. A delighted shout went up throughout their positions: "German aircraft!" They were the first German aircraft they had seen since the invasion—Ju-52 transports made available by 84th Corps. They dropped containers with ammunition for mortars and machine-pistols.

On the morning of June 11 the Americans succeeded in making deep penetrations on the right, on the left, and at the centre of the regiment. Von der Heydte had to withdraw some of his men from the front to use them for flank cover. As a result, the regiment's resistance was weakened. By noon the enemy had reached the outskirts of Carentan and gained a foothold in ruined buildings, gardens, and hedgerows. As a precautionary measure the regimental commander ordered the hills immediately to the south-west of the town to be reconnoitred for suitable alternative positions and for lines of retreat. The remnants of the 795th Georgian Battalion, which had placed itself under von der Heydte's command, were detailed to get those positions ready. In any case the Georgians were no longer up to the severe defensive fighting in the front line.

At noon the regimental commander made a personal reconnaissance of his alternative positions. On the road he met a staff car which signalled him to stop. It was the commander of the 17th S.S. Panzer Grenadier Division "Götz von Berlichingen," Brigadeführer[1] Ostendorff, and his chief of operations, Obersturmbannführer[2] Konrad. Von der Heydte made his report. He was informed that his regiment had been placed under Ostendorff's division, which was scheduled to make an attack on the American bridgehead on June 12. Ostendorff was in excellent spirits. "We'll get that little job cleaned up all right," he said optimistically. Von der Heydte, just to be on the safe side, requested that part of the division be sent into action at once to reinforce his parachutists outside Carentan. But Ostendorff refused. Naturally enough, he wanted to hold his division together for the full-scale attack which he felt confident would split up the bridgeheads. In vain did von der Heydte warn against an over-optimistic assessment of the situation. Ostendorff referred to his Russian experiences: "And surely those Yanks can't be tougher than the Russians."

"Not tougher," von der Heydte replied, "but considerably better equipped, with a veritable steamroller of tanks and guns."

The divisional commander cut short the argument with the words: "Herr Oberstleutnant, no doubt your parachutists will manage till to-morrow." They did not manage.

On returning to his battle headquarters von der Heydte learned that the fiercely contested farmhouse which had served as advanced headquarters during the past few days had fallen to the Americans. Immediate action had thus become imperative unless the entire regiment was to suffer the same fate as the 1st Battalion—encirclement and utter annihilation. Towards 1700

---

[1] Rank in S.S. troops equivalent to major-general.
[2] Rank in S.S. troops equivalent to lieutenant-colonel.

hours on June 11 the regimental commander therefore gave orders for the town to be evacuated and the troops to fall back to the reconnoitred and prepared positions south-west of Carentan. As dusk fell von der Heydte's parachutists disengaged themselves from the ruins of the violently contested town astride *route nationale* 13.

The battle for Carentan was over.

In vain did the 17th S.S. Panzer Grenadier Division try to recapture the town on the following day. The 2nd Parachute Battalion, with the regimental commander, was the only unit in the division to succeed once more in advancing to the outskirts of the town and digging in by the railway-station. For a while they held their position, but they were forced to abandon it again when the rest of Ostendorff's division remained pinned down by enemy fire. The road between Utah and Omaha was open.

"Bayeux must be retaken!"

What was the state of things in the British bridgehead near Caen, where we left the 25th Panzer Grenadier Regiment of the S.S. Panzer Division "Hitlerjugend" engaged in heavy fighting in the evening of June 7?

On June 8 the grenadiers and tank crews were still locked in fierce battle with the Canadians, who were vigorously pressing forward. A combat group with a company of *Panther* tanks of 12th S.S. Panzer Regiment and the reconnaissance company of 25th S.S. Panzer Grenadier Regiment captured Bretteville, overran the headquarters of the Regina Rifles, and held the village throughout the night. At dawn, however, Meyer was compelled to withdraw his combat group. Without infantry support the advanced position was no longer tenable. The enemy had grown too strong.

In the afternoon General von Geyr, the commander of Armoured Group West, turned up at Meyer's headquarters. Together, the general and the Standartenführer[1] climbed to the observation-post in the corner tower of the Ardenne abbey. Meyer reported on the situation. Geyr listened to him pessimistically, but finally announced that he would launch a full-scale attack with 21st Panzer Division on the right wing. 12th S.S. Panzer

---

[1] Rank in S.S. troops equivalent to lieutenant-colonel.

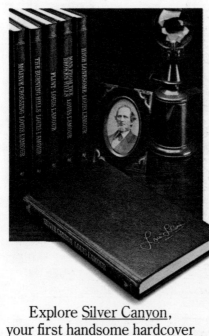

Enjoy the best of Louis L'Amour in special volumes made to last as long as your pleasure

As a reader of Louis L'Amour's tough and gritty tales of the Old West, you'll be delighted by The Louis L'Amour Collection— a series of hardcover editions of Louis L'Amour's exciting Western adventures.

The feel of rich leathers. Like a good saddle, these volumes are made to last—to be read, re-read and passed along to family and friends for years to come. Bound in rugged sierra-brown simulated leather with gold lettering, The Louis L'Amour Collection will be a handsome addition to your home library.

Silver Canyon opens the series. It's the memorable tale of Matt Brennan, gunfighter, and his lone battle against duelling ranchers in one of the bloodiest range wars the West had ever seen. After *Silver Canyon* you'll set out on a new adventure every month, as succeeding volumes in the Collection are conveniently mailed to your home.

Receive the full-color Louis L'Amour Western Calendar FREE —just for looking at *Silver Canyon* . Like every volume in The Louis L'Amour Collection, *Silver Canyon* is yours to examine without risk or obligation. If you're not satisfied, return it within 10 days and owe nothing. The calendar is yours to keep.

Send no money now . Simply complete the coupon opposite to enter your subscription to The Louis L'Amour Collection and receive your free calendar.

The newest volume....

The newest volume I placed on the shelf of my 8000-volume home research library was very special to me—the first copy of _Silver Canyon_ in the hardcover Collector's Edition put together by the folks at Bantam Books.

I'm very proud of this new collection of my books. They're handsome, permanent and what I like best of all, affordable.

I hope you'll take this opportunity to examine the books in the Collection and see their fine quality for yourself. I think you'll be as pleased as I am!

Louis L'Amour

Send no money now–but mail today!

☐ **YES!** Please send me _Silver Canyon_ for a 10-day free examination, along with my free Louis L'Amour Calendar, and enter my subscription to <u>The Louis L'Amour Collection</u>. If I decide to keep _Silver Canyon_, I will pay $7.95 plus shipping and handling and receive one additional volume per month on a fully returnable, 10-day free-examination basis. There is no minimum number of books to buy, and I may cancel my subscription at any time. The Calendar is mine whether or not I keep _Silver Canyon_.   85019

☐ I prefer the deluxe edition, bound in genuine leather, at only $24.95 each plus shipping and handling.   87015

Name _____ _(please print)_

Address _____

City _____ State _____ Zip _____

In Canada, mail to:
Bantam Books Canada, Inc.
60 St. Clair Avenue East, Suite 601
Toronto, Ontario M4T 1N5

Division in the centre, and Bayerlein's Panzer Lehr Division on the left wing. The objective would be a break-through to the coast along a broad front.

Break-through to the coast! "At long last," Meyer thought to himself.

On the left wing of the hastily established German line outside Caen units of Bayerlein's Panzer Lehr Division were already moving into their assembly areas. The general himself described these fateful days of June 8–11 as follows:

At first light on June 8 Colonel Scholze had reached the assembly area of Norrey with units of 901st Panzer Grenadier Regiment. Colonel Gutmann's combat group with units of the 902nd had to fight their way into the Brouay area since Canadian tanks had already occupied the village. Furious night fighting, with nobody able to tell friend or foe, resulted in heavy casualties. The artillery had still not taken up their positions. The regimental commander, Colonel Luxenburger, a dashing officer who had lost an arm in the First World War, and Lieutenant-Colonel Zeissler, the battalion commander, had driven ahead to reconnoitre with their headquarters personnel. Towards noon the two combat groups had taken up position. They were ready to join action. But the order for action did not come. They waited till the evening. Field-Marshal Rommel arrived at the battle headquarters in Le Mesnil-Patry. And presently it became clear that once again all plans were to be scrapped. Rommel angrily informed Bayerlein that the 50th British Division had taken Bayeux: "The 50th British Division, Bayerlein! Our very special friends from Africa!"

The field-marshal explained to the general that his division would have to redeploy both its combat groups from the Norrey–Brouay area into the area of Tilly during the night of June 8–9. Objective: "Attack on Bayeux in the morning of June 9. The town will be taken."

The town will be taken! The customary clear and optimistic order. Somehow it did not seem to match Rommel's general pessimism. "We shall suffer the same fate as in Africa, Bayerlein," he said irritably. "Instead of the Mediterranean we shall have the Rhine—and we shan't get anything across!"

All units to be redeployed once more! Bayerlein shook his head. Anyone would think they were on manoeuvres.

The movements began at nightfall. Undiscovered by the Canadians, but discovered, unfortunately, by the German Luftwaffe. And the Luftwaffe dropped its bombs on the German columns on

the move. Fortunately, not much damage was done. In the
morning of June 9 the redeployment was completed. The attack
on Bayeux could start. But British reconnaissance units and
armoured groups were already moving south on the Tilly-Bayeux
road. To avoid wasting strength in preliminary skirmishes the
German attack would have to take place to the west of the road.

The 2nd Battalion of the Panzer Lehr Regiment under Major
Prince Schönburg-Waldenburg participated in the attack with 1st
Company. Of the 1st Battalion, which Bayerlein had ordered
back from transfer to the Eastern front, there was still no sign.
The attack made good progress. Towards noon Ellon, in the Aure
Valley, was reached. Armoured scouting detachments on recon-
naissance had advanced as far as Arganchy, three miles south of
Bayeux.

Three miles from Bayeux! Bayerlein felt the excitement of
the hunt. He would teach the 50th British Division a lesson, just
as in the old days at Got El Ualeb, in Africa!

"Get a move on, chaps," he urged his staff officers.
Captain Hartdegen grinned. "It's going all right, Herr General.
It's going all right. It looks as if we might run straight into the
gap between the British and American sectors. With a little luck
we'll push through to the coast, neatly between Yanks and
Tommies, and stop them from linking up."

But—just as if there was a jinx on all German operations—a
moment later came the order: "Break off attack. Division to be
withdrawn to Tilly." Never before had there been so much
cursing among officers and other ranks of the Panzer Lehr
Division as at that moment.

What had happened?

A lightning thrust by powerful Canadian armoured forces
had created a critical situation at the joint between 12th S.S.
Panzer Division and Panzer Lehr Regiment, in the Tilly–Audrieu
–Cristot area. The 2nd Battalion, Panzer Lehr Regiment had to
counter-attack at once.

Again we notice this shortage of operational reserves. Again
a promising operation had to be broken off in order to stop a gap.
Once again operational planning had to be scrapped in favour of
improvisation.

The 8th Company, Panzer Lehr Regiment had spent the
night of June 8–9 in an orchard, well camouflaged. The harassing
fire directed at their area by long-range artillery had been
ineffectual. But with increasing light the Americans aimed their
fire more accurately. Captain Reche was sitting in the wireless-

operator's seat of his tank, his face ashen grey. He had been sick for several days. His crew were crouching by the side of the tank, trying to cook a hot meal with a blowlamp. Every time a shell came over everybody took cover—automatically, almost with an air of boredom. In spite of these interruptions they managed to get the potatoes cooked. They were dished out, together with hard-boiled eggs. As he gingerly peeled the hot jacket potatoes with his fingers Corporal Westphal softly muttered to himself, "For all we know this may be our last meal."

The 8th Company, Panzer Lehr Regiment were an experienced lot. Fine, battle-hardened men, every one of them. Many an evening as they sat about drinking Calvados, after they had downed their tenth tot, Westphal would suddenly call out, "Lance-Corporal Hämmerle, stoppage in forward m.g."

And pat, without a second's hesitation, would come the answer: "Turret to twelve o'clock."

Swivelling the turret to twelve o'clock was the way to get some daylight through the hatch for clearing any stoppages in the forward machine-gun.

Or the skipper would shout, "Release safety-catch!" And instantly everybody's left arm would reach out over their heads, for it was with the left hand that the safety-catch of the gun had

Mk. IV Tank

to be operated unless one wanted one's shoulder smashed by the gun's recoil. All this a good gun crew had to be able to do in their sleep. And so they practised in their sleep, or rather after their tenth Calvados. They were regular tank crews.

Towards 1400 Captain Reche arrived with orders from the battalion commander, Prince Schönburg-Waldenburg, for assembly in the Fontenay area. "Battalion will prepare to attack. Objective: to dislodge advanced enemy forces and push through to the coast. 8th Company on the left wing. Its task is flank protection." Once more an attack was to be launched to "push through to the coast."

Rumbling and clanking, the Mark IVs moved into position, the 8th Company without its commander. The M.O. had sent him to hospital. His place was taken by Lieutenant Walter, a schoolmaster from Pirmasens.

The assembly area was a favourable stretch of undulating ground. There was a good view of the area of attack: the village of Audrieu on the right, Chouain on the left. A mile ahead the undulating open ground was barred by two patches of dense wood. Between them was a narrow gap, no more than 200 to 300 yards wide. That was where the battalion had to get through.

"Tanks advance!"

Tank No. 801 was on the left wing. Its turret was in the ten-o'clock position. The skipper, Westphal, was staring hard at the gap between the two patches of wood. "We'll have to keep our fingers crossed hard."

Without stopping, the armoured detachment moved smoothly ahead in open formation over the waste heathland. For once there were no hedgerows and no fences. "Increase speed by one ratchet!"

They rumbled past freshly built, well-camouflaged British positions. The Tommies had hurriedly abandoned them at the sight of the advancing armoured armada. The leading troops were entering the neck between the woods. The ones behind them were closing up and slowing down.

Now they would know.

And there it was: concentrated artillery fire.

The very first salvoes were right on top of the formation. The tanks farther behind having closed up on the leaders, those in front were unable to move back. The tanks had got themselves jammed in the neck between the woods. The battalion commander had just reached a slight mound, Hill 103. Right in front of him an anti-tank gun barked. The shell pierced the turret. Prince

Schönburg-Waldenburg slumped over sideways, dead. All his crew were seriously injured. They tried to scramble out.

Captain Ritgen assumed command of the battalion. He remained in command until the end of the war and is now C.O. of the new Panzer Lehr Regiment of the Federal German Army in Munsterlager, with the rank of lieutenant-colonel.

The gap between the woods was closed by a tremendous curtain of gunfire. Anyone venturing in was done for.

In tank No. 801, which normally carried Captain Reche, the gun-layer was in charge. From the turret, through the scissor telescope, he spotted some enemy tanks outside the village of Chouain.

"Turret eleven o'clock."

"1200 metres."

"Armour-piercing!"

"Fire!"

"Fire!"

A hit.

But already the shells of a 20-millimetre gun were raining upon tank No. 801 from very close range. Damn! The fire was coming from the undulating ground. There—muzzle flashes. Luckily the shells had pierced only the outer plates.

"Turret nine o'clock!"

"Anti-personnel!"

"Fire!"

The turret machine-gun was likewise hammering away. Not another shot came from the British position.

Meanwhile the acting battalion commander had ordered the tanks back. No. 801 remained to give covering fire to the damaged tanks whose crews, many of them under fire, were carrying out repairs. As darkness settled over wood and heath, tank No. 801 also withdrew from the battlefield. Back to the orchard. Into hiding. Out in front the last burning tank was signalling yet another unsuccessful attack. Once more the push to the coast had been a flop.

"Hasn't it yet dawned on those chairborne gentlemen way back that we are facing a powerful enemy here who can't simply be thrown back into the sea just like that?" the skipper of one of the tanks asked.

It was a question asked by many.

In the evening of June 9, when it was obvious that a "thrust to the coast" was now out of the question with the forces available to individual divisions, Obergruppenführer Sepp Dietrich, the general commanding the 1st S.S. Armoured Corps, under whose command the Panzer Lehr had been placed as the only Army division, ordered Bayerlein at Lingèvres to prepare to defend the Tilly area. The line Cristot–Tilly–Verrières–La-Belle-Epine was to be held as the main front line at all costs.

There was no more talk about counter-attacking to the coast. It was a turning-point.

Dietrich's order was undoubtedly correct. It became obvious that the main weight of the British offensive was being switched to the Tilly area, since Montgomery had been unable, in spite of exceedingly heavy casualties, to capture by direct attack the important road centre of Caen.

Montgomery drew the inevitable conclusion. If he could not achieve his objective by frontal attack he must try to attack from the flank. This meant advancing from the Bayeux area to Tilly, gaining the high ground of Villers-Bocage, and thence wheeling towards Caen. A new chapter was opening in the battle of the invasion. Its name was Tilly.

4

THE BATTLE FOR TILLY

Forward Screen Duty

On June 9, when the Panzer Lehr Division was thrown into the defensive battle for Tilly, this modern fighting unit, wholly designed for mobile armoured warfare, was faced with unexpected tasks. Its zone of operation was the *bocage*—undulating ground criss-crossed by hedges, dotted with clumps of bushes, and interspersed with large apple orchards and pastures. It was not unfavourable terrain for defence. The high banks with their bushes or lines of trees parcelled up the landscape into hundreds of small rectangles, offering hiding-places and cover. But they also made observation difficult. Infantry units were able to establish themselves in the many sunken lanes. In this way the various defensive sectors could be set up in echelon. On the other hand, they had no contact with one another. The answer to these problems was the tank. The tank became the hub of defence. A weapon designed entirely for attack, assault, and rapid advance became a means of defence, an armoured anti-tank gun, or an armoured machine-gun. This new use gave rise presently to an entirely new fighting technique and also to a new type of fighter. The invasion battle was moulding tactics and fighting men no less than the battles of encirclement in the East, or the improvisations outside Moscow, on the Don, and on the Volga.

In Normandy the individual tank became the nucleus of infantry units. The infantry platoon, the company, the combat team—they were all based on the tank. Without tanks no position was taken. And without tanks no position could be held. Local counter-attacks against enemy penetrations or for the recapture of tactically important ground were almost invariably led by individual tanks.

The Panzer Lehr, to whom Guderian had once overconfidently assigned the proud task of throwing the Anglo-Americans back into the sea singlehanded, found itself forced into an entirely new mode of fighting. The division had been created as an élite unit for offence: now it was being expended as a defensive unit. Its splendid fleet of 750 armoured and superbly armed infantry carriers had to be put in store. They were being kept at a depot sixty miles behind the fighting front—750 armoured vehicles! Armoured divisions engaged in static defence—it was an exciting but also a depressing chapter in the history of the war. The episode that follows is typical of many.

"Outpost duty!"

Four Mark IVs moved off noisily. Their skippers had only pencilled sketch-maps to go by. And the order: "Position to be taken up along this road. Tanks to be well camouflaged. A good field of fire to be ensured. Sector must be held."

"Make sure you get into position before you're spotted by fighter-bombers!"

And then they were off. Five men were inside the tank. Outside, the infantrymen were clinging to the turret like a cluster of grapes. Tanks advance!

"Hard to the right—use that bank for cover." Nobody suspected that their little outing would last a fortnight. Fourteen days and nights on outpost duty. In the La-Belle-Epine area.

It was like a game of Red Indians—only deadly serious— this business of hide-and-seek to evade the sharp eyes of the fighter-bombers. Once a tank was spotted it was done for. Mercilessly it would be dive-bombed and attacked until a bomb or a volley of cannon-fire had finished it off. The enemy's superiority could be met only by cunning.

Corporal Westphal, the skipper of the tank, got out to reconnoitre along a sunken lane. He crawled through the hedges. He inspected every inch of ground. He had moved up and down the lane about a dozen times. "You'd think he was choosing a building plot," Lance-Corporal Hoffmann, the wireless-operator, said with a grin.

"Well, that's what it comes to," said Hämmerle, the loading number.

"Better a building plot than a tomb," Brettschneider, the gun-layer, agreed.

At last Westphal had found a spot to his liking. "Reece to

right and left!'' Two men moved off in opposite directions. They found their two neighbour tanks in well-camouflaged positions. To the left that of Corporal Schulz, to the right that of Corporal Pausch. Last in the line, with the fourth tank, was Captain Felmer. They were concealed in sunken lanes, in orchards, and in hayricks. The infantrymen around them were camouflaged by bushes, sheaves of oats, and broken-off branches and twigs.

The gaps between the tanks were rather wide. Even so, they had to try, in the event of an attack, to halt the enemy's armoured spearheads from their concealed positions. A mile behind them was the armoured reserve. If the outpost line was pierced, that reserve had to counter-attack.

The first few hours were spent in camouflage. Branches and twigs were carefully cut out of a hedge, and the tanks decorated with them until they seemed to have been spirited away. Time and time again a man would go off to see whether the camouflage looked genuine. Then he would say, ''A bit of the turret's still showing.'' Or ''A caterpillar link's still glittering in the sun.'' And so on, until at last he was satisfied. ''All right now.''

Next, the tank-tracks in the field of oats had to be obliterated—or they would be a clear signpost for any fighter-bomber. Laboriously each blade was bent back again and made to stand upright.

The first two days were tolerable. Water for washing and hot food were not yet missed. The men in the tank were not yet getting on each other's nerves. They still slipped cheerfully through the floor hatch and crawled out underneath the tank to replace the withered camouflage branches or get a breath of fresh air at night. Inside the tank two men stood or sat by the glass all the time, ceaselessly scanning the ground in front. ''What's the distance to that bushy-topped tree?'' There was some dispute and argument, then they agreed. ''And to that big bush in the hedgerow? To the far corner of the oat-field?'' Mentally they surveyed their whole field of fire. They became familiar with the distances. In an emergency they would not have to spend long calculating.

The time was 1400 hours on their third day.

''Alarm! Tommies!'' The men were galvanized into action. Lance-Corporal Ross, the driver, had his eyes glued to the glass. ''Ten Tommies with a man-handled anti-tank gun. They're crossing the field now. They're taking up position.''

''Two men coming up with ammunition-boxes.''

''Shrapnel,'' the skipper ordered calmly.

"400 metres."

"Fire!"

The 75-millimetre shell burst right in front of the anti-tank gun. Three British soldiers were still alive and were now racing towards an apple-tree with low, spreading branches.

"Turret eleven o'clock."

"Shrapnel."

"420 metres."

"Fire!"

The top of the tree was torn to pieces.

"Fire!" The tree-trunk was shattered.

"Fire!" There was nothing left but a tangle of smashed branches.

"Cease fire!"

They slid out through the floor hatch. They rearranged their camouflage. They were looking serious. They knew that things would soon be getting very hot for them.

An hour later the British artillery spotting-plane was above them. Circling round. Searching.

And then it came.

At first only a few roving guns did the ranging. But presently they were under concentrated fire. Hell was let loose. But it is not easy to hit a small tank in a big landscape. True, the field of oats was ploughed over. The hedge was torn to shreds. There was a continuous thumping against the sides of the tank. Death knocking at the door.

Shortly before sunrise the shelling increased in pitch until it was a veritable hurricane. The outer plates and the additional armour along the sides were riddled like sieves. The blankets draped around the turret with their twigs and greenery had been swept off.

"Smoke-shells!" Hämmerle called out.

The smoke-screen outside was thickening. Visibility was less than ten yards.

Any moment now they would come.

They could not see them, but they knew. "Fire!"

The four steel fortresses on which depended a stretch of the main front line outside Tilly were no longer concerned with camouflage. Now it was a time for fighting. The turrets swivelled. The guns belched forth their shells. Machine-guns ticked. Infantrymen fired from their foxholes, underneath the branches, and from behind trees. Fire and steel were hurled into the smoke-screen.

Open hatch. A quick look through the binoculars. "The barrage is creeping forward," said Westphal.

Now the infantry would come. They were not to be endangered by their own gunfire.

"Fire!"

The ground shook. The branches along the bank waved as in a hurricane from the blast of the gunfire. The summer sun of Normandy had vanished among clouds of dust and smoke. Gradually the smoke-screen dispersed. Where was the enemy? He did not come.

Four tank crews and a few dozen infantrymen heaved a sigh of relief. At once they set about replacing their camouflage.

It was their eighth night. The skipper had just changed places with the gun-layer to snatch a quick nap. His head resting against the eyepiece, Westphal dropped off immediately.

"Pass the shell-case over," the gun-layer said to Ross. None of them laughed any longer when they heard the intimate noise. Then the floor hatch was opened and their martial chamber-pot emptied. At the same moment there was a thud outside. *Crash!*

They jerked up. And again. *Crash!*

That was not artillery fire. Those were the shells of tank guns. One of them burst quite close. Start engine. Engage reverse. Full speed astern. Faster!

The skipper tried to get back into his seat but it was impossible. "Are we still following the hedge?"

Open hatch. "Yes."

Stop. They came to a halt beneath a massive, spreading oak. Shells were bursting in its boughs. Branches came clattering down. The next tank in the line was firing. Once. Twice. Three times. Then silence. Had they finished off the Tommy? Or had the Tommy merely made off? They could not ask because of the radio silence.

The thirteenth day dawned over the bank and the hedge. The men felt as if they had been put through the mill. They could no longer bear to see one another or to smell one another. Thirteen days of hardly being able to stretch. Thirteen days without a drop of water to wash in. Thirteen days crowded together in a steel coffin. Only their watchfulness remained.

Every day the skipper scanned the hedge through his binoculars. Foot by foot. Now he was looking at a small bulge. Surely that bulge had not been there yesterday? And one twig there seemed a lighter green. He focused his glasses carefully.

"So that's it—a Tommy." For an instant he could make out the flat steel helmet under the camouflage twigs. "Where there's one there are bound to be more."

The gun-layer ranged his gun. "On target?"

Karl Brettschneider nodded.

Load shrapnel. "Fire!"

"Forty metres less."

But now the barrel of an anti-tank gun emerged from the hedge. So that was it. They had better shoot accurately now.

The tank rang with the noise of the last shot. "Ten metres farther to the right. Can't you see the barrel?"

Now the British gun began to bark. It had aimed at the tank's muzzle-flash. The shell swished close past the turret. Which of them would be faster? For once Westphal's tank was lucky.

On the following morning, in the grey light of dawn, they were relieved.

Unless a man has spent fourteen days and fourteen nights in an evil-smelling tank on outpost duty he cannot know the simple bliss of returning to base, digging himself a comfortable hole in the ground, chucking in some blankets, and then rolling up in them and going to sleep. From afar came the sound of gunfire. The bark and swish of the fighter-bombers' rocket-shells. They did not care. They did not care the least bit, so long as they were not ordered: "Mount tanks. Immediate counterattack."

Tank Skirmishes

During the night of June 9–10 defence of the Tilly area was taken over by the units of the Panzer Lehr Division, all of which had at last arrived. The outpost line was at the same time the "main front line." It ran from Cristot (near the Caen-Bayeux highway) via Tilly-North and the châteaux of Verrières and Bernières, through La-Belle-Epine and Torteval, to Saint-Germain-d'Ectot and Anctoville. Thus a line of no less than ten miles had to be covered and held by a single division.

Divisional headquarters were in a farmhouse at Sermentot. Because of the danger from fighter-bombers elaborate precautions were necessary. The radio-transmitters had been set up a few miles away. This made it impossible for the enemy to pinpoint the headquarters by direction-finding. During the day no motor vehicle was allowed within a radius of 500 yards. All tracks and tyre marks had to be carefully obliterated. Only thus could a headquarters escape the attention of fighter-bombers and of artillery directed by spotter aircraft.

Only a few days previously the higher commands had been taught a terrible lesson. On June 8 Rommel, anxious to clarify the chain of command, had had General von Geyr appointed commander of the entire sector east of the Dives as far as Tilly. With the three armoured divisions now available to him—the 21st, the 12th S.S., and the Panzer Lehr—he was at long last to mount the counter-attack to the coast. "At last," the commanders in the field breathed. In the afternoon of June 9, however, the general's headquarters in the château of La Caine, four miles north-east of Thury-Harcourt, was attacked by fighter-bombers and wiped out by carpet bombing. The enemy had pinpointed the headquarters by direction-finding of its radio traffic. The chief of staff, General von Dawans, and twelve staff officers were killed. General von Geyr and Major-General Pemsel, the Seventh Army chief of staff (now in command of a corps of the Federal German Army) escaped by a piece of good fortune. But the planned attack could not now be launched. It was the end of June before a new headquarters staff was set up and the officers were ready to take over their duties.

The land around Tilly did not favour defence by infantry. The grenadiers of the 1st and 3rd Companies of the 1st Battalion, 902nd Regiment, for instance, had taken up positions on slightly rising ground. Shortly before dawn Second Lieutenant Bohmbach had inspected the positions together with the battalion commander. He was not encouraged by what he saw. Because of the stony soil the grenadiers were not able to dig in adequately, and were lying instead in quite shallow troughs, laboriously scratched out of the hard earth, with only a few stones to protect their heads.

Things got going towards 0500 hours: sudden concentrated artillery bombardment. The hurricane of fire lasted forty-five minutes. Unprotected, the infantrymen were lying among the hail of shells. It broke their nerve. A few men leapt to their feet and ran back. Others followed. The position was in danger of crumbling. Lieutenant Ritter stood up to check the panic. He rallied the men and led them forward again. Fortunately the bombardment was not followed up by a charge.

Just before noon five tanks rumbled past the farmhouse where battalion headquarters were established. They looked like German *Panthers*. Then one of them halted. The turret was opened. The skipper looked at the conventional tactical sign marking the farmhouse as a battalion headquarters. The tank's barrel swung across. *Crash!*

Clearly these were not German *Panthers*. Now they were really in for it unless there was last-minute help. There was.

Second Lieutenant Werner with his company of Panzerjägers was in position near the farmhouse. A few days previously some new self-propelled guns had been delivered to him. Here was his chance to test them. Within fifteen minutes he had shot up three of the five British tanks from his hidden position. The others got stuck. Their crews bailed out. In vain they tried to fight their way back, past battalion headquarters, with pistols and sub-machine-guns.

After some of them had been killed, however, the remainder put up their hands. A second lieutenant with a face wound turned to Bohmbach, saluted, and in precise, school German declared: "I surrender."

About this time, as Second Lieutenant Werner was cracking the tanks of a Scottish regiment west of Tilly, General Bayerlein, driving round the open plain north of Tilly, spotted a strong force of British tanks bivouacking in the most peaceful manner.

"Hartdegen, go and get anything you can find." The

Panzerjäger

orderly officer dashed off. He mobilized four *Panthers* and two 88-millimetre guns, that old wonder-weapon which had ensured so many successes in Africa. Bayerlein was in his element. He positioned his force at a favourable range, well camouflaged. Then he commanded: "Fire!"

The British combat force was like a stirred-up antheap. The vehicles careered about in wild confusion, and into the mêlée smashed the shells from the *Panthers'* rapid-fire guns and from the 88s.

But the battle did not remain one-sided for long. The British blanketed Bayerlein's force with one of their characteristic artillery bombardments. Heaviest calibres, including naval guns. After all, they could afford it.

The *Panthers* and the 88-millimetre guns had to disappear in a hurry.

It was always the same. Cunning, gallantry, and even self-sacrifice invariably had to yield to superior power.

In the evening Lieutenant-Colonel Zeissler, the missing battalion commander in the Panzer Artillery Regiment, returned to Bayerlein's headquarters. Together with Colonel Luxenburger and the N.C.O.'s and men of a patrol, he had been surprised by a Candian tank detachment and taken prisoner.

For no obvious reason this Canadian detachment had behaved in the most brutal fashion. The violence and fanatical ferocity of the invasion battle, which led to excesses on both sides had culminated here in a particularly ugly incident. During the general beating-up of the German prisoners Zeissler had slipped away into the undergrowth and had later made his way back to the German lines. His account was borne out in a horrible and deplorable fashion on the following day.

The one-armed Colonel Luxenburger was found severely injured on top of a Canadian tank which had been knocked out by a German anti-tank gun. He had been tied to the turret. Three days later he died in a German field hospital.

Cherry to Lemon: "Come at once!"

The expected British full-scale offensive came on June 11. It began with a powerful tank attack on Tilly. Captain Philipps, now a parson in Gladbeck, repulsed the British with units of 901st Panzer Grenadier Regiment. A second thrust was aimed at Verrières-Lingèvres. Verrières was lost. British scouting-cars

were already emerging from the large patch of woodland north of
the town, advancing towards the road, and sneaking up through
pastures, fields, and orchards.

The armoured reserve of the Panzer Lehr Regiment now
mounted its counter-attack. The steel colossi of *Panthers* and
Tigers rattled through the narrow streets of Lingèvres. Screeching,
they swung on to the secondary road outside the shell-wrecked
church. They turned into a farm track and rumbled on towards a
patch of wood about 300 yards away.

"Action stations!"

"Close hatches!"

All they could see of the hedgerows and ditches, of the
fields and the edge of the forest, was a narrow strip through the
bullet-proof Kinon glass which covered the vision slits.

"Both guns loaded. Safety-catches on," the gun-layer reported
over the intercom. The machine-gun and the long 75-millimetre
flat-trajectory gun were ready for action.

Second Lieutenant Theo was a troop commander in the 6th
Company and the skipper of the third tank which bore the code
name Lemon. Attentively he watched his front. Ahead of him,
advancing in single file along the narrow farm track, were three
tanks of the company. Now they turned left. They skirted the
edge of the wood, rumbling past the tangle of tall hedgerows,
clumps of shrubs, thick patches of undergrowth, and gnarled old
apple-trees. Second Lieutenant Theo was following them. Now
the three tanks in front were bumping across an open field into
the wood. Instantly hell broke loose.

"Enemy armour! Turret 11 o'clock! Fire!" These were the
commands Second Lieutenant Theo heard in his earphones. They
were the orders of the skippers of the tanks ahead of him. A loud
bang. Theo entered the open field. And now he could see what
was happening. On the path leading into the wood stood a
smoking Cromwell tank shot up by Cherry. Billows of smoke
rising behind the wreck suggested that other Cromwells, those
new, highly mobile British tanks, were withdrawing under cover
of a smoke-screen. Suddenly a Sherman burst from the hedge on
the right, but immediately turned tail and vanished in the thick
undergrowth. Theo sent a shell behind him. Almost at once he
found himself under fire from the left. He turned his gun towards
the outlines of a tank just visible behind a hedge. Direct hit.
There was no movement from the direction of his victim.
Evidently the crew had already abandoned the tank.

The *Panthers* and *Tigers* stalked the enemy through the thick undergrowth, but opposition from the British was getting stronger. They were feeding reinforcements of tanks and anti-tank guns into the patch of wood.

The commander judged correctly that his task was not to allow his tanks to be knocked out one by one in the treacherous thicket, but to prevent the enemy from taking the village of Lingèvres. The battle swayed to and fro for days. Finally it looked as if the British had given up the attempt.

Lemon, Second Lieutenant Theo's tank, had taken up a rest position in a farmyard on the village street. Corporal Martens was in the kitchen, supervising the giant frying-pan in which an enormous peasant breakfast of fifteen eggs was being prepared for the five men. Abruptly the village came under heavy bombardment. At the same moment, over Lemon's radio, which was left permanently switched on, there came a desperate call for help from Cherry. "Cherry to Lemon. Am surrounded by enemy infantry. Am unable to move. Come at once, Lemon. Repeat. Come at once, Lemon."

The peasant breakfast was flung into the sink. Blankets, haversacks, and personal kits were snatched up and tossed into the tank. Engines started. Out from under cover. They got their weapons ready for action as the tank lurched out of the farmyard. Everything was done automatically.

They saw the trouble as soon as they reached the field track. Cherry, which had been on picket duty, was standing motionless by the hedge. British troops were all around the tank. Theo opened up at them with his machine-gun. And another burst. The tracer struck the muddy ground right in front of the tank. The British infantry scuttled back to the wood. But now armour-piercing weapons were opening up on Theo from the edge of the wood. Undeterred, Theo's men got out of the tank. Under direct fire they made fast the steel hawser to Cherry. The troop's second tank was now coming out of the village and took over fire cover. It received a hit at once, but it continued firing. The tow-line was secure. Off! Steady now. Even so, the tow-line snapped.

From the edge of the wood the enemy was firing as hard as he could. Every time, smack into the bank. "Why on earth don't they aim higher?" muttered the wireless-operator of the broken-down tank as, together with Second Lieutenant Theo, he pulled the steel hawser over the towing-hook. "Off!" Theo ran in front of the tank and directed the towing manoeuvre down the narrow field track and through the anti-tank barriers at the edge of the village.

The battle for Lingèvres was getting fiercer. The British were using phosphorus shells for the first time, which, in addition to their explosive effect, caused terrible burns from their three-foot-high searing flames.

In a counter-attack against British tanks which had broken through the line Cherry was finished for good. Lemon was also damaged. Two more of the company's tanks were set on fire by phosphorus shells. The crews bailed out. They rolled over in the dirt to extinguish their burning uniforms. Amid the crash and roar of the artillery fire the wounded were packed on top of the last still-mobile tank. The injured grenadiers and tank crews were cowering on top of its stern. Most of them had severe burns. Many of them were naked because helpful comrades had torn the burning uniforms off their skins and thrown a blanket over their raw flesh. They were screaming with pain as they bumped about on top of the tank, close to the hot exhaust pipes. Their screams did not cease until the hypodermic needle blissfully entered their veins at the main dressing-station.

When General Bayerlein arrived at the flanking strongpoint of Saint-Germain-d'Ectot in the afternoon of June 12, Lieutenant Thiess, the commander of the division's escort company, produced for him three prisoners. Bayerlein was amazed to see that they belonged to the 7th British Armoured Division. They displayed the red jerboa on their sleeves and on their captured vehicle, the divisional sign that Bayerlein knew so well from the African campaign. So Montgomery's Desert Rats, those tough and cunning desert fighters, had also turned up. This meant that except for the 51st Highland Division all Montgomery's élite troops were now in Normandy. And in the face of that evidence the German High Command continued to doubt that the operations in Normandy represented the Allies' main blow!

Bayerlein took the prisoners along in his Volkswagen jeep to his headquarters for his Intelligence officer to question them about the intentions of the 7th Armoured Division. Suddenly the general heard his orderly officer behind him roaring with laughter. "And what's so funny, Hartdegen?"

With a broad grin Hartdegen pointed to one of the prisoners with a face like a horse: "Herr General, do you know who that is?"

"How should I know?" Bayerlein grunted.

"This man," Hartdegen announced dramatically, "this man is the chief undertaker of a London cemetery."

"A great pity," the general remarked, "a great pity we've got other things to do. I should have enjoyed a chat with him." Instead, the Intelligence officer had a long chat with him. But he, of course, was interested not so much in the cemetery as in the undertaker's business as a member of the 7th British Armoured Division. The undertaker was a chatty man. He told his captors that the Desert Rats had already penetrated deep into the flank of the Panzer Lehr Division and were pushing farther and farther into the still empty gap between the British and American bridgeheads. "If that is so," the Intelligence officer remarked, "then our situation is damned serious. If the Desert Rats get into the rear of our division they may well cause our lines to collapse."

The very next day, June 13, confirmed his fears. While Montgomery was still battering against Tilly and Lingèvres with tanks of 50th Division, thus tying down Bayerlein's armoured reserves, a combat group of 7th Armoured Division quietly slipped past Bayerlein's flank and penetrated as far as Villers-Bocage.

The British advance was discovered by Obersturmführer[1] Michel Wittmann in a *Tiger* tank of 2nd Company, S.S. Heavy Tank Battalion, 501st Regiment. Wittmann, the company commander, was an experienced tank man. On the Russian front he had knocked out 119 enemy tanks. He held the Knight's Cross with Oak Leaves.

The strong detachment of *Tigers* had been moved from the Beauvais area via Paris to the invasion front on June 7. The 2nd Company had been caught by fighter-bombers near Versailles in the morning of June 8 and heavily bombed. Since then they had moved only at night. On June 12 they had reached the neighbourhood of Villers-Bocage. The morning of June 13 had been set aside for servicing and maintenance. Bomb damage had to be repaired and the transmissions overhauled after the heavy flogging they had suffered during the long journey.

Meanwhile, Obersturmführer Wittmann set out with his old gun-layer, Oberscharführer[2] Woll, to reconnoitre the ground. Emerging from a small patch of woodland, he noticed enemy tanks moving along the road towards Hill 213, north of Villers-

---

[1] Rank in S.S. troops equivalent to lieutenant.
[2] Rank in S.S. troops equivalent to corporal.

Bocage. Carefully Wittmann withdrew to the edge of the wood. He observed. He counted. That was no reconnaissance detachment; that was an entire assault force. And it was moving into the rear of the Panzer Lehr Division.

But what could a single *Tiger* tank do about it, or, for that matter, the company's four other *Tigers,* the only ones which Wittmann had still available for action after their forced march and the heavy bombing?

But Wittmann was no ditherer. This was an occasion not for calculation but for action.

One "Tiger" against a Whole Brigade

A British armoured column was driving through Villers-Bocage. Though Wittmann did not know it, it was the spearhead of the 7th British Armoured Division—namely, the 22nd Armoured Brigade and units of the 1st Infantry Brigade. Among them were the famous 8th Hussars, the 1st Tank Regiment, and the 5th Artillery Regiment. Through his binoculars Wittmann could see that the British were meeting no resistance in Villers-Bocage. The supply units which had been stationed in the little town had been overwhelmed the day before.

The bulk of the British force continued along the highroad, towards Hill 213, in the direction of Caen. It was a hazy day, and there were no fighter-bombers or reconnaissance aircraft in the sky. Even so, the British were displaying an astonishing degree of unconcern. One motorized infantry company had stopped by the roadside. It was A Company of the 1st Infantry Brigade. "They're acting as if they'd won the war already," Wittmann's gun-layer grumbled.

Wittmann nodded. "We're going to prove them wrong." Calmly, he issued his orders. As if by a thunderclap the quiet of the morning was rent by the *Tiger's* 88-millimetre gun.

The leading British tank—only eighty yards away—immediately went up in flames. Like a gigantic beast the *Tiger* burst out of the wood and swung on to the road. In top gear it raced straight for the enemy column.

Then it stopped. It fired. It moved on.

It stopped again. It fired. It moved on.

Wittmann drove past the armoured spearhead of the British brigade, shooting up the vehicles. Tanks, trucks, armoured infantry carriers were all in a jumble. The way ahead was barred by the shattered and blazing tanks in front. Behind them, the half-tracked vehicles had closed up too much. Wittmann was pounding the vehicles with his gun and machine-guns.

All the half-tracks, as well as a dozen tanks of regimental headquarters and the reconnaissance company, were reduced to scrap. A Cromwell tank swung its turret round. Its 75-millimetre shell slammed against the armour plating of Wittmann's *Tiger* without inflicting any damage on the giant. The *Tiger's* 88-millimetre gun finished off the Cromwell.

Gunfire was now also coming from Hill 213. It came from Wittmann's four remaining *Tigers*, which were knocking out the reconnaissance tanks of the 8th Hussars as they tried to give covering fire to their comrades.

Meanwhile the noise of battle had alerted the 1st *Tiger* Company. Hauptsturmführer[1] Möbius moved off with eight tanks which had been standing by. Together with Wittmann's tanks he first outflanked and then broke into Villers-Bocage and destroyed the Cromwell tanks still in the town. In vain did Major French,

Cromwell Tank

[1] Rank in S.S. troops equivalent to army captain.

the commander of a British anti-tank detachment, try to avert disaster. One of his guns was firing out of a narrow side-street. A *Tiger* swung towards it. It rammed the house on the corner. The house collapsed. The gun was buried under the masonry. The *Tiger* merely shrugged off the rubble and the beams and, moving in reverse, rumbled back to the main road. Only one of Major French's guns scored a lucky hit. The track of Wittmann's *Tiger* was blown off and the giant lay motionless. Wittmann commanded: "Bail out!" At the head of his crew he fought his way back to his company.

Möbius's tanks fought a running battle with British infantry in the township. The fighting surged through the narrow streets. The Tommies were resisting desperately. From basement windows and doorways they fired their bazookas—an infantry weapon not unlike the German *Panzerfaust*. Untersturmführer[1] Stamm's and Oberscharführer Krieg's *Tigers* received direct hits and were burnt out. There was no time for their crews to escape. Furiously their comrades swept through the streets.

This engagement in Villers-Bocage on June 13 remains one of the most spectacular episodes of the invasion battle: a dozen *Tigers* against an entire brigade, against Montgomery's famous Desert Rats. In the British record of the war the engagement appears as "the battle of Villers-Bocage." The British chroniclers claim seven *Tiger* tanks destroyed. Evidently they counted a few old Mark IVs left behind in Villers-Bocage as *Tigers*. A pardonable mistake, since defeats and retreats all too easily lead to incorrect counting and inaccurate reporting—on both sides.

But the numbers did not matter. The main point was that Montgomery's armoured thrust into the rear of the Tilly line had been stopped by Michel Wittmann's *Tigers*. A dozen *Tigers* had won a battle.

The British were still dazed by the pounding they had got from the tanks when in the early afternoon German infantry made a sudden charge against Villers-Bocage from several sides.

These were advanced units of General von Lüttwitz's 2nd Panzer Division which was being moved into the area between the British and American invasion sectors in order to reinforce the Panzer Lehr Division. Lüttwitz's infantry penetrated into the town from the south. From the north a combat group of the Panzer

---

[1] Rank in S.S. troops equivalent to sergeant.

Lehr Division attacked with two 88-millimetre guns and three field guns.

Lieutenant-Colonel Kaufmann, Bayerlein's energetic chief of operations, had realized the danger of the British flanking movement, hurriedly scraped together various rearward formations, and personally led them into attack against the British.

Street fighting in Villers-Bocage continued until the evening of June 13. Then the British abandoned the battlefield, withdrawing the remnants of their battered units to Livry. But they did not salvage much. The entire headquarters personnel, as well as A Company with twenty-seven tanks and all the tracked and wheeled vehicles of the armoured brigade, were lost. The brigadier, fifteen officers, and 176 other ranks had been killed. The 1st Infantry Brigade left four officers and sixty other ranks on the battlefield.

But Montgomery's plan had not been confined to the attack by 7th Armoured Division. The flanking thrust at Caen was linked with a direct attack on the Tilly line. This was to tie down Bayerlein's forces and thus divert them from the outflanking manoeuvre of 7th Armoured Division. It was this flanking movement against the rear of the Panzer Lehr Division which was to have been the main blow, bringing about the collapse of the German front. Now that the action at Villers-Bocage had

MG 42

ended in failure, Montgomery had to try to convert the pinning-down operation at Tilly into a break-through.

After a tremendous preliminary artillery and aerial bombardment the 50th British Division, reinforced by new armoured units, launched its full-scale attack in the morning of June 15.

The main brunt was borne by Captain Philipps, the defender of Tilly. With units of 901st Panzer Grenadier Regiment he repelled all attacks on the town. There was furious hand-to-hand fighting. It was a battle decided chiefly by the *Panzerfaust*—that new weapon of the grenadiers—the Mark-42 machine-gun, and hand-grenades. Tilly was held. But Lingèvres was lost.

La-Belle-Epine, though stubbornly defended by an armoured reconnaissance unit under Major von Fallois, likewise fell on the following day. The battle moved towards its climax. The men of the Panzer Lehr now heard the noise of battle on their right flank too. In the Putot-Brouay area, held by the 12th S.S. Panzer Division, the British were likewise attacking. It was their 49th Division.

On June 16 the British crossed the Tilly-Balleroy road on a broad front. Strong detachments captured Hottot, on the Caen–Caumont road. The situation was getting dangerous.

General Bayerlein was then at the headquarters of 902nd Regiment, in whose sector the enemy had made his penetration. The 1st Battalion, Panzer Lehr Regiment, subordinated to the 902nd, was under the command of Major Markowski.

"Markowski must retake Hottot," Bayerlein ordered. The major had not even waited for the order, but had at once alerted his battalion: "Prepare for counterattack."

After a brief preliminary bombardment fifteen *Panthers* rumbled off with grenadiers riding on top. Markowski was right in front. Furiously the long barrels thundered. The machine-guns chattered. The anti-tank guns barked. By nightfall Markowski had dislodged the British and retaken Hottot. He himself was seriously wounded. Casualties among the grenadiers were heavy.

Dusk fell. The ghostlike ruins of Tilly towered into the sunset of June 16. Without pause the 50th and 49th British divisions were charging the cornerstones of the German front as if there was nothing more important in all the world than to capture these bombed-out, gutted villages.

V-1s streak over the Front

At the very moment when the British were battering the defences of Tilly and Cristot the German High Command suddenly struck at London.

Britain's metropolis was in utter confusion. Air-raid sirens were wailing ceaselessly. Mysterious unmanned missiles were streaking through the air from the Calais–Dunkirk area at a speed of nearly 400 miles an hour and bursting in or outside London.

The V-1 had arrived. The rocket age had begun.[1]

A few minutes after midnight on June 15–16 Hitler had unleashed his latest hound of hell. Twenty-four feet long, with a short wingspan of sixteen feet, plain and squat—such were the fire-belching monsters which carried a ton of high explosive. For the first time in their history the British found their capital under bombardment from the Continent.

The attack did not take them by surprise. All along, the British secret service had been fairly well informed about the progress of German long-range rocket research and the development of the V-1. On August 17, 1943, the British struck. A force of 597 aircraft attacked Peenemünde, the centre of V-1 production. The effect was catastrophic. When the bomber fleet made off, the dead bodies of 735 men, including a number of leading technicians, were littering the wrecked site.

Production was thereupon switched to the Harz Mountains, some of it to underground, bomb-proof factories. But Churchill's secret service discovered the move and remained currently informed about progress.

The first V-1 was to have been launched in December 1943 However, British Intelligence located the launching ramps and smashed thirty-five of them with 3000 tons of bombs. The next German date was February 15, 1944. But the ramps were smashed again. Eventually Lieutenant-General Ernst Heinemann scheduled the beginning of the V-1 offensive for the night of June 12–13. Colonel Wachtel, the commander of 155th Flak Regiment, which was in charge of the V-1 operation, had misgivings. He wanted a few more tests on the steering mechanism. But Heinemann

---

[1] For the full story of Germany's V-weapons read "V-2" by Walter Dornberger, who was the head of the Peenemünde installation. Another volume in the Bantam War Book Series.

stuck to his date. That this date was anything but a secret is shown by the fact that a day previously, on Sunday, June 11, the planned operation was known in London. In the morning of June 12 the acting head of the British secret service informed the senior commands of the Royal Air Force that employment of the V-1 was imminent.

Meanwhile Colonel Wachtel's gunners worked feverishly. The first salvo was scheduled for twenty minutes before midnight. But firing had to be postponed to 0330 hours. At last, shortly before 0400, the first ten V-1s roared off their ramps. But it was a very unlucky start. Five of them exploded immediately after take-off. The rest only just managed to get across the Channel.

General Heinemann at once called off the operation and postponed the offensive to the night of June 15–16. This time all went well. The snorting monsters roared off fifty-five ramps. By daybreak seventy-three V-1s had burst in the area of the British south coast. A gloomy and anxious House of Commons heard the Home Secretary report about the attack of "malignant robots." The German High Command, however, placed all its hopes in the new wonder-weapon, the "retribution weapon No. 1," previously referred to in the blueprints as Fi-103 or under the code-item of Cherry-stone.

Hitler intended to break Britain's fighting morale by a ceaseless bombardment of her capital. He believed he could wear down the British Government into surrender. That was why he refused—and continued to refuse even in mid-June—to direct the first rocket in military history against the concentrations of invasion ships off the Normandy coast or against the embarkation ports in Southern England.

There the new weapon might have had military effects. It might have disrupted Allied supplies, or possibly even cut them off. At least the Allied naval units would have been forced to withdraw from the French coast, which would have eliminated the murderous naval bombardment that was ceaselessly pounding the German defences from 640 barrels. A V-1 bombardment of the landing beaches would anyway have had a severe psychological effect, especially as the Allied forces in the field were known to be sensitive to artillery and aerial bombardment. But no! London was to be softened up instead.

It was a fatal miscalculation on Hitler's part. The total absence of German operations against the enemy fleet off the invasion coast was ironically emphasized by the sudden concentrated fire which British naval guns opened on the divisional headquarters of the 12th S.S. Panzers, seventeen miles south-west of Caen, on that very June 16, the day that saw the opening of the V-1 offensive.

Sturmmann[1] Hans Matyska, a driver attached to divisional headquarters, had just driven Gruppenführer[2] Witt's command car into the forecourt of the château, after some minor repairs to it, when an artillery spotter-aircraft passed overhead at great altitude.

"I don't like the look of him," the sergeant-farrier said to Matyska. They both grabbed their mess-kits and ran across to the field kitchen to collect their midday meal. After all, one never knew. But the British artillery spotter's radio was even faster. Like a tornado the first salvo roared through the air. Heaviest naval calibre. Two hundred yards behind the château the shells came down. A wall of fire and dirt rose up as high as a house. Then silence. Then came the second salvo. The gable of the château crumbled and crashed down. Officers and other ranks came tumbling out of the doors and leapt into the anti-shrapnel slit trench which had been cut right across the forecourt. Gruppenführer Witt, the divisional commander, had just reached the trench. He glanced back to make sure none of his men had been left lying injured. When he saw Matyska pressed against the outside wall he shouted across to him, "Over here, Matyska, into the trench." Matyska raced across like a sprinter. The third salvo was coming over. He tripped and fell headlong into the trench. Now Witt jumped in himself. And then everything was swallowed up in noise, fire, and smoke.

When Matyska had dug his way out from underneath the rubble and dirt the first thing he saw was the dead body of his divisional commander. The effect of the 16½-inch shell was indescribable. It had burst right on the edge of the trench. Matyska staggered among the dead bodies. He took another step and then dropped into the vast void of unconsciousness.

This disastrous incident demonstrated the terrible threat which the heavy naval guns represented to the fighting line and to headquarters. But Hitler could not make up his mind to use the V-1 against the fleet. He continued to put his hope of political results above the most pressing military requirements.

Admittedly, the V-1 bombardment was beginning to unnerve

---

[1] Private of S.S. troops.
[2] Rank in S.S. troops equivalent to lieutenant-general.

the Londoners. Service mail captured by 84th Corps conveyed a good idea of the morale in England. An assistant in a department store, for instance, described to her fiancé the scene in London during the opening days: "Almost noiselessly"—her account ran—"like little aeroplanes the missiles come gliding over. They burst first in one place, then in another, scattered all over London, and make large craters. Buildings collapse. It's terrible." Another letter revealed the emergence of a general sense of insecurity. Extensive areas of Central London were being evacuated. One woman correspondent gave as her new address a small town on the Tyne, near the Scottish border. The British public was demanding that the danger should be eliminated by the capture of the launching sites. Highly critical remarks were being made about the "inch-by-inch offensive." For once the placid English were grumbling quite a lot.

Hitler, however, refused to see that the V-1 offensive—if only because of their inadequate numbers and their insufficient accuracy against specific targets—would never induce a resolute British Government to ask for terms. Even on June 17, the date of his first and last visit to the invasion front, he still believed that the V-1 bombardment of London could decide the war. Again he declined to use the weapon against the English south-coast ports. It was incomprehensible. Rommel warned. Rundstedt warned. But Hitler viewed the situation optimistically. "We only have to keep our heads," he harangued the marshals. As for the situation on the Russian front, he believed that there was no serious danger there. "Hold the enemy in the East, defeat the enemy in the West," was Hitler's strategy. "If we ward off the invasion Britain will sue for peace under the effect of the V-weapons."

But even while Hitler tried to inspire his marshals with this thesis, the first explosive charges were already being detonated in Russia on roads, bridges, railway-tracks, and supply depots. With these explosions the Soviet partisan detachments were ringing up the curtain on the Russian summer offensive on the central sector of the Eastern front. Four days later this offensive burst forth on both sides of the Smolensk–Minsk supply artery and caused the collapse of the line held by Army Group Centre.

Where are our Airmen?

In the early hours of June 18 the troops in their foxholes on the Tilly front were woken up by a tremendous concentrated artillery bombardment. The earth was shaking. Then came two British divisions of the VIII British Corps, reinforced by newly landed armoured brigades. Under cover of the naval guns' creeping barrage and the aerial bombardment the British attacked. The first wave broke against the ruins of Tilly. All day long fighting raged around the shattered walls. In the evening they were lost. Cristot was lost also. But the enemy had not yet broken through. The main line, withdrawn behind the ruined towns, was still intact.

Again and again each yard of ground was contested in bloody hand-to-hand fighting. Again and again there was concentrated shelling, fighter-bomber attacks, and aerial bombardment. Casualties were mounting. It was only a matter of time before the Panzer Lehr Division and the 12th S.S. Panzer Division would be annihilated. The ceaseless artillery bombardment and the continuous waves of aerial attack would slowly but surely wipe them out. Whenever enemy aircraft streaked low over their positions, whenever bomber squadrons droned overhead in formation, the wretched troops would curse, grumble, or groan in despair, "Where on earth are our airmen? Where the hell is that damned Luftwaffe of Goering's?"

To this day former participants in the invasion battles find their hackles rising when they think back to those days. They felt let down by the German Luftwaffe, betrayed and sold out. It was a rare event even to see a single German fighter or bomber anywhere over the front.

But then, what could the German airmen take up? There is an illuminating passage in a secret analysis of the invasion battle, submitted to the Chief of the Luftwaffe General Staff:

> The 2nd Fighter *Geschwader* had an average of thirty machines available. But there were days when of the entire *Geschwader* only eight machines were operational. The majority of the fighter aircraft not operational could have been got ready for action within forty-eight hours provided the necessary spares had been available. But these had been withdrawn from depots in Western France because of the priority given to the fighter defence of the Reich.

And with what results? These too are mercilessly exposed in the report.

We read for instance:

The air officer commanding 3rd Air Fleet reports: Ground installations being systematically smashed, especially all fighter fields.

The chief of operations of 3rd Air Fleet reports: Enemy carpet-bombing raids by four-engined formations at first only in daytime, but now also by night, especially against transport installations. Ratio of air strength: generally 1 to 20, during major operations about 1 to 40.

The 2nd Fighter Corps reports: Own fighter operations now only conditionally possible. Effective reconnaissance and fighter operations entirely ruled out in the invasion area. Thirty Anglo-American airfields already constructed and operational in the bridgehead.

It was complete surrender in the air. The German Luftwaffe in the West was a neglected, broken tool. Here was the main reason for the German defeat on the invasion front. But does this mean that the Luftwaffe Command can therefore be exempted from all responsibility? Was there no opportunity for improvisation?

We have before us another report of the Luftwaffe Command, compiled from the most important operation logs, accounts of experience, and analyses. This attaches much importance to the German failure to carry out large-scale aerial mining of the sea along the invasion coast. It says:

It has been shown in both world wars that close mine barrages, even in the open sea, restrict the operations of naval forces and the movements of shipping, diverting them into definite areas. In the Second World War, minefields planted from the air outside ports and inlets proved to be even more effective obstacles to the enemy, entailing a considerable effort in terms of mine clearance. It may therefore be safely assumed that a large-scale strategic and tactical programme of mine infestation from the air would have been a considerable deterrent to an invading enemy. Our weak air forces, in particular, could have given considerable support in this way to our defensive forces at the moment of invasion. Mining of approaches would have had to be done as a strategic measure. It would have needed to have been applied over a considerable period in all areas where the enemy might have been expected, or where coastal defences and troop concentrations were less strong. A thick mine barrage would have greatly interfered with the movement of transports and warships. The accurate intervention of Allied battleships in the ground fighting around Caen would have been made considerably less effective, and the defence generally, as well as the preparations for a counter-attack, would have been greatly facilitated. . . .

The report finally points out that the sweeping of a close mine barrage laid from the air, which would have required a considerable effort by Allied naval units, would, moreover, have been an important indication of where the main blow of the invasion might be expected.

The Luftwaffe Command failed to grasp this task. Thus, while it may have been the innocent victim of a mistaken and inadequate defence policy, it must nevertheless be found guilty of a great many mistakes of its own. But then in war misfortune frequently becomes guilt, just as honour and glory are often no more than a free bonus of good fortune.

5

THE BATTLE FOR CHERBOURG

Operation Heinrich

The old hog-pen where Major Friedrich Wilhelm Küppers, the commander of Artillery Group Montebourg, had his battle headquarters was well camouflaged. The date was June 19. Küppers was sitting on a stool in his well-camouflaged tent, his map table and artillery board on his knees.

The Americans had brought up four divisions to force their breakout from the Utah bridgehead to the north and west. Küppers glanced up as the flap of his headquarters tent was pushed aside. In the opening, haggard from lack of sleep, smeared with blood and dirt, stood Lieutenant Staake of the 5th Battery, 1262nd Army Coastal Artillery Regiment. He had come from the O.P. on Hill 117. Küppers was prepared for bad news.

"What's up, Staake? Just look at yourself!"

In spite of his wound Lieutenant Staake made a precise report. "The enemy tank attack at the level-crossing was stopped by our gunfire. But the Americans then made a surprise thrust along a sunken lane right into the little wood of Montebourg. Armoured units are pushing past the town centre on both sides. The infantry which followed in their wake is now being engaged in fierce fighting by the grenadiers of combat group Berg, which is holding the town centre, and by units of combat group Hoffmann. Things are looking ugly," Staake concluded his report. Then he added, "If we are lucky the penetration can be sealed off. Otherwise we're in the trap. We'll have to get out of here, Herr Major, or else we'll be bagged by the Americans."

Major Küppers regarded his lieutenant. He's right, of course, he thought. But Quineville–Montebourg–Gorse Hill was the last position barring the road to Cherbourg, which had no proper landward defences. Once that position was breached there would be no hope for Cherbourg. That was why, for several days running now, every order had insisted: "If Montebourg falls the road to Cherbourg will be open. Montebourg must be held."

Mentally Küppers reviewed the past eight days.

On June 12 he had assumed command of the newly organized artillery group formed for the defence of Montebourg from five batteries of different artillery units. Its nineteen guns included four 122-millimetre guns, two 105-millimetre guns, and one 150-millimetre self-propelled gun; together with flak group König and with Major Rassner's batteries of 100th Mortar Regiment, it represented a considerable fire-power. Its purpose was to give support to 919th Grenadier Regiment, which had been in action ever since June 6 and had now been forced back to the edge of Montebourg, and to the combat groups Hoffmann and Müller of 243rd Infantry Division.

The battle for Cherbourg had thus in fact begun, for a naval port, or any fortress, must be defended in the forefield. This lesson was borne out by every single landing operation from North Africa to Sicily and Italy; and it had been proved even earlier by the fall of Singapore. But the artillery commanders had waited in vain for the guns which were not needed in the west and north of the Cotentin peninsula to be switched to its eastern

Bieber 150 mm. Self-Propelled Gun

coast, so that the American bridgehead could be hammered and smashed by concentrated fire. But Guderian's slogan "Not driblets, but mass" was being disregarded in the artillery too. Available resources were scattered about in driblets. The fear of further Allied landings, a fear nurtured by the German High Command and now haunting many headquarters, resulted in half-measures or less than half-measures. One battery would be sent to one place, and a couple of guns to another—to oppose enemy armour.

At Montebourg, at long last, things were to be different. Here the German units containing the Utah bridgeheads, units locked in exceedingly hard fighting, were to be given a really solid artillery backing. This backing was to be provided by Küpper's group. And, indeed, its batteries were firing to capacity. The Americans were beating their heads against the wall of Montebourg, the gorse hill of La Pernelle, and Quineville. During the day Küppers maintained what he called "cunning fire"—highly concentrated fire of very short duration, so as to make things difficult for the enemy's aerial spotting, sound-ranging, and muzzle-flash observation. At night he laid on "sprinkling fire"—a kind of harassing fire with all guns firing simultaneously as a concentrated salvo, but each gun at its own separate pinpoint target. This method yielded good returns, both materially and psychologically. The Americans were nervously probing the whole neighbourhood with artillery and naval guns. Spotter-aircraft were continually flying to and fro over the lines of the combat groups and their hinterland. The moment they spotted anything that looked like a gun-position hell was at once let loose.

But the gunners had become experts at camouflage. The gun-positions were real masterpieces of blending into the background. Any artilleryman vastly prefers a well-camouflaged, mobile field position to a static pill-box. Those blocks of concrete only limited one's field of fire; they could not really be concealed; they were ready-made conspicuous targets, and at the same time did not provide complete protection against bombs or naval guns. They were, in fact, for the guns and their crews.

The artillerymen in the field positions lay in one-man foxholes, just like the grenadiers of combat groups Müller, Keil, Berg, and Hoffmann in the main line farther forward. Thus even the heaviest bombardments could be survived. To do any damage a shell would have to strike right into a foxhole. And that happened very rarely. After all, a one-man foxhole was very small. And, what was more, it was almost completely invisible from the air. During the day everybody remained under cover. Supplies, spares, ammunition, food—all these came up at night. The men became experienced nightwalkers.

This co-operation between infantry combat groups and concentrated artillery directed in a modern manner proved exceedingly successful at Montebourg. Although the enemy was attacking with three divisions, the line held and the coastal roads to the north and north-west remained barred.

Farther south, however, things went wrong. Major Küppers recalled the dramatic telephone conversations he had had on June 16 and 17 with his regimental commander Colonel Reiter, on whose staff was also Lieutenant Professor Walter Hallstein, now the Chairman of the European Economic Community. "The Americans have broken out to the west from their bridgehead." Reiter had told him. It was quite true. With two divisions Major-General Collins had thrust to the west, traversed the picturesque Douve valley, crossed the river, and captured the battered little town of Saint-Sauveur-le-Vicomte. An important bridgehead had thus been established.

But worse was to follow. General Hellmich's combat group, with the 77th Infantry Division newly brought up from Brittany, was unable to halt the Americans' breakout from their beach or to iron out their new bridgehead. The 9th U.S. Infantry Division and units of the 82nd U.S. Airborne Division were pressing towards the western coast in an attempt to cut the Cotentin peninsula in half, split up the German forces there, and cut Cherbourg's overland communications to the south.

General Collins's manoeuvre succeeded. The Americans reached the western coast at Barneville. Thus an American corridor had been established in the forefield of Cherbourg, running across the peninsula, and compelling the German forces of 84th Corps to establish a northern and southern defensive front.

One operation that stands out from the general disaster of the collapse of the German defensive front west of Utah Beach is the 77th German Infantry Division's break-through to the south, right across the American line.

Units of this division, under General Stegmann, were to have covered the right flank of Schlieben's Cherbourg front. However, 84th Corps realized that the main danger was in the south. Schlieben had just been discussing the details with Stegmann in the afternoon of June 17 when the order came through: "Disengagement towards the south!" Stegmann was not sorry: he did not believe that Cherbourg's landward front could possibly be held by exhausted troops. Nor did he think very much of the idea of falling back on Cherbourg, which, in his opinion, was not tenable as a fortress in the long run. He was perfectly right.

General Stegmann therefore tried to lead his division to the south as fast as possible, in battle-worthy groups, through the enemy front. However, the horse-drawn units of the division were intercepted by fighter-bombers near the village of Bricquebec in the early morning of June 18. There was terrible confusion. Stegmann was driving down the road, trying to bring order into the chaos. Just then a fighter-bomber swooped down and opened fire on the general's car. The 20-millimetre shells tore straight into the vehicle. The general was killed instantly: the fourth general to be killed in action on the invasion front.

On the day before, General Hellmich, the commander of 243rd Infantry Division, had lost his life in similar circumstances. He too had been struck and instantly killed by a 20-millimetre shell.

"Death by fighter-bomber" was what the men called it in the front line. Death by fighter-bomber. General of Artillery Marcks, the exemplary and popular commander of 84th Corps, had also bled to death in a roadside ditch west of Saint-Lô on June 12, after being shot up by a fighter-bomber.

Command of 77th Infantry Division was taken over by the division's senior regimental commander, Colonel Bacherer, O.C. 1049th Infantry Regiment. He summoned the unit commanders to a conference. "What's to be done?"

"Give up," some suggested.

"Fall back to the north, into Cherbourg fortress," advised others.

But Bacherer asked, "Are 1500 to 2000 men to go into captivity at a time when, down in the south, every rifle is needed for the establishment of a new line of resistance?"

The columns moved off during the night of June 18–19. They were making for the south. Captain Dr Schreihage, the Intelligence officer, gives the following account of the phantom march of the 77th through the American front:

The few Volswagens and radio-vans that were still intact sneaked through the enemy lines in dread secrecy. In the grey light of dawn the marching columns were passing through enemy-occupied villages. The American sentries got quite a fright when they saw the silent processions, and were quickly disarmed. They joined the marching columns as prisoners. Keep moving. The signals detachment dismantled and nearly coiled up the wires of American telephone connexions—partly to cut the enemy's communications and partly to help themselves to badly needed material. A thick cloud cover and fine drizzle provided protection against fighter-bombers. Towards 1100 hours the force camped in a sunken lane. Patrols sent out to reconnoitre the immediate neighbourhood discovered an American field encampment less than 500 yards away.

But the men simply could not march another step. It had to be risked.

"Not a sound," was the order. "Rest for sleeping."

The men dropped in their tracks. On the banks of the sunken lane sentries lay on the ground, their eyes glued to binoculars. Would the Americans spot them? They did not.

In the late afternoon they moved on. Colonel Bacherer had a radio-signal sent to the units of 243rd Division lying to the south, beyond the American corridor: "We are pushing towards Villot. Let us pass through your blocking position. Can you help us by counter-attack?" Presently a handful of self-propelled guns of 243rd Division punched a clear passage through Villot for the 77th. But when they got to the little river Ollande it looked as if all their efforts had been in vain. The crossings were blocked by a strong American position.

Bacherer was not going to give up with success almost in sight. Now they would have to fight for it. The 1st Battalion, 1050th Infantry Regiment charged against the enemy-held bridge-head in the old-fashioned manner, with fixed bayonets, under cover of a light machine-gun. They took the bridge, smashed the 2nd Battalion, 47th U.S. Infantry Regiment and took a large number of prisoners. With all their wounded, with 250 prisoners, and with twelve captured jeeps the regiments reached the German lines.

All this, of course, Major of Artillery Friedrich Wilhelm Küppers in his well-camouflaged hog-pen north of Montebourg did not yet know on the morning of June 19.

But he did know that the Montebourg sector was 'hanging in the air.' And a sector was not just a stretch of land, but the grenadiers of combat groups Hoffmann, Keil, and Müller in their forward foxholes, the nineteen guns of his five batteries and the guns of 30th Flak Regiment, Major Rassner's mortars, and the anti-tank troops of the 709th Panzerjägers under Captain Hümmerich. This entire force was, in German Army parlance, 'hanging in the air'—its flanks were unprotected and it was apt to be bagged by the enemy at any moment. Küppers knew that Lieutenant Staake, standing in front of him, was quite right when he said, "We've got to get out of here, Herr Major; we're in a trap."

Küppers called for his driver, Corporal Johann Koch. "Have we got any brandy left for the lieutenant? He's earned a drink."

Koch produced a bottle. There was about two fingers left in it. The aluminium beaker would have to do for a glass.

"Thank you, Herr Major." Staake smiled. He raised his stubbly chin and knocked back the drink. "Has Operation Heinrich not yet been ordered, Herr Major?" he asked.

"No. Our orders are to hold out."

Operation Heinrich was the secret code-name for the withdrawal into the fortified area of Cherbourg.

Once the Americans had broken through at Saint-Sauveur and pushed across to the western coast of the Cotentin peninsula. Schlieben's right wing was no longer covered. Seventh Army therefore planned to withdraw these forces to the landward front of Cherbourg. Unless this was done there was a danger that the Americans might swing north from the western coast, cutting off those of Schlieben's forces which stood at Montebourg. To avert this danger, and also to keep the initiative, a gradual withdrawal was to be carried out sector by sector upon the cue Heinrich. But when the Führer's headquarters learnt of the plan Hitler flew into a rage and strictly forbade any withdrawal whatever. "The present positions are to be held at all costs," was the familiar order.

But reality proved stronger. At any rate, Schlieben's front had already been torn open to the west; so there was nothing left to hold. Rommel had remonstrated with Rundstedt by telephone, and Rundstedt had explained to Hitler the gravity of the situation. Thereupon his decision had been amended: "The fortress of Cherbourg is to be held at all costs. A fighting withdrawal of units to the south of it is authorized provided the enemy's advance is slowed down. Withdrawal in one single movement is forbidden." The officers commanding the smaller units were suitably instructed. Now their responsibility was weighing heavily upon them. For, translated into the plain language of the fighting front, the order demanded: "Hold out until further resistance is impossible. Only then, at the very last moment, may you withdraw under irresistible enemy pressure to avoid capture."

But when was this last moment? How would they recognize it if they had no idea of the situation on the next sector? To meet the local conditions and to clarify chains of command the German forces were reorganized. The 709th Division and the 922nd Grenadier Regiment of 243rd Division were formed into a Battle Group Cherbourg and taken out of 84th Corps. Thus responsibility for the Cherbourg area rested entirely with General von Schlieben. In his account of his anxieties he says:

"I remember fairly accurately a signal sent to me by Field-Marshal Rommel. It certainly did not suffer from any dearth of suggestions. Roughly it ran like this: 'Schlieben's group will hold out in front; it will retire only under heavy enemy pressure; it will not allow the enemy to outflank it; it will deceive the enemy by resourceful operations, and it will reach the landward front in good time.' Yet all I had was an entirely battered division, with horse-drawn transport, and almost immobile, while the enemy was far better and more generously motorized than even our armoured formations were at the beginning of the Russian campaign. The enemy, moroeover, had an air force which prevented all movement during daytime.

Another order [Schlieben's account continues] pointed out that in accordance with latest orders from O.K.W. the line Saint-Vaast-de-la-Hague–Le Theil—landward front of Cherbourg–Vauville had to be held at any price. This meant a barrier across the entire northern half of the peninsula.

Yet another radioed signal demanded that not only the landward front but the Jobourg peninsula in the north-western corner had also to be held at all costs.

The same demand was moreover made with regard to the hills at Brix. I had the impression that the High Command had stopped using a map or dividers. The road network on the Cotentin peninsula was so extensive and so superbly engineered that a mobile motorized force could quite easily by-pass any local opposition. On paper I had been given a free hand. But in reality orders were piling in one on top of another.

Thus it came about that because of this kind of "hold on" order the grenadiers and artillerymen were still lying in their foxholes in the Montebourg area on June 19, although on the western side of the peninsula American tanks were already moving towards Cherbourg.

Let us return again to Major Küppers in his hog-pen north of Montebourg. Küppers picked up the telephone and talked to the combat group headquarters. "First we've got to seal off the penetration," was their opinion, "otherwise we're dished."

Küppers therefore commanded: "Concentrated fire on the various penetration points." The batteries started roaring. Rassner's mortars started lobbing their salvoes. And a miracle happened. The artillery bombardment and the mortar salvoes made the Americans hesitate. They suspected stronger forces than were in fact available, and they shrank from the risk of pushing on. But how long could they be fooled?

Towards midday a telephone connexion with Division was restored by mere chance. While mending a line severed by gunfire the signallers had come across the wire leading to General von Schlieben's headquarters. Major Förster, the Intelligence officer of Schlieben's 709th Division, was startled. "You're still there? We thought you'd moved back during the night." At that point the line was cut again. Half an hour later an avalanche of bad news began to pour into Küppers's headquarters. The catastrophe was beginning to take shape. Captain Hümmerich's unit of Panzerjägers had lost so many anti-tank guns that the right flank could no longer be protected. Lieutenant König, the liaison officer with 30th Flak Regiment, reported that the gun-emplacements were all noticing approaching noise of battle and finding themselves under fire from mortars and tanks. Lieutenant Storz, commanding the 1st Battery, 1709th Artillery Regiment, reported from his O.P. on top of the Huberville church tower: "American armoured units are forming up for attack on both sides of Montebourg."

The 4th U.S. Division thrust into the open right flank of the German positions, while the 79th Division advanced towards Montebourg, its tanks by-passing the town centre and reaching the roads to Valognes.

Again Major Küppers rang through to the commanders of those combat groups to whom he had still a line. Lieutenant-Colonel Hoffmann, Major Rassner, and Lieutenant Schmidt had just turned up at his hog-pen: they had been shelled out of their headquarters north of the Montebourg–Valognes road.

What was to be done? Should they allow their flank to be

rolled up and themselves to be cut to pieces? Should they surrender? Or should they retreat—which meant that they would be at the mercy of the fighter-bombers?

The heavens were merciful. A gale-force wind sprang up, driving low cloud before it. A fine drizzle began to fall. This was the kind of weather they needed. Here was a chance of escape from their trap.

Once more their guns thundered and their mortars screamed. The ammunition they could not take with them was used up against the penetration points, simulating a counter-attack. This ruse enabled the combat groups to detach themselves from the enemy unnoticed. The difficult operation was brought off. Even the grenadiers in the town centre pulled out unnoticed.

In accordance with orders, no "withdrawal into the fortress in one movement" was carried out, but an intermediate line was taken up in the Le Mont area. At 1830 hours the combat groups were again in position, their guns ready for action. Only a soldier who has experienced for himself the kind of continuous fighting undergone by these men can appreciate the degree of discipline, obedience, and courage implied in the simple phrase: again in position.

On the following day the combat groups of Montebourg were incorporated in the landward defences of Cherbourg.

The curtain was going up on the last act.

Führer's Orders: Resistance to the Last Round

Some of the battalions moving into strongpoints along the landward front of Cherbourg had been reduced to 90–180 men. If only they still had their heavy AA guns which had proved so effective against tanks! But the guns, including a good many 88-millimetre ones, had been left behind in their positions. As bad luck would have it the gun limbers and tractors had been concentrated right in the middle of the American parachutists' dropping zone in the area of Saint-Mère-Eglise. The flak officer responsible had simply abandoned the tractor depot and 'disengaged himself.' The result was disastrous. The four weakened combat groups had to defend a thirty-mile arc round Cherbourg against six attacking divisions—in ordinary field positions and with practically no armour-piercing weapons.

The Jobourg peninsula with its outer strongpoint Westeck

was held by 922nd Grenadier Regiment organized as a combat group. Next, as far as strongpoint 463, came the combat group Keil with 919th Grenadier Regiment and the 17th MG Battalion. The centre of the line was held by 739th Grenadier Regiment under Lieutenant-Colonel Köhn; and the eastern sector, from strongpoint 436 down to Cap Levy, was manned by the combat group Rohrbach, together with 729th Grenadier Regiment The nerve centre of the town's defences and of the landward front was in an underground command-post at Octeville, a suburb of Cherbourg. There too was the headquarters of Admiral Hennecke, the Naval Commander Normandy.

General von Schlieben realized that there was no hope of prolonged resistance against a modern motorized army. The important thing was to gain time. Time to destroy the harbour so as to make it useless for American unloading operations for a long while to come. Time to enable a German defensive line to be established in the south so as to tie down the enemy forces aiming at Cherbourg for as long as possible.

Schlieben spoke frankly to the commanders of his combat groups. "Dig in and hold" was the slogan for the strongpoints. The men did their best.

In the corridors of the underground command headquarters there was hardly room enough to swing a cat. Nearly a thousand men were now inhabiting the subterranean galleries, sitting or lying around stretched out on cases, kitbags, and ammunition-boxes—sleeping, dozing, or cursing irritably. Naval gunners, the crews of harbour-patrol boats, building workers of the Todt Organization, men of the Labour Service, and Luftwaffe ground staff. There was a stench of gunpowder, rotting cloth, exhaust fumes from the various motors, and human sweat. The air-conditioning system was no longer working.

From the gallery exits came the crash of shell-bursts. Now and again the electric light would flicker, and a moment later would be an explosion.

A corporal who had found safety in the command bunker but an hour ago, after his position had been overrun, knew what the bangs were. The Americans had reached the top of the hill, above the command-post. They were now using enormous drilling rigs to bore holes into the ground and were filling them with explosive. "If we don't surrender soon they'll turn us into pulp," he observed challengingly.

Sub-Lieutenant Blume, Admiral Hennecke's orderly officer, was laboriously picking his way to the situation room. The situation, of course, was revealed more clearly by conditions within the command-post than on the maps. The troops hardly bothered to move their legs out of the way to let the sub-lieutenant pass. That was the measure of their weariness, their battle fatigue, but also their demoralization and recalcitrance. Blume no longer paid any attention to it. He had just been to the general's command-post. His chief of operations had told him enough. There was no hope.

In the situation room Blume was met by Lieutenant Schierhorn, Hennecke's A.D.C. "What news?" he asked. Blume shrugged his shoulders. "Fort-du-Roule fell two hours ago. So now the Americans on the high ground at the southern edge of the town command every corner of the fortress." Schierhorn was shocked. "What happened? How could a powerful fort like that fall? Surely that rock fortress with its 150-millimeter guns was considered impregnable?"

Blume again shrugged his shoulders. "The Americans had positioned their guns near a field hospital. With his batteries built into the rock and pointing seaward towards the harbour the commander of the fort could not do anything useful anyway. And he dared not use his automatic weapons for fear of shooting up the hospital. His guns were silenced at point-blank range by hits through the apertures."

Schierhorn walked up to the map. "And how long can we hold out in here?" Blume answered without hesitation. "They've already encircled our hill. They're blocking the southern exit by blasting, and are drilling down into the rock above us from the top. They are also dropping assault charges down our ventilation shafts. These may not hurt us much, but since the air-conditioning has packed up it means that our air is being fouled by nitrous fumes. If they don't blast us out of our burrow they'll smoke us out."

The sub-lieutenant fell silent. The A.D.C. was silent too. The rumbling of the artillery sounded eerie and evil in this twentieth-century dungeon. Blume reached under his desk. "That's the last of it," he said as he poured out two glasses of cognac.

Divided from Blume's situation room by only a few feet of rock and soil, Lieutenant-General von Schlieben, the commander of the fortress of Cherbourg and the entire Cherbourg front, was likewise standing in front of his map in his panelled room, gazing at the tangle of blue lines and red arrows. The date was Sunday, June 25, and the time was 1552 hours. There was a knock at the door. Major Förster, the chief of operations, entered.

In his hand was a slip of paper. "Army Group's reply to our signal, Herr General."

Schlieben turned. He said nothing, but his eyes tried to read in Förster's face the decision taken by Army Group in response to the signal he had sent that morning:

> Enemy superiority in material and enemy domination of the air overwhelming. Most of our own batteries out of ammunition or smashed. Troops badly exhausted, confined to narrowest space, their backs against the sea. Harbour and all other important installations effectively destroyed. Loss of the town unavoidable in nearest future as enemy has already penetrated outskirts. Have 2000 wounded without possibility of moving them. Is there any point, in view of the overall situation, in having our remaining forces entirely wiped out, as seems inevitable in the absence of effective counter-weapons? Request urgent instructions.

Schlieben remembered every word. Especially the final question. He had taken some care with Förster to phrase it. Surely they must give him a free hand! "Well?" he asked. "What's their reply?"

Major Förster read out: "In accordance with the Führer's orders you are to continue fighting to the last round. Rommel, Field-Marshal."

"Is that all?"

"That is all, Herr General."

The general glanced at the situation-map on the wall. He had stared a hundred times at the jumble of lines and arrows. And a hundred times he had realized the basic fact that the fortress of Cherbourg had its face to the sea. That was the direction in which all the guns of the naval defences, of the army coastal artillery and of the fortress artillery were facing. That was the direction from which the enemy had been expected. That he might come from behind, from the landward side, had been steadfastly and confidently discounted by the senior German Command—in spite of many a warning. They were now about to pay for their mistake. The fate suffered in 1942 by the British in Singapore, the world's strongest naval fortress, was about to befall the Germans at Cherbourg—invasion through the back door.

Major Förster and the Intelligence officer were entering the latest reports about enemy penetrations on the situation-map. Everywhere the red arrows were piercing the blue lines and circles of the German defensive positions. And every intersection by a red arrow represented a tragedy. Many of the strongpoints and defensive positions were not even connected by telephone. Neighbouring strongpoints often lacked visual contact with one another over the difficult ground. The ring of interior forts around the city centre were outmoded. Only the two newly built outer fortifications, Westeck and Osteck, were modern constructions by the Todt Organization. But even they were inadequately equipped for defence against attack from the landward side. This, then, was Cherbourg's landward front line, a line which might conceivably be held by crack units, but never by the exhausted remnants of two infantry divisions and the medley of men without battle experience: airfield ground personnel, Luftwaffe transport units, fortification engineers, elderly naval ratings, the office staff of Field Kommandantur No. 583, middle-aged pay-masters from the fortress's depot personnel, employees of the Labour Service, the Todt Organization, and Georgian battalions.

On May 1, 1944, about five weeks before the invasion, General Marcks had proved in the course of an exercise that the fortress could be overrun from the landward side: in a surprise attack the Assault Battalion Messerschmitt had broken through its defences. It was a piece of tragic irony that the first real enemy penetration was made in exactly the same spot where Marcks's assault battalion had broken through in the exercise—at the joint between strongpoints 422 and 426. The lesson of the manoeuvres had been confirmed by grim reality. And how could it have been otherwise? How could strongpoints manned by veterinary officers and their staffs, or by half-trained teen-age parachutists, stand up to attacks by enemy armour?

The Line is carved up

What concentrated gunfire and aerial bombardment had failed to achieve was achieved in next to no time by infantry charges with tank support. The men abandoned their positions and sought safety inside the concrete bunkers of the city. But some strongpoints resisted fanatically. Thus eighteen-year-old men of the Labour Service defended their strongpoint at Gonneville with stubborn courage. The ground was unfavourable. Artillery observation was difficult and the guns could not be brought to bear effectively against the attacking armour. Nevertheless the young boys stood as firm in their trenches as battle-hardened grenadiers, and even fought the American infantrymen with their spades. But what could they achieve against tanks? They fired their *Panzerfaust* bazookas while they had any left, and then put up their hands.

But even the experienced combat groups were powerless against the Americans, who were equipped with every conceivable technical means. Keil's men, the 919th Grenadier Regiment from Hesse and Thuringia, the 17th MG Battalion, and Müller's combat group of the 922nd—none of them were able to stand their ground. Köhn's 739th Grenadiers and Rohrbach's 729th likewise had to yield. Thanks to their material superiority the American assault regiments simply carved up the front.

Lieutenant-Colonel Keil reports: The American attacks on all the strongpoints, however small, invariably followed the same pattern. First, bombing by fifty aircraft. Second, pasting by mortar fire. Then the charge by assault troops. The Americans carried first-rate walkie-talkie sets. They reported back immediately on the success or failure of their operation. Before the German company commander was even informed by runner that the enemy had established himself in one of his strongpoints the commander of the American assault force would have called up reinforcements by radio. As soon as they had captured a strongpoint they organized themselves for all-round defence and waited for the German counter-attack. They then repulsed it, and followed up at once. Hours would pass before regimental headquarters got a clear picture of what was heppening and before counter-measures of any scope could even begin to be taken. In the meantime the same drill would be carried out at some other strongpoint. In this way, at the cost of a colossal expenditure of *matériel,* the German landward front was being crushed and atomized.

General von Schlieben was thinking of his appointment as fortress commander by Hitler on June 23. The Führer had sent him a telegram. It had contained the sentence: "If the worst is to happen, then Cherbourg must fall into enemy hands only as a heap of rubble." A heap of rubble!

Schlieben stood gazing at the map. It recorded clearly the unrolling of events.

On June 20, at 1400 hours, a signal had come from Artillery Group South: "Enemy spearhead on Valognes–Cherbourg road has reached southern outpost. Request permission to open fire."

Late in the afternoon, towards 1745 hours, the Americans reached the landward front on the eastern sector also, near the village of Le Theil. They probed the German defences, but withdrew again when the salvoes of 5th and 8th Batteries, 1709th Artillery Regiment crashed down on the armoured spearheads. That had been the overture.

The curtain was rung up on the first act on the morning of June 21. An air raid of tremendous force, by several waves of 1000 machines, battered the German lines. It was followed by concentrated artillery fire and by attacks from low-flying aircraft. Eventually the tanks rumbled forward. From Saint-Pierre-Eglise a detachment advanced cautiously towards the airfield at Gonneville, within the area of strongpoints 410 to 420.

Captain Zdralek, in charge of the 9th Battery, acted as artillery observer in strongpoint 416, directing the fire of his guns against the American tanks. Direct hit! The tanks turned tail. Presently they came back, intent on forcing the break-through this time. But they were again unable to get through the barrage of gunfire. Once more they withdrew.

However, they succeeded elsewhere.

"Alarm!" the shout went up in strongpoints 425 and 426. But already the tanks were upon them, having crept up over ground that was difficult to observe. A parachute company composed of young men from a training battalion, with only six weeks' training and with no fighting experience, was overrun. The enemy, as a result, gained a foothold right inside the German lines. True enough, Second Lieutenant Kadau of the 729th Grenadiers succeeded in holding strongpoints 421 and 424 with his company. But what use was that? The American tanks simply drove through the gap at strongpoint 425.

At 1615 hours they were outside the gun-position of Second Lieutenant Ohlmeier's 5th Battery, 1261st Artillery Regiment. The regimental battery of the 1709th, under Lieutenant Bauer, had been overrun, and Bauer and most of his gunners had been killed. The position of 11th Battery, under Lieutenant Schwalbe, was defended in furious hand-to-hand fighting. Gun after gun was eliminated by the tanks. The horses in the transport park were mown down. Lieutenant Schwalbe, though wounded, reached the Osteck fort and made his report.

Artillery reconnaissance parties of 8th, 10th, and 11th Batteries entered the threatened area. They reported back: "Enemy spearheads with armoured support have already reached the Cherbourg–Théville main road, west of the airfield. Second

Lieutenant Kadau is still holding out in the main line. Apart from the gap torn into it at strongpoint 425 the main line is still intact. Captain Walter with his 8th Battery, 1709th Artillery Regiment is encircled by the enemy and has organized all-round defence.''

It was the great hour of the artillery. The infantry's counter-attacks were supported by concentrated gunfire. Every barrel was firing to capacity.

As if by a miracle the field telephone lines to the encircled 8th Battery, running through the switchboard of the overrun regimental battery, had remained intact. The unmanned exchange, with the connexions set for fire control, thus continued to function in a sunken lane which had long since been captured by the enemy.

"Hang on!" was the message the men of 8th Battery heard again and again. And they hung on. Lieutenant Frey, with a battalion of 729th Grenadier Regiment, fought his way right up to the battery in a surprise counter-attack. Corporal Rühl knocked out two enemy tanks with *Panzerfausts*. The Americans opened fire with phosphorus shells. But 8th Battery, encircled from three sides, held out. In vain Frey tried to seal off the lost strongpoints 423 to 425. Captain Hallmann, repeating the attempt with a parachute company, was no more successful. The danger persisted.

For another three days 8th Battery stood its ground. Then the position had to be abandoned. They blew up their guns. The crews by then had been reduced to twenty-two men.

All that was reflected on the situation-map in General Schlieben's command-post—in straight and curved arrows, in discontinuous and dotted lines, in conventional tactical signs for batteries, regiments, companies, headquarters, and all kinds of units. The great battle was transformed here into an abstract mural. But for anyone who knew how to read it, each line was pregnant with life and death.

On June 22 the Americans forced deep penetrations into the western and southern parts of the front.

By June 23 Major-General Collins's assault regiments had driven four wedges into the German defences. The main German line collapsed in many places. In the areas of all four German combat groups American tanks were striking at artillery positions now forced to defend themselves from all directions.

On June 24 the enemy had established himself in the suburbs of Tourlaville and Octeville, and at the Fort-du-Roule. Thus the underground command bunker of Schlieben, Hennecke, and the artillery commander Reiter found itself within the immediate combat zone.

A Captain crosses the Lines

On June 25, towards 1000 hours, a squadron of enemy warships appeared off the fortress, just as if they were taking part in a naval exercise. Battleships, cruisers, and destroyers. Was Cherbourg to be cracked from the sea after all?

In the wireless-room of Fort Homat Captain Witt, the harbour commandant, sat behind the vision slits of the concrete bunker which looked almost like the bridge of a cruiser. "Lattice masts," he said, his eyes glued to the telescope. That meant battleships of an older American type. Now the fleet opened fire. Out of a wall of smoke and fumes the salvoes came roaring over. Not since the Battle of Jutland had Witt seen a squadron in action with all its guns blazing. Fascinated, he watched the spectacle. In any event that was all he could do. The units were keeping well out of range of his 150-millimetre battery in Fort Homat.

The shells churned up the ground. Direct hits in the Fort-des-Flamands. Stocks of ammunition going up. Big fires.

The squadron sailed up and down in front of the fortress. East of the harbour it came a little closer inshore. "Surely Hamburg battery ought to be able to get them now," Witt was thinking. At the same instant he could see the muzzle flashes: the heavy coastal batteries York, Brommy, and Hamburg were firing at the American naval units. York Battery scored hits on *Texas*, on a light cruiser, and on a destroyer. At the Hamburg battery Lieutenant Gelbhaar opened up with his four 240-millimetre guns and scored hits aboard two cruisers of the Cumberland class. True, the British Admiralty denied the loss of a cruiser, as assumed on the German side, but there were plenty of witnesses to confirm that highly effective direct hits had been scored—including army coastal artillery officers who would certainly be the last persons to credit the naval gunners with any unearned success. According to information released by the U.S. Navy Department on March 4, 1954, the German batteries engaging in duel with the Allied naval force scored direct hits on H.M.S. *Glasgow*, U.S.S. *Texas*, U.S.S. *Brien*, *U.S.S. Bardon*, and U.S.S. *Laffey*.

Towards 1200 the Allied squadron withdrew beyond the range of the German coastal batteries. Mass formations of Lightning bombers came screaming over to attack the German gun-positions.

By grid-pattern fire the naval fortress guns and the flak between them succeeded in shooting down eighty aircraft.

An hour later Schlieben's Intelligence officer made a highly significant entry on his situation-map: Fort-du-Roule had fallen.

It was obvious at a glance that the approach roads from the south were no longer covered: they were open to the enemy. The town and harbour had become a prize ready to be plucked by the Americans. Their heavy artillery was pounding the encircled heights of the suburb of Octeville below which lay the network of subterranean bunkers which housed the German command-posts.

American engineers were trying to blast these command-posts and thus paralyse the nerve centre of the German defence. That was the moment when Schlieben had sent out his urgent signal into the ether, asking the higher command whether there was still any need for the destruction of such forces as remained in Cherbourg. We already know Rommel's reply, logged in at 1548 and handed to Schlieben at 1552 hours: "In accordance with the Führer's orders you are to continue fighting to the last round."

The next few hours were charged with dramatic tension.

From the hill came the detonations of the charges intended to blast and block the southern exit gallery.

"We ought to blast the Americans off the hill-top, Herr Admiral!" Hennecke regarded the lieutenant doubtfully. Boldly the lieutenant continued: "I did the same thing at Saint-Marcouf—and successfully too. It was our only chance. I got our neighbouring battery at Azeville to open up at my bunker—enemy assault troops had got on top of it and were trying to force us out."

The man giving the admiral this somewhat unorthodox advice was Lieutenant Ohmsen. He had been brought to Hennecke's headquarters office by Blume, the admiral's orderly and situation officer. Hennecke reflected a while.

"Have you still got a line to the Cap de la Hague batteries, Blume?"

"Yes, Herr Admiral."

"Send a signal instructing them to pound our hill with their 250-millimetre long-barrel or their 203-millimetre cruiser guns. And inform General von Schlieben!"

But this time Ohmsen's recipe did not work. The Cap de la

Hague batteries had taken a heavy pasting from big-calibre naval guns and aerial bombs. The adjustment of the guns had been upset too much, and the battery commander was afraid of hitting the German defenders. Thus the Americans were able to carry on undisturbed with their drilling operations on top of the hill of Octeville.

Some 2000 wounded were lying in the hospitals of the compact town. Red Cross signs could not stop the shells. A slightly wounded, captured American captain asked the medical corps lieutenant to take him to Schlieben: he offered to cross the lines, to point out the location of the hospitals to the American commander, and to return with medical supplies.

Schlieben let him go. Maybe the captain was merely trying to dodge the inferno, but then, again, maybe he really would help. And help he did. Towards 1700 hours the captain returned with a consignment of pain-killing drugs and with a letter from the American commanding general. In it the general called on Schlieben to surrender: "You and your troops have resisted stubbornly and gallantly, but you are in a hopeless situation. The moment has come for you to capitulate. Send your reply by radio, on a frequency of 1520 kilocycles, and show a white flag or fire white signal-flares from the naval hospital or the Pasteur clinic. After that, send a staff officer under a flag of truce to the farmhouse on the road to Fort-du-Roule, to accept the terms of surrender."

Schlieben sent word to the captain that he had nothing to reply to the letter. He was playing for time—time to complete the last big demolitions in the harbour that would rule out the unloading of transports at Cherbourg for many months to come.

At exactly 1900 hours a tremendous tremor ran through the fortress. Captain Witt, the harbour commandant, had blown up the dock railway-station in accordance with orders. Piers and jetties were wrecked by thirty-five tons of dynamite. The old tower, Cherbourg's famous landmark, was also toppled into the harbour basin. Schlieben had hesitated for a long time about blowing up the tower. But military considerations had prevailed in the end. Its masonry would represent an additional complication to the restoration of the harbour basin to normal use. Cherbourg's famous silhouette had gone.

By 1910 hours assault troops of American engineers with flame-throwers and bunker-demolition charges had got to within a hundred yards of the northern exits of the underground head-quarters galleries. The general gave orders for all secret papers to be burnt. At 1932 his orderly officer, Lieutenant Kruspe, dispatched the last signal: "Last phase of fighting begun. General fighting side by side with his men."

Seventh Army bombastically replied: "We are with you." Schlieben could only smile resignedly as he read the signal.

Octeville surrenders

The underground galleries were chock-full with troops who had gained the safety of the bunker. They were utterly finished and were waiting for the end. Only corporals and sergeants were still pushing their way through the galleries, lugging ammunition-boxes to the exits where the commanding officers and their staffs were resisting with carbines, machine-pistols, and machine-guns in accordance with the order: "To the last round."

As Sub-Lieutenant Blume opened the steel door to the hospital gallery he was met by a stench that nearly took his breath away. Ursula Bräutigam, his efficient auxiliary, almost collided with him. She was helping in the hospital. At night she still kept the operations log.

"How are things here, Ursula?" Blume asked.

The girl made a resigned gesture. "Three hundred men crammed tight in the gallery. And, what's worse, they've been dying off like flies since yesterday."

"Why?" Blume inquired. Ursula Bräutigam shrugged her shoulders. "Better ask the chief medical officer."

A surgeon-ensign was coming along with blood-transfusion equipment. Blume asked him, "D'you know where the chief is?"

"He's been operating for the past five hours." The young doctor was anxious to get along. But Blume held him. "Why are the men dying?"

"Because the ventilation's packed up. The wounded are simply being poisoned. They are dying because the air is poor in oxygen, but full of gases and cordite fumes that have come down through the ventilation shafts from the demolitions and the explosions."

"And what can be done about it?"

"Nothing," replied the doctor. "Even gas-masks would be useless."

Blume returned to the exit of the right-hand northern gallery, where Schlieben and Hennecke, armed with carbines, were standing behind improvised breastworks. The Americans had just started lobbing mortar-shells at the concrete canopy above the gallery exits.

The sub-lieutenant reported on the situation in the hospital.

The two commanders withdrew a few steps down the gallery. They were talking. The others could hear the word "orders." And then Schlieben's voice, clearly: "If my superiors thought fit to make me a general, then they've got to accept the fact that I will act in accordance with the situation and with my conscience." This was not the first time that Karl Wilhelm von Schlieben had behaved in this way. In July 1943, while commanding the 18th Panzer Division in Russia, he had led his troops out of encirclement to freedom by defying orders. Now he was determined to save at least the bare lives of his men.

Then the words "flag of truce" were heard. The news spread through the galleries like wildfire: "The old man is sending off an officer under a flag of truce! He's putting an end to it!" It was like a great sigh of relief.

As the white sheet tied to a rifle was held out of the bunker entrance the enemy fire fell silent. It was a terrifying silence that was suddenly brooding over the tormented town. Two officers walked out with the white flag. The time was a little after 1400 hours on June 26.

The battle for the nerve centre of the fortress of Cherbourg was over. The hillside spewed out a long stream of soldiers, sailors, officers, and administrative officials.

Schlieben and Hennecke were taken over by American officers at the exit of the gallery and conducted to General Eddy, the commander of the 9th U.S. Division on top of the hill of Octeville. Eddy drove off with the two Germans to General Collins's corps headquarters, nineteen miles south of Cherbourg. The photographers were already lined up. Cameras clicked. And presently thousands of copies of the picture were dropped by enemy propaganda units over the lines where the Germans were still resisting. That, too, was a part of modern warfare.

Meanwhile, an interesting argument was taking place behind the scenes. A number of American officers suggested to First Army that General Bradley should invite Schlieben to supper. There was much argument in favour and against at U.S. headquarters. In the end Bradley himself settled the issue with typically American logic: "If Schlieben had surrendered four days earlier I'd have asked him. But now that he has cost us a pile of human lives—no!" Well, Bradley was to have a good deal more annoyance from similar characters before he was through with them.

As far as the troops and the regimental officers were concerned, there was no argument among the Americans about asking them to dinner. The loudspeakers blared: "Keep moving!" and the G.I.'s shouted: "Mak snell!"

Ursula Bräutigam, the padre, and Frau Wist—the same Frau Wist who had given a recital in the Cherbourg officers' mess on June 5—were loaded on a lorry and subsequently exchanged for British nurses in German captivity.

Sub-Lieutenant Blume, Lieutenant Kruspe, and Corporal Kröhne from Sand near Kassel were taken from the P.O.W. collection point and packed into a jeep. Their destination was U.S. headquarters at Yvetot to join Schlieben and Hennecke.

Off they went, heavily guarded like dangerous criminals. An American sergeant was sitting on the edge of the jeep, his finger on the trigger of his tommy-gun.

"Look at the road they're taking us!" exclaimed Kruspe. Blume looked round. Then, in his best school English, he said to the escort officer, who was sitting next to the driver, "You are driving along a mined road."

"Shut up, son-of-a-bitch!" the American snarled. The bang occurred almost instantaneously. They had hit a mine.

The shock and the jolt caused the sergeant to squeeze the trigger. The burst of fire killed the two Americans and the German corporal. The sergeant himself had his belly ripped open by a splinter. Only Kruspe and Blume got away with their lives, though heavily wounded. Blume had a tommy-gun bullet in his head.

The fall of Octeville, of course, did not mean that the whole of the large town and harbour were in American hands. Schlieben had expressly surrendered only his own headquarters. The commanders of the various districts, especially in the strongly fortified arsenal, had to make their own decisions. They all knew that what mattered most was to gain time.

It was obvious, however, that any prolonged resistance was out of the question. Panic was rife. The fighting morale nearly everywhere was at zero. True, behind the ramparts of the naval arsenal there were still strong and effective units under Major-General Sattler, the town commandant. But unlike Captain Witt, the harbour commandant, Sattler did not believe in further resistance. He surrendered on the morning of June 27 and, together with 400 men, was taken into captivity.

Captain Witt, on the other hand, did not give up yet. He ordered a Labour Service unit to seal off the rampart along the dock basin, personally saw to the last demolitions, and, on the receding tide, with eight officers and thirty other ranks, crossed to the fortifications on the outer mole in a yacht and two dinghies. There, at Fort West, was the firing-panel for the still intact minefields off the big western harbour entrance. Whoever had his finger on the button there could block the entrance.

Naval Group West in Paris were considerably surprised when they received a signal as late as June 27: "Battle headquarters of harbour commandant now at Fort West. Mine detonation panel ready for action."

Back came an astonished signal from Paris: "How was move made to Fort West?"

Laconically, Witt replied: "Aboard yacht and two dinghies at first light."

The captain could not have foreseen that this exchange of signals would provide the material for a heroic broadcast account of his exploit. It was a stirring tale. Its only weakness was that the Americans monitored it.

General Collins, whose lightning victories scored with his 25th U.S. Division over the Japanese had earned him the flattering nickname of "Lightning Joe," was already furious at the delay of his Cherbourg operation. His reputation was beginning to suffer. He could not afford any heroics by German centres of resistance. The battle against Witt became a matter of prestige for him.

Nevertheless, it took the Americans three days to subdue the fortifications on the outer mole by artillery and aerial bombardment. Only when the mine detonation panel in Fort West had been smashed by concrete-piercing shells did Witt, now wounded, give in.

On the western sector of the Cherbourg front, in the "communications peninsula"—so called because of the numerous pieces of telecommunication equipment installed there by the Navy and the Luftwaffe for the observation of the English south coast—resistance also continued for some time. The units involved there were the combat group Keil with the regimental headquarters and 2nd Battalion, 919th Grenadier Regiment, the Assault Battalion Messerschmitt, and the 17th MG Battalion. Artillery support was provided by the Artillery Group West under Major Quittnat and the light flak-gunners of the 932nd. Farther to the west the combat group Müller was holding out with parts of 922nd Grenadier Regiment and two batteries of 243rd Artillery Regiment.

They gave the 9th American Division a good run for their money. Every single strongpoint was stubbornly contested. Not until June 30 did the remaining centres of resistance on the west coast of the Jobourg peninsula capitulate.

On the other end of the front, seven and a half miles from the city centre, fighting continued until June 28. That was where the powerful Osteck fortification, built by the Todt Organization, commanded the airfield and the coast.

Gunners against Tanks

In his command-post, right in the centre of a well-camouflaged network of underground bunkers, communication trenches, anti-tank obstacles, and minefields, Major Küppers stood with his eyes glued to the periscope, like a captain of a submarine going into action on the high seas.

Enemy tanks were cautiously advancing. But this would be no walkover. The modern strongpoint with its cunning tank-traps, its automatically touched-off banks of mortars and flame-throwers, its radar and wireless devices, was still barring the VII American Corps's advance to the northern coast of the Cotentin peninsula.

Staff Lance-Corporal Johann Koch was in the signals bunker on June 26 when the last message came through from General Schlieben's headquarters. The artillery commander Cherbourg signalled to his group commander of the sector "East": "We're giving up. Can do no more. All the best. Reiter."

"Nip over to the commander," Staff Sergeant Wittwer said to Koch, "and give him the signal."

"What is it?" asked Küppers without taking his eyes from the periscope's eyepiece.

"Signal from Colonel Reiter," the lance-corporal repeated.

The date was June 26 and the time exactly 1400 hours. Küppers read out the signal in a subdued voice. The officers and N.C.O.'s present realized that this was the beginning of the end also for Osteck, for the left flank of the fortress of Cherbourg with its super-battery Hamburg, its coastal strongpoint Seeadler, and its flak strongpoint Ritter.

Küppers telephoned to the communications bunker and

inquired if the artillery commander Cherbourg had passed on the frequencies for radio communication with Corps or with Army.

The answer was no. "We tried to put an inquiry through ourselves, but there's no reply from the Octeville command-post." It was too late for radio contact. The Americans were at all the exits of the galleries under the hill of Saint-Sauveur, frisking the German troops as they filed out.

"See if you can make contact with any headquarters," Küppers ordered the signallers. The wireless-operators slowly turned the dials to their receivers. They listened. They retuned. They listened again.

At last a contact was made with 319th Infantry Division stationed on Guernsey, and eventually also with a naval headquarters in Le Havre. That night, over both circuits, the combat group Osteck sent out a coded report on the situation for retransmission to 84th Corps and Seventh Army. To anyone reading the report it must have been clear that in spite of its powerful guns Cherbourg's Osteck could not hope to hold out much longer.

Küppers's report stated: 9th and 10th Batteries, 1709th Artillery Regiment and 7th Battery, 1261st Army Coastal Artillery Regiment at Tourlaville–Bretteville overrun by enemy armour.

"Overrun!" It sounds cool and factual. "7th, 9th, and 10th Batteries." Just a few figures. But behind these figures is the fate of a few hundred men—unnamed companions who had been manning guns—and of their horses and transport.

Küppers's report continued: 5th Battery, 1709th and flak battery Hamburg ready for action. A flanking gun of Gelbhaar's 240-millimetre naval target battery Hamburg converted for operation against land targets by the blasting away of the concrete roof-slab.

Any officers and men who succeeded in reaching Osteck from lost or disbanded batteries of the 1261st and 1262nd Army Coastal Artillery Regiments were immediately organized into infantry units. Among them were also the survivors of 11th Battery, 1709th, and 5th Battery, 1262nd. They were brought into Osteck by Staff-Sergeant Schneider and Second Lieutenant Schwulst. The fate of the grenadiers of Katzmann's battalion, which had been holding the position outside Gonneville and along the airfield, remained unknown.

In the early hours of June 27 American infantry were seen through the periscope to be swarming over the high ground, making for the western side of Ritter's flak strongpoint which barred the road from the airfield. Tanks were rumbling along amidst the charging infantry. Ritter's flak battery was blazing away furiously.

The first tank was knocked out. The second was in flames. But already three or four others were bursting into the strongpoint. Now was the moment for Sergeant Gradert and his men of the 11th Battery. They had been lying in ambush as tank-destruction parties. In short leaps and bounds, from cover to cover, they were now making for the Shermans, their *Panzerfausts* tucked under their arms.

Another twenty yards. Steady now.

The American tank was opening up with its machine-gun. Another ten yards. Now. Hissing, the fiery rocket streaked from the barrel. Its explosive head smacked against the turret.

A flash like lightning. A crash. The Sherman was blazing like a torch. Its crew tried to bail out. They crumpled in the submachine-gun fire.

Corporal Kühnast also got a tank right in front of his bazooka. It was the leading tank. Direct hit below the turret. Evidently right in the ammunition stack, since it blew up at once. The two remaining Shermans turned tail and made off. The accompanying infantry surged back or was mown down by machine-gun fire.

"Enemy attack against eastern land front," Second Lieuten-

Sherman

ant Czychon, on periscope watch, called out half an hour later.

Major Küppers peered into the eyepiece. Sure enough. The Americans were now attempting a different method. They were trying to overrun the remaining strongpoints on the eastern sector of the landward front, between Nos. 410 and 418, from the rear, and so to capture the position of Hamburg battery.

Mines without Detonators

There was an excellent view through the periscope. The fire of artillery and flak batteries could be neatly and accurately controlled without endangering one's own troops.

The 240-millimetre flanking gun of Hamburg battery was keeping the enemy's supplies under harassing fire. Enemy fighter-bombers were trying to silence this annoying obstacle. The naval guns were aiming their shells at the emplacement. But for once Gelbhaar's useful spitfire was fortunate.

The flak and field guns of the German artillery group were putting up a continuous barrage in front of the American armoured spearhead. It was a fantastic fireworks display—a blazing curtain of fire. When the third American tank went up in flames the rest turned away. The accompanying infantry withdrew.

But instantly the American commander switched his attack to the other side. Once more U.S. armour charged the high ground around Maupertus along the coastal road. But this attack, too, was halted by well-aimed gunfire.

Furiously, the American naval gunners fired salvo after salvo upon Osteck and the Hamburg battery.

From the north-east a strong enemy column was now approaching. They took up position in an enclosed field, quite unconcerned, their vehicles all bunched together. Like a gigantic fist the shells of Küppers's 5th Battery and the Hamburg flak crashed down upon them. Losses must have been heavy. But already another powerful armoured formation was approaching from the south. This American army was truly inexhaustible, like some modern hydra. Whenever one armoured head was cut off, another two, three, or half a dozen appeared immediately.

The "six-embrasure turret South" received a direct hit. The two machine mortars near by were put out of action. Suddenly the enemy tanks were within the strongpoint site.

"White flag on six-embrasure turret South," the man at the periscope reported. Its depot personnel had hoisted the flag of surrender. Their commanding officer, Lieutenant Zerban, summoned by Major Küppers to the command-post, merely shrugged his shoulders. "What can you expect of elderly reservists who aren't used to fighting?" he asked resignedly. Küppers glared at him, then pressed his eyes against the periscope. His thoughts were reflected by the command he gave through to 5th Battery: "Open fire at six-embrasure turret South!" Küppers personally directed the salvoes until the white flag had been shot off its staff.

Lieutenant Schwalbe was ordered to clear up the penetration at the southern anti-tank ditch with his tank-demolition party. Lieutenant Staake and his men were likewise employed against the south-westerly area, in the direction of the six-embrasure turret.

"How do the enemy tanks manage to get through the minefield without any losses?" Küppers asked in astonishment. Lieutenant Zerban was able to explain the miracle. The mines did not have detonators. Not enough detonators had been supplied for priming all the mines. Naturally enough, more and more tanks were now pushing through this gap into the outer strongpoint after some initial losses at other spots.

"A fine mess," Sergeant Planer grumbled. "I'd like to send whoever is responsible down to the anti-tank ditch right now!" But then, who was responsible for this and for much else in the Cotentin peninsula? Who? The question was being asked by the living, and it was being asked by the dead in the unending rows of graves all along the road from Carentan to Osteck via Sainte-Mère-Eglise–Montebourg–Valognes–Théville.

Tanks now also attacked the six-embrasure turret East and with well-aimed fire silenced it.

"All personnel into the bunkers for close-combat defence!"

Lieutenant Schwalbe and his men were holding the anti-tank gun-bunker at the eastern entrance, and Lieutenant Staake with his gunners of 5th Battery mopped up the area around the radar bunker. But what was the use of it? American infantry in company strength had in the meantime rushed across the unprimed mine-belt and got across the anti-tank ditch. The depot personnel of the mortar emplacement had already surrendered. Küppers now applied the well-tried recipe of ordering 5th Battery, 1709th and the Hamburg battery to direct their fire upon his own position. The American infantry were pinned down in front and on top of the bunkers. The tank crews were getting jumpy. But Osteck was not to be cleared of the enemy in this way.

Right on top of the grass-covered periscope bunker the Americans, all unsuspecting, set up an observer-post to direct their fire against the Hamburg battery. The Americans had not yet spotted the carefully camouflaged periscope, but Küppers had spotted them. He called up Lieutenant Gruber, the C.O. of 5th Battery. With its third round Gruber's roving gun scored a direct hit. A slight tremor was felt inside the bunker. On top, the American O.P. had been blown away.

Jeep with White Flag

By about 2100 hours American engineers had moved up to the periscope bunker and were trying to blast open the entrances.

"We'll have to shake them off, Herr Major!" Sergeant Planer remarked. Küppers nodded. "Get an assault party together!"

Küppers took charge of it personally. Like a pack of devils they burst out of the gallery. Corporal Panschütz with his machine-gun cleared the road for them. Sergeant Planer, Corporal Koch, and Corporal Notermanns kept the Americans down with hand-grenades. Küppers with three men drove off the demolition party. Then a burst of carbine fire hit them from the flank. Panschütz dropped in his tracks. His machine-gun fell silent. The others scuttled back into the gallery.

The Americans were becoming more cautious. At dusk they retired as the result of artillery fire. But by 2145 hours the Germans had spent their last shells. All they had left was twenty smoke-shells.

Then began a war of nerves. From a captured bunker the Americans telephoned through to the command-post and demanded its surrender. "To-morrow morning we'll bomb everything to smithereens. Then it will be too late to surrender," the voice on the telephone said in broken German. Loudspeakers started blaring outside the bunkers. They reported the fall of Cherbourg.

Küppers knew that his resistance could only be short-lived. He consulted his officers. "Let's wait till the morning," was their decision.

Towards 0300 on June 28 an American jeep with a white flag drove up to the periscope bunker. Its occupant, a lieutenant bearing a flag of truce, was met at the main entrance. He demanded "unconditional surrender."

"For that we don't need a parley under a flag of truce," returned Küppers. "Tell that to your commanding officer. And tell him also that I am prepared to discuss with him fair terms of surrender, if only in order to settle the question of care for the wounded and the handing over of our American prisoners."

The American lieutenant made no reply and roared off.

Shortly after 0800 hours Lieutenant Czychon, on periscope watch, called out, "Several jeeps under a white flag approaching Osteck entrance!"

This time it was the commander of the 4th U.S. Division, Major-General Barton. He had come, accompanied by his personal staff, to propose surrender to Major Küppers.

The general had been fortress commandant of Ehrenbreitstein after the First World War. He evidently had pleasant memories of Germany, and when he heard that Küppers's home was in Wiesbaden a friendly private conversation got going immediately.

"Time is running short," one of his staff officers finally reminded him. Barton nodded, asked for his general staff map, and spread it out in front of Küppers. The large-scale attack scheduled for June 28 was clearly marked on it. "I'll be quite frank with you and show you just what's going to happen the moment our negotiations break down." The general pointed to the map, which contained details of the forces earmarked for the attack. They were the reinforced 22nd Infantry Regiment, the 5th Ranger Battalion, the 24th Tank Battalion, as well as divisional and corps artillery.

"The map doesn't show what's going to hit you from the air and from the sea, but I think you have a pretty good idea. So why resist any further? I admire the fighting spirit of your troops, and I have been truly amazed by the skill of your artillery group with which I've been involved all the way from Montebourg. Your people have given me a lot of trouble."

"May I have a look at the map?" Küppers asked.

"Go right ahead," Barton replied with a smile.

Küppers understood why the general could afford to smile. The entire network of German positions was shown on the map with absolute accuracy, and in far greater detail than on their own maps. On the back were listed precise data about the types of weapons and ammunition at each emplacement and bunker, as well as the names of all strongpoint commanders, and of the battalion and regimental commanders to whom they were responsible. The adjoining sheet covered the former defence

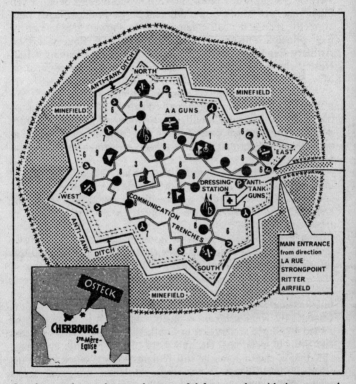

Osteck, a modern underground system of defence works, with the command-post of Artillery Group East under Major Küppers. Küppers held the eastern landward front until June 28. Key to the numbers: 1. Periscope bunker. 2. Command-post of strongpoint commander. 3. Radar station. 4. Communication-posts. 5. Six-embrasure turrets North, West, South, and East. 6. Mortar positions with automatic fire control. 7. Flame-thrower positions. 8. Troops' bunkers. 9. Observation-post facing Cherbourg harbour.

sector. "East," in the Saint-Pierre-Eglise area outside the Cherbourg fortified zone.

To his amazement Küppers found that on this sheet, too, the German positions had been entered down to the last detail. Even the numbers of troops in the different billets in the villages were correctly recorded. All command-posts showed the names of their principal officers. True, the entry for 11th Battery, 1709th Artillery Regiment still listed as its commander Lieutenant Ralf Neste, who had lost his life in an accident with a *Panzerfaust* on May 5, 1944—but that seemed to be the only mistake.

General Barton noticed Küppers's tremendous surprise. "We left nothing to chance," he remarked calmly. "Before we started out on the invasion our Intelligence service had got hold of every detail of the German coastal defences, complete with the measures listed in your detailed area schedules, straight from original German plans."

There was silence inside the bunker. There was silence outside. Not a shot rang out. Not a single voice called out for a stretcher. Küppers's mind was revolving round and round the same question: How had the enemy been able to find out all these details?

And yet the answer was by no means difficult. An army of agents in occupied France had been collecting the information— information provided by careless talk, by thoughtless actions, and by traitors. The French Resistance fighters had done the rest. All the information picked up, overheard, or nosed out by billetors and by "willing helpers" had been taken across the Channel by countless carrier-pigeons to the pigeon-lofts of the Allied Intelligence services in Southern England. Their success had been tremendous. The full story of this gigantic espionage and Intelligence operation still remains to be written. It is the story of the Alliance of Animals, that most important secret intelligence organization of the Allies in France; the story of "Panther," the French Colonel Alamichel who set up the organization; the story of Colonel Fay, who was known as "Lion"; and of Marie-Madeleine Merrie, that young, pretty, and courageous Frenchwoman who oddly enough bore the code-name of *Chérisson* ("Hedgehog").

The Alliance had 2000 regular, paid collaborators in France: principal agents, agents, wireless-operators, couriers, and liaison men. These had woven a vast information-gathering network over the whole of France. They were installed in the Todt

Organization, in the billeting-offices, and in the town halls. They were employed as charwomen in the living-quarters and staff offices of the German army of occupation. They smiled at them as waiters in canteens and Forces clubs. They acted as interpreters. They even included German traitors, misguided or blackmailed. The chief of the Alliance had three headquarters in Paris for his staff of officers and for his British chief radio-operator, "Magpie." One of these headquarters was the contact point for couriers, the second was an alternative headquarters for emergencies, and the third, in the Rue Charles Lafitte, was headed by "Odette," the famous Odette. At these headquarters all the information converged. Here it was sorted according to Army, Navy, Air Force, political or economic, and photographed on microfilm. Urgent information was radioed to London in code. Contact with London was also provided by aircraft and speedboats in league with the skippers of small coastal craft and fishing trawlers. The Alliance of Animals represented an exciting chapter of the secret war in France: cunning, brutal, self-sacrificing, bold, and dirty—all at the same time.

General Barton's maps were a result of that work—one among many.

Küppers's consultation with his officers did not take long. Every one of them knew that to continue the struggle under those conditions was useless. Common sense demanded that it should be ended.

At 1330 hours General Barton shook hands with Major Küppers. The date was June 28. At Osteck and in the battery positions the war was over. The men wearily retraced the path by which they had come—all the way back to Utah Beach. There the latest casualties joined the first. Many an exhausted, elderly soldier was drowned because he lacked the strength to breast the water as they waded out to the waiting transports.

The end was gloomy, just as the whole battle for Cherbourg had been. When the German communiqué announced the fall of the naval fortress the officers and men at the headquarters in Le Havre and the Channel Islands merely shook their heads in despair. For weeks they had been onlookers in a grandstand, watching the inadequate German forces being swallowed up piecemeal in the vortex of the battle. They still failed to grasp the colossal mistake committed by the German military command when it allowed crack divisions to stand by idly on the Channel instead of throwing them into the battle of the beach-heads.

To us to-day the blunder seems almost inconceivable. And yet it proves that modern war, for all its technical complexity, is decided as much by miscalculations as by weapons. There is a lesson in that for those who think of power only in terms of technical superiority.

The Cost of Miscalculation

At the time of the fall of Cherbourg there were more German divisions standing inactive in their quarters between the Seine and the Scheldt alone than were engaging the enemy on the invasion front. Why? Because the Führer's headquarters and the German High Command was obsessed by the idea that the Normandy landing was no more than a diversionary manoeuvre, and that the main blow was yet to fall at the narrowest point of the Channel, in the Pas de Calais.

It was this mistake that determined the German counter-measures from the very first day of the Allied landing.

An army group, consisting of two armies with twenty-four infantry and five Luftwaffe field divisions, as well as an armoured group of six armoured divisions, had been standing ready for action in Northern France, Belgium, and the Netherlands at the beginning of June. But forty-eight hours after Allied assault forces had landed on three separate coastal sectors in Normandy, the German counter-measures were still only on the scale of regiments, battalions, and combat groups. Even when divisions were involved in the operations only some of their units were in fact in the line. These units fought magnificently well, but—paradoxical as this may sound when one thinks of the thirty-five German divisions—they were invariably outnumbered owing to the attacker's creation of local centres of gravity and because of the German strategy of makeshifts and stopgaps. Even during the first two days of the invasion the German Command incessantly offended against Guderian's slogan of "Not driblets, but mass!" In a war of driblets the German defensive positions, small tactical reserves, and combat groups were written off one by one. And that in spite of their successful resistance which often brought the enemy to the very brink of defeat.

But the German Command missed its opportunities. It was weighed down by the nightmarish fear that further large-scale landing operations might, indeed were bound to, take place at other points of the coast. The dummy fleet in the British ports and the cardboard-and-plywood army encampments in Kent, mistaken for the real things by German reconnaissance crews, served to confirm the High Command in its *idée fixe*. Moreover, the rules governing amphibious operations were unknown to the generals of the German High Command. Divisions were allowed to stand to on the west coast of France for fear of further landings, although such landings were in fact impossible in those areas because of weather and beach conditions. Thus, the paradoxical situation arose that by the end of June the Americans alone had landed on their sector of the front four corps with fourteen divisions, which were opposed on the German side by only three intact divisions and the remnants of three shattered divisions and five regiments—a fighting force roughly equivalent, allowing for its equipment, to five divisions. Yet entire armies were helplessly watching the German tragedy from their quarters on the southern and western coasts of France and in the seaside resorts of Belgium and Holland: pinned down by orders based on a total misreading of the situation.

The Australian author Chester Wilmot, by far the most outstanding of Allied war reporters, has this to say about it:

> By June 26th, when Cherbourg fell, there were 25 Allied divisions in the bridgehead. . . . In the United Kingdom there were 15 divisions awaiting shipment to Normandy, and half a dozen training divisions supplying reinforcements for the British Army on all fronts. Yet on this same day the best German Intelligence opinion was that "The enemy is employing 27 to 31 divisions in the bridgehead and a large number of G.H.Q. troops. . . . *In England another 67 major formations are standing to, of which 57 at the very least can be employed for a large-scale operation.*"
>
> The 42 non-existent divisions which German Intelligence placed in Eisenhower's reserve were the brainchildren of British guile and German stupidity. Allied agents had had no difficulty in 'selling' the Germans an absurdly inflated Anglo-American Order of Battle, for . . . the Intelligence Branch at O.K.H. had been eager to buy. . . . These spurious divisions clouded the

judgment of the German High Command and helped to distort its strategy.

Cherbourg was the first fruit of this distorted German strategy. It was not the only one.

6

BETWEEN CAEN AND SAINT-LÔ

Hill 112

Between the Orne and *route nationale* 175, leading from Avranches to Caen, flows the Odon. It is a little stream, running into the Orne south of Caen. Not many people had heard of it prior to 1944. But to-day tens of thousands of former German and British soldiers remember that fateful stream only too well. On some days its flow was dammed by the piled-up dead bodies of men killed in action.

And on some days this little river and its bridges were more cursed about than even the blood-drenched Hill 112, the pivoting point of Montgomery's Odon offensive.

The British did not want to be outdone by the Americans when Eisenhower's VII Corps was attacking Cherbourg. They wanted their own victory. And they wanted it where it had been denied them for many weeks, at Caen, which had been scheduled in Montgomery's timetable for capture on D+1, the second day of the invasion. By this time it was D+16.

On June 22 the British and Canadian units opened their offensive after an unimaginable artillery barrage. They intended to strike across the little Odon river to the Orne, occupying the strategically important Hill 112, and then capture the town by an outflanking attack. That was the plan.

The British came up against the 12th S.S. Panzer Division "Hitlerjugend." The battle that followed was one of the most frightful of the entire Second World War. Some battalions were overrun. Companies were crushed to pulp. The tanks of the 11th British Armoured Division charged furiously against the German anti-tank gun-positions. They achieved a penetration. If the break-through across the Odon valley could now also be accomplished, then Caen must fall and the German front in Normandy would be cracked wide open.

Montgomery's armoured divisions were opposed only by remnants of German formations, by small groups, and by individual grenadiers lying in sunken lanes, their *Panzerfaust* at the ready. And here were the Shermans. One, two, three, four of them. Now was the moment when an individual might still engage in battle against a modern war machine, perhaps for the last time in military history.

One such individual was Emil Dürr, a young man of twenty. He burst from out of the hedge. With his *Panzerfaust* he set the Sherman on fire. He then grabbed his sticky bomb[1] and flung it against the side of the second tank. But the bomb dropped off. Dürr snatched it up and held it against the steel plate. The tank blew up. Emil Dürr was killed. The third Sherman was knocked out by the anti-tank gun. The fourth was finished off by another *Panzerfaust*. But what were four tanks? Over by the reconnaissance company another group was approaching. They overran the last German anti-tank gun, wheeled on top of the firing pits, and crushed the cannon together with its crew. British infantry, riding on the tanks, kept up furious small-arms fire and thus prevented *Panzerfaust* attacks. The commander of the 12th S.S. Panzer Division, Meyer, was right in front with his division escort company, himself carrying a *Panzerfaust*. Suddenly a tremendous roar was heard above the crash of the shellbursts. And there it was—a German *Tiger*, that armoured miracle weapon of the Second World War. Just one *Tiger*. But its 88-millimetre cannon stopped the Shermans. They turned away. But for how long?

North of Caen, where the grenadiers and tanks of 21st Panzer Division had been in position since June 6, the situation was also beginning to look ugly.

During the night of June 22–23 a British assault unit, after a heavy preliminary bombardment, broke into the defensive position of 5th Company, 192nd Panzer Grenadier Regiment on the road from Douvres to Caen. The road-block was thus swept away and the road into Caen was open.

The disastrous news brought Major Vierzig out of his bed in the little Château de la Londe. ''Immediate counter-attack!'' he commanded.

---

[1] Sticky bombs: explosive charges in adhesive-coated containers.

Lieutenant Meyer, with some of the headquarters company of the 2nd Panzer Battalion, again dislodged the British from the German position. But no sooner was this danger averted than a new one arose along the Périers-Caen road, north-west of the Château de la Londe. The grenadiers had fallen back to the château. The road was clear. The British might tear open the picket line of the 2nd Panzer Battalion.

Vierzig got hold of his orderly officer, Second Lieutenant Lotze, a man of twenty-two. "You'll have to put things right, Lotze. But because of the uncertainty of the situation I can't spare you more than ten men." Lotze was not exactly enthusiastic, but since the penetration was believed to be only in platoon strength he thought that with one sergeant and ten men, whom he presently picked from the headquarters company and 220th Panzer Pioneer Battalion, he might manage.

They set out at first light. Cover on the left was provided by Sergeant Dietsch with a machine-pistol, on the right by Lance-Corporal Moller with a machine-gun. They worked their way forward right up to the trench occupied by the Tommies. Lotze intended to do the job in the traditional infantry way: leap up, yell wildly, open fire, and down into the trench. And then enfilade with the machine-gun.

He talked encouragingly to his men. He knew that this was necessary: the days of going into battle cheering had long since passed. He made them see that this was their only chance against an enemy who outnumbered them by, probably, thirty men. So off they went. Lotze leapt up first. He yelled. And the others yelled and banged away as if a whole battalion was charging.

The British sentry fired. Moller was hit in the thigh. But he got to the edge of the trench and hammered away with his machine-gun. The others were already lying at the parapet, firing down into the trench. Lotze's pistol barked. The hand-grenades crashed into their short length of trench. Suddenly a whistle shrilled and the first arms reached up.

"Cease fire," Lotze shouted. "Hands up!"

All arms flew up inside the trench.

Lotze and Dietsch got to their feet.

"Good heavens!" The fright nearly made them fling themselves down again. Before them they saw not twenty or thirty men, but a whole company. Half a dozen were lying in the trench dead or wounded, and the others were standing up with their hands above their heads.

Lotze grabbed the British lieutenant round whose neck dangled the whistle. "How many men?" he asked him.

"Eighty-four," the officer replied.

Lotze felt slightly sick at the thought of his little band of ten men. "Only needs a couple of lunatics in that lot, and our little party'll be over," he was thinking.

He made the lieutenant stand beside him and, gesturing with his pistol, made him understand that if any of his men tried anything it would be the end of him, the lieutenant. The British officer nodded. He ordered his men to fall in, and in marching order they went off along the road to German headquarters. Major Vierzig's eyes nearly popped out when he saw the procession approaching.

The Panzer battalion's report to Division on June 23, which survives in the original—though slightly singed at the edges—contains the passage: "In this operation the enemy, including his dead, lost about one company. At 0700 hours the defensive position of 5th Company, 192nd was again in our hands."

"Yes, indeed," Oskar Lotze, now an engineer in Southern Germany, reminisced. "We were slightly mad. And when the British lieutenant held out his hand to me back at headquarters I did not even understand what he wanted. Our twenty-two heroic years had not left any room in our minds for the realization that after a sensibly concluded battle the opponents might shake hands just like after a football match. I'm still hoping I might meet the man again one day in order to shake both his hands."

In the afternoon of June 27, just as the battle of Cherbourg was nearing its conclusion, the British succeeded in establishing a bridgehead at Caen across the Odon with their 11th Armoured Division. A few tanks penetrated as far as Meyer's divisional battle headquarters at Verson. The headquarters staff were already crouching in foxholes clutching their *Panzerfausts*. Farther south, too, the British had succeeded in seizing a bridge over the Odon. Slowly they were worming their way towards Hill 112, the key position to the whole sector.

"Hill 112 must be held," was the order from Corps. Max Wünsche's Panzer regiment was to occupy it in order to prevent the threatening enemy break-through to the Orne bridges.

At last, in the evening of June 28, reinforcements arrived for the German counter-attack: three more S.S. Panzer divisions. It sounded most promising. But that was about all. For while several Panzer divisions were idly standing by in Holland and in the south of France in order to meet the imaginary second invasion, the German High Command had pulled out the 9th and 10th S.S. Panzer Divisions from heavy defensive fighting in Poland in order to employ them in Normandy. The badly mauled 1st S.S. Panzer Division had been transferred from Russia to Belgium for rest and replenishment.

It was with these—by no means fully operational—units that the general commanding the 2nd S.S. Panzer Corps, Obergruppenführer[1] Hausser, was to mount his offensive on June 29 against Montgomery's strong assault divisions in order to turn the tide. Hitler and the German High Command placed their hopes in the S.S. divisions hardened on the Eastern front.

June 29 was ushered in by the roar of British heavy naval guns. Their shells crashed down on Caen. "To-day's going to be lively," the troops were saying, glancing up at the sky. Fighter-bombers were hovering above, ready to strike. The moment anything moved, down they pounced. British artillery, moreover, was trying to get the range of Hill 112. Slowly at first, but intensively before long. "Damn!" the grenadiers cursed. They had an uneasy feeling that there was worse to come.

The fighter-bombers were hanging in the clear sky like a swarm of hornets. The naval guns were roaring ceaselessly, sending over salvo upon salvo, until it was almost impossible to hear oneself speak.

"That's a fine start!" the men in their positions were shouting to one another. It was the morning of June 29. The divisional headquarters of "Panzer" Meyer was at Verson. An armoured car was racing through the narrow streets. Like a sparrow-hawk the "duty fighter-bomber" plummeted down from the sky. Its cannon stuttered. The burst tore open the pavement and straddled its target. The ammunition in the vehicle blew up. An ambulance was treated with no more respect. In an instant it was blazing fiercely. It was impossible to save the wounded. "Oh damn! Damn! Damn!" screamed the medical corporal. He buried his face in his burnt hands. He was crying.

Hill 112 was under concentrated artillery bombardment. "Suppose the British have anticipated us? Suppose they, too, are launching an offensive to-day, and their attack strikes at our assembly positions?" the troops were speculating. And, true enough, tanks of the 2nd British Armoured Division were already climbing up the slopes of the Odon valley, moving in the direction of Hill 112. The top of the hill was no longer visible.

---

[1] Rank in S.S. troops equivalent to general.

Heavey-calibre shells were ploughing over the fertile Norman soil, yard by yard.

There could be no doubt any longer. The British had forestalled the attack by Hausser's divisions. Ceaseless artillery fire and aerial bombardment thundered down on the German formations in their assembly positions: the very worst thing that can happen to troops and to army commanders.

Shortly after 0900 hours the field telephone rang at the position of the 6th Battery, 83rd Mortar Regiment, barely 800 yards behind Hill 112. Sergeant Doorn lifted the receiver. He listened. He replaced it and raced over to Captain Gengl, who was just then with the battery. "Herr Hauptmann, telephone message from the O.P. on Hill 112. Gunner Kuschow reports that enemy tanks are at the top. There is a Sherman within five yards of his foxhole. He asks that he should not be rung up. He's going to try to make his way back through the enemy lines. He does not know what has become of Lieutenant Wernicke, Second Lieutenant Nitschmann, or the other three men of the O.P. Probably overrun."

"That's not too good, Doorn," muttered Gengl. Then he ordered: "Battery personnel, with the exception of six men, will get ready for infantry action. Form two tank-demolition parties."

The gunners got within a hundred yards of Hill 112. Sergeant Doorn's tank-demolition party even got a little farther. But then the British machine-guns began to rake the cornfield through which the gunners were advancing. The first to be hit was Lance-Corporal Trautz, the next was Gunner Krautz. Doorn and Lance-Corporal Lübbe had great difficulty in getting their wounded companions out of the line of fire. The others, too, were forced to withdraw. The British were holding the hill not just with a few tanks, but already with anti-tank guns and part of a machine-gun battalion.

Hill 112 was lost. The British had gained the key to further operations against the Orne bridges. They had a clear field of vision over the whole area. No movement on the German side could escape their notice. This could well be fatal.

The heavy howitzer battalion of 12th S.S. Artillery Regiment and the mortar batteries of Colonel Tzschökell's 7th Mortar Brigade opened up on the British spearheads. The Tommies got a heavy pasting. But would it help?

It was easy to calculate exactly when the enemy would have brought up sufficient reserves to wheel from Hill 112 towards the town. "Panzer" Meyer was already regrouping the remnants of his divisions for the all-round defence of Caen. He was going to try to hold at least the town itself.

But Gruppenführer[1] Bittrich, the new commander of the 2nd S.S. Panzer Corps, refused to write off the offensive so easily. He ordered Hill 112 to be retaken.

In the grey dawn of June 30 the hill was the target of concentrated German artillery fire and especially of mortar fire. Max Wünsche ordered his tanks to creep ahead under cover of the slight haze. Steady! Not too much noise! It was almost as if the tanks were crouching. They waited for the pauses in the artillery fire. Then they burst forward. They had their well-tried technique. This technique demanded: drive on regardless, firing anti-personnel shells into the general confusion.

The British gunners spotted the attack too late. They tried to smash it. They fired from every barrel. But Wünsche's tanks were faster. They reached the hill-top. They knocked out the anti-tank guns. A motorized machine-gun company was confused by the mortar fire and was overrun. The survivors were taken prisoner. The operation had been successful. The British had again lost the strategically vital Hill 112. Like torches, the wrecked tanks blazed against the evening sky. The paint was blistering on the steel. Gunpowder fumes drifted over the tortured earth where the dead were lying and the wounded were crying for help. There was not a yard of ground that had not been ploughed over by bombs and shells. But Caen had been saved.

A particular share in preventing the British break-through belonged to Colonel Tzschökell's 7th Mortar Brigade, with its 83rd and 84th Regiments. The brigade had held covering positions of its own, to both sides of Hill 112. The units of the two regiments had been pounding the hill with about 300 barrels.

These mortars, the *Nebelwerfer* or "smoke mortars," were employed on all fronts. Their shells had wrought havoc on Lake Ladoga, in the Caucasus, and at Stalingrad. In the battle for Normandy three mortar brigades were likewise engaged at the key-points of operations. The 7th Brigade alone fired some 8000 tons of mortar-shells in the Caen area. And yet the achievements of this splendid branch of the army have not so far had the acknowledgment and publicity they deserve.

The designation "smoke troops" had surrounded the mortar

---

[1] Rank in S.S. troops equivalent to lieutenant-general.

Nebelwerfer

units with a multitude of legends and misconceptions. The term
"smoke mortar" was in fact no more than a camouflage name
from the days of the Reichswehr, when Germany was forbidden
under the Treaty of Versailles to have armour or armour-piercing
weapons, but was allowed non-toxic smoke-screen equipment.
Consequently, a weapon for laying smoke-screens by large-
calibre missiles was developed, with a rapid rate of fire. Very
soon, however, this development led in an entirely different
direction—to rockets.

During the Second World War the "smoke mortars"—apart
from a few units which used up their old stocks of 105-millimetre
smoke-shells during the German campaign in France—had nothing whatever to do with smoke. The "smoke mortar," in fact,
was the German Wehrmacht's first rocket weapon. Its designer
was General Dornberger, who now works in the U.S.A. His
collaborators included Major-General Zanssen and Wernher von
Braun, whose work eventually led to the V-2. The old name

"smoke mortar," however, survived, and was even encouraged for reasons of security.

The first mortar regiment was given the number 51. It was followed, in the spring of 1941, by the 52nd and 53rd Mortar Regiments.

At the beginning of the Eastern campaign there were three mortar regiments in existence. By the end of the war there were twenty brigades of two regiments each—a total of forty regiments—employed on all fronts. Their calibres were 150, 210, and 300 millimetres. The 210-millimetre shells had the most powerful propellant charge and could carry over six miles. The penetration of the shells was somewhat less than that of artillery-shells, but their fragmentation effect was far greater.

The mortars were fired from the cover of a hole in the ground by an electric ignition device. The powerful jets of fire caused considerable dust clouds which made frequent changes of position necessary in order to escape spotting by the enemy. The noise when a mortar was fired was frightful. Whenever a camouflaged mortar battery went into action everybody ran in terror for cover.

These highly effective mortars were employed in a variety of versions. Thus, the "Mark 40 mortar" was no more than a grid of wooden and iron rods which served at the same time as the packaging of the 184-pound shells. The "mule" was a ten-barrel mortar mounted on a track-laying armoured vehicle.

The mortars rendered vital assistance to the infantry. Organized as G.H.O. troops, they were employed at all key-points, close behind the fighting line, since their range was considerably less than that of artillery. Their range, in fact, was roughly between one and six miles. This employment near the fighting line entailed casualties that were every bit as high as those of the infantry. This fact alone is an eloquent tribute to the fighting morale and courage of the formations with the curious name.

Panzer Lehr transferred to Saint-Lô

On June 30 Max Wünsche recaptured Hill 112 from the British. The battle for Caen had been stabilized. The line was holding. It was also holding in the neighbouring sector to the west, near the much-contested Tilly. There Bayerlein's Panzer Lehr Division was locked in combat with three of Montgomery's crack divisions. As at Caen, the grenadiers were lying in their foxholes in the ground, in front of the anti-tank guns, or else sitting inside their tanks and not budging an inch. They stood their ground at Hottot and Vendes. Again and again they repulsed the armour and infantry of Montgomery's 49th, 50th, and his 2nd Armoured Divisions.

On July 2, an unpleasant day, the funeral of Colonel-General Dollmann, the G.O.C. Seventh Army, took place. He had died of a stroke—it was said from bitterness over the interrogations to which he had been subjected after the success of the Allied landings. The news that Hitler had demanded his recall could not now reach him. His successor was an S.S. general, Obergruppenführer Paul Hausser, a man who came from the old Reichswehr, where he had held the rank of lieutenant-general. He now became the first Waffen S.S. officer to command an army.

Field-Marshal von Rundstedt also received his letter of dismissal on July 2. His successor, von Kluge, was already on his way to take over.

General Geyr von Schweppenburg was likewise relieved of his command of Armoured Group West on July 2. A truly dramatic day, a day of scapegoats!

It was a fateful day also for General Bayerlein. He received the following order: Your positions in the Tilly area are to be handed over to an infantry division at once. Your division will leave behind one-third of its tanks, tank grenadiers, and artillery, and then transfer to the American front in the area of Saint-Lô.

Bayerlein could not believe his eyes. What on earth could induce C.-in-C. West to order such a splitting-up of a battle-worthy division? Were things going that badly in the Saint-Lô area? And even if they were—was there really no other solution?

Rommel's war diary reflects the anxiety felt at Army Group. What the pivoting point of Caen was to the British sector, Saint-Lô was to the U.S. sector of the invasion front.

The principal town of the Cotentin *département*, Saint-Lô, was a tactically important road junction. Four *routes nationales*, as well as several secondary roads, intersected there. Coming down the hills flanking the deep Vire valley, they all crossed the river near the railway-station by the only bridge. Only by way of this bridge could forces be switched from one bank to the other, from the Tilly-Bayeux area to the Carentan-Périers area. In spite of repeated bombing this strategic artery had suffered only insignificant damage. Everything around the bridge had been reduced to rubble—the railway-station, the Hotel Normandie, the corps abattoir. But the bridge had survived. Was the enemy now trying to capture it? He was indeed, and things were looking rather black.

Among the men who were stationed in the peninsula there cannot be one who does not remember Saint-Lô. Prior to June 6 much army pay was spent there during off-duty visits on Norman roast mutton or fillet beef, followed by a few glasses of Calvados.

The cathedral towered in silent majesty. The half-timbered houses breathed peace. But peace was no more than a memory by July 6. Heavenly peace had been supplanted by hell.

As a farewell gift the British prepared a special surprise for the Panzer Lehr, just before their departure from the Tilly front. Bayerlein's headquarters in a small farmhouse near Monts, left unmolested for the past twenty days, suddenly found itself under exceedingly heavy bombardment at 2200 hours. Concentrated salvo upon salvo. The shells burst among the vehicles lined up for departure. Two Volkswagen jeeps were in flames at once. "Everybody under cover!" Staff officers, runners, drivers, radio-operators, all leapt into trenches and foxholes. The bombardment lasted two hours. Connexion with the division's units was cut. Eventually they used a pause in the fire to move off.

On the morning of July 3 Bayerlein had his staff together again. His new headquarters was at Villers-Bocage, near the spot where his personal driver, Corporal Kartheus, had been killed by a fighter-bomber attack on Bayerlein's staff car during the first few days of the invasion. That had been four weeks ago. And now the division was back again. It was like a merry-go-round. A savage merry-go-round. For how long would it turn this time?

The question the troops were asking was more matter-of-fact: "Have we really escaped that hell of Tilly, or are we only being transferred to another?" Major Wrede, the head of divisional administration, overheard the question. "I fear that we shall find we've jumped out of the frying pan into the fire," he remarked. Events were to prove him right.

The tanks did not abandon their positions until after dusk. "Careful! Don't make the Tommies suspicious!" was the slogan. The men were cursing under their breath. Soldiers detest any break with normal routine. The tank men were curiously regarding the newcomers from the infantry, who in turn were watching the tank men's preparations for departure with mixed feelings. At last they were off. A few miles behind their own lines they turned west.

It was dark. It was a difficult journey. Often they could drive only at walking pace. The skippers of the tanks would then walk in front of their vehicles. The distant gunfire was like midsummer lightning or like the firing of photographic flash-bulbs. "Like a New Year's Eve fireworks," grunted Corporal Westphal in the second tank of 8th Company. "A fine New Year's Eve," Lance-Corporal Linke said, laughing. "Well, here's a happy New Year to you!" Kordass, the driver, shouted over the intercom.

No one knew exactly where they were going. Nor could they estimate the distance they were covering during the night. All the time it was a case of starting, stopping, and starting again.

No lights allowed. No cigarettes. No pocket torches. The hooded identification-lights on the rear of the vehicle were only faintly visible. To prevent the driver from dozing off, Westphal, up in the turret, pulled his mouth-organ from his pocket. He tapped it twice against his palm to shake out the breadcrumbs, and then started up the favourite song of 8th Company: *Under an Umbrella in the Twilight*. Softly the music came over the earphones of his crew.

The night gave way to a cool, hazy morning. As soon as the outlines of the tanks began to be visible aircraft look-outs were posted. Then came the signal to halt. A brief conference. Orders were: "Keep moving whatever happens, even during air-raid alarms. The column must keep going. Vehicles dropping out will not be towed away as that would reduce travelling speed. In the event of air attack fire will be opened by all weapons. Anti-tank guns will also be used against fighter-bombers. All crews aboard! Column will advance!"

Low clouds were drifting across the sky. Weary, the aircraft look-outs were crouching on top of the tanks. Corporal Westphal handed over to his gun-layer and leant against the 'rucksack,' the metal box with their food supplies, which was bolted to the back of the turret. He pulled his greatcoat over him. Now for a quick shut-eye. Towards 1100 he was jerked from his sleep. A fighter-bomber. No more than seventy feet above their column. It was now going for the tank in front of them. Westphal had leapt up drowsily. He lost his balance and fell from the tank. But it was not his tumble that infuriated him. It was the thought that those cursed planes were here even though the clouds were practically trailing along the ground. Muttering angrily, he climbed back on his tank. "Close hatches! Stand by! Anti-aircraft machine-gun!"

In front they could already hear the smack of shells and bullets. But Tank 812 was lucky this time. The shells from the aircraft cannon slammed into the roadside ditch. And now the pilot was turning away. "Fire!" The chatter of the machine-gun followed him for a brief instant.

However, he was certain to come back. Probably bring along a few friends. "Come on, step on it!" For once they were in luck. And luck is every bit as important to a soldier as his daily bread-ration. The haze, the low cloud, and the rain which was beginning to fall acted like a magic hood, making them invisible. As soon as the weather cleared up they drove into some orchards and camouflaged their vehicles with branches and entire tree-tops. Towards the evening, and without any losses, they reached the area of Saint-Lô. It was a miracle.

The Fall of Caen

The disastrous consequences of the strategy of stopgaps and operating with insufficient divisions were seen within twenty-four hours of Bayerlein's departure from the Tilly front. His last units had not even reached Saint-Lô when a large-scale British offensive struck against the recently abandoned Tilly–Caumont sector and against the positions of 16th Luftwaffe Field Division and 12th S.S. Panzer Division outside Caen. For days the battle ebbed and flowed. The Luftwaffe Field Division, inadequately trained for infantry combat, had lost the bulk of its flak, many of its officers, and more than 800 of its other ranks during the first aerial bombardment. Now it was smashed. Desperately a few isolated infantry companies held out in their positions without contact to Division. General Sievers, the divisional commander, was seen wandering about the north-eastern edge of Caen—a lonely man looking for his regiments.

On July 9 the British penetrated into the northern suburbs of Caen. West of the town, too, the line was beginning to give, even though the S.S. units there were fighting with a determination such as had not been encountered, according to Allied reports, since the beginning of the invasion. They were prepared to implement Hitler's order: "Caen must be defended to the last man."

At the airfield fifty grenadiers—the remnants of a company of 1st Battalion, 26th S.S. Panzer Grenadier Regiment—were dug in among large, solid blocks of stone, the ruins of an old

Norman farming village. They did not let the British advance by a single step.

An exceptional instance of heroism, however, was the fight of 1st Flak Battery, 12th Flak Battalion at Ardenne. The British had to capture each gun separately in costly close combat. Captain Ritzel acted as gun-layer for his last surviving 88-millimetre gun. He quickly knocked out three Shermans. He then defended his position in close combat, together with six men. They fought with spades and rifle-butts. They died, riddled by submachine-gun bullets, in bloody hand-to-hand fighting.

A senseless sacrifice? Not according to the operations report of the divisional commander. The block set up by this battery, the report states, enabled all the wounded to be moved from the Ardenne abbey.

But even if the entire "Hitlerjugend" Division had let themselves be killed, Montgomery's superior forces were no longer to be halted at Caen. In vain did 84th Corps, referring to the Führer's orders, refuse permission to Meyer, the divisional commander, to evacuate the parts of the town situated west and north of the Orne. For once Meyer, usually a most obedient soldier, defied orders and prepared for evacuation. "We were

88 mm. Gun

meant to die in Caen," he has said since, "but one just couldn't watch those youngsters being sacrificed to a senseless order."

At 0300 Corps eventually authorized the evacuation of the totally wrecked northern and western parts of the town. Strongpoints were blown up. The exhausted units were ferried across the Orne. In the afternoon the first British patrols cautiously advanced into the ruined town. At long last Montgomery was in Caen, where he had wanted to be as long ago as June 7. It had taken him over a month to cover the eight miles that his timetable of operations had scheduled to be covered on the first day of invasion. His casualties had been heavier than the figure estimated by the British General Staff for the entire campaign right into Berlin. At any rate Caen had fallen. But Montgomery had still not achieved his break-through and thrust across the Orne. He had not yet gained the open terrain he needed for a tank battle. The German front was once more becoming stabilized. In haste. Rommel was setting up a defensive position in depth.

Mont Castre and Saint-Jean-de-Daye

In accordance with his policy of switching pressure between the eastern and western wing of his invasion front, Eisenhower had used the tying down of German reserves at Caen for deploying the U.S. First Army on the right wing of the Cotentin peninsula. Allied strategy was based upon this continuous alternation of the centre of gravity. The German Command, as a result, was compelled to keep its reserves of heavy armour permanently on the move, as a kind of fire-brigade, and thus expend their strength prematurely. There simply was not enough armour available for both fronts. When it was engaged at Caen the Americans at Saint-Lô had things all their way. And when it was concentrated in the Saint-Lô area things at once began to look precarious on the Caen front.

There was every justification for Rommel's grumblings about the O.K.W. during the critical days of early July: "How can they expect me to hold out with a quarter-division when three American divisions are attacking?"

The forest of Mont Castre was to justify Rommel's remonstrations. In the history of the 353rd Infantry Division and the 15th Parachute Regiment this forest holds a particular place—as one of the bloodiest battlefields.

The Americans overran the weak German outposts. The

15th Parachute Regiment under Colonel Gröschke was sent forward to steady the reeling front. They were young recruits, trained in a hurry. But they stood their ground and sealed off the penetration.

The main blow of the attack fell upon 353rd Division under Lieutenant-General Mahlmann. The division was holding a line nine miles long, to both sides of La Haye-du-Puits. Nine miles were to be defended by four infantry battalions and two artillery battalions! The town of La Haye itself was held by the Pioneer Battalion of the 353rd under Captain Pillmann. Like a breakwater, the engineers stood up against an enemy who outnumbered them by ten to one. There were only forty of them left when the Americans at last gained a foothold in the northern part of the town.

July 7 started hazy. That was the kind of weather the troops loved. They would be reasonably safe from fighter-bombers. But they were to get a different surprise instead.

Before the German artillery observers even noticed that anything was afoot in the grey, hazy light, assault units of the 30th and 9th U.S. Divisions effected a surprise crossing of the Vire–Taute canal at 0430 hours by way of a temporarily repaired bridge. At a second point the Americans dashed across the canal in assault boats. Saint-Jean-de-Daye was soon taken. The American push went right through to Le Désert. Eisenhower's intention was clear. The Germans were to be squeezed out of Saint-Lô by a big pincer movement of the two divisions.

At first, things seemed to be going well for the Americans. Eisenhower therefore also sent in the 3rd U.S. Armoured Division. It steam-rolled its way through the cornfields north-west of Saint-Lô. However, the American advance was halted on July 9 by an attack of the 2nd S.S. Panzer Division. A further attack, by the Panzer Lehr Division, was scheduled for July 11. The objective was to cut off the American forces which had crossed the Vire.

It was a bold plan. And at first everything went well. Colonel Gutmann launched a frontal attack against the 30th U.S. Division with his 902nd Panzer Grenadier Regiment and twenty tanks. On his left, Colonel Scholze with his 901st Panzer Grenadier Regiment struck at the deep flank of the 9th U.S. Division. Twelve *Panthers* and an anti-tank-gun company lent his attack striking-power. "It's working again at last!" the tank commanders were calling to each other over the radio-telephone.

And indeed it was working again. By 0630 hours Captain

Philipps with his tanks was two miles behind the enemy lines. He had overrun two battalion command-posts. He had encircled and captured part of an infantry regiment belonging to the 9th U.S. Division. And he was still making good speed towards the Vire canal. At Le Désert Bayerlein's grenadiers were tying down large American forces, which would all be in the bag when Captain Philipps's tanks reached the canal. When!...

The battle ebbed and flowed across orchards and sunken lanes. Often the tanks were facing each other at no more than 100 to 150 yards. But again—as on so many other occasions—it turned out that the German High Command had employed insufficient forces for so bold a plan. The Panzer Lehr Division, for one thing, was a division on paper only. In reality it had shrunk in the costly battles of the past few weeks to about a third of its effective strength. And this third was expected to dislodge three American divisions.

In the afternoon the weather cleared. And at once the fighter-bombers appeared. They roared over fields and roads. They forced the grenadiers to go to ground. The superior range of the German tanks was of no avail now. The grenadiers were unable to follow up. The operation ground to a standstill. By nightfall, of the thirty-two German tanks, twenty had been knocked out by the fighter-bombers. Casualties among the troops exceeded 500. Captain Philipps, that experienced and resourceful commander of 1st Battalion, Panzer Lehr Regiment, was taken prisoner. Despairing and resigned, the grenadiers were lying behind hedgerows, below earth banks, in sunken lanes, and among the crops in the fields. "Will nothing go right these days?" they were asking each other. No, nothing was going right these days.

Even so, a heavy blow had been dealt to the Allied Command at Saint-Lô and in the forest of Mont Castre. The American offensive was to have led to the break-out from the Cotentin peninsula. This the Americans had failed to achieve. Moreover, the U.S. divisions had suffered very heavy casualties.

And what was the situation at the other end of the front—at Caen?

There, too, the Allied offensive was failing to make further headway. Montgomery's divisions had ground to a halt. They did not succeed in crossing the Orne and breaking out of the *bocage* into the open plain of Falaise.

The extent to which these reverses and disappointed hopes

were preying on the nerves of the Allied authorities soon became obvious. The Allied top-level staffs in London and Washington were talking of a crisis. To-day, when it is widely believed that the Allied victory in Normandy had never for a moment been in doubt and could not have been prevented by anything, it is instructive to read the official American and British reports and communiqués of those days.

Even Eisenhower was worried. If the Germans were to bring up their infantry from the south of France—and they now had the time to do it—almost anything might happen. The Allies might still be pinned down in their bridgeheads at the outbreak of winter, incapable of large-scale operational movements. The weather would deteriorate. The bombers—and especially the fighter-bombers—would be grounded. This would mean that the Allies would lose their decisive weapon. They would find themselves outmanoeuvred by "General Weather"!

Such were the gloomy thoughts of the Allied staffs. They were haunted by the bogy of a 'petrified front.' The American Press was publishing articles whose impatience and irritation were unmistakable.

Of all this the German troops were unaware—which, of course, is not surprising. What is rather more surprising is that the German High Command was equally unaware of it. Further proof of the failure of the German Intelligence service.

It seems hardly credible—but the German Command down to C.-in-C. West continued to believe firmly in a second invasion in the Pas de Calais. They continued to keep strong German divisions standing to on that part of the coast instead of switching them to the fighting front as Eisenhower feared. It was absurd.

The Allied Supreme Command could not believe what it saw, and continued to be greatly worried by the thought that effective German Panzer divisions might turn up on the American front at any moment. Such a move would have greatly jeopardized the plan of Allied headquarters, which provided for a break-out on the right wing. Indeed, General George S. Patton was already poised for this move with his newly brought up U.S. Third Army. The German High Command and the Führer's headquarters had made things easy for him. If his victory was, nevertheless, hard-won, the credit must go to the courage and fighting spirit of the German troops in the line.

Goodwood

What's the enemy up to? This question stands at the beginning of all strategy. It provides a livelihood for entire armies of spies. And the centres of these secret organizations are known as Intelligence. The fighting front, too, needs its own Intelligence apparatus. Patrols, aerial reconnaissance, radio monitoring, reconnaissance in force (involving the taking of prisoners and interpretation of captured documents)—all these are practised in the field to produce the answer to the question: What are the enemy's intentions? All information converges on the desk of the Intelligence officer, the man whose job it is to piece together, from countless scraps of information, a general picture of the enemy's intentions. The Intelligence officer is a kind of alchemist. In his laboratory he tests the material brought to him and divides the genuine gold from merely glittering base metal. His most important qualities are imagination and mistrust.

Unfortunately, the German Command did not always attach to this kind of work the attention it deserved. The professional soldiers did not think much of the 'specialists.' From regiment downward the work was done as a sideline by the orderly officer. Things were very different on the enemy side. The Americans had full-time Intelligence officers down to battalion level. The Chief of Intelligence on the staff of C.-in-C. West, Lieutenant-Colonel Meyer-Detring, had only nine officers on his establishment. His opposite number, the Chief Intelligence Officer of the American forces, operated with ten times that number. A significant difference!

In a sunken lane on the American sector of the front, south-east of Périers, a German command car was standing. It bore the familiar camouflage paint of green and brown patches and stripes. It belonged to 84th Corps headquarters. Its windows were spattered with mud from near misses by the enemy's guns, which were probing the neighbourhood on a lavish scale.

All radio traffic was at once pinpointed by direction-finding equipment. All foot tracks on the ground were photographed from the air. And then the fighter-bombers would be sent over, or else the artillery would open up. After all, the enemy could afford it.

On this July 13 enemy fighter-bombers were again continuously circling overhead. Major Hayn, the 84th Corps Intelligence officer, accompanied by his orderly, was cautiously ducking through the tall grass and across apple orchards towards the bus in which Lieutenant-Colonel von Criegern, the corps's chief of operations, had his office. Hayn's quarters were in a small, isolated farm, a little over half a mile farther west.

General Dietrich von Choltitz, who had succeeded General Wilhelm Fahrmbacher as corps commander on June 15, greeted his Intelligence officer with the words: "Well, Hayn. And what bad news have you for us to-day?"

The major put two sketch-maps down on the table.

"These, Herr General, are the findings for yesterday—July 12." His finger moved along the thick band indicating the main fighting line and stopped at a sector of the American front that had been shaded red. "This entire area south of Carentan is keeping radio silence. The area, as we know, is that of the XIX and VII U.S. Corps. This suggests some regrouping. In the north considerable radio traffic has been taking place on the sector of our 243rd and 353rd Divisions. And here, immediately to the south of it, newly positioned enemy batteries have been ranging their guns. On the right wing the 1st U.S. Division has not been identified for a few days. It has evidently been relieved."

The general was studying the sketch attentively. "And how about to-day's findings?"

"Quite a few changes," the major replied. "Agents report heavy traffic across the neck of the flooded area near Baupte, towards the south-east. Many newly positioned batteries have begun ranging their guns also in the Sainteny area. Two prisoners wore the shoulder-flash of the 3rd U.S. Armoured Division. One enemy killed had on him letters postmarked A.P.O. 1—that is to say, Army Post Office 1st Division. This would suggest that the unit has not been relieved, but switched to the centre of our front. Enemy papers captured by men of the 17th S.S. Panzer Grenadier Division "Götz von Berlichingen" show that the front sector of the VII U.S. Corps has been considerably narrowed down. New enemy radio frequency: 2201 kilocycles. Of interest, finally, are the numerous flash-light photographs made by enemy reconnaissance aircraft between Périers and Hill 146 last night. Another significant point is the heavy enemy bombardment of the more obvious hills in the centre of the corps's zone. Evidently they are trying to eliminate our O.P.'s Even isolated farms have been shelled for the first time."

Hayn thought of Alphonse Lelu, his 'landlord,' whom the previous day's shelling had driven from his orchard to his cellar.

The old ex-Foreign Legionary had cursed the liberators' guns with astonishing vigour.

"And how do you interpret the situation?" Choltitz asked.

"Clear preparations for an offensive, Herr General. The main effort at Sainteny, in the direction of Coutances—what we've been calling the lesser Cotentin solution. This agrees also with C.-in-C. West's assessment of the situation. They suggested last week that, with enemy forces made available by the fall of Cherbourg, a resumption of attacks against the front of 84th Corps was to be expected not later than mid-July."

Choltitz nodded agreement. He walked over to a small cupboard and produced a bottle of Martell. Pouring the cognac, he said to Hayn, "In your evening report to Army you'd better harp a little on the danger of an enemy attack. Looking worried is part of our job, Hayn—or else the gentlemen in Le Mans may decide that some one else needs supplies and ammunition more urgently than we do!"

Outside, dusk was beginning to fall. The major and his orderly melted into the shadows under the apple-trees. From afar came the rumble of the front: the inevitable signal of battle.

Five days later. Second Lieutenant Hans Höller was about to shave when the look-out yelled down into the garden: "Enemy aircraft!" Höller dropped his brush and wiped the lather off his chin with his hand as he raced over to his self-propelled 20-millimetre gun. A glance at the sky revealed blue flares. Fighter-bombers! Pathfinders. "Bad sign," Höller was thinking.

It was only on the day before, on July 17, that the 8th Company, 192nd Panzer Grenadier Regiment, had been moved from the fighting at Caen over to the right bank of the Orne. Posted on the southern outskirts of the town, Höller's grenadiers were to stop any surprise attacks launched from the 6th British Airborne Division's bridgeheads across the Orne. To the north of them was the 1st Company, 32nd Luftwaffe Panzerjäger Regiment. The 1st Battalion of this regiment was one of the last operational units left of the 16th Luftwaffe Field Division.

Second Lieutenant Höller found his self-propelled gun ready for action. His men all had the same question in their eyes. Are things now starting in earnest for us too? They certainly were.

Eisenhower had instructed Montgomery to launch his offensive with three armoured divisions, two Canadian infantry divisions, and one armoured brigade. They were to force a break-out on the Caen front, engage and annihilate the bulk of the German Panzer divisions deployed around Caen, and in this way enable the Americans to achieve the decisive break-through on the Saint-Lô front. Montgomery's plan was straightforward. It was the Second World War version of the great battle of *matériel*. First of all a huge air armada was to tear a gap in the line by bombing. Infantry of the 2nd Canadian and 3rd British Divisions was then to push through along the flanks of the gap and secure the corridor through which the tanks of the 7th, the 11th, and the Guards Armoured Divisions would then drive down towards the south, if possible straight into the Paris area.

Carpet bombing began at 0500 hours exactly. Three air fleets, two American and one British, attacked with 2100 bombers. Unending processions of aircraft were moving high up across the sky. In perfect fly-past formation. They released their bombs. They let their seeds of death fall, whining, towards the earth. As they turned away they dropped their smoke-markers. A signal for the next wave—This is where we unloaded our cargo!

Ceaselessly, for four hours, this execution of villages, forests, and fields continued. For miles around the air was full of smoke and dust. There were no farm tracks left, and no orchards— only craters. A 20-millimetre flak-gun was hurled some sixty feet, even though it had been well dug in.

Machine-gun posts were levelled. Anti-tank-gun positions were torn to shreds. Infantry trenches were buried with everything that was in them.

The last fifty tanks of the 22nd Panzer Regiment, which had been forming up at Emiéville, were blasted out of their camouflaged positions and many of them smashed. The rest found themselves trapped in deep bomb craters. Feverishly the men tried to dig them free.

Suddenly everything was quiet.

A moment later came the tanks and the infantry. Montgomery's offensive was under way in the strength of two corps.

The flood surged against the German lines, against the 272nd Infantry Division, which had not a single tank or any armour-piercing weapons, and against the 21st Panzer Division with the remnants of 16th Luftwaffe Field Division and part of 1st S.S. Panzer Division. Available reserves consisted of two combat groups of the decimated 12th S.S. Panzer Division "Hitlerjugend."

The code-name for the offensive was Goodwood. Just an exciting sporting event!

Second Lieutenant Höller, in charge of the 8th Company's

heavy platoon, and Lieutenant Braatz, the company commander, knew the positions at the north-eastern corner of Caen like the backs of their hands. They had been established there from June 6 to July 8. It was there they had had their first brush with British parachutists on D-Day. It was there they had buried their battalion commander, Major Zippe. There also was the grave of Atteneder, their runner, a model lance-corporal. There, too, were the graves of many other men of 1st and 2nd Battalions, 192nd Panzer Grenadier Regiment, the regiment which had gained fame by pushing right through the British bridgehead down to the coast on D-Day. Unfortunately, no other unit had joined them.

"That pitted ground is holding up the progress of the tanks," Lieutenant Braatz called over to Höller. Höller, too, put his binoculars to his eyes. They were both lying at the open end of a machine shop in Colombelles, watching the ground in front. The British were sitting in the bomb craters, anxiously waiting for tank support.

The sound of machine-gun fire was coming from the positions of the 1st Luftwaffe Panzerjäger Company in front of Colombelles. So Lieutenant Koschwitz's men were still resisting. The two officers scuttled back and gave the alarm through to Company.

Such infantry guns as were still intact were at once aimed at the enemy's spearhead spotted among the craters. Surprising that anything should still be intact after the pounding they had had from the air.

Höller so directed the positioning of one of his 75-millimetre anti-tank guns that it covered the exit road from Caen. And almost immediately it uttered its first bark. The cautiously advancing Canadian tanks faltered in face of the bursting 75-millimetre shells. "Good," Höller grunted. "Good." But already the first shells were crashing down some eighty yards from the gun. Enemy artillery was finding its range. There must be a British artillery-spotter somewhere among the ruined factories of Colombelles. Maybe even on one of the smokestacks. The next salvo landed quite close to Höller's anti-tank gun. "What's the matter with them? Don't they see what's happening?" the lieutenant thought in despair.

"Runner!"

"Herr Leutnant?"

"Skip across to the anti-tank gun. Order: change position at once!"

The lance-corporal raced off. He had covered a hundred yards when the next salvo came droning over.

"Down, man, down!" Höller screamed. But the runner did not hear him. How could he possibly hear him? He seemed to be leaping straight into the bursting shell. And the next salvo landed within ten feet of the gun. The gun was silenced, together with its crew.

Slowly, very slowly, the Canadians advanced. They filtered through the thin German lines. They thrust forward also from the southern part of Caen. The German field guns were silenced by the Canadian artillery. Höller's company and the entire 2nd Battalion were forced back towards Mondeville.

Koschwitz's Panzerjäger company was also smashed. Corporal Poggenbruch, its tank specialist, managed to knock out a Sherman, but was nevertheless forced to abandon the road-block on the way to Mondeville. Schwarzenberg, the wireless-operator, tried desperately to make contact with Battalion, but there was no reply. Battalion headquarters had long since been overrun. Second Lieutenant Langenberg's 2nd Company came through once more on the telephone from the old Château de Colombelles. Then this connexion too was cut off. By about 1400 Koschwitz was left with nineteen men. He ordered: "Fall back! Rendezvous point: the park by the château." But the Canadian tanks had got there before them. So the troops went on, scuttling through sunken lanes and crawling along ditches, until they came upon the remnants of Second Lieutenant Langenberg's 2nd Company in the iron-works of Mondeville. They found regimental battle headquarters by the railway embankment. Mondeville was encircled. Heino König, the map draughtsman of 1st Panzerjäger Company, led the remnants of 31st and 32nd Panzerjäger Regiments through a pedestrian tunnel in the embankment. They all met in a fortified position of 12th S.S. Panzer Division.

To begin with, the commander of the 2nd Battalion, 192nd Panzer Grenadier Regiment would not hear of breaking out from Mondeville. He sent a signal to Division: "2nd Battalion encircled. Fighting to the end." Eventually, however, common sense prevailed. A favourable moment was seized upon. With great verve the battalion fought its way through the Canadian lines. They got through with scarcely any casualties and were incorporated in the new defensive front some ten miles farther to the south-east.

Deep in the right wing of 21st Panzer Division, among the artillery and flak-positions of the 16th Luftwaffe Field Division, the aerial bombardment did not have the same devastating effect as at the centre of the offensive. Most of the scattered batteries escaped without direct hits. In particular the many 88-millimetre flak batteries which had become available after the evacuation of Caen and had been thrown into the ground fighting by Rommel for use against armour wrought havoc among the British and Canadians. The tanks of their 29th Armoured Brigade ran straight into the line of fire of seventy-eight of these formidable guns. They responded at once. The air reverberated with the metallic sound of the 88s. With smoke pouring from them the tanks lay motionless in the cornfields. Some burst into flame. Others blew up. Startled by such vigorous resistance, the British advanced hesitantly towards the Caen–Vimont railway-line. Only a few of their units crossed the embankment. The bulk were caught in the deeply echeloned defences of 21st Panzer and 1st Panzer Divisions.

What was not knocked out by the 88s was shot up by the *Tiger* tanks of the 2nd S.S. Panzer Corps. Before long combat groups of 12th S.S. Panzer Division, brought forward again, were once more dug in along the road and the Cagny-Frénouville railway.

Meyer's grenadiers, equipped with *Panzerfaust* and sticky bombs, set up an insuperable barrier across the path of the British armoured divisions, whose thrust had by then lost its momentum. At nightfall Brigadeführer[1] Wisch sent in the *Panthers* of his 1st S.S. Panzer Division. Their superior fire-power inflicted terrible losses on the British. Soon eighty British tanks were lying wrecked on this sector alone, burning and smouldering in cornfields and patches of wood. Montgomery's famous 11th Division alone lost 126 tanks on that day—more than half of its total strength.

The Guards Armoured Division lost sixty tanks on the Caen–Vimont road, all of them to the 88-millimetre guns. A terrible bleeding. The backbone of the British offensive was broken. It ground to a standstill. The attempt to burst open the barrier around the bridgehead between Orne and Dives had once more been foiled. Operation Goodwood had not been such a good day's racing after all.

On the high ground south of Caen the German units were strengthening their defences. Montgomery pulled back his battered armoured divisions. The British lion was licking his wounds. The British Press muttered angrily.

---

[1] Rank in S.S. troops equivalent to major-general.

*   *   *

Yet the British scored one victory which perhaps more than outweighed the German defensive success. A British fighter-bomber chose for its victim the man on whom were pinned the hopes of the German troops.

In the afternoon of July 17 Field-Marshal Rommel visited the front and called at the battle headquarters of 1st S.S. Panzer Corps. He discussed the situation with Oberstgruppenführer[1] Sepp Dietrich. "Panzer" Meyer had also been summoned to make a report.

As Rommel was about to drive back to La Roche-Guyon, some time towards 1600 hours, Dietrich advised him to exchange his big staff car for a more manoeuvrable Volkswagen jeep because of the fighter-bombers. But Rommel, smiling, dismissed the suggestion. By the time he left the sky had cleared.

"Step on it," Rommel ordered his driver, Daniel.

At Livarot Daniel had turned into a side-road. But three miles from Vimoutiers he had to rejoin the main raod. A moment later Sergeant Holke called out, "Low-flying aircraft!"

The fighter-bombers were sweeping up from behind, along the road from Livarot. They were less than a hundred feet up.

"Try to make the village," Rommel called to Corporal Daniel. Daniel stepped on the accelerator. He roared into the bend. But the aircraft was faster. A burst of 20-millimetre shells tore into the car. They went through the upholstery and ripped open the left side of the vehicle.

Daniel was hit in the shoulder. He slumped forward over the wheel. The car swerved to the right and crashed into a tree-trunk. It then spun round to the left and fetched up broadside across the road.

Rommel, who had struck his head against the windscreen and was bleeding heavily, was flung out of the car. He hit the road with a crash. His skull was broken.

The hero of Africa, the great hope of Normandy, had fallen victim to a British fighter-bomber like countless other men on the invasion front. Captain Lang, Major Niehaus, and Sergeant Holke escaped without injuries. They ran back along the road. They dragged Rommel behind a hedge. As soon as the fighter-bombers had disappeared they brought the field-marshal to the nearest village. Its name, by an ironic twist of fate, was Saint-Foy-de-Montgomery.

---

[1] Rank in S.S. troops equivalent to colonel-general.

Rommel was not replaced in his post. Field-Marshal Hans von Kluge, Rundstedt's successor as C.-in-C. West, personally assumed command of Army Group B.

"Clever Hans," as the brilliant General Staff officer was universally called, in a pun on his name, had been transferred to Normandy from the Eastern front at the beginning of July to replace Rundstedt and to "stabilize the front." Almost at once he had driven to Rommel's headquarters and in the course of their conversation had told him sharply, "Even you will have to get used to obeying orders!" Kluge had felt sure that clear centralized power and a strong hand were all that was needed to master the situation.

A fortnight had been enough to convince him that even he could no longer reverse the fate of the invasion front. The personality of the German commander in the West had ceased to matter. Eisenhower had already won an irretrievable lead both strategically and in terms of military strength. And Kluge had already been allotted a different place in history: that of becoming the tragic symbol of the German generals' corps in its struggle against the High Command's mistaken interference with its own decisions.

On July 20 a tremendous thunderstorm swept over Normandy. The gutted ruins of towns and villages were lit up by flashes of lightning and shaken by crashes of thunder. Rain and hail turned the land into a swamp. Small streams swelled into violent torrents. Tracks became impassable watercourses. Into this unleashed fury of nature dropped the sensational headlines: ATTEMPT ON THE FÜHRER'S LIFE. The effect produced by the news from Paris, Berlin, and Rastenburg on the different headquarters varied a good deal: excitement, alarm, but also hope that the war might now perhaps be over soon. But the formations locked in battle, whether officers or other ranks, had no time for political arguments. This is how General Bayerlein described the reaction among the divisions at Saint-Lô: "Our eyes were more on the fighter-bombers than on the Führer's headquarters." The remark clearly shows how utterly the troops had been drained of all vitality, how their minds had become focused on one thing alone. Survival.

Break-through at Saint-Lô

On July 19 the Americans fought their way into the streets of Saint-Lô against the remnants of the 30th Fast Brigade. The brigade commander, Freiherr von Aufsess, one of the most gallant officers of 84th Corps, had been killed in house-to-house fighting on the outskirts. It was a savage and costly struggle. The official account of the 29th U.S. Division conveys a picture of the action. Only step by step, in small groups of five men advancing under cover of tanks, was it possible to gain possession of the ruins of buildings and of the roads blocked by wreckage. The leader of the American spearhead, Major Thomas Howie of the 3rd Battalion, 116th U.S. Infantry Regiment, was among those killed.

Five days later the following scene took place at the battle headquarters of the Panzer Lehr Division, south-west of Saint-Lô.

"When do you think the Americans will renew their attacks on our sector?" General Bayerlein asked Kaufmann, his chief of operations. Kaufmann looked up. The flies were buzzing in the kitchen of the old smoke-stained farmhouse near Canisy. "Things may start again at any moment, Herr General. The enemy's certainly ready. That much is obvious. I think the weather is the only factor that's stopped him so far."

"But Army still thinks the main offensive won't be here but at Caen," Beyerlein objected.

At that moment the telephone rang. Report from 901st headquarters: "Heavy bombing raids."

Bayerlein looked at Kaufmann. "I believe this is it."

It was the morning of July 24. All units were alerted at once. Telephones were ringing. Runners were coming and going. Everybody was waiting for something to happen. Again the telephone rang. Another report from battle headquarters of 901st Panzer Grenadier Regiment: "Bombs being dropped in front of our lines. American infantry moving back."

Moving back? What did that mean? The day passed. There was no attack. The night too was quiet. July 25 dawned.

At 0700 hours an advanced company of 902nd Panzer Grenadier Regiment reported by telephone: "American infantry in front of our trenches are abandoning their positions. They are withdrawing everywhere."

Soon the same news came from every sector of the division.

"Looks as if they've got cold feet," Kaufmann laughed. "Perhaps Army is right after all."

A few minutes later Seventh Army reaffirmed its view that the enemy offensive would not come at Saint-Lô. Bayerlein was notified that 2nd Panzer Division was to be taken out of the line, to be transferred to positions south of Caen where Seventh Army headquarters expected the enemy to launch his offensive. The place of the relieved armoured division was taken by Lieutenant-General Drabich-Waechter's 326th Infantry Division, until then stationed in the Pas de Calais. The switch was performed without much upheaval.

An hour later, at 0940, the telephones in the farmhouse at Canisy started ringing again. The same report was coming through from all formations in the line, from positions well behind the front, and from every village and hamlet where armoured reserves were stationed: "Bombing attacks by endless waves of aircraft. Fighter-bomber attacks on bridges and artillery positions." There could be no doubt left: this was it.

So it was the Saint-Lô front after all!

And meanwhile the 2nd Panzer Division was driving away from the battlefield over to Caen where nothing was happening.

But why, in that case, had the American infantry been pulled back yesterday and again earlier to-day? At the time the move was interpreted as a ruse. To-day we know that it had a much more trivial explanation.

General Bradley had intended to attack on July 24. Because of bad weather he countermanded his order at the last moment. He was afraid the bomber fleet might drop its bombs inaccurately because of poor visibility. However, Bradley's order countermanding the offensive came too late to reach some of the formations. The bombers took off and, as feared, dropped their bombs among their own lines. Panic broke out. The G.I.'s, totally unaccustomed to aerial bombardment, hastily abandoned their positions. That was the 'withdrawal' reported by 901st Grenadier Regiment.

Even after Bradley had scheduled the offensive for July 25 some of his regimental commanders, made distrustful by the previous day's events, continued to pull their battalions back from the front line. After all, the weather was not so much better than the day before. These were the withdrawals reported to Bayerlein by 902nd Grenadier Regiment on July 25.

In point of fact, the cautious commanders were proved right. In several places the American aircraft again dropped their bombs on their own lines. The 47th and 120th Infantry Regiments suffered heavy losses. The 12th Field Artillery Regiment was completely smashed. General McNair, the Inspector of U.S. Land Forces and a personal friend of Eisenhower's, was blown up in his scouting car. Even so, quite a number were dropped on the German lines.

For another hour Bayerlein's headquarters maintained telephone and radio contact with the forward formations in spite of the hail of bombs. Then all contact ceased.

But the entries made during that hour in the situation-map at divisional headquarters spoke volumes. More than 2000 bombers had turned the sector of the Panzer Lehr and the neighbouring 13th and 15th Parachute Regiments into a corridor of death four miles wide and two miles deep. Everything had been churned up. Trenches had been buried. Anti-tank-gun positions had been wiped out. Stores of fuel, ammunition, and supplies had been set on fire. That 2000 bombers were attacking on a front of four miles meant that each bomber had only to plough a strip about ten feet wide. It explained the appearance of the ground at 1000 hours where but an hour before the Panzer Lehr Division had been positioned with 5000 men.

At least half the division had been put out of action: killed, wounded, buried alive, or driven insane. Tanks and guns in the forward line had been smashed to pulp. The roads were impassable.

But that was not yet enough for General Bradley. "Safety first" was his first principle. At 1000 hours precisely he therefore sent in another 400 fighter-bombers which pounced on anything that was still moving.

Even that was not enough. At 1030 hours medium bombers made a precision attack on the roads to Saint-Gilles and Marigny.

Only then came the VII U.S. Corps infantry. The three infantry divisions were little more than peacemakers to clear and secure the corridor for the motorized units that followed behind.

The bombers had done their job thoroughly. Too thoroughly. The G.I.'s with their bulky equipment were making only slow and laborious progress across the lunar landscape of bomb craters, uprooted trees, wire, and masonry. The tanks, at first, were not able to move at all. Engineers had to clear a path for them with bulldozers.

Bayerlein rode over to the battle headquarters of 901st Regiment on a motor-cycle. Colonel von Hausser was sitting in the basement of an ancient stone tower.

A second lieutenant was just running down the stairs into the vaulted room: he had been sent forward to reconnoitre. "Here you can have it first hand," the colonel said to the general. And the general listened to the lieutenant's account. "I did not find a single strongpoint that was intact. The main fighting line has vanished. Where it used to be is now a zone of death."

By noon the Americans had crossed the Saint-Lô–Périers

road. But on the following day, July 26, they encountered
German resistance at Marigny. Heaven knows how some of the
positions had managed to survive the inferno. At any rate, they
were now firing at the Americans.

Bradley immediately ordered 400 medium bombers to put
down a bomb carpet. Before long the 2nd U.S. Armoured
Division broke through on the right wing and thrust on to
Saint-Gilles. By the evening it had reached Canisy. Bayerlein's
headquarters had pulled out just in time.

It was a hot, sultry day. Weary, hungry, and dirty, Bayerlein
was sitting in his new battle headquarters near Dangy, three
miles farther south, together with his chief of operations and his
orderly officer.

The sentry reported a German staff car. A General Staff
officer had been sent by Field-Marshal von Kluge, C.-in-C.
West, looking for the Panzer Lehr. He was greatly relieved at
finding the divisional commander in person. Was he bringing
help? No. He was bringing an order.

In his spotless uniform with the scarlet stripes down the
seam of his trousers the lieutenant-colonel was a little embarrassed
as he stood before the general and his officers who had not
shaved or seen a hot meal for several days, let alone had any
water to wash in. He could imagine what these men must have
gone through. But what was the use? He had an order to deliver.

"Herr General," he said. "Herr General, the field-marshal
demands that the line from Saint-Lô to Périers be held."

There was silence in the room. Kaufmann was watching
Bayerlein. Major Wrede was staring out of the window.

"The line from Saint-Lô to Périers is to be held," Bayerlein
repeated. "May I ask with what?"

The lieutenant-colonel ignored the question. "What I am
passing on to you is an order, Herr General," he replied.
"You've got to hold out. Not a single man is to leave his
position!" As if by way of apology, he added, "A battalion of
S.S. *Panther* tanks will be striking at the American flank to
relieve you."

Not a single man was to leave his position!

Bayerlein stared at the officer. An oppressive silence hung
in the air. Somewhere outside a stable door slammed.

The general felt the blood drumming in his temples. The
man who had gone through the mill of El Alamein with Rommel
and had witnessed the collapse of the German Afrika Korps
among the sandhills of Tel el Mampsra and in Tunisia without

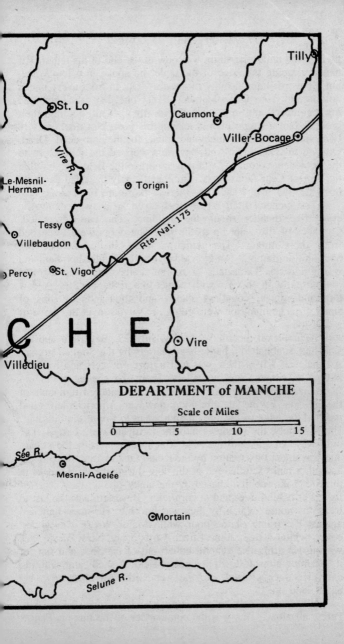

giving way under the strain was now at the end of his tether. His hands gripping the edge of the table, he spoke in a low voice, but his words hung heavily in the air: "Out in front every one is holding out, Herr Oberstleutnant. Every one. My grenadiers and my engineers and my tank crews—they're all holding their ground. Not a single man is leaving his post. Not one! They're lying in their foxholes mute and silent, for they are dead. Dead. Do you understand?" And Bayerlein stepped up quite close to the lieutenant-colonel. "You may report to the field-marshal that the Panzer Lehr Division is annihilated. Only the dead can now hold the line. But I shall stay here if those are my orders."

The General Staff officer was saved an answer. A terrific crash like thunder shook the building. The earth trembled. Cascades of fire leapt up to the sky. The doors were wrenched from their hinges. The windows were shattered. The big ammunition-dump at Dangy had been hit by fighter-bombers and was going up. Thousands of mortar-shells were swishing and roaring through the air with comet-like trails of fire. A few thousand mines, countless shells, and thousands of tons of small-arms ammunition were going up: salvoes over the grave of a division.

At noon on the following day, July 27, Bayerlein and his staff had established a battle headquarters by the Soulles stream. All that was left of them was half a dozen officers and fourteen N.C.O.'s, runners and signallers. From the shelter of an old farmhouse they were trying to collect the scattered remnants of the division. By the late afternoon, however, American tanks had reached the edge of the stream and began to fire at the building. Unfortunately, the windows into the farmyard were barred. The only way out was into the road which ran alongside the stream and was under observation by the tanks. One by one, the officers and other ranks scuttled out of the door during the brief breaks in the fire. Like rabbits, chased by the tanks' shells, they scurried for cover behind trees and in cornfields. Bayerlein was the last to leave the house, which by then was burning. He stood flattened against the frame of the door while Major Wrede was taking cover behind a tree, some fifteen yards away. Now Wrede was waving his arm. The general bolted out of the door and ran for it. He flung himself down in a potato field. A shell came whining over. His face pressed into the wet earth. All clear now. Up again, and on.

When dusk fell he was seen walking down the road to Percy, all alone. This was the commander of the famous Panzer

Lehr Division, of which Guderian had said only three months before, "With this division alone you will throw the Anglo-Americans back into the sea!" And now he was foot-slogging down a French road. At the Führer's headquarters a little flag was taken off the big situation-map.

The Front snaps

At about the same time as General Fritz Bayerlein eventually came up against units of the 2nd Parachute Corps, another dramatic conversation was taking place at that corps's headquarters, near Saint-Vigor, six miles east of Percy. It, too, illustrated both the situation and the mood at forward headquarters.

This time it was General Meindl, commanding the 2nd Parachute Corps, who had a heated exchange with an emissary of Field-Marshal von Kluge. The emissary was the field-marshal's own son, Lieutenant-Colonel von Kluge, who had been sent to Meindl to find out what the situation was. The son thus became the butt for the corps commander's anger. Meindl was apprehensive. What was Kluge's spy after? Was he bringing more "hold out" orders? And even further demands?

Meindl's corps was holding positions on the flank of the American thrust to the south. A reconnaissance unit of his 12th Panzerjäger Regiment, under Captain Goetsche, had arrived at the crossroads of Le Mesnil Herman in the nick of time to knock out an armoured spearhead aiming at the divisional headquarters of General Kraiss's 352nd Infantry Division, and thus saved the divisional staff from being taken prisoners. Goetsche set up a 'hedgehog' position and for twenty-four hours held the important road to the south against all attacks by American armour. Half a dozen smouldering Shermans lay wrecked outside his position. But what use was heroism at the Le Mesnil Herman crossroads? It could not close the enormous gap caused by the loss of the Panzer Lehr Division.

Nor could that gap be closed by the battalions of Count Schulenburg's 13th Parachute Regiment who hung on grimly in the Marigny area. Besides, Meuth's 2nd Battalion had shrunk from 800 to 100 men. No. The cracked front needed help of a different kind. To provide such help the Seventh Army commander, Colonel-General of S.S. Troops Hausser, had ordered the 2nd and 116th Panzer Divisions to launch, from out of the threatened flank of the 2nd Parachute Corps, an attack on a broad front against the rapidly advancing Americans, to break through their lines, and, if possible, to re-establish contact with the western coast of the peninsula. The 2nd Panzer Division was commanded by General von Lüttwitz and the 116th by General Count Schwerin. The overall command of the operation had been given to General of Armoured Troops Freiherr von Funck. General Meindl had just been informed by Hausser of this plan.

Meindl's drive back to his headquarters showed more clearly than anything else the true situation in the area of operations. Along the nine miles from Seventh Army headquarters to his own battle headquarters the general was chased out of his Volkswagen by fighter-bombers about thirty times. Thirty times he was forced to dive into the ditch or behind some bank. In order to facilitate this manoeuvre the doors had been taken off the Volkswagen jeep. ''Scuttle-car'' was the name the men had given the vehicle.

A journey that used to take thirty minutes required a full four hours. This utter helplessness was enough to make a man cry. And under these conditions they were to launch a tank attack on a broad front the following day! Would the higher commands never learn?

It was in this mood that the general found young Kluge waiting for him at his battle headquarters. Meindl's surmise proved correct. Young Kluge had been sent to convey his father's reminder to ''hold out.'' At this, General Meindl exploded, just as General Bayerlein had exploded twenty-four hours earlier. ''Kindly convey to your father exactly what I am going to say to you.'' Meindl began icily. ''The time has come when Normandy can no longer be held. It cannot be held because the troops are exhausted. This is the fault mainly of orders to hold out in hopeless positions; but we are still being ordered to hold out even now. The enemy will break through to the west of us and outflank us. And what's going to happen then? Everything is now being staked on those few Panzer divisions! But I can tell you already that these two divisions with their old methods won't get anywhere. It would have been far better to organize the tanks into a mobile armoured defence force, instead of moving them against imaginary objectives as if this were a tactical exercise on a map! If your father knew what it means to operate against an enemy with a downright fabulous command of the air, then he would know that our only chance of doing anything useful at all is by attacking at night. To-morrow's tank attack is going to be a failure, because it is scheduled on too broad a front and because it isn't going to start until dawn, which means it will take place in daylight. Those tanks are destined to be smashed. And all that's left for the grenadiers to do is to lie down and sacrifice their lives. It's heartbreaking to have to stand by and watch!''

Meindl was right in every respect, including his prediction that the attempt to strike at the enemy's flank with two Panzer divisions must end in failure. The enemy was simply far too strong in the air and on the ground.

Things happened as they were bound to happen. True, Meindl's parachute corps continued to hold the right flank of the front, but the entire left wing of 84th Corps was cut off. The Americans swept through to the south between the two corps, entirely unmolested. If they wheeled round to the coast the whole of 84th Corps would be trapped. If they wheeled to the east, Meindl's divisions would be threatened with encirclement. And if they continued southward, without being stopped, then they would burst into the wide-open expanse of France and threaten the entire Seventh Army.

Faced with this situation, Colonel-General Hausser decided to order 84th Corps to break through towards the south-east and link up with the 2nd Parachute Corps. There was no time and no facility left for agreeing with Kluge about any operations in support of this move. When a telephone contact was eventually established it was broken off again after the first few words.

Naturally the withdrawal of 84th Corps left the west coast of the Cotentin peninsula unprotected. It opened for the Americans the gap of Avranches and gave them their chance for a break-out. For this reason Choltitz opposed the plan. He rang through to Army and asked to speak to Hausser personally. But Army insisted on the execution of the move. It feared the loss of the entire corps if the battered units were left behind on the coast.

Field-Marshal von Kluge countermanded the order and demanded a gradual withdrawal to the south, while holding on to the western coast, so as to gain time. Hold on. Hold on. But the corps's movements towards the south-east had already got under way and could no longer be halted.

One cannot help noticing that Field-Marshal von Kluge, that shrewd strategist, acted throughout those weeks as a zealous champion of the orders given out by the Führer's headquarters. One wonders why. It may be that against his better judgment he had lost the courage to contradict orders from above because he sensed that Hitler mistrusted him and suspected him of having sympathized with the conspirators of July 20.

Whatever the reason, the men in the fighting line who had expected new and revolutionary decisions from the highly respected strategist, decisions that would take the actual situation into account, now lost their faith in Kluge too. After all, the men in the fighting line could see what was going on, and how divisions and regiments were melting away like snow under the sun.

General Mahlmann's experienced 353rd Infantry Division, which had been saved from encirclement by 941st Grenadier Regiment on the Sienne river on July 28, was reduced by July 30 to a mere 800 men. Combat groups formed of several divisions, such as the combat group Heinz, had shrunk to barely company strength. The well-tried 6th Parachute Regiment, which has been cropping up in our chronicle of events ever since June 6, was down to forty men. Forty men out of 1000! That was the situation. And the enemy made the most of it.

On the evening of July 28 packs of American tanks and motorized columns swarmed towards the south along all roads between the Vire and the Atlantic coast. There was no cohesive German line left ahead of them.

And what about the Caen front? Would it not have been possible to withdraw units from there and switch them to Saint-Lô? The answer is no. The strategy of the Allied Supreme Command was well co-ordinated. As soon as the American offensive got going at Saint-Lô the Canadians attacked at the other end of the line, at Caen, and engaged the Armoured Group West in heavy defensive fighting. The release of any formations was thus impossible. After all, this was the decisive strategic importance of the Caen front—to pin down German forces, and to draw one Panzer division after another, while down at Saint-Lô the great break-through was being prepared which eventually was to trap the German Seventh Army.

It was really well done. The strategy of the Allied Supreme Command was the deliberate exploitation of their material superiority in the field. It was an astonishing organizational achievement, both before and during the invasion. Science and technology had made an amazing contribution to the creation of that superiority and continued to strengthen it every day.

As a result, Eisenhower could afford a great many things which, in the event of defeat, would have been marked down by history as military mistakes. With his fully motorized units he was able to form centres of gravity rapidly and equally rapidly to switch them. Conversely, he was able to contain German counter-attacks which produced critical situations. He saved his soldiers the strains and stresses which had gradually become the German troops' daily bread—marching at night and fighting during the day, always being hunted from the air, without pause, without relief, and without hope. Officers and troops of the German Army who remembered the First World War realized in Normandy that the nature of war had fundamentally changed. *Matériel* and sweat had become more important than spirit and blood.

7

THE BIG TRAP

The Bridge of Pontaubault

Dramatic developments in military history are invariably the result of some unusual decision by a military leader. General Guderian's revolutionary tank tactics, with their bold disregard for conventional flak cover, brought about the gigantic victories in the battles of encirclement during the early phases of the war in Russia. Field-Marshal Rommel in Africa applied the principles of naval battle to the desert. He feinted, he sent outflanking columns across desert considered impassable, and he cut off the enemy's front-line troops from the supply bases and their few roads. In this way he defeated the British armies which, though greatly superior to him in number, were fighting along conservative lines until another military leader opposed him with a new principle. Montgomery gave a demonstration of the tactics of attrition—the rich man's war.

The battle for France saw the emergence of another revolutionary army leader. Not on the German side, but on General Eisenhower's.

George S. Patton, a tank leader commanding the U.S. Third Army, became the real victor in the West. He was a kind of American Guderian and Rommel rolled into one. At the end of July 1944 he seized the chance of injecting new life into the concept of the armoured *Blitzkrieg*.[1]

Patton drove his VIII Corps down through the narrow corridor between the German flanking position and the Atlantic coast. "Drive on," he ordered his unit commanders. And if they

---

[1] For George S. Patton's own battle account, read "WAR AS I KNEW IT." Another volume in The Bantam War Book Series.

asked about flank cover, he would snarl at them, "You worry about your objective, not your flanks!" For the Americans these were bold, almost reckless tactics.

The 4th U.S. Armoured Division reached Avranches in the evening of July 30. On the following day it took Pontaubault and established a bridgehead over the Sélune. Thus Patton had burst open the door for the break-out into the unconfined expanse of France.

The climax of the invasion battle had arrived. Would Patton be able to keep the door open? Everything depended on one road and one bridge, for only a single road with a single bridge led from Avranches over the Sélune into Brittany. And to complete the picture Field-Marshal von Kluge had only the remnants of one single division at his disposal for averting the impending disaster. This was the 77th Infantry Division under Colonel Bacherer, an experienced commander. The division had suffered heavily in July and had been moved into the area west of Pontaubault for rest and replenishment.

One could have heard a pin drop at Bacherer's battle headquarters when, on the evening of Sunday, July 30, his chief of operations read out a signal from Kluge: "Avranches is to be taken and held at all costs. It is the keystone of our defence. On it hinges the decision in the West."

So the decision in the West now hinged on a single bridge, on a single road, and on the remnants of a single division!

Bacherer was a man of action. He scraped together everything he could lay his hands on. Not only his own formations of 77th Infantry Division, but also fourteen self-propelled guns, some units of 5th Parachute Division, and such stragglers as turned up at the various rallying points.

With this combat group, Bacherer on the morning of July 31 struck at Pontaubault, took the town, and immediately moved on towards Avranches. The grenadiers penetrated into the town. They captured house after house. The self-propelled guns pounded the American strongpoints and kept the American tanks away from the German battalions. There was low cloud and drizzle. Not a fighter-bomber was in the sky. The battle continued to rage. Things were not going at all badly for Bacherer's combat group.

But towards noon the weather cleared. It was the same old story. The men of Albert Allgaier's 1st Battalion, 1050th Infantry Regiment had begun to glance anxiously up at the sky. They did not have to wait long. "Fighter-bombers!" the cry went up.

Like vultures the machines hurled themselves out of the sky. An unending succession of them. Within a short time, in less than an hour, all fourteen self-propelled guns had been wrecked. The American tanks, now unobstructed, rumbled forward into the line, scattered the grenadiers, and forced the combat group to fall back towards the south and the west.

"Demolition party to blow up the Sélune bridge," Bacherer commanded. At least he was going to deprive the Americans of the only bridge leading out of the bottleneck into Brittany. But that damned bridge seemed to have a charmed life. The first demolition party was shot up. The second ran into an ambush and all its men were taken prisoners. The bridge remained intact. American tanks were racing over it. By the evening of July 31 they were outside Bacherer's battle headquarters. At the last moment the colonel and his staff slipped away along a sunken lane. General Patton had reached his objective. After eight weeks' incessant fighting the Americans had gained the exit from the narrow Cotentin peninsula. Nothing now stood in their way.

In vain the Luftwaffe tried to hit and destroy the bridge of Pontaubault. It attacked it by day and night from August 3 to August 7. But except for one minor hit all the bombs went wide. And across that bridge Patton was whipping on his divisions. The bottleneck, the road from Avranches to Pontaubault, became a solid moving mass of tanks and motorized formations. Beefy officers stood at the bridges, their Colts in their fists. "Keep going, keep going!" They ordered one unit after another into the bottleneck. Fighters and anti-aircraft guns shielded the corridor from the air. And underneath that umbrella flowed an uninterrupted stream of tanks, track-laying and wheeled vehicles, and marching troops. With lordly disregard for all operational plans and safety regulations Patton ferried through no fewer than seven divisions within the span of seventy-two hours—all of them along that single road. It was a total of over 100,000 men and more than 15,000 motor vehicles! A fantastic feat of organization.

This force burst into the wide-open expanse of France and at once fanned out. Patton never hesitated to expose his flanks. He acted in accordance with Guderian's principle: "The protection of our flanks is the business of the infantry that is following behind. Our objective is in front."

On August 4 Rennes fell. The 4th Armoured Division thrust across the peninsula as far as its southern coast at Vannes. The strategic objective was the fortress of Brest, nearly 200 miles from Avranches Patton sent in the 6th Armoured Division.

However, it allowed itself to be delayed at Dinan, south of Saint-Malo, by Bacherer's combat units which were threatening the American flank. Patton had the divisional commander summoned to the telephone: "Keep going. Keep going regardless of your flanks until you've reached Brest!" he fumed. Another instance of how boldness or caution can decide the outcome of a battle. A precious twenty-four hours had been lost. The German garrisons of Brest and Saint-Malo had time to prepare to defend themselves. Brest could no longer be taken by a coup.

Operation Lüttich

While Patton's Third Army was racing through Brittany and towards the south the U.S. First Army under Hodges continued its offensive in an easterly and south-easterly direction in order to widen the corridor of Avranches. General Hodges's VIII Corps took Mortain with its commanding high ground. A pivot had been established for the impending large-scale wheeling of the entire front towards Paris.

"Unless the door of Avranches is pushed shut again the German front in France will collapse," General von Choltitz said to Colonel-General Hausser, the Seventh Army commander, early in August. But Army and Army Group were quite aware of the magnitude of the disaster. An attempt had to be made at all costs to seal the big gap of Avranches and to cut off Patton's army from its rearward lines of communications.

At the Führer's headquarters, too, the danger of the open door of Avranches was by now realized. General Patton's bold manoeuvre had been watched with dismay and amazement. "Just look at that crazy cowboy general," Hitler grumbled, "driving down to the south and into Brittany along a single road and over a single bridge with an entire army. He doesn't care about the risk, and acts as if he owned the world! It doesn't seem possible!"

Why then was it possible?

If one remembered the triumphs of the once-so-powerful German Army it really seemed incredible that this American general could now be playing cat-and-mouse with it in this manner. How was it possible? Surely there were some strong Panzer divisions left in France? And were these divisions unable to cut off a bottleneck of sixteen to nineteen miles? Was the entire campaign in the West to depend on a mere sixteen miles?

It seemed absurd. Surely this must be the great chance for the German Command? Surely this could become the great turning-point, just when the enemy had banked a little too recklessly and contemptuously on his run of good luck? That, at any rate, was Hitler's idea. It was shared by Colonel-General Jodl, Hitler's chief of staff.

On August 2, General Warlimont, the deputy chief of the O.K.W. staff, arrived at Field-Marshal von Kluge's headquarters. He brought with him Hitler's order for Operation Lüttich—a thrust from Mortain against Avranches. Hitler demanded that of the nine Panzer divisions engaged in Normandy eight should be got ready for the attack. The Luftwaffe, too, was to throw into the battle "all available reserves, including 1000 fighters."

So far so good. But what about the date? Field-Marshal von Kluge wanted to strike at once. Hitler wanted to postpone the launching of the offensive until "every tank, every gun, and every aircraft have been rounded up."

Kluge telephoned Jodl: "We've got to strike at once. The enemy is getting stronger every day. He's already got an entire army through the Avranches gap!"

Jodl's reply reflected an astonishingly over-optimistic assessment of the situation: "Don't worry about the Americans who have broken through. The more there are through the more will be cut off." An answer fit for a history primer. One is reminded of the reply reputedly made by Leonidas, the leader of the Greek troops at Thermopylae, when informed that the Persians' volley of spears and arrows would darken the sun. "So much the better," he said, "then we'll be fighting in the shade!"

Field-Marshal von Kluge and Colonel-General Hausser did not share Jodl's optimism. They knew that any further delay would be the death warrant for their army. They therefore decided to start the offensive during the night of August 6–7. The entire hopes of the Western front rested upon Operation Lüttich.

Four panzer divisions—the 2nd under General von Lüttwitz, the 116th under Count Schwerin, some units of the 1st S.S. "Leibstandarte" under Brigadeführer[1] Wisch, and the 2nd S.S. "Das Reich" under Gruppenführer[2] Lammerding—as well as a combat group of the 17th S.S. Panzer Grenadier Division "Götz

---

[1] Rank in S.S. troops equivalent to major-general.
[2] Rank in S.S. troops equivalent to lieutenant-general.

von Berlichingen" and the remnants of the Panzer Lehr smashed at Saint-Lô made up the offensive force which was placed under the overall command of 47th Panzer Corps.

General Freiherr von Funck, the corps commander, wanted to use the night for the first big armoured thrust. He hoped to cover half the distance to Avranches in darkness. His 120 tanks were ready to advance along a ridge of high ground between the valleys of the See and Sélune; these streams, as it were, providing natural flank cover against enemy interference.

The 2nd Panzer Division was ordered to move off at 2400 hours. But only the right-hand assault group was in fact moving. The attack on the left wing was delayed by a bad hold-up. The tanks of the 1st S.S. Panzer Division had not turned up. On its way to the jumping-off line the Panzer regiment had got into a sunken lane a mile and a half long. As bad luck would have it, an enemy fighter-bomber which had been shot down crashed on top of the leading tank and completely blocked the road. A bad omen. In reverse gear the tanks had to back out of the lane. The manoeuvre took hours. Not till daybreak was the left-hand assault group ready to move into action.

The right-hand group, meanwhile, had raced on ahead with two tank battalions, Panzerjägers, and 304th Panzer Grenadier Regiment. The Panzer grenadiers and engineers were riding on top of the tanks.

Then they came up against American anti-tank barriers on the roads. A quick burst of shell-fire. Attack by grenadiers on the American outposts. And forward again. The American main fighting line was overrun.

At Dove the 1st Battalion of the Panzer regiment ran into a mine-belt. Major Schneider-Kostalsky, the regimental commander, was killed by a mine. Engineers cleared the road. On again. Mesnil Dove fell. But there was an anti-tank gun left by the church, well under cover. That damned gun was holding up the entire attack. At last a 75-millimetre shell swept it away.

On again.

Mesnil Adelée fell. The group was within four miles of its objective for the day. Once there, half the distance to Avranches would be covered. The armoured spearheads swept on towards the west.

Then the day dawned.

The left-hand assault group of Lüttwitz's Panzer division had not started out from its base line till shortly after 0200, because of the belated arrival of the S.S. "Leibstandarte" tanks.

It thus lost the element of surprise. Soon it began to get light. True, a haze hung over the ground. The hills were shrouded in thick mist. Crossroads vanished from sight. But at least the fighter-bombers were being kept away from the battlefield.

Like Spectres, the massive Mark IVs, the sleek *Panthers*, and formidable *Tigers* materialized out of the mist in front of the American lines. The 2nd Panzer Grenadier Regiment took the stubbornly defended little town of Saint-Barthélemy by storm. A hundred prisoners were taken. But then the tanks of the "Leibstandarte" got stuck in front of a powerful barrier on the main road to Avranches. Strong formations of the 3rd U.S. Armoured Division refused to be dislodged.

Meanwhile the 2nd S.S. Panzer Division had broken into Mortain and overrun the anti-tank gun positions of the 30th U.S. Division. It was now storming the high ground outside the town.

But the heights could not be taken at the first rush. And then the momentum was lost. It became a tough struggle for

Republic Thunderbolt

every foot of ground. On the other wing, on the right flank of the offensive, the 116th Panzer Division ran into an anti-tank position of the Americans who had occupied the area around Périers on the preceding day. It could not make another yard's progress.

Even so, by the time the morning haze lifted, Lüttwitz's right-hand assault group was deep inside the Mortain-Avranches corridor. One more such push and the bottleneck would be sealed. Whether it could be kept sealed with the weak forces available was another question, but at least the vital artery of Patton's army would be cut for a while. That might produce a sensational turn in the fortunes of war.

"Bad weather is what we need, Herr General. Then everything will work out all right," Lüttwitz's chief of operations said to him. But his wish was not granted. The early haze dispersed quickly. August 7 was ushered in with a cloudless sky. And in this sky, presently, appeared Eisenhower's wonder weapons: fighter-bombers, Thunderbolt bombers, and rocket fighters. Innumerable swarms of them. They pounced on the columns of the 2nd Panzer Division at Le Coudray, half-way to Avranches. They swept over the roads and drove grenadiers, Panzerjägers, and engineers under cover. With uncanny precision the rocket-shells of the Typhoons smashed into their targets. Against this weapon even the otherwise invincible *Tigers* of 1st Panzer Division were helpless. Desperately the tank crews ducked inside their steel boxes. The grenadiers lay in the fields, motionless, so as not to become targets. Rarely had the absent Luftwaffe been cursed as much as along this road to Avranches.

"How can the Luftwaffe be absent from such a vital operation as this?" the commanders in the field were asking each other. The troops, in simpler words, asked, "If they're not coming out for this, what *are* they waiting for?"

And why did they not come out?

Seventh Army knew, of course, that the offensive could not succeed without air cover against the enemy's fighter-bombers. Air-General Bülowius had promised to make 300 fighters available. "In ceaseless sorties," he had assured Hausser, "they will keep the skies clear above the area of operations."

Yet not a single German aircraft showed up. Not, by any means, because Bülowius had gone back on his word. The fighter formations had indeed taken off from their airfields around Paris. But British and American fighters had intercepted them and engaged them in aerial combat immediately above their bases. Not a single unit reached the air space over the fighting front between Mortain and Avranches. With complete impunity the Allied airmen were able to hunt down the tanks, anti-tank guns, and grenadiers of the assault group of 47th Panzer Corps, and, thus it came about that, for the first time in military history, a vigorous and successful land offensive was eventually halted from the air.

The German regiments were still defending the ground they had gained, contesting every patch of wood, every farmhouse, and every sunken lane. But the offensive had been broken— smashed from the air. Admittedly, General Bradley had to employ his entire VIII Corps against the German combat groups in order to exorcise the mortal danger; but exorcise it he did. After forty-eight hours the German grenadiers reeled back into their jumping-off positions, which they had left so hopefully during the night of August 6.

Attack by 600 Tanks

The British forces in the meantime had not remained idle. To support the American defensive operations in the Avranches-Mortain corridor, Montgomery sent in the II Canadian Corps south of Caen to engage as many German forces as possible. It was the old technique of alternate emphasis.

The operation bore the code name Totalize. This suggested that Montgomery intended a major blow. His idea was to break through the German front, press on to Falaise, and attack from the rear the German armoured forces aiming at Avranches.

On August 7, after nightfall, the Canadian divisions assembled south of Caen and prepared to move off. Armour and motorized infantry formations were to attack in six wedges west and east of the Caen–Falaise main road, force a break-through, and take Falaise in the afternoon.

Towards midnight the first aerial bombardment of the forward German lines began. Behind this hail of fire the Canadians moved off with more than 1000 armoured vehicles. Ahead of them flew over 1000 Flying Fortresses which once more smashed up the positions of the 272nd Grenadier Division and of the 89th Infantry Division which had only just been brought over from Norway. Then came the tanks. They cleared narrow passages. Through these narrow passages Canadian infantry aboard self-propelled carriers roared into the rear of the German positions.

They dismounted, fanned out, and attacked the German strong-points from behind.

To crack open the six-mile-wide arc of German positions south of Caen, Montgomery threw in everything he had got on the ground and in the air. On the flanks of the front arc 500 heavy bombers turned the ground into a landscape of huge craters. Crater upon crater, with no level ground left anywhere. It was a new, cunning device to prevent the tanks of 12th S.S. Panzer Division from making relief attacks from the flanks.

Smoke and dust hung in the air. To add to the inferno 700 American aircraft made a direct frontal attack on the most forward German strongpoints. They dropped on them a new type of high-explosive bomb. Squadrons of Typhoon fighters with rocket cannon ranged over the hinterland, intercepting all traffic to the front and pinning down anti-tank and 88-millimetre positions. The 89th Infantry Division, which had been transferred from an idyllic existence in Norway straight into the inferno of the great decisive battle in the West, bore the brunt of the attack. It cracked. Some units panicked. But other sectors of the front stood up to the Canadian attacks until midnight. Things were looking ugly. The British and Canadian assault units were three miles inside the German defences. The 4th Canadian and 1st Polish Armoured Divisions were still being kept in reserve on either side of the Caen–Falaise road. They only had to move, and disaster would be complete. All there was to oppose them was two combat groups of 12th S.S. Panzer Division with fifty tanks.

Kurt Meyer realized the danger. He rallied his forces and, together with Sturmbannführer[1] Waldmüller, went forward to get a picture of the situation. Through his binoculars he saw the packed tank columns along the Caen–Falaise road.

"Great heavens," he said to Waldmüller. "Suppose they move in now?" They could not understand why they were not moving in.

The reason was simply that their commanders lacked experience and would not risk thrusting past the German strongpoints which were still holding out.

Meyer realized that an attack by the enemy's armour must be prevented unless the whole front was to collapse. The only method was defence within the front line, centring on Cintheaux,

---

[1] Rank in S.S. troops equivalent to major.

combined with an enveloping attack by German armour. Meyer calculated. It should be possible to get ready by 1230. "Attack at 1230 hours," he commanded.

Just then things were livening up in the air. Enemy reconnaissance planes. That was dangerous. Wherever those fellows showed up, bombing raids followed. And an aerial bombardment of his assembly positions in the neighbouring villages was the last thing Meyer wanted. There was only one way out. Immediate attack. Off!

Once again Michel Wittmann's *Tigers* rumbled northward. Great hopes were pinned upon them. The grenadiers followed.

Everything happened the way Meyer had foreseen. The 8th U.S. Air Force made a carpet-bombing attack with several hundred bombers and levelled the villages where the grenadiers had been stationed a little while before. Meyer's men laughed maliciously. The fireworks display had not hurt them. They took Cintheaux and established themselves among the ruins. Wittmann's *Tigers* gave them flank cover against enemy tank attacks and themselves wrought havoc among the Canadian armoured companies. The Canadian attacks, launched piecemeal and half-heartedly, time and again fizzled out in the German defensive fire. In vain did General Simonds, the commander of the II Canadian Corps, try to revive the momentum of his offensive. The attacks of his armada of 600 tanks broke against the wall of Cintheaux and Wittmann's *Tigers*.

"The front is holding," the communiqués proclaimed. The front! Much too grand a term. There was no front. There was only a shell-torn, pitted, ravaged strip of land six miles wide. Half-buried, the last grenadiers and machine-gun sections were lying in their foxholes. Death and destruction had been showered on them by 1900 bombers and 1800 fighters.

In the afternoon the Canadians took Bretteville, which had been stubbornly defended by remnants of 89th Infantry Division without armour-piercing weapons. The rest of the division, which still used horse-drawn transport, was overrun and shot up.

The fighting for Cintheaux raged until nightfall. However, with the fall of Bretteville the defenders' flank was exposed. Combat group Waldmüller and Wittmann's tanks therefore broke off contact with the enemy and withdrew to the Laison river. The *Tigers* were placed in ambush in the forest of Quesnay. Michel Wittmann, the much-feared tank killer, was no longer with them. He had met his death in action.

To save Totalize, the offensive that had begun so promisingly, the Canadian commander decided on a bold stroke. He dispatched a mixed assault group with 28th Tank Regiment to occupy the tactically important Hill 195, a good distance to the south, by a night attack. In this way he would gain control of the strip of ground between the Laison and Laize rivers, and the German defensive positions would find themselves outflanked.

The move turned into a dramatic episode. The British assault force lost its way. Instead of Hill 195, it occupied Hill 140, about four miles farther to the east, without encountering resistance. But Hill 140 happened to be the defensive position chosen for Waldmüller's combat group after its withdrawal from Cintheaux.

Waldmüller meanwhile had been overtaken by the enemy and forced away from his objective. Thus, when Obersturmführer[1] Meitzel drove up the hill in a scout car in order to link up with Waldmüller he suddenly found himself under fire from tanks in a clump of trees. Zigzagging wildly he raced back.

Kurt Meyer had watched the incident in astonishment through his binoculars from a neighbouring hill. "What are those tanks doing up there, firing? Did Waldmüller mistake Meitzel for a Tommy?" But almost at once Meitzel's report came through from the Panzer regiment. "Hill 140 occupied not by German forces but by enemy tanks."

Meyer felt a shiver run down his spine. How on earth had enemy tanks got to Hill 140? And where was Waldmüller?"

Meitzel was again sent out to reconnoitre. This time he did not return. His vehicle was knocked out and, although he was now on Hill 140, he was there as a prisoner of the Canadians.

Max Wünsche had also ordered a reconnaissance to be made of the hill. The result was beyond doubt. The hill was being held by strong enemy forces. Their tank guns commanded the Laison valley. But this valley was the last possible defensive position north of Falaise. Moreover, a new formation, Lieutenant-General Chill's 85th Infantry Division, was already on its way to take up positions there. Action was imperative. The enemy had to be dislodged from the hill.

Meyer assembled fifteen *Panthers* to storm the hill from the east, and a few *Tigers* to storm it from the west. Artillery and mortars opened up on the target. The *Tigers* crept up to the hillside under cover of the bushes. Their 88-millimetre shells

---

[1] Rank in S.S. troops equivalent to lieutenant.

Royal Tiger

crashed into the clumps of trees and undergrowth. Enormous pillars of smoke signalled direct hits. One Sherman after another was blown up or left lying a smouldering wreck. And now the first *Panthers* were coming up from the east. Just then the familiar opponents appeared on the scene. Enemy fighter-bombers pouncing down from the sky. Against them even *Tigers* and *Panthers* were helpless. ''Damn,'' cursed Meyer. ''Damn. Are we going to lose this round as well?'' But for once Montgomery's flying artillery ranged itself as an ally on the side of the German ground forces. The fighter-bombers directed their shells not at the *Tigers* and *Panthers* but at the Canadian tanks. In a flash Max Wünsche sent his tanks up the hill. There they found a vast tank cemetery. From behind their smouldering wreckage and from foxholes in the ground the Canadians offered desperate resistance. With the help of two bicycle companies of 85th Infantry Division, which had just appeared on the scene as their division's vanguard, the Canadians were being increasingly crowded together. One batch after another, they surrendered.

Obersturmführer Meitzel arrived with twenty-three Canadians of 28th Tank Regiment. A little while before he had been their prisoner. Now they were his. In this war roles were exchanged very quickly. Forty-seven tanks littered the ground, smouldering.

On Hill 195, tanks and grenadiers of the combat group Olbotter stood their ground against furious attacks by Canadian Highlanders. On the right wing Obersturmführer Hurdelbrink's hurriedly summoned Panzerjäger company with its 75-millimetre *Panther* guns on self-propelled chassis repulsed the 1st Polish Armoured Division's attempt to strike across the Laison river. The Poles lost forty tanks. In dismay, Montgomery's divisions withdrew towards the north.

Falaise was once more saved. Totalized had been stopped.

Utterly exhausted, nearly dropping with fatigue, the men of 12th S.S. Panzer Division handed over their positions to 85th Infantry Division. They were not to know that their magnificent defensive success would prove an expensive victory, a victory that would lead the German Command into fatal miscalculations.

Since the danger of a British break-through towards Falaise now seemed to have been averted, Field-Marshal von Kluge yielded to pressure from the Führer's headquarters and ordered another offensive towards Avranches with a view to closing the bottleneck after all. It was a dangerous, a disastrous gamble. It meant that Kluge was keeping the bulk of Army Group B in an exposed position which, on operational grounds, it ought to have abandoned long ago. He closed his eyes to the fact that Patton's army was already streaming past Le Mans. He refused to see that the opportunity of encircling and annihilating the German forces was being positively forced upon the Americans unless the front line was taken back at once.

Things happened as they were bound to happen. On August 10 the XV U.S. Corps wheeled left via Alençon to Argentan, into the deep flank of the Seventh Army. Thus, with the Canadian thrust to the Laison river, the big pocket in which Kluge's divisions with their 150,000 men found themselves was beginning to take shape. Unless they pulled out to the east in a hurry, between Argentan and Falaise, while the anti-tank positions on the Laison were still holding out, they would meet with disaster.

Guderian once defined the task of modern tank armies as follows: "The objective of the armoured troops is always the enemy's capital." General Patton was now applying this principle. He was whipping on his divisions towards the Seine and Paris.

Simultaneously he increased his pressure on Central France, racing on towards Tours and Orléans.

General Wilck's 708th Infantry Division, which tried to stem the southward surge of the American motorized divisions, was overrun.

New formations, including the well-equipped 9th Panzer Division, were hurriedly brought up from the south of France. Now that it was too late they were being sent into action one by one, when during the first week of the invasion—if only they had been moved up to the front in time—they might have reversed the course of events.

Again the O.K.W. ordered: "The southern front must be held!" The strategic idea was to hold in the south and to strike back towards the west. The German High Command rigidly clung to its plan to launch one more thrust towards Avranches, close the corridor, and cut off the American forces which by now were well to the south. The operation was to be accomplished by General Eberbach's armoured group.

But even that excellent tank commander could not work miracles.

In the meantime, what was the situation in the fighting line? For the past four weeks all divisions of Seventh Army had been in action. And action meant heavy fighting during the day and marching at night without respite. Since the beginning of August none of the units had been receiving regular supplies. Stores had fallen into enemy hands. Whenever a supply column, running on its last drop of fuel, arrived at a store or fuel dump it would find it wrecked or occupied by the enemy. The result was that the vehicles, in particular the artillery tractors, were no longer getting any fuel.

The picture was the same among the armoured units. And in this condition the troops were being ceaselessly harassed and kept on the defensive by a mobile enemy with an abundance of supplies and equipment.

On August 12 it was clear that the second thrust from Mortain to Avranches, ordered by the O.K.W., was no longer possible. All hopes had been abandoned of halting Patton's Third Army and of chopping off the jaws of the pincers which were beginning to close round Seventh Army. There was only one thing left: get out of the pincers as fast as possible. Retreat across the Dives.

The horse-drawn divisions moved off. The motorized formations covered the withdrawal.

"Family men, two steps forward!"

August 13 was a Sunday. The remnants of the Panzer Lehr Division, now only a "combat group Panzer Lehr," were in position in the Habloville area, north-west of Argentan. The roads were jammed with shot-up horse-drawn transport. Motorized units were worming their way through. A mortar battery took up position on the edge of the village. At 0900 hours precisely, when the morning haze had given way to a brilliant summer sky, the fighter-bombers appeared. They swept over the road. They combed the small patches of wood and set fire to the farms and barns where grenadiers and gunners had sought shelter during the day.

General Bayerlein and his staff officers were in a slit trench near the edge of an orchard. The farmhouse which had housed his battle headquarters was on fire. A fighter-bomber roared up from the road towards the orchard. Barely thirty feet up it skimmed over the tops of the apple-trees. It banked. The pilot was peering out of the cockpit. He was looking straight into the slit trench. Bayerlein could see his face. He saw his eyes. The pilot seemed to be laughing and saying, "Just stay put. I'm coming back in a minute!" He completed his turn and was back in an instant. Stuttering, his cannon sent its 20-millimetre shells into the trench. With a crash, two bombs followed. An avalanche of earth and tree branches came down on Bayerlein and his officers. Those who were still alive dug their way out. Not one of them had escaped uninjured.

Some ninety miles west of the Habloville orchard, over on the Atlantic, another dramatic scene took place at the same time. In the courtyard of the fortress of Saint-Malo, on Hill 26, Colonel Bacherer was addressing his men. There were 700 of them left. There was no longer enough water or food for all. That was what Bacherer told them.

"Family men, two steps forward!" he commanded. And he let those who had wives and children at home fall out and march into captivity. For those who remained began the final chapter of the fortress.

The Americans battered the strongpoints and penetrated into the outer defences.

Early in the morning of August 15 the telephone rang in Bacherer's underground headquarters. Surprised, the colonel picked up the receiver. "This is Major-General Macon," a voice said. Bacherer was speechless. "I am inviting you to surrender. We are already inside your strongpoints," the American commander continued through an interpreter.

Bacherer replied, "I see no cause for surrender, but I would request you to take over my wounded who are no longer capable of fighting."

Macon agreed. An hour's cease-fire was arranged. The bulkhead doors of the fortifications swung open. American ambulances drove up and took over the German wounded. For one hour humanity prevailed over the war.

Then the doors of the galleries on top of Paulus Hill were closed once more. The final round began. Towards 1400 hours the Americans began to use phosphorus shells. The ammunition dump was hit and an explosion followed. Fire broke out. Burning liquid phosphorus set fire to the straw in the troops' dormitories, and since there was no ventilation plant the galleries were soon filled with smoke and fumes.

At that stage Bacherer ordered a white flag to be hoisted, and 350 survivors marched off into captivity. Paulus Hill had fallen.

Over on the other side, ninety miles farther east, in the Falaise area, the remnants of fifteen divisions—over 100,000 men—continued to resist annihilation in a vast pocket, the "pocket of Falaise."

"Keep moving, let's get out of the trap," was the order of the day. But that was more easily said than done. There was but a single bridge over the Orne across which the divisions of the 84th Corps and the 2nd Parachute Corps could escape. Vehicle behind vehicle, nose to tail, endless columns were queuing up on the road to the bridge throughout the night and well into the morning. Whoever got across was saved. Those who were still on the western bank when day dawned had to seek what cover they could in the open ground. For during the day, throughout the hours of daylight, enemy fighter-bombers, Typhoons, and medium bombers would try to wreck the bridge, that last road to salvation, apart from a few rather insecure emergency bridges suitable only for infantry. Oddly enough, they did not succeed.

"Where is Field-Marshal von Kluge?"

The date was August 17. It was to prove a fateful day for the campaign in the West. Hitler had mistrusted Kluge for some

time; since he had been informed that the field-marshal had
sympathized with the conspirators of July 20. On August 15
Kluge had left his headquarters for the front to consult with
General Eberbach, but failed to arrive at Nécy, their agreed
meeting-place. Hours passed. Army Group B sent a signal to all
divisional headquarters: "Where is Field-Marshal von Kluge?"
Later in the evening Eberbach received a signal direct from the
Führer's headquarters: "Establish whereabouts of Field-Marshal
Kluge. Report back every hour." This keen interest did not
spring from any solicitude for the C.-in-C.'s fate. An ugly
suspicion was haunting the German High Command at Rastenburg.
"Kluge has gone off for secret surrender talks with the enemy,"
it was whispered. The rumour, however, was totally unfounded.
It was merely a product of Hitler's uneasy conscience. In reality,
Kluge had got caught in an enemy fighter-bomber attack. His car
and his two wireless-transmitters had been shot up. After that the
field-marshal had found himself trapped in the chaotic night
traffic on the congested roads. For hours on end he drifted
helplessly in the slow moving current of a defeated army. Finally,
at midnight, after a twelve-hour absence from his headquarters,
he turned up at Eberbach's command-post in Nécy.

At the Führer's headquarters, however, his story was not
believed. Instead, a man who enjoyed a reputation of unconditional loyalty to Hitler, of ruthless severity, tremendous willpower,
and fanatical personal courage was picked up by aircraft from the
Russian front and appointed to succeed Kluge. Thus, on August
17, Field-Marshal Walter Model turned up quite unexpectedly at

Douglas B-26

the headquarters of the Army Group, with a handwritten note from Hitler, and took over the command in the West.

As Model came out of the map room after his first conversation with Kluge he nearly collided with General Bayerlein. "What on earth are you doing here?" Model asked.

"I was going to report to Field-Marshal von Kluge. The remnants of my division are to be pulled out of the line for a rest," Bayerlein answered.

Model's reply reflected the spirit of the merciless war in Russia: "My dear Bayerlein, in the East our divisions take their rests in the front line. And that's how things are going to be done here in the future. You will stay with your formations where you are." He saluted and was gone.

Presently, Field-Marshal von Kluge was gone too. He dispatched a letter to Hitler, and departed. He had explained in his letter: "My Führer. When you receive these lines I shall be no more. I cannot bear the accusation of having brought about the fate of our armies in the West by mistaken measures, and I have no means of defending myself. I am therefore taking the only action I can, and shall go where thousands of my companions have preceded me. . . ."

In a concise military critique Kluge then outlined the reasons for the failure of the Mortain offensive. Inadequate armour, no antidote to the Allied air monopoly, a German army in the West that was inferior to the Allies both in numbers and in equipment. In conclusion, Kluge implored Adolf Hitler to end the war: "I do not know whether Field-Marshal Model, a man of proved ability, can still save the situation. I wish him success with all my heart. But if he does not succeed, and if your anxiously awaited new weapons—especially those of the Luftwaffe—do not prove decisive, then, my Führer, I appeal to you to end the war. The German people have undergone such unspeakable sufferings that it is time to put an end to the horror. . . . Display now the greatness that will be necessary for calling a halt to a war that has become hopeless."

Near Metz, Kluge swallowed a phial containing poison.

Model was unable to save the situation. He could not avert the fate that was to befall the troops in the Argentan–Falaise pocket.

On the very day that he took over the command of the Western front the American divisions at Argentan moved off towards the north. The British and Canadians at Falaise struck towards the south. The aim was a linkup and the closing of the pocket. The Seventh Army and the 5th Panzer Army were to be caught in the trap. Some 100,000 men—the remnants of fifteen divisions—were herded together in an area twenty-two miles wide and eleven miles deep. Ceaselessly, artillery and bomber squadrons pounded the troops in the pocket. Many formations disintegrated. The men, sick with despair, wandered about aimlessly or lay under cover anywhere, waiting for the end. Others were determined to fight their way out. There was only a narrow gap left, between Saint-Lambert and Chambois, where escape might still be possible.

The Hell of Falaise

The 2nd Canadian Infantry Division was to take Falaise, the "hinge" of the door, and then strike at Trun and slam the door shut.

In Falaise, however, S.S. troops were established. The 6th Canadian Brigade had to capture it house by house from a small combat group of 12th S.S. Panzer Division. In the end sixty grenadiers held out inside the *Ecole Supérieure* for three days. Only four of them were taken prisoners, and they were wounded. The rest had been killed one by one. During the final night two S.S. privates, boys of eighteen and nineteen, chosen by lot, had sneaked through the Canadian lines to report to Division the annihilation of their combat group.

When they got there the wireless-transmitters were just about to be blown up. There were no tanks left. The last two *Tigers* had held up the spearhead of the 53rd British Infantry Division for a while and had then been knocked out.

Obersturmführer Meitzel was taken prisoner with his men—all of them wounded. Standartenführer Max Wünsche came up with his last few tanks against a strong enemy anti-tank position. His tanks were destroyed. Wünsche managed to escape, but was taken prisoner five days later. "Panzer" Meyer was left with a mere handful of men, only some hundred from what was once a powerful and impressive division. Were they all—they and the other divisions in the big trap between Falaise and Argentan—doomed to suffer a Norman Stalingrad?

On August 18 Major-General von Gersdorff, representing Seventh Army, arranged with General Eberbach, of Armoured Group West, that Bittirich's 2nd S.S. Panzer Corps, in position outside the pocket, would support Seventh Army in its break-out attempt by striking at the British flank from the Vimoutiers area. Bittrich was still without motor fuel and ammunition on the afternoon of August 19, but he hoped nevertheless to be ready to move by the morning of August 20.

Consequently Colonel-General Hausser, the Seventh Army commander, ordered all units still capable of action to break out during the night of August 19–20.

General Elfeldt, commanding 84th Corps, formulated the order briefly as follows: "Individual combat groups will break out independently from the pocket. The 84th Corps staff will cover these operations with the remaining fragmentary groups from the northern front and will follow 2nd Parachute Corps as rearguard."

A corps staff covering the break-out of its last battle-worthy units! It must be an order without parallel in the history of general staffs.

Early on August 20 General Wisch moved off with two divisions. Two divisions! It sounds impressive. But in fact he had a total of twenty tanks—two less than the normal strength of a tank company. The infantry of the two divisions comprised three battalions. Nevertheless, the attack made sufficiently good progress to begin with. Soon, however, it got stuck. The troops were able to take the high ground north of Coudehard, but that was all. All the corps could do was establish a supporting line for the formations trying to break out from the pocket.

The break-out battle, meanwhile, was in full swing.

The remnants of 353rd Grenadier Division, under the leadership of their experienced and prudent commander, General Mahlmann, broke out between Moissy and Chambois. The general personally reconnoitred the routes and led the local operations against the enemy forces covering those routes.

General Meindl, the commander of 2nd Parachute Corps, in a dramatic march led the 3rd Parachute Division, parts of 12th S.S. Panzer Division, and the headquarters personnel of Seventh Army out of the trap. Reconnaissance had confirmed that the pocket was by then completely closed. Meindl ordered two assault wedges to be organized. He personally assumed command of one of them. The other was led by his chief of staff, Colonel Blauensteiner.

Army had intended to place 277th Infantry Division and 12th S.S. Panzer Division also under Meindl's command. This did not come off because there was no longer any contact with these formations. However, in the late afternoon Meindl had informed "Panzer" Meyer of his plan in a personal telephone conversation. Meyer's headquarters personnel and Krause's group were to follow the infantry. The motorized units of 12th S.S. Panzer Division were to break out via Chambois together with 1st S.S. Panzer Division.

At 2230 hours the forward scouts of the parachute units slipped away into the night like shadows from their assembly positions in a small wood. The order was: "If possible avoid contact with the enemy." Accordingly Meindl and his men crawled over ploughed fields, crept past enemy armour, and sprinted along underneath the line of fire of Canadian machine-guns. Towards midnight they reached the Dives. The bridges were held by the enemy. There was but one way across—to swim. The river was five or six feet deep, the banks sloped steeply and were overgrown with brambles, and above, upon the bank, there lurked three enemy tanks. A few feet at a time, the infantrymen in their dripping-wet uniforms crawled past them along the furrows of a potato field. All the time they moved underneath a curtain of enemy machine-gun fire. Over on the other side, in Saint-Lambert, a few houses were on fire, lighting up the scene. The noise of battle floated across the river. Enemy tanks rumbled past. Horse-drawn vehicles, wrecked by enemy fire, littered the hedges and the roads.

The commander of the 3rd Parachute Division, Lieutenant-General Schimpf, was seriously wounded in the leg by a 20-millimetre shell. Colonel-General Hausser, who had lost his right eye near Moscow, was marching along with his men, a machine-pistol slung round his neck. He was struck by shrapnel and again seriously wounded in the face. But this officer of the old school, a graduate of the Prussian Cadet College, did not give in. Propped up on the stern of a tank of 1st S.S. Panzer Division, he eventually escaped from the pocket after an adventurous journey.

Contact between Meindl's two assault wedges had been lost during the crossing of the Dives.

Colonel Blauensteiner with his group held the high ground of Coudehard. At daybreak he attacked the hill with the chapel on it. But the barrier established there by the 1st Polish Armoured Division was too strong. Blauensteiner was unable to pierce it. Major Stephan, the experienced commander of 9th Parachute Regiment, was severely wounded. With the onset of daylight the infantry took cover behind hedges, in ditches, and in farm buildings. As dusk fell they turned to the south, broke through the enemy ring, and moved on towards Orville.

General Meindl himself, together with a few officers and twenty men, had got through all enemy barriers. But towards dawn they happened to come across the line of advance of an enemy armoured column. Three tanks pulled up within a few yards of the trench in which Meindl and his men were lying. They could hear the tank crews talking. They were speaking Polish. For an hour and a half the small group remained pinned down, motionless and in complete silence. At last a few shells burst near by, and the tanks moved to another position. The slight drizzle which had been falling during the morning and which had somewhat mitigated their thirst now ceased. The sun came out. It grew hot. Under the hedges the heat was like that of a greenhouse. At last Meindl made out the rattle of German Mark 42 machine-guns—Blauensteiner's attack on the high ground of Coudehard.

Meindl now also assembled his force. He rounded up whatever stragglers of 9th and 15 Parachute Regiments he could find. And supported by three tanks of the S.S. Panzer Division "Das Reich" the attack on the enemy's barrier position east of Coudehard got under way.

Towards 1600 hours they had burst open a hole one or two miles wide. At 1700 the first German trucks drove out of the pocket towards the east along the winding road of Coudehard. Shortly after 1900 Meindl arranged for all wounded within reach to be driven out through the gap by a hurriedly assembled Red Cross column, with Red Cross flags prominently displayed. For all other vehicles the general declared the road closed. His correct behaviour was duly rewarded. Enemy fighter-bombers swooped down but, seeing the column, swung away. As soon as general traffic was resumed at 2000 hours the fighter-bombers promptly returned and opened up at the columns. Only nightfall put an end to their strafing.

Troops and vehicles were streaming out of the pocket through the gap at Coudehard until shortly before midnight. Of the 3rd Parachute Division, about 4000 men, including corps troops, escaped from the inferno. When an armoured reconnaissance detachment reported that there was nobody behind them Meindl ordered the positions along the edges of the gap to be abandoned. Wind and rain drowned the noise of these movements. At 0500 hours the gap was closed up again. Enemy tanks were moving over the high ground. Anyone attempting to slip out north-west of Saint-Lambert now would run straight into a barrier of Canadian armour.

In the grey dawn of August 20 yet another hole was punched into the ring of encirclement. The Seventh Army chief of staff, Major-General Freiherr von Gersdorff, had reached the Trun-Chambois main road hard by the village of Saint-Lambert, on the eastern bank of the Dives, with his combat group which included part of 1st S.S. Panzer Division. Enemy anti-tank guns covered the road. Gersdorff sent forward two tanks. They fought down the anti-tank guns and crossed the road. Immediately German scout cars, self-propelled guns, and trucks broke from every conceivable kind of cover and raced through the gap towards the east—but unfortunately smack into a position held by the 90th U.S. Division. The Americans, flushed with the certainty of victory, were completely taken by surprise. They put up their hands. But what was one to do with them? Take them along? That was impossible. They were disarmed and left where they were.

Two energetic officers, Major Bochnik of the 116th Panzers and Sturmbannführer Brinkmann of the 12th S.S. Panzer Division, organized a new combat group on the spot and with it attempted a further break-out. They widened the gateway to salvation and made the "breakout point army commander" the most important gap on the eastern edge of the pocket.

"Panzer" Meyer had assembled his combat group in a few farm buildings towards midnight. Together with General Elfeldt and his chief of staff, von Criegern, the leading team moved off. At Chambois they met an armoured column of 1st S.S. Panzer Division, which was just then getting ready for attack. Meyer's group joined them. But the enemy anti-tank barrier proved too strong. They fell back. They rallied again. They launched another attack. This time they were successful. They swam across the Dives. On the hillside sloping down to the river the enemy was established and was firing down at them. The river-bed had become a death-trap for the horse-drawn artillery. Dead horses, limbers, guns, with human bodies scattered along them—that was the scene on the muddy banks of the Dives.

The group moved on. Canadian infantry was overrun. Meyer with his 200 men tore through the enemy positions like a ghostly hunt. The men did not yell. Almost without a sound they burst from the hedges. The Canadians, in panic, fell back in the face of this assault. It was led by the commander himself, his head in a bloody bandage and his pistol in his fist. Charging alongside him, with a machine-pistol, was Mikhail, a Cossack from Dnepropetrovsk who had accompanied Meyer throughout the campaign. Hubert Meyer, the divisional chief of operations, ran with a carbine under his arm. Obersturmführer Köhn had an old haversack dangling from his neck, crammed full with hand-grenades.

They leapt over a ditch full of German dead.

Out! That was their one thought. Out of this inferno.

In his account of the break-out, Kurt Meyer says, ''When we had got through we turned and looked back and cursed the men who had senselessly sacrificed two German armies.''

The 2nd Panzer Division, under its wounded commander von Lüttwitz, likewise fought its way out of the pocket. With his last fifteen tanks and his divisional artillery Lüttwitz mounted his attack south-east of Saint-Lambert at dawn on August 20. The 304th Panzer Grenadier Regiment and the last of the Panzerjägers covered the thrust. The armoured spearhead and the 2nd Panzer Grenadier Regiment battered their way through Saint-Lambert and kept the gap towards Trun and Chambois open for a few hours, until the rest of the division had passed through.

The 116th Panzer Division freed itself from encirclement in savage fighting and got fifty fighting vehicles safely out of the pocket.

Meanwhile, Major Hayn, the 84th Corps Intelligence officer, was stuck with Corporal Volland in the middle of a horse-drawn column outside Chambois. The bridge down in the valley was already in sight when the enemy tanks opened fire on the column. The drivers slewed off the road to the right and left, trying to find cover in some patches of wood. One group found refuge in the old Château d'Aubry. Hayn and Captain Pfeifer of 47th Panzer Corps decided to follow the dictates of common sense and conscience. They organized parties to bring in the many wounded who were lying behind hedges, in the fields, in sunken lanes, and near their vehicles. Before long the château and its park had become a major collecting post for the wounded. Lieutenant Tillmann, the medical officer of 988th Infantry Regiment, and Lieutenant Dieter Müller, the medical officer of the ''Hitler-jugend'' Division, arrived on the scene and took charge. In vain, however, did Hayn send out radio signals in clear, declaring the château a field hospital. In vain were big sheets laid out on the lawns in front of the buildings. British artillery slammed into the turrets and the forecourts. At long last, early in the morning of August 21, American reconnaissance units drove into the courtyard.

Hayn handed over the wounded to a captain of 90th U.S. Division. Outside the château American infantry had taken up position—men from Texas and Oklahoma. Curiously they eyed the German officer. One of the men was playing a mouth-organ. He broke off and called over to the major in German. "Know this one?" And, more appositely than he realized, he played the old tune: *Ach, du lieber Augustin*. Hayn felt the tears rising to his eyes. But he did not turn his head.

General Elfeldt and Lieutenant-Colonel von Criegern had lost contact with Meyer's group during the crossing of the river. Until 0300 the general waited for news about the situation at the break-out points. But the only news that reached him was a signal that he had been relieved of his command. It ran: "Relieved. Corps headquarters personnel to assemble north of Mont Ormel. Re-employment in an intercepting line near Amiens."

Shortly after 0300 General Elfeldt led a small combat group, which he had organized from stragglers, into attack towards Saint-Lambert. Their road was barred by the outposts of an enemy tank battalion. Elfeldt tried to by-pass it along a sunken lane. Too late. A column of the 1st Polish Armoured Division engaged the group and shot it up. Whoever was not killed was taken prisoner.

Thus General Elfeldt and his staff were left behind in the pocket, in the Stalingrad of Normandy. Left behind with him were 40,000 prisoners of war and 10,000 killed. But 50,000 men had fought their way out.

8

THE BEGINNING OF THE END

The Crossing of the Seine

"Blauensteiner!" General Meindl exclaimed joyfully when he ran into his chief of staff and chief of operations at Orville towards noon on August 21. The colonel laughed and saluted. "Present and correct, Herr General—after slipping out of the trap."

The officers and men looked like gipsies. Their uniforms were in shreds from the thorn hedges along the sunken roads. The men were covered with dirt, and most of them were wounded. But no one who had survived this break-out would ever again be afraid of anything.

"What now, Herr General?" Blauensteiner asked his corps commander.

"I found what's left of Seventh Army headquarters personnel this morning. We are to move to the Seine in two nightly marches and wait there to be ferried across. The retreat will be covered by an armoured formation of the S.S. Panzer Division 'Das Reich'."

"That's most reassuring, Herr General," Blauensteiner said sarcastically.

Meindl looked at his chief of staff. He made no reply. No reply was necessary.

Ever since June 7 the spectre of a big Allied break-through had been hovering over the map table at corps headquarters. At first, Army Group B had lacked the necessary strength to prevent a landing. Then it had not received sufficient reinforcements to split up the enemy's bridgeheads by counter-attacks and to throw the enemy back into the sea. Costly though they were, the counter-attacks of Seventh Army had always been only just sufficient to clean up penetrations and patch up the crumbling front. One Panzer division after another had been decimated. Protected by their air forces, the Allies had gained enough time to land such vast quantities of men and *matériel* that anybody could calculate for himself when this flood was bound to burst through the weak dam. And now the time had come. For two months the collapse had been delayed. Now it had taken place. Admittedly, there had been no large-scale surrender in the Falaise pocket. One-third of Seventh Army had been able to escape and to avoid annihilation. But the armoured troops, the backbone of all offensive operations, had been smashed. Their remnants were, at best, suitable for defensive fighting. After Falaise, Army Group B was composed of 100 tanks in fighting order. A mere 100 tanks!

Meindl recalled the information sheet which had been sent to him from the Führer's headquarters in December 1943. According to shorthand record No. 35, page 24, Hitler had confidently and optimistically told a conference on December 20, 1943: ''The decisive point is that, at the moment of landing, the enemy will have bombs dropping on his head. We shall then compel him to take cover. And so long as there is even a single aircraft in the sky he must remain under cover. In this way he will lose time hour by hour. Within half a day, however, our reserves will be moving up. If the enemy is pinned down on the beach for only six or eight hours you can well imagine what this will mean for us.''

Hitler's calculation had been wrong. True, the enemy had been pinned down upon landing for six hours or more, even without the Luftwaffe, but the reserves had never turned up. At first they had been mobilized only in driblets and too late. And then they had been employed wrongly and with insufficient artillery support. They had not been able to move in during the day because they had no roof over their heads. The skies had been controlled by the fighter-bombers, the medium bombers, and the heavy bombers of the Allies. And these had barred the way to all German operational reserves. They had made nonsense of Hitler's calculations.

The war in the West was decided by Allied superiority in the air. This was the second time that Rommel had been defeated by Allied airmen. The first time was in Africa. It was from the air, and from the air alone, that Rommel's tank army was defeated in North Africa, at the very moment when his hand was on the door to Cairo and to the fabulous oilfields of the Middle

East. The complete dislocation of German supplies caused the Afrika Korps to be without fuel and without vehicles during the decisive battle of El Alamein. Thus the chance of capturing North Africa and the Middle East, and of making Britain ready to sue for peace, had been lost.

The German U-boats had likewise been eliminated from the air. The offensive of the "Grey Wolves" had been stopped by bomber aircraft controlled by radar. They had inflicted heavy losses on the U-boats, outmanoeuvred them, and forced them to stay submerged.

It was from the air again that the manufacture and employment of the V-1 and V-2, the first two rocket weapons in military history, had time and again been delayed. The centres of production and research in Germany, as well as the launching ramps in the front-line area, had been wrecked repeatedly by bombing.

This Allied superiority in the air grew into a complete air monopoly at the time of the invasion, and thus into the decisive prerequisite for victory in the West. Carpet bombing and fighter-bomber attacks pulverized coastal fortifications and wrecked the French railway network, cut off reinforcements and supplies, smashed armoured divisions and artillery, and rendered the infantry helpless victims.

This, then, was the real, bitter truth about the Second World War. Meindl knew it, and Blauensteiner knew it too. It was not the fault of the Luftwaffe officers or staff that the German bomber and fighter squadrons were so hopelessly outnumbered during the latter part of the war. The fact was that the German armaments industry was simply not capable of handling a war against the West and the East. It could supply either aircraft or tanks. It could not provide both.

"What now?" Colonel Blauensteiner asked his corps commander.

"Our great hope is the Seine," Meindl replied.

The Seine! A big river, certainly. But even a big river was no longer an insuperable obstacle to a modern, technically well-equipped army. Prefabricated bridges, special pontoons, and assault boats enabled entire divisions to cross a river in a matter of hours, provided, of course, that its banks were not defended by highly mobile troops, heavy artillery, self-propelled guns, and tanks, which could nip every attempt at crossing in the bud. In the absence of such opposition a river was no more than a ditch. The German armies had proved this in the Russian campaign.

Why should the Americans, who had successfully crossed the Channel, be more helpless on the Seine?

They were, of course, anything but helpless. General Patton once again displayed the boldness he had already shown at Avranches. Heedless of the enemy, he raced his divisions through Northern France. The roads to Paris were open, undefended, and intact.

The German High Command believed that it could defend Paris and cover the German retreat to the Seine with only three divisions of Fifteenth Army. Once again a clear case of too little and too late. Patton was sweeping along with three armoured divisions and three fully motorized infantry divisions. Luckily for the German retreat it was bad flying weather. The fighter-bombers were grounded. Thus the remnants of the 2nd Parachute Corps reached the Seine at Louviers without losses.

Major-General Kurt Meyer also turned up at the headquarters of 1st S.S. Panzer Corps with the remnants of his 12th S.S. Panzer Division and was greeted like a man returned from the dead. Whatever had managed to escape from the pocket was ferried across the Seine at Rouen in boats and barges. Formations of the division already on the Seine for rest and replenishment were deployed to delay the enemy.

A truck jolted along with the survivors of 1st Battalion, 25th Panzer Grenadier Regiment, the hard core of the combat group Waldmüller. Among them were a dozen men of 1st Company. A mere dozen.

In the grey light of dawn on June 7, 1st Company had clambered aboard their vehicles at Caen. They had been 250 men. Andreas Schnell remembers clearly how, throughout their journey, Unterscharführer Grenzow kept saying to him: "When I shout 'Stop' you slam on your foot-brake and hand-brake at the same time." It had worked perfectly all the way. No fighter-bomber had got Schnell's troop carrier. But a bullet had got Grenzow. And all the others had caught their packet too. All but a mere dozen, the twelve men who were now riding on top of the truck. Only five of them had been with the company in Caen on June 7. Five survivors of their original lot.

The 21st Panzer Division was engaged in fighting with advancing American units along the road to the Seine: thrown in at one spot, then rushed to another, always expected to patch up the holes punched by the enemy into the weak, mobile covering-line and to prevent the formations falling back to the Seine from being cut off once more. The division had been in action ever since June 6. Until the end of August all the reinforcements it received amounted to two draft-conducting battalions. Most of the tanks had dropped out at Caen. The division had made its break-out from the pocket with only eight Mark IVs. Not one of them got across the Dives. The Panzer grenadier regiments had shrunk to forty or fifty men. Artillery, self-propelled gun units. Panzerjägers, and flak units had lost most of their weapons and vehicles. Numbers do not convey the extent of pain and suffering. But they do reflect the technical disaster that defeat means in a modern battle. They reflect the extent of the loss of military equipment without which a soldier becomes impotent no matter how brave he is.

Between June 6 and the end of August the formations of Army Group B lost 1300 tanks, 20,000 trucks and motor-cars, 500 self-propelled guns, 1500 field guns and howitzers, and several thousand anti-tank and anti-aircraft guns. Casualties totalled 400,000 killed, wounded, or taken prisoners. Some 200,000 filed into P.O.W. camps in Britain, Canada, and the U.S.A.

The god of war had swept the human and technical strength of two armies from the theatre of war. The remnants were now rallying on the banks of the Seine.

The 3rd Company of the engineer battalion of 21st Panzer Division were building a bridge over the river near Rouen. They worked like men possessed, since ever new formations were piling up on the river-bank, waiting for ferries, barges, and boats. The bridge-building operations proceeded without interference from the air. The weather was favourable.

Parties of officers were standing by the ramp. Pistol in hand they directed the crossing and checked panic and chaos. Here the remnants could be seen of all the battle-tested divisions that had shed their blood in Normandy: the 21st, the 2nd, and the 116th Panzer Divisions. The 2nd, 9th, 10th, and 12th S.S. Panzer Divisions. The 17th S.S. Panzer Grenadier Division, and men from parachute divisions, infantry divisions, Luftwaffe field divisions, and flak divisions who had fought with so much courage and even bravado among the orchards, the hedgerows, and the sunken lanes of the *bocage*.

Only one formation was absent—the 6th Parachute Regiment which had made the first promising counter-attacks on the Utah Beach sector on the very first day of the landings, and which had been in action continuously since June 6. The fate of this regiment was typical of the action and the extinction of many regiments.

After the evacuation of Carentan, von der Heydte's parachutists had fought in the sectors of various divisions on the Cotentin peninsula. About the middle of July the regiment's name once more figured prominently in the Seventh Army communiqué after its bicycle company of only twenty men had jointly with a Mark IV tank of 2nd S.S. Panzer Division "Das Reich" captured an American infantry battalion of thirteen officers and 600 men.

The regiment was subsequently caught up in the vortex of the American break-through at Saint-Lô and, with a combat group of 2nd S.S. Panzer Division, fought its way out to the south from the Coutances pocket, to the intercepting positions of 353rd Division. No one who took part in this action will ever forget it. Throughout the night, in single file, they had moved stealthily along secondary roads and secret paths, while, from the main road, the rumble of American tanks was borne over to them. Von der Heydte himself led the regiment's spearhead like a Red Indian chief. His cunning outwitted the fully motorized Americans. His regiment got through. But what was there left of this once proud regiment? A few hundred men. Nearly all of them sick or wounded. Most of them had to be sent down "hospital alley," as the troops called the road to the military hospital in Alençon.

Sixty men were left, a mere sixty. They were pulled out of the line, and at Lisieux caught up with the sick and wounded of the regiment, altogether 1007 men. From this single regiment 3000 officers and men had been killed in action or were missing.

The columns had been hurrying over the bridge at Rouen for barely two hours when the weather cleared. And with the sun came the lords of the battle of France—the Allied airmen.

Again not a single German aircraft was covering the crossing. The end was as the beginning had been. Only a few flak-guns were hurling their shells into the sky. But they could not avert the catastrophe. The fighter-bombers swept low over the bridge. They tore the pontoons apart with their shells. They dropped their bombs into the gaps. The Seine had its victims.

Meanwhile the fortunes of war had dealt a decisive trump card to General Patton three miles upstream from Paris. Near the little town of Mantes Gassicourt, nineteen miles north-west of Paris, German engineers had been blowing up the weir. Before they had finished their task they received the order to leave at once and tear up the important main road from Dreux into Paris, to mine it and to make it impassable for armour. The infantry units in position along the Seine in the Mantes area were likewise ordered to move off immediately to cover the road into Paris. The German High Command believed that General Patton would press straight on to the French capital with a view to capturing it as quickly as possible. And that had to be prevented.

Hitler was stubbornly clinging to the idea of defending Paris to the last house. That was why, from remote Rastenburg, thirty-seven miles from the Russian front, he was issuing detailed orders for every operation on the French battlefield, nearly 1000 miles away. He was conducting the war from a map, unable to take account of local conditions, but insisting that every withdrawal be authorized by him in person. As a result, much valuable time was constantly being lost, time that could have been vital in view of the rapidly changing situation. Hitler—that much seems clear from surviving sections of the O.K.W. war diary and from the accounts supplied by experienced staff officers to the compilers of the American history of the war—was by no means blind to the dangerous developments in the West. He had given more thought than anyone to the mechanization of warfare and understood the problems arising from American superiority. But—and this was his crucial error—he believed that the quality of the German troops could make up for that handicap. He expected far too much of the German front-line soldier.

Paris did not become another Warsaw

The American plan did not originally envisage the capture of Paris, as was assumed at the Führer's headquarters, but merely its encirclement. Eisenhower was averse to costly street-fighting.

Consequently, General Patton's 79th Infantry Division did not turn towards Paris at all, but, under cover of night, got to within three miles of Mantes without seeing a single German grenadier. On the following morning a patrol cautiously reconnoitred towards the river. No one on the American side dreamt that the Seine might not be held.

Everything was as quiet as the grave. The Americans saw the demolished weir. But a narrow footbridge was still passable. Provided, of course, that there was no German machine-gun on the opposite bank. One single machine-gun with two men would have been enough to deny the bridge to the Americans.

Sergeant White decided to chance it. With three volunteers he raced over the footbridge. Now they were across. Nothing happened. They waved. A patrol followed them across and cautiously probed the neighbourhood.

"Whatever you do, don't make any more noise than you have to," White reminded his men. They got two heavy machine-guns across the river. And then a few mortars.

They had gained their bridgehead. They radioed the news to General Patton. Patton immediately came in person. He had a look for himself. Then he raced off to Bradley, the C.-in-C. A few hours later he rang through to 79th Division: "Get the 313th Regiment over the river!"

The troops were roused from their sleep. They hurried over the footbridge, panting under their heavy weapons. They extend-

Browning H.M.G.

ed the bridge with girders and planks and presently drove their trucks across. By daybreak, when the first German troops out of the Falaise pocket were being ferried across the river at Rouen to establish a new defensive line behind the Seine, some twenty miles west of Paris General Patton already had a strong bridgehead over that river, a bridgehead that could no longer be reduced.

The incident of the bridge of Mantes—one of the many fateful bridges of the last war—was further evidence of how the German Command was losing control. Nothing was going right any longer, nothing at all. Fortune had definitely turned her back upon the German armies.

On August 23 Patton, with units of his 7th Armoured Division, also succeeded in establishing a bridgehead south-east of Paris, near Mclun. The Seine was conquered even before Paris had fallen.

"The objective of armour must always be the enemy's capital," had been one of Guderian's strategic principles. Eisenhower intended to disregard this principle in order to spare Paris. He wanted to encircle the city and subsequently compel the Germans to surrender. Soon, however, political considerations forced his hand.

On August 19 the palpable defeat of the German Army in the field had induced some 3000 Paris gendarmes to revolt and seize the police prefecture. That was the spark that touched off the powder barrel. The Resistance openly took up arms. *En avant!* Chase the Germans out of Paris!

Faced with this situation all the liaison officers at Allied headquarters were helpless. Appeals to common sense were of no avail, neither were references to strategic requirements. *Aux armes!* The cry went up through the suburbs. It was a matter of politics. None of the various Resistance organizations, from the Communists to the Nationalists, wanted to be outshone by any other. The City Hall, the Palais de Justice, the War Ministry were all occupied. The streets rang with the crack of rifles. Machine-guns rattled from basement windows. From the roofs hand-grenades were tossed down on German patrols.

General von Choltitz, commandant of Paris since August 7, was faced with a difficult decision. The Führer's order was: "The bridges over the Seine are to be blown up. The city is to be defended to the last house."

The general knew what this would mean—for the city, for

the civilian population, for the troops and the German headquarters, for the administrative authorities and the supply organizations.

The risks of the situation were highlighted by events on the far side of the European front, where the Warsaw rising of August 1 had led to savage and protracted fighting. The people of Warsaw had likewise taken up arms in expectation of their liberators. When the Russians failed to arrive Warsaw was reduced to ruins.

Choltitz did not want Paris to become another Warsaw. He negotiated with agents of the Resistance. There was a good deal of haggling. The general was on the horns of a dilemma. On the one hand he had to conduct his negotiations with the representatives of the Resistance and their liaison officers in such a way that not a whisper of it reached Hitler's headquarters. On the other he had to reach an agreement that would save him from having to surrender to the unpredictable forces of the Resistance. In the end a truce was arranged until August 23.

But the leaders of a Resistance movement combining so many different sections did not have full control over their rank and file. Many groups waged war independently. Attacks on German patrols and strongpoints continued, and counter-measures had to be taken in the face of provocation.

Choltitz could not allow the situation to drift any further. Chaos was imminent. The scene was already dominated by the attendants of the Horsemen of the Apocalypse—looters, irresponsible elements, and political wire-pullers. Many headquarters troops took off their uniforms in the hope of hiding out in civilian clothing with their girl-friends. Some of them succeeded. Others paid for their attempts with their lives, because the Resistance regarded them—and their girl-friends—as spies.

How was catastrophe to be averted? The German regular forces were far too few, and the hurriedly organized units of office personnel and transport staffs dissolved as quickly as they were formed. All battle-worthy Gestapo and police units had left the city. Nevertheless, urgent orders kept coming in for industrial plants and important strategic objectives in the city to be blown up. Choltitz tried to arrest the drift by sharply worded broadcast announcements. But the sharp words only further inflamed the heated tempers and led the Resistance to believe that the Germans had broken the truce. There was not a single responsible man in Paris in those days—from the German Ambassador, Otto Abetz, down to the commanding officers of the various Service units—who was not guided by the wish to save Paris from destruction.

In those hours of peril for the French capital many threads were woven between the opposing fronts in the hope of finding an acceptable solution.

It was found. In view of the reasonable German attitude Eisenhower decided—against his original intention—to let the V Corps with the 4th U.S. Infantry Division and the 2nd French Armoured Division march into the city. Choltitz now had a partner with whom the question of surrender could be discussed in an orderly military manner.

The Last Act

While the Resistance was hunting down German stragglers, climbing over the roofs and crawling through the sewers to surround and wipe out such German centres as were still holding out, the camp-followers of a twentieth-century war were streaming eastward out of the city in endless columns: civilian and semi-military officials, collaborators, units of French Militia, people who had made all kinds of deals with the Germans, and black-marketeers. Wedged in among these crowds were German headquarters personnel with their trucks piled high with office equipment, furniture, and young women auxiliaries. It was a sad procession.

The German garrison held out north of the Seine until the afternoon of August 25. Then General Choltitz surrendered with 10,000 men. But for many soldiers, and in particular for a great many officers, this was merely the beginning of a terrible ordeal. Freedom was triumphant, but, as usual, hatred was simmering not far beneath the surface. The fall of Paris was the final seal on the German defeat in the battle for France. The curtain was going up on the last act of the Second World War.

For the German army in the field the only hope left, the last hope, was the West Wall on the frontiers of the Reich—but this had long been stripped of all heavy weapons. It was a poor hope.

Nevertheless, the regiments trudged on towards it. "Their road was not yet at an end," a Canadian observer writes in the most recent official history of the war. And he adds this judgment:

> Although there is no doubt that in the higher
> levels of command the Allies' operations in Normandy

were far better conducted than the Germans', the same cannot be said with confidence about the operations on the actual battlefield. The German soldier and field commander showed themselves, as so often before, to be excellent practitioners of their trade. The German fighting soldier was courageous, tenacious, and skillful. He was sometimes a fanatic, occasionally a brutal thug: but he was almost always a formidable fighting man who gave a good account of himself, even under conditions as adverse as those in Normandy certainly were. German commanders and staff officers were in general highly competent. Man for man and unit for unit it cannot be said that it was by tactical superiority that we won the Battle of Normandy.

This is the exact truth. Victory was won by better organization, by superior air power, by superlative technical equipment, and by the inexhaustible wealth of production potential and manpower. The German armed forces had been burnt to cinders in the crushing battles of *matériel* in the West and in the murderous campaigns in Russia. Defeat was inevitable.

BIBLIOGRAPHY

Bekker, Cajus: *Radar–Duell im Dunkel* (Oldenburg/Hamburg: Gerhard Stalling Verlag).

Collier, Basil: *The Defence of the United Kingdom* (London: H.M. Stationery Office, 1957).

Ehrman, John: *Grand Strategy*, Vol. V (London: H.M. Stationery Office, 1956).

Eisenhower, Dwight D: *Crusade in Europe* (New York: Doubleday and Company, 1948. London: Heinemann, 1949).

Görlitz, Walter: *Der zweite Weltkrieg*, Bd. (Stuttgart: Steingrüben Verlag).

Guderian, Heinz: *Erinnerungen eines Soldaten* (Heidelberg: Kurt Vowinckel Verlag).

Harrison, Gordon A.: *Cross-Channel Attack—The European Theatre of Operations* (Washington, D.C.: Office of the Chief of Military History Department of the Army, 1951).

Hayn, Friedrich: *Die Invasion—Von Cotentin bis Falaise* (Heidelberg: Kurt Vowinckel Verlag).

Howarth, David: *Dawn of D-Day* (London: Collins, 1959. New York: McGraw-Hill, 1959).

Lusar, Rudolf: *Die deutschen Waffen und Geheimwaffen des 2. Weltkrieges und ihre Weiterentwicklung.* (München: J. F. Lehmanns Verlag). *German Secret Weapons of World War II* (Los Angeles, Calif.: Borden Publishing Co., 1959).

Meyer, Kurt ("Panzer" Meyer): *Grenadiere* (München-Lochhausen: Schild-Verlag).

Montgomery, Field-Marshal Viscount: *Memoirs* (London: Collins, 1958. Cleveland, Ohio: World Publishing Co., 1958).

Omaha Beachhead (War Department, Historical Division).

Ruge, Friedrich: *Rommel and die Invasion* (Stuttgart: K. F. Koehler Verlag).

Ryan, Cornelius: *The Longest Day* (New York: Simon and Schuster, 1959. London: Gollane, Gollancz, 1960).
Speidel, Hans: *Invasion 1944* (Tübingen and Stuttgart: Rainer Wunderlich Verlag. Chicago: Henry Regnery and Co., 1944).

Stacey, Colonel C. P.: *The Canadian Army 1939–45* (Ottawa: Edmond Cloutier, King's Printer, 1948).

Stjernfelt, Bertil: *Alarm i Atlantvallen* (Stockholm: Hörsta Förlag A.B.).

Verney, Major-General G.L.,: *The Desert Rats, The History of the 7th Armoured Division* (London: Hutchinson, 1954).

Wehr-Wissenschaftliche Rundschau: 9. Jahrgang, Heft 6, June 1959 (Frankfurt/Berlin: E. S. Mittler and Sohn GmbH).

Wilmot, Chester: *The Struggle for Europe* (London: Collins, 1952, New York: Harper and Brothers, 1952).

Also unpublished manuscripts, war diaries, and military studies in private possession and in German and foreign archives.

THE AVIATOR'S BOOKSHELF

THE CLASSICS OF FLYING

The books that aviators, test pilots, and astronauts feel tell the most about the skills that launched mankind on the adventure of flight. These books bridge man's amazing progress, from the Wright brothers to the first moonwalk.

☐ **THE WRIGHT BROTHERS by Fred C. Kelly** (23962-7 • $2.95)
Their inventive genius was enhanced by their ability to learn how to fly their machines.

☐ **THE FLYING NORTH by Jean Potter** (23946-5 • $2.95)
The Alaskan bush pilots flew in impossible weather, frequently landing on sandbars or improvised landing strips, flying the early planes in largely uninhabited and unexplored land.

☐ **THE SKY BEYOND by Sir Gordon Taylor** (23949-X • $2.95)
Transcontinental flight required new machines piloted by skilled navigators who could pinpoint tiny islands in the vast Pacific—before there were radio beacons and directional flying aids.

☐ **THE WORLD ALOFT by Guy Murchie** (23947-3 • $2.95)
The book recognized as *The Sea Round Us* for the vaster domain—the Air. Mr. Murchie, a flyer, draws from history, mythology and many sciences. The sky is an ocean, filled with currents and wildlife of its own. A tribute to, and a celebration of, the flyers' environment.

☐ **CARRYING THE FIRE by Michael Collins** (23948-1 • $3.50)
"The best written book yet by any of the astronauts."—*Time Magazine*. Collins, the Gemini 10 and Apollo 11 astronaut, gives us a picture of the joys of flight and the close-in details of the first manned moon landing.

☐ **THE LONELY SKY by William Bridgeman with Jacqueline Hazard** (23950-3 • $3.50)
The test pilot who flew the fastest and the highest. The excitement of going where no one has ever flown before by a pilot whose careful study and preparation was matched by his courage.

Read all of the books in THE AVIATOR'S BOOKSHELF

Prices and availability subject to change without notice

Buy them at your bookstore or use this handy coupon for ordering:

Join the Allies on the Road to Victory
BANTAM WAR BOOKS

☐	24164	INVASION—THEY'RE COMING! Paul Carel	$3.95
☐	23843	AS EAGLES SCREAM Donald Burgett	$2.95
☐	23549	FLY FOR YOUR LIFE L. Forrester	$3.50
☐	20308	THOUSAND MILE WAR B. Garfield	$3.50
☐	22832	D DAY: THE SIXTH OF JUNE, 1944 D. Howarth	$2.95
☐	22703	LONDON CALLING NORTH POLE H. J. Giskes	$2.50
☐	20749	BREAKOUT J. Potter*	$2.50
☐	23833	COMPANY COMMANDER C. MacDonald	$3.50
☐	24104	A SENSE OF HUMOR J. Webb	$3.50
☐	23820	WAR AS I KNEW IT Patton, Jr.	$3.95

*Cannot be sold to Canadian Residents.
Prices and availability subject to change without notice.

Buy them at your local bookstore or use this handy coupon for ordering:

SPECIAL
MONEY SAVING
OFFER

Now you can have an up-to-date listing of Bantam's hundreds of titles plus take advantage of our unique and exciting bonus book offer. A special offer which gives you the opportunity to purchase a Bantam book for only 50¢. Here's how!

By ordering any five books at the regular price per order, you can also choose any other single book listed (up to a $4.95 value) for just 50¢. Some restrictions do apply, but for further details why not send for Bantam's listing of titles today!

Just send us your name and address plus 50¢ to defray the postage and handling costs.